Introduction

How to Be a Millionaire
Colorado Springs, 1881. Penny Joshua's brother needs a loan to purchase a promising mine, but he doesn't have much to recommend himself. Then Penny meets Justin Van der Meer, an apparent waiter, and decides to convince him to pose as a millionaire to go with Farley for a meeting with a banker. Will a case of mistaken identity lead to a hot spring of shame or heat up to a romance over the Christmas season?

Love by Accident
Running W Ranch, 1882. When a small train is caught in an avalanche near Liza Wainwright's home, her family takes in a group of strangers over Christmas. But when her handsome neighbor, Garrett Anderson, arrives with food, his help is unwelcome. Will an old family feud stifle Christian charity or awaken a chance for holiday romance?

A Wife in Name Only
Masten Ranch, 1884. When Katherine Priestly seeks a job to help support her destitute family, a local ranch needs a cook, but the owner, Brett Masten, will only hire a married woman to work among his men. Desperate, Katherine claims she is a married woman at the tender age of eighteen. Will her charade become a barrier to true love and send her home penniless at Christmastime?

Colorado
CHRISTMAS

Love Comes in Three Unexpected Packages
During the 1880s

ROSEY DOW

BARBOUR
PUBLISHING

©2007 by Rosey Dow

ISBN 978-1-59789-818-8

All scripture quotations are taken from the King James Version of the Bible.

This book is a work of fiction. Names, characters, places, and incidents are either products of the author's imagination or used fictitiously. Any similarity to actual people, organizations, and/or events is purely coincidental.

Cover image: Ron Dahlquist

Published by Barbour Publishing, Inc., P.O. Box 719, Uhrichsville, Ohio 44683, www.barbourbooks.com

Our mission is to publish and distribute inspirational products offering exceptional value and biblical encouragement to the masses.

ecpa Member of the
Evangelical Christian
Publishers Association

Printed in the United States of America.

How to Be
a Millionaire

Dedication

To my daughter, Miriam Dow,
who helps me with those pesky plot twists.

Chapter 1

Colorado Springs, Colorado, December 1890

A t a small table near the kitchen door of their father's stylish restaurant, Penny Joshua leaned across the small table and said, "How much time will Mr. Campbell give you to find a backer for the mine?"

Worry in every line on his young face, her brother, Farley, replied, "The longest Campbell can give me is New Year's Day. After that, he'll have to start looking elsewhere. Otherwise, he won't make his production deadline in April. He has to get the equipment up here and hire a crew." He flung his hand down in an impatient gesture. "I'm going to be twenty-five years old in three more months. It's time I married Diane and got a start in life. Who knows how long it'll be before another chance like this comes up?"

The bell over the front door jangled as a matronly woman entered, followed by a slim man in a bowler hat. Penny slid her chair back. "I wish Campbell had come to you last June instead of a week before Christmas," she said, irritated. "Colorado Springs is a ghost town at Christmas time. Where are we going to find anyone to buy a one-third share in a copper mine?"

Before she could stand, Farley reached out to grab her hand. "That's not it, Penny. I think Willoughby Matthews may spring for it, but I have to convince him it's a good deal. I have the geology report, but I need an edge. Something that will pull Matthews in."

Penny pulled her fingers loose from his grasp. "Let me think about it," she told him. "I've got to wait on the Wilsons." She stood, smoothed her flowing skirts, and scooped a notepad from her starched apron pocket.

Smiling a welcome, she hurried to the first patrons for lunch that day, and Farley returned to the kitchen. Farley and their father, Michael, cooked and cleaned behind the scenes while Penny waited tables and tended the twelve-table dining room. During the peak season, Penny managed four waitresses. From September to May, she had no trouble working both shifts alone.

Farley's problem hovered in her mind. How could they convince Willoughby Matthews to turn loose his cash?

Matthews owned the Regal Astoria, one of the largest hotels in a town that catered to millionaires. Complete with hot-spring spas, riding stables, and suites the size of the Joshuas' entire house, the Regal Astoria had an international reputation. Willoughby Matthews could well afford to plunge a little. Unfortunately, he had a reputation for being inherently reluctant when it came to speculating.

Beginning at three that afternoon, Penny had two hours free before supper began. Bundling into her dark green coat and matching hat, she left the Joshua House of Fine Dining and headed toward the center of town. She wanted to get out into the air so she could think.

Daddy had opened the restaurant when Farley was ten and she was eight. Penny had been clearing tables and sweeping floors ever since. After Mama had died four years later, Penny had become a waitress at the restaurant six days a week. Later, she became Daddy's bookkeeper as well.

They lived comfortably, but they had no savings. What if something happened to Daddy? Farley didn't want to run the restaurant, and neither did Penny. She had other plans for her life, dreams of being a writer with a steady flow of royalty checks and fan mail. No one in the whole world knew about Penny's writing—she wasn't quite ready to share this dream with her family yet as she wasn't sure of their reactions—but she was a steady contributor to the *Colorado Springs Summit*. Writing under the name of Gregory Landis, she wrote novellas of five to ten chapters with one chapter printed each week. The paper was small, but she did get a penny for every ten words. It added up to as much as $2.50 a week, an amount she hoarded in a savings account. What she was saving for, she hadn't decided yet.

If only Farley could buy a share of the copper mine. He could marry Diane and they could have a life of their own without being tied to a commercial kitchen. Diane was a sweet, steady girl. She and Farley had been engaged for more than a year, but Farley wouldn't set a date. He wanted more for his bride than one cramped room over the restaurant, and he couldn't afford a place of his own.

She passed the grocer's shop and nodded to Mr. Connors. His delivery boy kept the Joshuas' restaurant supplied with a daily supply of goods.

What would give Willoughby Matthews confidence that the copper mine was a good investment? Verbal promises wouldn't impress him. The geology report would help but...

A middle-aged gentleman in a dark suit passed her on the sidewalk.

Suddenly, she had an inspiration. What if Willoughby Matthews learned that someone else was investing in this venture? Someone Matthews would naturally respect?

"Hey! Wait up!"

Farley's voice behind her brought Penny to a stop in front of the Crabtree Feed and Grain Store. The sidewalk was littered with small bits of cracked corn and oats. She waited for Farley to reach her before she said, "What is it? Is something wrong?"

White gusts puffed from his mouth. He paused to catch his breath then said, "I need to talk to you." He took off his beaver hat and readjusted it on his head. "Have you thought of a way to get Campbell to come in on the deal?" he asked.

She reached out to take his arm. "Do you know of anyone else who's also investing?" she asked, falling in step with him.

He shook his head. "The Campbell Company works through silent partners. There's no published list of investors."

"Too bad. We could get one of them to go with you to see Matthews. Just having someone important there would give you more credibility." They took four steps in silence. Her eyes narrowed as she gazed toward the steely sky. "Unless. . ."

"Sis? I get nervous when I see that look on your face."

"What if. . .what if we can find someone who *looks* important to go with you? What if Matthews only *thinks* the man is rich and backing the mine?"

Farley frowned at her. "That's dishonest. We could never get away with it."

"Can you tell a lie if you never open your mouth?" she challenged. "I don't mean to have someone spin a yarn to Matthews. All we need is someone who can make an impression without saying a word. You can introduce him as an associate and leave it at that."

He wasn't convinced. "It would take a lot of doing. You'd have to find someone willing, and then you'd have to bring him up to par—expensive clothes, the right bearing. . .and that's just the beginning."

Smiling at him like he was a three-year-old, she patted his cheek with her gloved hand. "Leave those things to me," she said. Looking both ways, she stepped off the sidewalk. "I'll be back by five." With short, quick steps she crossed the street and headed up the other side, leaving Farley staring after her.

Doing some quick mental calculations, she figured she had about fifty dollars to pull off the ruse. That should be enough. The problem would be finding a man who looked right and who would be desperate enough for some ready cash to go along with the plan.

Where could she find a well-formed-yet-poor man? He had to have a touch of aristocracy and good looks. Or did he? Well. . .he had to be intelligent, at least.

She turned into the main thoroughfare where the best hotels and restaurants lined the street. Maybe a waiter or a bellboy. Pulling her watch from her handbag, she quickened her pace. It was already four o'clock.

In the penthouse of the Olympia Hotel, twenty-six-year-old Justin Van der Meer adjusted his coat and black bowtie as he left his dressing room. He crossed the master bedroom and strode into a dining room glittering with gold and crystal.

Seated at a small table near the wide dining room window, his valet, Albert Wessel, looked up from his Parchessi game board and immediately stood. "Are you going down so early, sir?" he asked in clipped British consonants. He was an egg-shaped man, from his full-length silhouette to the form of his balding head. He had deep creases around his full mouth and twinkling brown eyes.

Reaching into his pocket for a small horsehair brush, he circled Justin's slim frame and swished at his dinner jacket, a tailored creation of pure lamb's wool with silk lapels.

"Why shouldn't I eat when I want?" Justin demanded with mock severity. "I'm hungry, and there's no one joining me. You know I'd much rather be alone in the dining room anyway, Vessel." For more than thirty years, Albert Wessel had been valet to Justin's grandfather, salt-mine multimillionaire Gustaf Van der Meer. Gustaf never lost his heavy Dutch accent, so Wessel had been "Vessel" to the family since the valet had traveled from Great Britain to join the Van der Meer household.

Waving the whisking brush away from his collar, the younger man approached the game board. "How is it going? Finish the tournament yet?" Since discovering Parchessi on their last trip to New York, the valet passed his every spare moment playing the game. When he couldn't convince anyone to join him, he played against himself.

"I'm on the last game," Vessel said, resuming his seat. "The far side is winning, 3-2. If the near side wins this round, we'll have to play a tiebreaker."

Justin laughed. "We? You're the only one playing," he said with a teasing light in his dark eyes. "Wouldn't you like to join me in the dining room for supper? No one will be there to see my *disgrace*."

Vessel's reply was the gentle scolding reserved for a favorite son of the house. That's exactly what Justin had been until his grandfather's death the previous year. "Master Justin," he replied primly, slipping into Justin's old title, "it just isn't done."

"I know. I know." The younger man stepped away. He fluffed the back of his close-cropped hair with his fingertips and immediately smoothed it down. He paused to say, "I'll send you up a supper tray with some mulled cider and a big piece of cheesecake."

Vessel's expression brightened. "Very good, sir. Thank you, sir." He was back at his game before Justin closed the apartment door.

With his hands deep in his pockets and whistling a jaunty tune, Justin waited for the clanging, groaning elevator. His grandmother, Heidi, would have scolded him for the bad habits he'd picked up at Berkeley during the four years he'd lived in the dormitory. Remembering her guttural voice, he straightened and smoothed his coat.

Justin's father, Heinrich, was the only child of Gustaf and Heidi Van der Meer. Against his parents' wishes, Heinrich had married an actress with no social ties and little talent. When he contracted consumption less than two years after the wedding, Heinrich came home to be nursed by those he trusted and loved. His wife stayed only long enough to see her husband and their tiny son settled into the mansion. A few days later, she disappeared into the night and never returned.

All Justin knew of her was that her name was Rosalind, and she also died of consumption while she was in Europe. He was three years old at the time. All he had of his parents was an old tintype, too faded to make out their faces.

Gustaf and Heidi doted on Justin. They raised him with all the structure and strictness of their Christian Dutch heritage, determined that this boy would not become heedless and self-willed like his father. Justin grew up in a twenty-room mansion with leather-covered walls and priceless antiques, but he had few toys and no allowance. He had daily kitchen chores and worked in the stables on Saturdays.

Justin entered the empty dining room to the welcoming aroma of a well-cooked roast or stew. No waiter was in sight. He stepped toward the kitchen door, hoping to catch someone's eye, but no one appeared.

A few minutes later, he wondered if he should return to his room and come back in an hour. But what was there for him to do? Watch Vessel rolling dice and moving pawns? At least the scenery here was different. He had chosen Colorado Springs because it was off-season and he wanted some peace from the frantic partying of the young rich. With three days still remaining until Christmas, peace was beginning to seem horribly boring.

A crash in the kitchen startled Justin. He whirled around and backed into a large rack full of clean silverware. Lunging to catch it before it toppled over, he couldn't stop the disaster. The second crash followed close behind the first.

His face flaming, he bent over to salvage as much of the clean silverware as he could, carefully lifting those that had not touched the floor.

Penny entered the lobby of the Olympia Hotel and looked around for prospects. The elderly gentleman behind the desk was certainly not a candidate for her purpose. No bellboys in sight. Moving across the wide, silent room, she entered the restaurant.

Was the entire hotel empty? Letting out a frustrated sigh, she turned to leave when a movement caught her eye. A tall, dark-haired young man was working over a silverware rack near the kitchen door. He was slim and had a straight set to his shoulders. Intrigued, Penny moved closer.

He must have felt the intensity of her stare because he turned to look at her before she reached him.

Penny's pulse quickened. He was handsome but not too pretty. Good carriage but not arrogant. He could have been an actor instead of a waiter. Maybe he would be before much longer.

Before she had time to second-guess herself, she strode up to him. "Good afternoon," she said breathlessly. "I have a job for you on Saturday at three o'clock. It will take about an hour, and I'll pay you twenty dollars." She paused and looked at him anxiously. "Do you have to work on Saturday?"

He gaped at her. "Excuse me, miss. Do you know me?"

"I'm sorry. I don't have time to wait for introductions. I need someone who looks rich to attend a business meeting at a high-class hotel on Saturday. It's at three-thirty. You won't have to say a word. My brother will introduce you to his associate. That's it. Do you want the job?" She scrutinized his jacket. "I'll have to find you something better to wear than that waiter's uniform, but I can manage that."

She paused to glance at his face, impatient now. "Will you do it? If you have to work that afternoon, I need to know right away so I can find someone else."

Dropping a handful of knives into a slot on the rack, the hint of a smile twitched his cheeks. He nodded in a highbrow fashion and said, "I'm free on Saturday, so that will be agreeable."

Penny let out a relieved sigh. She pulled open the top of her purse and found two coins. "Here's fifty cents. Get yourself a haircut and a shave and meet me at the Joshua House of Fine Dining this evening at eight o'clock. Do you know where that is?"

"I'll find it, Miss. . ."

"Penny Joshua," she said. "And your name?"

"Justin. . .Avery."

Stepping back, she looked him over again. "We'll need to work on you a bit, but I think you'll do fine." She gave him a glowing smile. "We'll see you at eight." Glancing at her watch, she rushed out.

The moment Penny disappeared through the doors, Justin sank into the nearest chair and began to laugh. Too well bred to shout or guffaw, he chuckled and chuckled until his eyes watered and his stomach ached.

He rubbed the two quarters together in his palm. What a lark. If only Teddy, Max, and the rest of the gang at Berkeley could see him now. It would have been the talk of the school for weeks.

Finally, a craggy-faced waiter emerged from the kitchen and approached his table. "May I help you, sir?" he asked.

Pulling out a handkerchief to wipe his eyes, Justin drew in a breath and tried to regain his composure. "Bring me whatever smells so good. It's beef, I think."

"Right away, sir." The waiter strode into the kitchen.

Staring at six pairs of gold velvet drapes lined up on the opposite wall of the massive room, Justin savored the memory of a sweet pixie face, flashing eyes, and the most gorgeous blond hair he had ever seen. Suddenly, his boring Christmas holiday had become intensely fascinating.

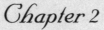

Chapter 2

Justin finished his early supper in short order, chewing through a slab of succulent roast beef and gravy-covered mashed potatoes, barely tasting them. He ordered Vessel's meal, signed a bill, and headed for the street without his coat. The barbershop was just next door, and he didn't want to answer Vessel's questions about his sudden urge to go out.

Thirty minutes later, he returned to the hotel. He punched the button on the elevator, rocked on his heels, and chuckled again. Every time he thought of it, he had to laugh. Sometime between now and eight o'clock he had to get this laughing out of his system or he'd never make it through the evening. Miss Joshua would wonder if he'd had a drop too many if she saw him in this state.

Justin had always enjoyed a good joke. He picked up that trait from his many hours playing with stable boys, hearing the banter of the kitchen help, and playing dozens of games with Vessel. The old retainer had been like a second grandfather to Justin ever since he could remember—a favored grandfather because Gustaf was too involved with his business to be much fun. Vessel, on the other hand, had afternoons free to teach him croquet, whist, horseshoes, chess, and a ridiculous parlor game called Blind Man's Bluff, the house staff's favorite.

Entering the penthouse door, Justin tossed the key into a nearby crystal dish. Vessel's empty supper tray sat nearby, waiting for room service to pick it up.

Whistling, Justin headed for his room. He wanted a few minutes alone to compose himself.

However, when he passed Vessel's ongoing tournament, the older man cried out, "What—Ho! Sir, what happened to your hair?"

Justin stopped in mid-stride. He fluffed the bristly back of his head and smoothed it down. Pasting on a sober face, he slowly turned to the valet. "I stepped out and got a haircut," he said, as though it were a weekly event.

Vessel became instantly offended. "Master Justin, do you find my haircuts lacking in some way? All you have to do is tell me, and I will correct any deficiencies." He circled Justin to inspect the damage. "Is this your pleasure from now on? I'm not sure I can duplicate it. The back is too short, the crown stands up, and the front. . ." He craned his head for a closer look.

With his mind moving at lightning speed, Justin tried to come up with an answer that would satisfy the old fellow. Vessel had been cutting Justin's hair since he wore short pants. He forced a solemn look, knowing that it would squelch any further questions. He was, after all, the new master. "It's nothing I'm ready to discuss," he said shortly and quickly retired to his room.

He strode to the mirror to take a closer look at his head and winced. Inspecting from several angles the dark stubble covering his scalp, he picked up his brush and tried to comb it down. When he finished, it looked exactly as it had before. He set the brush back on the dressing table. Oh well, in a couple of weeks Vessel could put it to rights.

Penny skipped back to the restaurant. Excitement gave her wings. Her plan might just work after all.

Inside the back door, she shrugged out of her coat and pulled her hatpin from her narrow-brimmed hat. The cooking smells from that evening's menu—creamy onion soup and Beef Wellington—warmed the air. She placed her hat neatly on a shelf and hung the coat on a peg beneath it. Pausing to check her hair in a small mirror there, she hurried to the kitchen door and leaned inside. Their father was bent over the sink with his back to her.

She spotted her brother stirring a simmering five-gallon pot. "Farley," she called in a stage whisper and waved him closer.

Farley hooked the curved spoon handle over the edge of the pot and hurried to her. Stepping into the hall, he closed the door after him.

"I found him!" Penny bounced with every word. "He's going to meet us here tonight after we close."

Farley sucked in a quick breath. "You didn't!" He shook his head in warning. "I don't know about this, sis. You may be in over your head this time."

She grabbed his sleeve with both hands and shook it. "He's a waiter at the Olympia. He's a bit young, but he fits the part perfectly. And he said he'd do it for twenty dollars."

Farley frowned.

Turning him loose, she glanced at the clock in the hall and set off toward the dining room. "I'm late setting up for supper," she said airily. "We'll talk about it later."

At six-thirty that evening, stretched out on his bed with his hands under his head, Justin Van der Meer was in a dilemma. He had to meet Penny in ninety minutes. If he wore his usual dinner clothes, her brother might spot him as a rich fraud straightaway. The problem was he didn't own anything shabby enough for a waiter's wardrobe, and every store in town closed by six, most shops by five.

He shifted the pillow a little lower and moved up to rest his back against the sewn-leather headboard. On the other hand, Penny had assumed that his two-hundred-dollar dinner jacket was a waiter's uniform. Maybe her brother would, too. That's the best he could do tonight. But tomorrow. . .

He hopped off the bed and crossed fifty feet of rose-covered carpet in shades of pink, crimson, and burgundy. "Vessel, I need you to do something for me tomorrow morning. The shops open at eight, don't they?"

Vessel stood and moved away from the game board. "Yes, I believe eight it is. What's your pleasure, sir?" The old retainer's gaze wandered over Justin's newly shorn head.

The younger man pulled a folded wad of bills from his pocket and peeled off several of them. "I know you're going to think it's strange, but please humor me." He fended off Vessel's expression of growing alarm with a wave of his hand. "It's just a lark. I don't want to go into it right now, Vessel, so please don't ask."

"Does it involve a pretty girl?" Vessel asked dryly, as he took the money from Justin's hand.

"As a matter of fact. . ."

Resigned and patient, Vessel replied, "Say no more, young sir. Say no more."

"I want you to find a cheap clothier and buy me a dark suit off the shelf. I'll need everything—shirt, shoes, hat, gloves, and overcoat. Well-cut if you can manage, but coarse, not fine."

"Very good, sir." Tucking the cash inside his vest pocket, Vessel returned to the Parchessi game. "We're in the tiebreaker. The far side has it so far, 3-1."

Justin inspected the board. "Would you like me to sit in for the far side?"

Vessel looked dutifully solemn. "If you will, sir."

Smiling, Justin backed away. "I just remembered I have a sketch to finish. Let me know when you're ready to start a new game."

Returning to his room, Justin chuckled. Vessel would rather cut off his nose than deny Justin anything, but coming in on the winning side at the end of the tournament would be like filching the last bite of the last piece of chocolate cake from his plate. The fact was Justin couldn't resist teasing the old fellow now and then.

Both Penny and Farley worked like Trojans to get the restaurant cleaned and in order before Justin arrived. Their father was scouring the monster stove in the kitchen.

"I hope he comes," Penny told Farley when he joined her in the dining room where she was filling small bowls with moist salt. All around her, chairs perched upside down on bare tabletops.

Rolling down his sleeves and buttoning them, he retorted, "I'm tired, and I need a bath. I almost hope he doesn't come."

"You ungrateful wretch." She picked up a neatly folded white napkin from a stack nearby and threw it at him. "I'm doing this for you, remember?"

He picked up the cloth napkin from where it fell at his feet. Holding it by opposite corners, he flipped it around to make a lumpy rope. Stretching it taut, he aimed it toward her arm. "Not for me, for us." With a teasing grin and a threatening gleam in his eye, he said, "Say it."

Completely unimpressed with his posturing, she said, "I know—for us." She grabbed the napkin away from him and dropped it into the canvas laundry bag propped nearby. It was stuffed with tablecloths and napkins. A young man from the Chinese laundry would come by to pick it up in the morning.

A knock sent her hurrying to unlock the front door. Pulling it open, she said, "Justin, please come in." A frigid gust blew her words back in her face and made her flinch.

Shivering in only his dinner jacket, he bounded inside. "Thanks for coming right away," he gasped. "I didn't realize how cold it was when I set off." He rubbed his hands together and blew on them.

"There's still hot coffee on the burner," Penny told him, closing the door and turning the lock. "I'll fetch you a cup." She waved toward her brother. "This is Farley Joshua, my brother, the one who got us into this."

She gave him just a second to shake Farley's hand, then said, "Let's use this table next to the radiator where it's warm," and hurried through the swinging doors into the inner sanctum of Joshua's House of Fine Dining. It had a massive Empire stove, a stone oven for baking bread, and three sinks on the left side. In the center stood a thick oak table and four chairs, and on the right was a long work counter lined with knife blocks and crocks filled with long-handled utensils.

With his enormous back bent over the stove, his meaty right arm in rhythmic motion over the black grill, Michael

Joshua glanced over when Penny lifted the coffeepot from the far burner.

"A little late for that, ain't it?" he grunted.

"It's not for me, Daddy," Penny told him. "A friend just stopped by, and he's almost frozen. I thought this would warm him up."

"David Langstrom?" he asked slyly.

"Daddy! Why would *he* come over?"

He sent her a teasing smile. "You tell me, Penny."

Refusing to lower herself to answer such a ridiculous question, she turned her shoulder toward him and poured coffee from a gallon-sized enamel pot, emptying it. "Perfect. I always hate to waste it." She deposited the pot into a deep metal sink and left the kitchen. As the door swung shut, she heard her father's deep-throated chuckle.

David Langstrom was a deacon's son, just back from the university. Every unattached girl above the age of twelve had her cap set for him. Every one except Penny, that is. She thought David Langstrom was full of himself. She wanted a man who was more down to earth—kind and approachable like her dad.

She brought Justin's coffee to the table. "Please, sit down," she told Justin, who was still standing some distance away. She looked him over as he crossed the room. "See what I mean, Farley? That waiter's jacket won't do at all." She turned to Justin. "Do you have anything better than that?"

He looked at her with an uncertain expression.

Taking his hesitation for a no, she said, "I wonder if I can borrow one..."

Farley shook his head. "From whom?" he demanded. "That's why we're in this predicament, remember? Everyone's out of town."

"How could I forget?" she asked archly. She studied Justin's shoulders and said, "Stand up to Farley, so I can judge your size." She glanced from one to the other. "Just a tad narrower, I think. I'll take one of Farley's suits over to Bernard's in the morning and ask him if he has a ready-made suit the right size."

Taking a seat across from Justin, Penny said, "I hope you don't think we're awful for doing this. Farley has a chance to buy a large share of a new copper mine northwest of Denver. He's got the geology reports to prove it's a good investment, but he doesn't have enough money for a full share. He's looking for a backer to stake him for the rest of it in exchange for thirty percent of the profits." She paused to meet his eyes. "We're not trying to cheat anyone. It's just that our contact is so tight-fisted that we wanted a little extra persuasion to convince him to come in on the deal."

Justin turned to Farley. "Would you mind if I saw the report?"

Surprised, Farley shrugged. "Why not? It's all legit. I've got it in my jacket." He hustled into the hall and was back soon with a folded document.

He handed it to Justin, who looked over it.

Farley continued, "As you can see, there's no risk. The copper deposit is wide and deep. How can I lose?"

Justin slowly folded the report and handed it back. "You've got something there, Farley. It's worth pursuing."

Penny said, "We can't get anywhere without enough money." She smiled. "That's where you come in. We need your help, Justin. It means a lot to us."

Chapter 3

Justin grinned at Penny. She had the most fascinating almond-shaped blue eyes he had ever seen. "That's what I'm here for," he said. He glanced from her to Farley and back again. Pushing his empty cup away, he asked, "Where do we start?"

"Let's pretend that you're coming into the restaurant with Farley," she replied. "He'll introduce you to Mr. Matthews." Waving her hand toward the front doors, she said, "I'll be Mr. Matthews. Pretend to go outside and come back in."

The men walked most of the way across the dining room. When they were out of Penny's hearing range, Farley said, "You're a sport to do this, Avery."

"Twenty dollars is twenty dollars," Justin replied wisely.

With Farley leading the way, the men approached the table.

Penny stood and stretched out her small hand. "How do you do, Mr. Joshua? It's good to see you."

Farley shook her hand. "Good afternoon, Mr. Matthews. I'd like you to meet my associate, Justin Avery."

Uncomfortable with the playacting, Justin hesitated.

Penny shook her head and gently scolded, "You're a millionaire, Justin. You're confident and relaxed. Mr. Matthews is just another man like you are, so don't act nervous." She sat down. "Let's try that again."

The men retired to the other side of the dining room. Farley put out a few of the gas lamps as they moved, leaving them in a pleasantly dim atmosphere.

When they had gone far enough, they stood waiting for her signal to approach. Farley sighed. "It could be a long night. When Penny gets her teeth into something, she's like a puppy going after an old sock."

"I'll try to get it right this time," Justin said and followed Farley's winding return path among the chair-topped tables. His elbow caught a leaning leg and the chair crashed to the floor, totally unnerving him. He stood staring at it.

Farley rushed back to pick it up. "Don't worry. These old things have seen more wear than a forty-niner's seen dirt." He set it back on the table.

Pulling his coat straight, Justin lifted his chin and drew in a slow breath. This time he minded his elbows and arrived at the table without incident.

"How do you do, Justin?" Penny asked, her voice extra deep.

Justin was quick to step up, look Penny in the eye, and firmly shake her tiny hand.

The men sat down, and Penny dashed to the hostess station for three menus. She came skipping back and dropped one in front of each place, then quickly resumed her seat and pasted on a blank expression.

In her deepest voice, she said, "I'll have the vichyssoise and coffee, please." She turned to Farley expectantly.

He cleared his throat, glanced at the cardboard in front of

him, and said, "I'll have the same."

All eyes were now on Justin. He scanned the menu, and one item caught his eye. "Sauerkraut and sausages with boiled potatoes and kale," he said.

Penny stared. "You would go into a high-class restaurant and order *that*?"

Defensive now, he glanced at Farley. "It's one of my favorite meals. Why shouldn't I order it? Besides, what if I can't read the foreign words written on there?"

Penny's eyes narrowed. "How can you work at the Olympia Restaurant and not know the names of European dishes?"

He quickly explained, "I know the ones on that menu, sure. But both menus won't be exactly the same. I'd have to figure something out in a split second."

Actually, Justin was well read in Latin, French, and German, but he had to play dumb on this point. Besides, Grandma Van der Meer had believed that simple foods built strong bodies, so Justin had a distinct disliking for anything highly spiced, rich, or unrecognizable. He hardly looked at a menu whenever he ate out. He found it a boring waste of time when he had four or five favorites and almost always chose one of them.

With a sigh of great patience, Penny said, "What would you like, sir?"

Justin looked at her calmly and said, "I'll have the same."

Farley let out a loud hoot. "That's the best bet, old man. Whatever it is, we'll have to suffer through it."

Penny made a point of ignoring his sarcasm. "What about drinks?"

Justin held up his hands, palms outward. "I have a religious belief about temperance. I've never tasted alcohol, and even twenty dollars isn't enough to get me to try it."

She looked at him, surprised. "Are you a Christian?" she asked.

"Yes, I am." Justin felt a blush coming on and despised himself for it. "I wonder if I shouldn't stop this charade right now," he faltered. "I want to help you kids, but. . ."

"Penny's a Christian," Farley told him. "She goes to meetings at the tabernacle north of town."

It was Penny's turn to look uncomfortable. "That's why I don't want you to tell any untruths, Justin," she said, glancing at her hands then upward toward him. "We're just trying to create an impression, not lead Mr. Matthews down the merry path. Farley has the geology report. . ."

"It's a good prospect," Justin broke in, glad for a valid reason to go ahead with their plan. "That's why I'm with you. You kids deserve a break."

Penny sighed. "I wish we had an actual meal so we could practice table manners."

Farley yawned. "Don't you think that's enough for tonight, sis? I'm beat."

She nodded. "Let's meet tomorrow at three while the restaurant is closed for the afternoon. Can you arrange that, Justin?" When he nodded, she went on, "We'll actually eat a meal together, so we can work on table etiquette." She gave Farley a pointed look. "You need practice on that as much as Justin does."

Farley groaned.

Pushing his chair away from the table, he stood, bade Justin good night, and trudged toward the back stairs.

Justin watched him go with a sinking feeling. He wasn't at all ready for the night to end.

"Daddy is finishing up in the kitchen," Penny said. "How about a cup of hot cocoa before you go back into the cold?" She seemed to have another thought. "You know, Farley has an old coat he uses to go out to the ice house. Why don't you borrow it until tomorrow? I can't stand to see you go back into that cold again. You'll catch something dreadful for sure."

"Why, thank you," Justin said, "for the cocoa *and* the coat. That's very kind of you."

She stood, and he did, too. He followed her to the kitchen door. When she paused just outside, he hesitated, uncertain of what she expected of him.

"A gentleman always opens a door for a lady," she said.

Feeling another blush coming on, Justin hurried to push the swinging door inward. He'd been well versed in that bit of etiquette since he could walk, but he'd never seen it applied to a kitchen door before.

Once inside, Penny dropped all signs of pretense. "Daddy, this is Justin Avery," she said.

Michael Joshua was rinsing his grill stone under the faucet. He turned to greet Justin and then showed him his greasy hands. "I'd shake hands with you, but. . ."

"That's all right, Mr. Joshua," the young man replied with a smile. "Thank you for allowing me into your kitchen."

"We'd like some hot chocolate," Penny said. "Is the stove still hot?"

"That it is," her father replied. "There's still plenty of hot water in the reservoir, too."

The big man glanced at Justin with renewed interest, sizing him up, and Justin squirmed. He wondered if Penny's father had ideas about Justin's designs on his daughter.

Penny moved quickly around the kitchen, opening cabinet doors and lifting a small pot from a hook overhead. Watching her graceful movements, it occurred to Justin that Mr. Joshua might not be far off the beam.

In a few minutes, she had three warm cups on the oak table. "Can you sit down with us, Daddy?" she asked. "I've made a cup for you, too."

"You're a sweet child," he said, smiling sadly at Penny. Mr. Joshua washed his hands and wiped them on a towel. Pulling back the thick straight chair, he eased his wide girth onto the seat. "Penny is the image of her dear mother at that young age," he told Justin. "She was as blond as an angel and as tiny as a hummingbird."

"She passed away when I was twelve," Penny told him. She reached out to squeeze her father's hand. "Daddy's been mother and father to me and Farley. And a good job he's done of it, too." A warm look passed between them.

"My parents died when I was a baby," Justin said. "My father before I turned one and my mother when I was three. They both had consumption."

"How sad!" Penny said. She glanced at her father. "At least Farley and I both remember Mama." She spoke to Justin. "Who took care of you?"

"My grandparents raised me," Justin said. "They were good people."

"Were?" Penny asked.

He nodded. "Unfortunately, they were already old when I was born. They're both gone now."

"Do you mean you're going to be alone at Christmas?" Penny asked, alarmed.

"Well, we have an old family...friend...who has never married. I'm planning to spend the day with him."

She glanced at her father, then back at Justin. "Why don't you come and spend the day with us?" she asked. "We're going to be alone, too, the three of us, and it can be rather depressing. It would be fun to have someone in for a change." She turned toward her father. "Wouldn't it, Daddy?"

Setting down his cup, he looked blankly at his daughter for a moment then suddenly burst out, "Of course, of course. We'd be delighted to have you, young man."

Justin hesitated. "Would you mind if I bring my friend along? I'd hate to leave him all alone."

"That goes without saying," Penny told him. "Come early and stay late. Daddy cooks several turkeys for our Christmas Eve menu, and we enjoy the leftovers the next day. There'll be plenty to spare."

"That's kind of you," Justin said, feeling a strange warmth inside. "Very kind."

She beamed at him. "Did your family have any special Christmas traditions?" she asked. "We hardly do anything special for Christmas since Mama passed away. What did your family do?"

"My grandparents were from Holland, and they stayed with the Dutch traditions all their lives. We exchanged gifts on December 5 and only went to church on December 25."

"Did you do anything else on December 5?" Penny asked. The light of the lamp overhead shone in her eyes.

"We always had a huge tree lit with dozens of white candles," he said, smiling softly. "We'd string cranberries to wrap around the tree and then decorate the limbs with glass balls. And Grandma would always hide a pickle."

Penny wrinkled her tiny nose. "A pickle?"

He chuckled. "It was my job to find the pickle hidden among the branches. Then I'd get a special chocolate truffle all to myself."

"Did you always find it?"

"Almost always," he said. "When I was eleven, I couldn't find it because it was tied to the trunk under a wide branch. I was so disappointed that the cook. . ." He gulped. "That is. . . they cooked me a special cake the next day."

Penny sipped the last of her chocolate. "We used to make paper snowflakes and pinwheels and tie them to the tree with silk thread. And we'd string popcorn because Mama didn't like cranberries. She said they were too expensive and stained our clothes besides."

"You don't do that anymore?" Justin asked.

She patted her father's hand. "After Mama died, we just couldn't do the same things. Whenever I thought of pulling out the old Christmas decorations or putting up a tree, I wanted to cry. So, we never did." She smiled at her father. "What do you think, Daddy? Could we do some things this year?"

His fleshy face, so like Farley's, curved into a smile. "There's no harm in it," he told her, patting her cheek. "Do what you will."

She beamed at him, then turned to cast the glow of her smile upon Justin. "Tomorrow is Christmas Eve. We'll practice here from three o'clock to five o'clock then Farley and I will have to serve dinner. We close at seven thirty. Why don't you come around at eight? And bring your friend. It will be fun."

Her enthusiasm was contagious. "All right. I will."

Mr. Joshua got heavily to his feet, weariness in every move. "I'm going to write out my grocery order to leave for the delivery boy, and then I'm off to bed. You young people have to excuse the old man who needs his rest." With a wink for Penny, he pulled off his apron and disappeared through the swinging doors.

Justin pulled out his watch. Eleven o'clock. "I've kept you too late," he said, standing.

"Not at all." She smiled up at him. "I wonder that we haven't met before. Farley and I don't get out much, but we do know a lot of the food service staff in the hotel restaurants. Most of them have worked for us at one time or another."

Holding the kitchen door for her to pass, Justin left her comment unanswered. He'd almost tripped himself up once tonight. He didn't want to take a second chance.

Outside the door, she scurried down the hall and pulled a worn quilted coat from a peg and brought it back to him. "This is Farley's coat. You can wear it home and bring it back tomorrow."

"Thanks," he said, shrugging into it. The collar was worn through at the front edge, and it smelled of grease and old straw. But it was soft and warm. He buttoned it closely around his neck as they crossed the dining room.

At the door, Penny said, "Before work in the morning, I'll see if Bernard has a suit that he'll let me rent for a day. That shouldn't cost too awfully much." She held out her hand. "Thank you for helping us, Justin," she said with a soft smile.

She gazed into his eyes, and Justin's world stood still.

The young girls in his circle were pampered and powdered, with agendas and innuendoes in every word, every action. This lovely creature was sweet and unspoiled, her only agenda to help her brother get a start in life.

And to think, if he hadn't knocked over that silverware rack, he might have never met her.

Chapter 4

A few seconds later, Penny locked the restaurant door behind Justin. She took her time crossing the dining room, shutting down each burning gas lamp as she came to it. Standing in the comforting dimness of the last lamp, she took a few moments to gaze into her memories of the evening.

Something about Justin Avery had captured her interest from the first time she met him. What was it? She couldn't quite tell. . .but he was charming.

Pulling a sheaf of paper from a locked cabinet below the waitress station, she found a pencil stub in her apron pocket and sat down to write. It was a new story about a tall young man with dark hair and lively eyes.

During his mad dash back to the Olympia penthouse, Justin shivered and scolded his feet for not moving faster. Even with Farley's coat, he was still freezing. His ermine-lined overcoat was much warmer, but it was also a dead giveaway, and he'd been forced to leave it behind. Vessel would have to find him a warm coat in the morning. He couldn't take this kind of punishment for the next three days without catching something dreadful.

Outside the hotel, he pulled the jacket off and turned it inside out. Rolling it into a bundle, he held it under his trembling arm and dashed indoors. Inside the hotel lobby, he strode to the elevator, still shivering in spite of the warmth cascading over him. What a wonderful thing central heating was. He made a mental note to have a system installed in the Milwaukee mansion right away. He rarely went there in the winter, but even the spring and fall were uncomfortably cool in that part of the country. He was scheduled to arrive there in March. Pulling a notepad from his inner pocket, he jotted a few words.

Vessel was in his own room when Justin reached the penthouse. The rooms were silent except for the slight hissing of a single gas lamp on the wall near the front door. Lit only by that lamp and a single candle in a brass holder, the apartment stretched out gloomily before him. Justin quickly turned off the gas and picked up the candle to find his way to his quarters.

He stowed the old coat in a back corner of his wardrobe and hurried out of his clothes. Within minutes he was soaking in a warm bath.

He started chuckling. Then he laughed loud and long. No sauerkraut and pork indeed. Was that more barbaric than eating snails and fish eggs? He let the hot water course over his face, soaking in the warmth. Penny Joshua was as cute as a blueberry muffin on a china plate. He could hardly wait to hear what sweet morsels would flow from her soft lips when he saw her tomorrow.

Say, since he was invited to their place for Christmas Day, didn't that mean presents, at least one for the family? What should he bring? He immediately imagined expensive hats and canes for the men and glittering jewelry or a fur wrap for Penny.

Shaking the water out of his eyes, he groaned. He was supposed to be a "poor man." He couldn't afford anything more than a few cents. And he had little time to shop. The stores would close at noon tomorrow. What was he going to do? Justin Van der Meer spent most of the night tossing and muttering to himself.

Bernard had been friends with Michael Joshua since Penny was a small girl. He was Michael's mentor in business and his formidable chess opponent on cold, windy evenings. Penny reached Bernard's tailor shop at five minutes past eight the next morning, but she was still the second customer in the store. When she stepped inside, a portly man in a dark overcoat was staring at a dinner jacket and discussing something urgent with the tailor.

Bent and trembling, Bernard resembled a beaver standing on hind legs, wavering in the breeze. He wore a sagging suit with a cloth measuring tape draped around his neck and thick glasses on his wide nose.

"This is a very economical fabric," he was telling the customer. "Only fifty dollars for both coat and pants. The lining is cotton instead of silk, as you can see." He flipped back the hem of the jacket.

Interested, Penny stepped forward and stopped beside a rack holding twenty rolls of suit material.

"Is that the very cheapest suit you have?" the customer asked, doubtfully. "I'm actually looking for a coarser fabric than that."

With an affronted expression, the clothier straightened to his full height of five feet, three inches and smoothed the dark cloth with his shaking hand. "That's the cheapest, Mr. Wessel," he quavered, "though I can't imagine why Mr. Van der Meer would want something worse instead of better."

The patron glanced toward Penny and took a step toward the door. "I won't keep you, Bernard, when you have other customers. There has to be another shop in town that sells cheap suits."

Penny spoke up. "If you go three streets over to Fourth Avenue, there's a place called Maxine's. She may have what you need."

Bernard sniffed. "Imported from Mexico or China," he said. "Nothing for a gentleman there, Penny, my dear."

Penny raised her shapely eyebrows. "For your information, Mr. Bernard, my father buys all his suits there, and he looks just fine." Her sparkling eyes softened her rebuke. It was an old argument between the friends.

"Is that so?" the man asked, pleased. "I'll go right over. You say it's three streets to the west?"

"That's correct," she said, smiling sweetly.

"Good day, miss," he said, with a small bow from the waist. "Thank you for your kindness." He nodded toward the shop owner. "Bernard." With a nod, he placed his bowler hat on his round head and trudged away.

"Miss Joshua," Bernard wheezed, "what can I do for you this fine day?"

She stepped closer and held out Farley's best suit. "I brought this to judge the size. I want to rent a gentleman's suit for one day." She peered at him anxiously. "Is that possible?"

He hesitated, his rheumy eyes searching her face. "For anyone else, I'd say no. But for you, Miss Penny, I'll see what I can do. I don't have many ready-made outfits available." He held up Farley's jacket for a closer look.

"A bit narrower in the shoulders," she told him. "And a tad longer in the leg. The waists are about the same."

Leaving Farley's suit on a nearby table, Bernard disappeared through a curtained doorway. He returned a few minutes later carrying a jacket on a wooden hanger. "Someone ordered this one last fall and never came to pick it up." He shook his head. "I'll never understand. No matter how much money a person has, it's so wasteful to pay for something and not make arrangements to claim it."

He held the suit toward her for a closer look. "One hundred percent wool. Hand worked with a silk lining. You'll not get much finer than this." He looked at the pants. "I can take down the hem in a matter of minutes. The rest should fit fine."

"How much to rent it for one day only?" Waiting for the answer, she held her breath.

"The customer paid one hundred dollars to have it made. For one day? Ten dollars." The firm set of his lips told her that the price was not negotiable.

"I'll need a shirt and some shoes. . ." Now that she thought about it, the shoes Justin had worn last night would be fine for the meeting. "Just a shirt," she amended. "And a nice-looking necktie."

"Fifteen dollars," he said. "I'll have it all delivered to the restaurant by noon."

She pulled open the drawstring on her purse. "Thank you, Bernard."

"Tell your father to stop by some afternoon for a game of chess," he said. "I haven't seen him for months. He's got to take time to relax during the off-season. You can tell him that for me." He tucked the money into his jacket pocket and winked.

Penny smiled. "I'll tell him," she promised. "It would do him good to get away from the restaurant for a few hours." Since her mother's death, he spent more and more time in the restaurant until finally he only worked and then slept and awoke to do it again.

Pulling her coat closer about her, Penny huddled her neck deeper into the collar as she stepped into the winter wind. Well, that detail was taken care of. If she hurried, she still had time to borrow a copy of Thomas Hill's etiquette book from the pastor's wife.

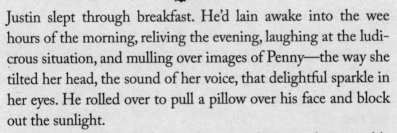

Justin slept through breakfast. He'd lain awake into the wee hours of the morning, reliving the evening, laughing at the ludicrous situation, and mulling over images of Penny—the way she tilted her head, the sound of her voice, that delightful sparkle in her eyes. He rolled over to pull a pillow over his face and block out the sunlight.

It was no good. He had to figure out how to take a suitable Christmas gift to the Joshua home without spending a dime. Time was wasting.

The sound of the apartment door closing brought him full awake. Reaching for his dressing gown, he was at the bedroom door before Vessel reached the dining room.

"What do you have there?" Justin asked, eyeing a bulky package in the valet's hands.

"Your evening wear, sir," Vessel said in his most proper voice. He always became irritatingly polite when he disapproved of something. "Straight from Mexico," he added. His voice took on the barest tinge of disdain. "It has a tag sewn in the back of the neck to say so. . .which I will remove immediately, of course."

"Is it that awful?" Justin asked with delicious horror.

Vessel handed him the bundle.

A few minutes later, Justin buttoned the suit jacket and turned in front of the full-length mirror. A double-breasted gray pinstripe, it was at the height of fashion about two years before. "Not bad. Not bad at all." He picked up the overcoat and slid into it. It was black and bulky, not fashionable but wonderfully warm.

"I got the entire ensemble from a place about six blocks from here," Vessel told him, pulling the back of the overcoat straight. "A young lady at Bernard's put me onto the place. It was a stroke of luck that she was there because Bernard had nothing that would have. . .pleased you."

Justin came alert. "A young lady?"

"She came in at a few minutes past eight, just after I did." He nodded. "An eyeful, that one."

The younger man turned to glance at Vessel. "Did you get her name?"

Standing back a little to frown at the overall effect of the suit, the valet said, "I remember it because it was unusual. Bernard called her Penny."

Justin paused, then casually unbuttoned the coat and handed it to Vessel. "Thank you, Vessel. Just order a light brunch because I'm going to dine early again today. That will be all for now, but we're invited to a Christmas Eve supper tonight at eight o'clock."

"*We*, sir?"

"Don't look so shocked," Justin said, grinning. "This isn't a gala affair. It's a light supper at the home of one of the restaurant owners in town. I recently met the family, and they are very nice people." He opened the wardrobe to pull out one of his own white shirts. "Don't be such a snob, Vessel," he told the valet.

"We'll have a wonderful time."

"Master Justin," Vessel said, exasperated, "when are you going to tell me what you are doing? You must be careful. Your status—"

"Can be a real bore," Justin finished. He chuckled and sent a Cheshire-cat grin toward the old man. "Don't worry. I'm having the time of my life. When you meet the Joshua clan you'll see what I mean."

He finished unbuttoning the new shirt and threw it on the bed. Vessel picked it up. Justin was slipping his arms into the sleeves of his own shirt when he noticed Vessel's disturbed expression. "All right," he said. "I guess I'll have to fill you in before we go over there this evening." He nodded toward a chair. "You may as well sit down. This will take a few minutes."

Chapter 5

Vessel moved into the blue wingback chair a short distance from the bed. He wore a slightly worried expression but didn't say anything more.

Justin finished dressing in a leisurely manner as he spoke. He started the tale at the beginning with his visit to the hotel restaurant on the day before and ended with Penny's invitation.

"We're supposed to be there at eight o'clock for supper," he finished.

Vessel continued to watch Justin's face without speaking. He simply sat there with his hands on his lap, unmoving.

Justin tied a white satin scarf loosely around his neck and pulled on a black smoking jacket, his morning loungewear. Shoving his hands deeply into his pockets, he did a complete turnaround to survey his room.

"I need you to help me out, if you don't mind," he said, ignoring Vessel's quiet disapproval. "I have no gift to give the family on Christmas morning, and I can't spend any money without giving myself away."

Vessel sniffed. "It seems you've put yourself in the position of the vast majority of all the world," he said. "They manage to figure out a solution. I'm sure you will, too." With that he stood and politely left the room.

Justin pulled out his bureau drawers and fingered through their contents. He'd brought five large trunks with him to Colorado Springs, but now they seemed so little. If only he were at home in Nevada, he'd have unlimited options for trinkets to give away. As it was...

Almost an hour later, he gave up in despair. A fellow couldn't give just anything to a family...all right, a girl...he'd met only recently. Frowning and chewing his lower lip, he opened his teak jewelry case looking for some bauble that might serve. Finally, he let the lid drop. Nothing there.

He opened his closet doors and stood back. Every item hanging inside was purchased for a specific purpose that was very male. Nothing there either.

He flung himself back on the bed with his hands clasped behind his head. What did a fellow give a girl he was interested in, one that would please her and yet be casual enough so as not to scare her away?

After obtaining the etiquette book from the pastor's wife, Penny Joshua continued her morning errands. She was looking for Christmas treats and some gifts. She stopped at the bank to make a small withdrawal from her secret savings account. For three years she had hoarded her magazine paychecks with no specific purpose in mind. Occasionally she would make a withdrawal for a pair of shoes or some gloves when she needed them.

Penny visited the local grocer, Mr. Connors. When she arrived, he was putting the final oranges on a tall display of Christmas apples and oranges in a bin just inside the front door.

Tall and lanky with a craggy face and beard that made him look something like Honest Abe, the shopkeeper looked up when the bell on the door jangled.

"Good morning, Penny. What brings you out so early?"

Penny smiled. "Merry Christmas, Mr. Connors. I've come to fetch some things for our Christmas dinner." She looked at the oranges and apples. "Those look so good. How much are they?"

"A penny apiece. That's a new shipment of oranges just come in from California. And are they good! The apples are some I've had in cold storage, but they're still crisp and sweet."

"I'll take six oranges," she said, feeling extravagant and liking it, "half a pound of popcorn, and a gallon of apple cider." She handed him her basket and walked toward the end of the counter to peer into a thick glass crock. "Is that cinnamon?" she asked, delighted.

Adding oranges to the basket, he nodded. "Bought 'em from a peddler last week. The feller always comes around before Christmas with a sack full of spices from the Orient. If you're interested, you'd better get some while you can. They won't last long."

She looked at the small square card in front of the crock reading, "5 Cents/Stick," considered for three seconds, and plunged. "I'll take one stick of cinnamon," she said and moved on. Her father kept cinnamon in a locked cabinet. He'd never allow her to use even a smidgen for the family. That would be eating up the profits.

Her shoes sounded loud on the floor as she circled the U-shaped counter, looking for gifts. This year she wanted four instead of two. Finally, she decided on three items.

"Anything else, Penny?" Mr. Connors asked as he wrapped her choices.

"That will be all," she said, pulling at the strings on her purse. "Can you have those things sent around to my house in about two hours? Not the restaurant, the house. If they go to the restaurant kitchen, there'll be no surprises on Christmas morning." She grinned as she handed him some coins and lifted her heavy basket from the counter.

Dropping the money into a metal box with small dividers in it, Mr. Connors smiled and his beard grew wider. "Tell your old dad to stop by and shoot the breeze sometime. All I ever see of him anymore is the grocery list the delivery boy brings in."

Penny smiled. "I'll tell him." She tucked her small cloth purse into a deep pocket hidden in the folds of her skirt. "Have a wonderful Christmas. And tell Mrs. Connors I said hello."

"The same to you and yours!"

Penny let herself out and headed up the street. She'd always tried to get a little gift for Farley and her father, but she wanted this year to be special. It was the first year since her mother died they'd actually had Christmas dinner with all the trimmings and guests as well. Maybe she could talk Farley into cutting them a tree this afternoon. Wouldn't it be fun to decorate a tree tonight? She and Farley…and Justin? The image brought a soft smile to her face and made her feet move a little faster.

She spent the next hour completing her shopping and arrived home in plenty of time to hide her bundles. She placed two long, slim sheets of stiff paper on her dressing table. This evening she'd cut out the printed forms and sew together four ornaments, ornate six-sided spheres with a different winter scene on each side. She'd gotten them for a steal and couldn't resist.

Glancing at the clock on the mantel shelf in her room, she

hurried to her chifforobe to find a clean work dress. She had to be in the dining room in thirty minutes.

At five minutes past three that afternoon, Farley unlocked the door to let Justin into the restaurant.

Stepping inside, Justin handed him the old coat that he'd borrowed the night before.

"Thanks," Farley said. "That was perfect timing." He turned it around and slid his arms into it. "I'm going out," Farley told him with a look of intense relief. "Penny has it in her head that we need a Christmas tree to decorate tonight, and I am the one to find it, chop it down, and bring it home."

His grin showed that his next words were totally insincere. "I'm awfully sorry. You'll have to face the lion alone. Don't let her wear you out, old man. You have my sympathies."

He re-opened the door and paused to say, "I'm picking up Diane, my fiancée, on my way out of town." With another delighted grin, he sent Justin a nodding salute and closed the door firmly behind him.

Not at all disappointed, Justin unbuttoned the front of his new overcoat as he crossed the dining room. The afternoon had just become promising.

Penny stepped through the swinging doors and stopped, watching him critically as he moved toward her. "Would you do me a favor?" she called.

Justin paused in mid-stride. That was an unusual way to greet a guest. Should he say hello or answer her question?

She didn't wait for his response. "Would you mind going back to the door and walking in again? I'd like to look at your deportment before you take off your coat. And please don't unbutton until you reach the coat room attendant."

She was all business, that one. Pulling in his lips and pressing them together while he had his back to her, he did his best to stifle the smile that was determined to betray him.

Careful to keep his chin up and his expression blank, he made it back to her without having to do a third run.

"May I take your coat, sir?" Penny asked, primly.

"Thank you," Justin said carefully. He loosened his buttons with methodical accuracy, shrugged out of it, and handed it to her carefully folded over one arm.

She took the coat by its collar and hung it on a peg nearby. "Your table is ready. Please follow me." She led him to the same table where they'd practiced the night before. It was set up with two meals: baked chicken on a bed of rice with some kind of cabbage salad and green beans.

Moving quickly, Justin stepped behind a chair and pulled it out, bowing slightly toward her to show that he would like to seat her.

Penny looked surprised and at a loss for moment, but she quickly recovered and sat down with a murmured "Thank you."

Justin took his own seat across from her and looked into her gorgeous eyes. Had it been sixteen whole hours since he'd seen her last? It seemed like a lifetime.

She lifted her napkin, shook it out, and draped it over her navy skirt. Justin imitated her actions. He picked up his fork two seconds after she did, tasted when she did, and then complimented the meal.

Without touching the chicken with their fingers, they carefully pried up tiny bits of flesh with their forks. The entire process was intensely tedious. He could understand Farley's glee at being excused.

It was a challenging game to see how long he could continue without her rebuke. His grandmother had been a stickler for table etiquette. Since he was a small child, Justin had been schooled in which fork to use, what to say to a lady at the dinner table, and the proper expression reserved for servants in the dining room. Of course, at Berkeley he'd relaxed some of that after being with the American students who knew nothing of the strict Dutch society he'd grown up in.

In the year since he'd inherited the family fortune, he'd been amazed at the rude, uncouth behavior of about half the rich people he came in contact with. They seemed to think that their money gave them the right to be unpleasant. In Justin's mind, acting like a millionaire meant flinging cigar ash over everyone and everything within range, shouting orders, and being outrageous when the mood hit.

Fifteen minutes later, they were deftly scooping the last grains of rice from their plates and discussing the weather in excruciating detail.

When Justin drained his coffee cup, Penny asked, "Would you like another cup? We're having Napoleons for dessert, Farley's specialty. Daddy sent him to a French cooking school in New Orleans last year."

"Thank you. I believe I will have another cup of coffee."

She hurried away and returned with a tray holding two dessert plates and the coffeepot. She served the food, poured coffee, and hurried away with the pot.

Justin waited for her to join him before touching the food.

When Penny returned, he quickly stood to seat her again.

"Thank you, Justin," she said sweetly. "You're doing amazingly well. All you need to work on is your enunciation. From time to time I hear a sort of guttural tone to your words."

Justin stiffened. "As I said, my grandparents were from Holland," he told her. "They both spoke with a heavy Dutch influence to their pronunciation. We also have a good friend who is British. I'm afraid I picked up some of each accent—a curious combination, but I'm stuck with it."

She nodded. "Well, that's all right. It's not a major problem."

He hid a sigh of relief. There was nothing he could do about the way he spoke. After all the teasing from his friends at college, he'd tried to talk more like they did and succeeded to a degree, but his Dutch heritage would be with him for the rest of his life. He'd had to accept that years before.

She took a careful bite of her pastry. Swallowing and touching her mouth with her napkin, she asked, "I haven't seen you around Colorado Springs before. Where are you from originally?"

"Nevada. My grandfather was in mining there until he died last year."

"He was a miner?" Penny asked. "No wonder you were interested in Farley's report. Have you done any mining yourself?"

Skating on thin ice, he decided to stall. He didn't want to tell any lies, but she was making it very difficult. "Tell me about your mother," he said. "She must have been a very special person to have such creative and responsible children."

"She was," Penny said softly. "She was very hard-working. She helped Daddy build this restaurant." She looked around at the green-flocked wallpaper, the tin tiles on the ceiling, and back to him as she went on. "She'd hold while he nailed. She'd plumb while he set a stud. They were always together. That's why my dad has been so lost since she's been gone. He's never been able to get his feet under him again."

"I kind of know how he feels," Justin said, unable to hold

back the sadness in his voice. "First my grandmother passed away and six months later my grandfather. I guess I still feel like I'm drifting. They left me the family house in Nevada, but I don't go there much. Staying there feels like sleeping in a museum. It's nice enough, but empty and cold."

Penny nodded. "Without the Lord's help, I don't know how I would have survived," she said. "Neither Farley nor Daddy is a Christian. Mama was, though. She loved the Lord, and she made me promise that I would keep a Christian testimony in the house."

Her eyes filled with sudden tears. "I don't know what it will take for Daddy and Farley to accept Christ. I know Daddy wants to be with Mama more than anything in the world, but he won't humble himself and ask Christ to save him. Whenever I mention anything about the Lord to him, he puts me off by saying he's tired or he's too busy to talk about it right now."

Justin wanted to reach out and comfort her more than anything he'd ever wanted in his life.

With a chagrined look, she dabbed at her eyes with her fingertips. "I'm sorry. I didn't mean to get all weepy on you." She sipped her coffee. "Tell me, what are your plans? Surely you don't want to be a waiter all your life."

A short laugh burst from Justin's lips. Quickly, he swallowed to stifle the mirth. "You're right about that. I've never wanted to be a waiter." He grew more serious. "Actually, I haven't come to the answer of that question. What are my plans? My grandfather took it for granted that I'd follow him in mining, but I'm not sure that's the best for me."

He hesitated for just a second then plunged ahead. "My real passion is art. I was an only child, and I spent many hours alone. When I was drawing, the time would go so quickly that

I'd hardly realize it. My grandparents thought art was a useless pastime, totally unworthy of being a profession, so I've never pursued it."

"What medium do you use?" she asked.

Intrigued at her knowledge of the subject, he said, "Pencil and charcoal, sometimes alone and sometimes together." He warmed to the subject. "I like doing landscapes and animals. I'd spend hours in the stable sketching the horses, the dogs, and the cats out there."

He set down his fork. "I took a couple of classes without my grandparents' knowledge. I didn't like sneaking around to do it, but something inside me made me press ahead." He grinned like a bad schoolboy. "I have to admit that I loved every minute of it."

Her eyes alive with interest, she asked, "Do you have any of your drawings with you?"

Embarrassed now, he shrugged. "I have a couple of sketchbooks in my room. I've never shown them to anyone. They're probably not very good."

"An artist never values his own work, unless he's extremely arrogant," she said. She rested her forearm on the table. "Would you mind bringing some of your works with you tonight? I'd love to see them."

He drew back a little. "They're probably not very good, Penny. You'll be disappointed."

Her lips drew together in a daring expression. "How about if we make a deal?" She paused then quickly said, "If you'll show me your drawings, I'll show you my. . .writing."

"Your writing?" He tried not to be shocked. It wasn't unheard of for a woman to write for publication—Louisa May Alcott and Harriet Beecher Stowe had been very successful—but he was having a hard time fitting this new piece of information in with the young woman who sat across from him. He focused in on her and lowered his voice. "Do you mean stories for your family?"

Her chin lifted a fraction. "I mean stories for the newspaper. That's all I'm going to tell you now. Bring your sketchbooks tonight, and you'll get the rest of the story."

He shook his head, smiling at her audacity in spite of himself. "Farley was right. When you get your teeth into something, you don't let go."

"Do we have a deal?"

He held out his hand to shake. "Deal. But no one sees them except you."

She clasped his hand in a firm grip. "Agreed, under the same conditions." She smiled, the victor. "The restaurant closes early because it's Christmas Eve, so we'll have dinner at seven thirty." She gave him an arch look with a teasing smile. "Be sure to bring your friend along and don't be late."

Chapter 6

At quarter to five, Justin headed back to his hotel with his head whirling and his heart thumping like the pistons on a steam engine. Show his drawings to a girl he'd only met a couple of days ago? Before he met Penny, he would never have considered it. But today, he was excited at the prospect. Would she like his work? Somehow he knew she would, and it had nothing to do with the sureness of his lines or the delicateness of his shading.

Vessel was still tiresomely polite when Justin reached the penthouse. Ignoring him, Justin retired to his room and closed the door. He had too much to think about for the next two hours. And he had yet to come up with a suitable gift for that lovely girl.

He looked through his trunk for the fifth time. Bother! Nothing would suit. What was he going to do? Unless. . . His gaze paused on something on top of his dressing table. Lunging to his feet, he swiped it up with a delighted gasp.

Penny was setting up the waitress station for the dinner crowd when Farley swept in from the cold, his cheeks and nose brilliant red.

She set down the spoon she was holding and dashed toward him.

"What's with you, sis?" Farley demanded, pulling off his coat. "I'm the one who's been freezing in the cold woods, but you have rosy cheeks just the same."

With a small giggle, she pressed both palms against her face. "Did you get it?" she asked.

"A tree?" he replied, delaying his answer.

"Farley!"

"Yes, Miss Joshua. I cut down a spruce up on Blackbird Hill. It's about five-and-a-half feet tall." Pulling off his coat, he showed her his scratched wrists. "That thing was a bear. I had an awful time loading it on the wagon. If it weren't for Diane's help. . ." He clamped his jaw shut.

"Diane?" She pushed him in the chest. "Now who's holding out? No wonder you didn't complain about going!" She peered out the window of the back door. "Did you take her home already? I'd like to see her. We haven't talked for ages."

He nodded. "Her parents are having lots of family over for dinner tonight so she had to get home. I may slip over there later this evening and say my howdys."

"See if you can bring her back with you for a few minutes," Penny said. She reached up to kiss his cheek. "You're a dear." She turned away to rush back to her work, calling over her shoulder, "Daddy's waiting for you to cut the pies. You'd best get moving."

The moment Penny unlocked the restaurant door, a dozen people poured inside—two couples and a family of eight. She stayed busy until the moment the last party went out at fifteen past seven.

Justin would arrive in fifteen minutes and she absolutely had to change clothes. Propping open the swinging doors, she called to her father and brother, "When Justin knocks, let him in. I'm going upstairs." Holding her skirts high, Penny made her way up the narrow steps with practiced grace and flew to her bedroom.

The family quarters were located over the restaurant with stairs both outside and inside. With three bedrooms and a modern bath, it was very comfortable. The kitchen was a tiny galley with only the barest essentials. But that was no problem for them since they ate at the restaurant three times a day.

Her dress, made from a dark green fabric with creamy white lace at the collar and cuffs and a green-and-red plaid sash around the waist, was hanging on a peg. As she was tucking up her hair, she realized she was excited about seeing Justin again.

Justin was dressed in his cheap suit and ready to leave at six forty-five. He stepped into the dining room and drew up when he saw Vessel still in his shirtsleeves and playing Parchessi.

"Vessel, we'll need to leave in thirty minutes," he said, worried. "You'll have to hurry so we won't be late."

The valet stood up, very straight, with his expression completely composed. "Begging your pardon, sir, but—"

"No, I'm begging," Justin interrupted. "*Please* come with me this time, Vessel. I'm asking you. . .please."

Vessel regarded the young man's face for a moment. "As you wish," he said and headed for his room. Ten minutes later, he reappeared wearing his dinner jacket, his overcoat on his arm.

They left without any further conversation. Carrying his sketchbooks in a thin leather case, Justin led the way, relieved to have Vessel with him. He wanted the old fellow to meet the Joshua family. Why it was so important to him, he didn't analyze. He just knew it was important.

When they stepped out of the clanking elevator and into the hotel lobby, a blond young man in a dark suit left the lobby desk and headed toward them. "Justin!" he cried. "I was hoping to catch you!"

Justin lost his breath for a moment. "Teddy!" he finally managed to croak. "What are you doing here?" Teddy Criswell was his old roommate and best friend from Berkeley.

Teddy shook his head and grimaced. "You won't believe what's happened to me since I saw you last summer."

"How did you find me?" Justin asked, still breathless.

"I sent a telegram to your house in San Francisco and got a reply that you were here." A faint note of desperation made his words sound tense.

Justin finally keyed in on what he was saying. "Are you in trouble, old man?" he asked.

"Not in trouble, no." His face became downcast. "I was in Denver to spend the holidays with Alice. I was all set to propose tomorrow morning. Had it all planned." He pulled a velvet box from his vest pocket and waved it toward Justin. "Then out of the blue she ended our courtship this morning. What was I going to do? Hang around her house for three more days? Not on your life." He shoved the box back into his pocket. "When I found out you were so close, I caught a stage."

"Teddy," Justin said, trying to think fast, "we're going out for a dinner engagement. Would you mind getting supper in the hotel here and waiting for me in our rooms?"

The other man nodded. "That's fine with me. I'm beat. A hot bath and a comfortable bed sound like heaven to me."

Justin handed him the key to the penthouse. "Vessel has a spare key to let us in later. Take the green room. Third door on the left of the hall."

"You're the greatest, Justin," he said, taking the key. He turned toward the dining room then turned back. "Who are you dining with?" he asked. "I thought no one was in town this time of year."

Ignoring Vessel's baleful stare, Justin said, "We'll talk about it later, Teddy. It's too complicated to go into now. I'll check in on you when we get back."

He headed toward the door with Vessel close at his heels. As they reached the tall outer doors of the hotel, Justin could have almost sworn he heard a *harrumph* from the valet, but Vessel was too well bred for that.

Teddy was a good sport and a lot of fun. He was also a great tease. He and Justin had played their share of pranks while they were at school together. The son of a moderately wealthy family who owned a chain of farm equipment stores, Teddy had majored in agricultural science. They had a standing joke that both he and Justin loved to dig in dirt: Justin for what he could get out of it and Teddy for what he could put into it.

When Justin first met Teddy, they were freshmen at Berkeley. The senior men had painted thin slabs of wood to match the school's restroom doors. They'd carefully covered the "WO" portion of the word women and then stood aside to watch the fun. Justin was headed inside when he met Teddy—red as raw beefsteak—bolting out to a chorus of shrill screams. The seniors had laughed themselves silly, but Justin had never mentioned the incident to Teddy since. Some things are just too painful.

If it hadn't been for Justin's involvement with the Joshua family, he would have been delighted to see his old friend,

Teddy. As it was, he felt a nervous twitch in his left jaw that wouldn't go away.

When Justin and Vessel arrived at the restaurant, Farley opened the front door, stepped out, and closed it behind him. He was carrying a lantern. "Let me show you how to get to the entrance of our apartment," he said, leading the way down the gravel-covered alley next to the building. "Then you'll know where to find our front door when you come again."

At the back corner of the structure, he turned left. The stairs slanted away from the building, and they reached the bottom step ten paces later.

Justin kept glancing back at Vessel, marching steadily after him for twenty stair risers. The older man never paused or changed his stoic expression. Justin was beginning to worry. He hadn't seen Vessel this reserved since Grandfather had sent him to Berkeley with a letter for the dean in an attempt to stave off a suspension threat.

During their sophomore year, Justin, Teddy, and their third roommate, Matt Jenkins, had greased every doorknob in North Hall, including the outer doors, and had ground the entire male student body to a halt. Not that the men had cared. They thought it was a lark, but the faculty was livid. Every first-hour class had started late.

Farley stepped into the apartment with Justin and Vessel behind him. They stopped in the front hall to take off their coats. Farley did the honors and then led them into the parlor. "My father's putting together our dinner and dealing with tonight's leftovers," he said. "I'd better help him out. Would you mind waiting here? Penny should be with you in a few minutes."

Justin made the right response and found a chair. Vessel did likewise and remained as still as a stone. Propping the leather case against the leg of the chair, Justin looked around.

The parlor was large enough for a short camel-backed sofa and three chairs with a secretary and a chest of drawers against two of the walls. A large alcove with four mullioned windows added light and space. Crocheted doilies and antimacassars covered almost every surface, even the arms of the chairs. A delicate hurricane lamp with a milky glass shade stood on a spindly round table in the center of the alcove, creating a gentle glow. It would have been a perfect subject for a still life, with the white gauze curtains billowing behind it.

On the other side of the room stood a dining table, already set for dinner with a white tablecloth and gold-rimmed china. The table had six Windsor chairs around it.

The men had been seated for a few moments when Penny entered the room. Her glossy blond hair shone against the dark green fabric. Lurching to his feet, Justin had to guard himself from staring. Every time he saw her she seemed more beautiful.

"Good evening, Justin," she said, beaming at him as she shook his hand. "I'm so glad to see you." She glanced at Vessel, who was also standing.

"This is Albert Wessel," Justin said.

Smiling a delighted welcome, she offered him her hand. "Mr. Wessel, how good of you to join us this evening." She took a seat on the plush sofa, and the men sat down in chairs across from her.

Penny told them of the Christmas tree that Farley had cut. "After supper, we'll haul it up here and put it in the alcove." She nodded toward the hurricane lamp. "I'll have to find another spot for that."

A knock at a nearby door brought Penny to her feet. "That's the men with the food," she said. She crossed the room and pulled open a door in the hall. Farley stepped through carrying a large platter of turkey with a bowl of stuffing balanced on top of it.

"Dad's behind me with a tray," he said, puffing a little. "I'm ready to say we should have eaten downstairs."

"Don't be a spoilsport," she chided. "We eat there every day of the year. Why can't we enjoy our own home for a change?"

Justin stood. "Can I help carry anything?"

Michael Joshua stepped into the hallway and nodded. "There's a pitcher of tea on the kitchen table," he wheezed.

Glad for something to do, Justin hustled down the steps and was soon back with the metal pitcher.

The five of them gathered around the table, and Penny introduced Vessel to her family.

"Please call me Vessel," he told them. "Everyone does."

Hearing the friendly note in the valet's voice, Justin sent a sly glance his way and caught Vessel softly smiling in Penny's direction while she talked to her father.

Justin stifled the urge to give the older man a nudge in the ribs. After all his disapproval, she'd smitten him, too. If that didn't beat all.

He must have been grinning, because Penny turned toward him and gave him an inquiring look. Sobering, he bowed for prayer as Mr. Joshua said the blessing.

When they raised their heads, Penny lifted a bowl of mashed potatoes and handed it to Vessel. "Tell me, Mr. . . ."

"Vessel," he repeated, smiling at her. "No mister. Just Vessel."

"Yes, um, Vessel, how do you like Colorado Springs this time of year?"

"The mountains are beautiful," he said, taking the dish from her hand. "But it's too cold for my liking, and too windy. I much prefer California."

"California?" she looked at Justin.

He looked at Vessel.

"I lived there years ago," Vessel said. "I like to go back to visit from time to time. Have you ever been there?"

"I haven't had the pleasure," she said.

Mr. Joshua added, "It's a dream of Penny's to see the ocean." He passed the platter of turkey. "Me, I'm content to stay at home."

"Justin tells me you're an old friend of his family," Penny said. "Are you in mining, too?"

Feeling his way along, Vessel slowly replaced his glass on the table.

"I told her about my grandfather being in mining," Justin told him, "and how he wanted me to follow in his trade."

"I'm in men's clothing," Vessel said, moderately dignified without being too stuffy.

"That's where I saw you!" Penny burst out. "Bernard's shop. I knew you looked familiar."

Chapter 7

Justin felt a surge of alarm.

"Did you find a proper suit for Mr. Van der Whoever?" Penny asked Vessel. "Bernard is a wonderful tailor, but he's so expensive."

"We're old chess players," Mr. Joshua added. "I haven't had a good game with Bernard for ages. Too long."

"He said to come by in the evening and have a game," Penny told him. "You really ought to, Daddy. It would do you good."

"Have you ever played Parchessi?" Vessel asked Mr. Joshua, his smooth face hopeful.

The big man frowned. "What did you call it?"

"Parchessi. It's the royal game of India, just come to the U.S. of A. It's marvelous fun."

"You don't say. I've never heard of it."

Vessel described the game in detail, finishing with, "It's a wonderful pastime."

Justin chuckled. "He ropes me into a game whenever he can. I'm sure he'd love to have some new competition."

"It sounds very interesting," Michael said, intrigued. "I'd love to try it."

"After the meal, why don't I go round and fetch the board?" Vessel asked. "It's just a few minutes' walk to my quarters."

"I'd hate for you to venture out in the cold and dark to get it," Penny said.

"Not at all, my dear. I'd be delighted."

Justin smiled to assure her. "He means it, Penny. It would be the highlight of his holiday."

"In that case, please do." She beamed at him again.

Vessel's smooth cheeks flushed a little.

Farley finished the last of his sweet potato and raised his napkin to his lips. "Sorry to be rude, but I've got to run. Diane is expecting me."

Penny laughed. "We wouldn't dream of keeping you," she said. "Not that we could if we tried."

He gave her a pat on the shoulder and headed for the outside stairs. "I'll be home before midnight," he called just before the door banged after him.

Mr. Joshua grunted. "He's young and in love. You'll have to excuse his manners." He helped himself to a second helping of potatoes.

When they finished the meal, Justin helped Penny clear the table and carry the dishes back to the restaurant kitchen. Vessel set out for the hotel, and Penny's father retired to his room for a much-needed break while he awaited Vessel's return.

Downstairs, Penny ran hot water into the deep metal sink while Justin scraped and stacked, an art he'd learned from his duties in the mansion's kitchen. Before long, they had a system in place and the dishwashing progressed with speed.

"I've got your suit," Penny said. "Bernard sent it over this afternoon. He's going to let me keep it until the meeting and only charge me for one day."

"Nice of him," Justin said, wiping a cup.

"You can take it home with you this evening, if you'd like," she said. They worked in comfortable silence for a few minutes. "Did you bring your sketches?" Penny asked, handing him the last plate to dry.

"Of course," he said, smiling into her eyes.

"In that case, I'll show you my writings before we go up. I keep them locked in a cabinet down here. My menfolk wouldn't dream of looking through the waitress station, you know."

Drying her hands, she led him through the swinging doors. He found a seat at their usual table while she fetched the pages.

He'd expected handwritten sheaves of paper, but she brought him copies of the *Colorado Springs Summit*, all folded back to reveal the stories of Gregory Landis.

He glanced through the stack. "You're Landis?" he asked, amazed.

"Have been for the past five years." She sat across from him, peering at his face to catch his reaction.

He wasn't sure if his response was obvious to her or not. He felt awed and impressed. Writing stories for the newspaper? She had more grit to her than he'd imagined.

He smiled, and her answering smile formed a warm arc between them, an invisible rainbow that held them and moved them and molded them until they forgot all else.

The spell lasted until Vessel's measured tread sounded over their heads.

"We'd best get back upstairs," Penny said, her cheeks delightfully pink. "You've still got to fulfill your end of the bargain, you know." Scooping up the bundle, she locked the newspapers back into the cabinet.

"Would you like to join the game of Parchessi?" Justin asked as they walked together down the hall. "It's great fun."

"If you want," she replied. Then after a small pause, "On the other hand, I think I'd rather sit in the parlor. It's been a long day, and I'm a little tired. Maybe tomorrow we can play."

"In that case, let's find a lamp and take a look at the sketchbooks. I brought both of them, so we could be awhile."

When they reached the parlor, the men were already in positions on opposite sides of the table, generals surveying their territory. Vessel was in his glory.

Sitting close together on the sofa with a lighted gas lamp on the wall behind them, Justin opened the satchel and drew out two wide weathered books. Their paper covers were wrinkled and smudged with charcoal.

He hesitated, running his hand over the top cover. "I have one favor to ask of you before we begin."

"Yes?" She turned to him expectantly and the light played across the smooth curve of her cheek.

"Be honest," he said, gently. "I want your true and unvarnished opinion. Agreed?"

"Of course." She smiled, and he thought his heart would stop.

Forcing himself to get to the matter at hand, he opened the book and moved it over so the binding fell between them, and they each held one side.

He kept turning pages at slow intervals. He'd expected to feel embarrassed or nervous, but instead he was at peace. She was a kindred spirit in the arts, something he'd never found before.

Suddenly her hand flew out to stop him from turning the page. Before them lay two kittens in the midst of a rough and tumble, a knot of legs and tails done in charcoal.

She didn't speak for a full minute, her expression intent as she studied the details. "This is marvelous," she murmured, glancing at him. "One is a calico and the other a tiger. How did you do that?"

"We had cats in the stable," he replied. "I loved to watch them play. These two scrappers were always going at it. One day I took my charcoals out and captured them." He gazed at the picture and pointed to the bottom right edge of the image. "I hide my name and the date within the picture itself. See here?" He checked the date and calculated. "I was twelve when I did this one."

"You did this when you were twelve?" she gasped. "I can't believe that. You have talent, Justin," she declared. "You must pursue this." She turned the page, eager now to see what lay ahead.

They spent the next two hours with the sketchbooks while the men exclaimed and complained over their game. Justin wanted the evening to last forever.

"Will you come back for Christmas breakfast with us?" she asked as they neared the end of the last volume.

"I don't want to intrude on your family time," he said, though he wanted it in the worst way.

"We'd love to have you and Vessel come for the day tomorrow."

Her father let out a roar, and she chuckled, turning to watch them.

"Set back again!" Mr. Joshua cried. He settled himself into the chair. "Don't look for any quarter from this side," he declared. "You're not getting any."

Vessel laughed. "Nor you from me, I promise you." He

shook the dice in their little black cup and poured them onto the board. "Five!"

"They're overgrown children," Penny said, still laughing.

"Warriors," Justin corrected. "There's a difference."

She tilted her head as an idea struck her. "You know, we should have a party tomorrow, invite some more people in and have a good time."

She counted on her fingers. "I'll have Farley bring Diane. He'll be delighted at that, believe me. I'll invite Margaret and Catherine, friends of mine from our church." She ticked them off. "You and Vessel." She turned to him. "Do you have any friends from the hotel that you'd like to bring along?"

Justin drew up. He'd like to bring Teddy in the worst way. What could be more heartless than to leave a good friend alone on Christmas while he himself was having a high old time? But could he trust Teddy to keep mum?

"What is it, Justin?" she asked. "You look worried."

He smiled. "Nothing could be wrong tonight," he murmured, leaning a little closer. "I was just thinking about who I could invite."

"You don't have to tell me now," she said, looking down at her six extended fingers. "You could bring two friends, and we'd still have room for everyone." She laughed again. "Or bring more, and we'll move down into the restaurant."

He laughed. "I'll remember that."

The lock rattled, and Farley kicked the outer door open. A blast of cold air brought Penny to her feet to see what her brother was doing. Justin came along behind her.

Farley had his back to them. He yanked hard on something out of sight, and a snowy Christmas tree slid into the hall.

"Oh, look at the wet!" Penny cried and ran to get some rags

to wipe up the floor.

Farley pulled the tree in far enough to get around it in the narrow hall, then hurried to fetch a bucket from the stoop and close the door. "Where do you want this?" he asked when Penny returned.

"In the parlor alcove," she said, "but not until it's drier. Oh, why didn't you bring it in *before* it started snowing."

Testily, he replied, "If I'd known it was going to snow, I would have."

She let out a frustrated gasp. "Oh well, there's no hope for it now. I'll put towels on the floor under it until it drips dry." She turned toward the galley kitchen. "We'll have to move the furniture to make way."

Farley took off his damp cap and coat and hung them up. He glanced at Justin. "Let's get that sofa moved and those two small tables."

The men set to work while Penny removed the hurricane lamp to her bedroom for safekeeping. Farley carried the bucket of sand to the alcove, and the men set the tree upright in it then filled it almost full of water. Penny quickly set towels on the wooden floor beneath it.

"It's beautiful even without any ornaments," she said as she smiled at Justin. "I guess we'd best get busy. I made popcorn to string up and some paper ornaments to put together."

"Candles?" Farley asked her.

"A dozen of them," she said then went on, "We're having a party here tomorrow afternoon at two o'clock. I'd like you to invite Diane, Catherine, and Margaret." She glanced at him. "You are going out in the morning, aren't you?"

He nodded. "I'm supposed to be at Diane's house around ten o'clock. I'll stop in to see the others on my way by." He flexed his shoulders and stretched his back. "I put a crick in my back pulling that thing up the stairs." He rotated one shoulder and then the other. Glancing at Penny, he asked, "So, what have you got planned for the party? Parlor games? Food?"

"Both!" she announced. "We've got plenty of cake left in the ice box. I'll make coffee, and we'll be set."

"Sounds like a great time," he said, pleased. "Now, where are the candles?"

"In the kitchen." She hurried to find them along with some strong thread and two needles. When she returned, she gave Farley the box of candles, then handed Justin a needle and a long length of thread. She placed a bowl of popcorn between her and Justin on the sofa.

Mr. Joshua whooped over some play in the game, and Farley headed over to see what was happening. In a few moments, he returned and they worked at decorating the tree for the next hour.

When his job was finished, Farley lifted the curtain and peered into the night. "It's really starting to come down out there."

"Is it?" Penny stopped sewing a paper ornament and joined him at the window. "I love to watch it snow."

Justin joined Penny at the window. Thick snowflakes swirled around the street lamps.

"We'd best get started home," he said, noticing a thin coating of white on the ground. "I hope this doesn't keep us away tomorrow."

"So do I," she murmured, gazing shyly up at him.

At that moment, Vessel cried, "That's it! Game point. You win this round, old man."

Farley stepped to the table. "I'd like to get in on the game tomorrow," he said.

"Tomorrow?" his father asked, a hearty note in his voice.

"Penny's got a party planned for the afternoon," Farley told him.

Penny added, "I've invited them to come for breakfast and stay for the day," she said.

"Excellent!" Mr. Joshua said. His round cheeks almost hid his eyes when he smiled.

Slipping the colored playing pieces into a small velvet pouch, Vessel said, "I'll leave the game here, if it's all right with you, Michael."

"Good idea," Justin put in. "It's snowing, and you'd get the box wet carrying it home."

Vessel became concerned. "Snowing? We'd best be going then." He flipped the board closed with a quick movement and had the box top in place within seconds.

Justin returned to their coats hanging in the hall. Penny followed him. "Maybe you'd better leave the suit here tonight," she said. "It'll get wet if you take it now."

"I'll leave the sketchbooks here, too," he told her. "No sense taking any chances with them either."

"Of course. I'll put them away in my room."

Vessel trundled into the hallway, and Penny moved to give him room to put on his coat.

"Thank you both for coming," she said warmly.

"Yes, thanks for coming," Mr. Joshua said, standing at the end of the hall. "I don't know when I've had such a good time."

The men shook hands all around and said their good nights. Justin clasped Penny's hand in his for a lingering moment. He had a difficult time pulling himself away from her.

"Tomorrow!" he whispered as he left her.

Her answering smile made his heart sing. "Ten o'clock," she said.

Carefully moving down the snowy stairs, Justin and Vessel hurried down the street, anxious to get out of the bitter cold and the biting wind.

"I owe you an apology," Vessel said when they paused at a street crossing.

"We differ on that," Justin said. "I should be apologizing. I put you in a difficult position tonight."

"Not at all. It was jolly good fun," he replied, stepping into the street. "What a marvelous family." He chuckled. "What a delightful young lady, Justin my boy."

Justin nodded, and his stomach turned into a leaden knot. What would she think of him when she learned who he really was? When she learned that he hadn't been honest with her?

Penny turned out the gaslights as she made her way to her room. Farley and Daddy had already turned in. It was close to midnight, and they were all exhausted.

She paused in the doorway to her room, leaning against the doorjamb with her head resting on the smooth woodwork. What a wonderful man Justin was. She'd never met anyone like him. . .and she probably never would again. He was sweet and thoughtful, kind and generous, talented. . .and a dedicated Christian. And so handsome with those brown eyes and that cute little dimple in his chin.

She sighed and pulled her door gently closed. She'd had a few crushes in her life, but never one steady beau. A couple of years ago, she would have been bouncing with excitement after spending the evening with an attractive gentleman, but tonight was different. Tonight, she felt a calm warmth deep within her. She wanted to hug it to herself and never let it go.

Slowly changing into her flannel nightgown, she turned out the last light, snuggled under the goose-down comforter, and soon fell into a deep sleep.

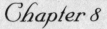

When Justin and Vessel arrived at the penthouse, Teddy came out of his room dressed in a thick blue robe and wearing slippers. His straw-like hair was tousled, and he looked like he was ten years old.

"Good morning," he said with a sleepy grin.

"Good night, Master Teddy," Vessel said and went straight to his quarters.

"Did you get any rest?" Justin asked, taking off his coat. He laid it over the arm of a nearby chair.

"About three hours," Teddy replied with a wide yawn. He rubbed his eyes. "I woke up a few minutes ago, starving." He gazed around the dining room. "Do you have a kitchen hereabouts?"

Justin shook his head. "Sorry. But I do have a loaf of bread and a piece of hard cheese. Vessel keeps some in a cupboard for an emergency."

"Well, I'd call this one," Teddy replied, rubbing his stomach. "I ate a big dinner. Can't imagine why I'm so famished."

Justin lit a lamp in the dining room and opened a cupboard door. "I'll bet you haven't eaten much the last day or so. Too wrought up."

The other man nodded. "You've pegged that right. Alice had me jumping through hoops. It wasn't pleasant, and that's a fact."

Justin set the food on the table and poured them both water from a carafe. "I'm glad you're up," he said, sitting across from Teddy at the table. He waited for his friend to cut a slab of cheese and chew for a moment before saying, "I'm in a sticky situation, Ted, and I'm going to have to call in a couple of favors."

Teddy stopped chewing. "You don't say," he said around his mouthful.

Justin started with the restaurant fiasco and Penny's mistaking him for a waiter. "She gave me fifty cents to get a haircut," he said ruefully.

Teddy's eyes grew round. "You are pulling my leg, Justin Van der Meer. You surely are."

"I am not!" he declared. "You can ask Vessel in the morning. He knows about this, too."

Teddy's expression became intent. "And you took it?"

Justin nodded. "I got the haircut, too."

Teddy pulled his left earlobe. "Okay, okay." He held up his hand to stop Justin's storytelling. "Let's go back for just a minute. You've left out a vital detail."

"What?"

"What does she look like?" he demanded.

"Penny?" Justin gazed into the yellow light reflected in the table's glossy top. "The top of her head comes up to here." He held his hand level at a point below his shoulder. "She has delicate features and the bluest eyes I've ever seen. Her hair is so blond it almost glows. She wears it up—" He had his hand over the top of his head then froze when he caught sight of Teddy's sardonic smile. Ignoring it, he went on, "She's spunky and smart. . ."

"Got it bad, I see," Teddy said, chuckling. He took another bite of bread and cheese.

"I've never met anyone like her," Justin said. Suddenly, he grew serious. "She still doesn't know who I am, Teddy. And she can't find out yet. You've got to help me keep it mum."

"Keep talking," he said, still chewing.

"We're invited to her house for Christmas Day. I want to take you along, but you have to promise me you'll watch what you say. Promise you won't give me away."

"That's a hard promise to make, Justin," Teddy said. "What if I slip up?"

"So far it hasn't been hard to avoid certain topics. When she asks something personal, I change the subject or make a comment that has nothing to do with what she asked. She hasn't seemed to notice."

"All I can promise is that I'll do my best." He squinted at Justin. "How many times have you seen this girl?"

Justin told of their two practice sessions and Christmas Eve at the Joshuas' apartment, leaving out the part about his sketches and her writing. "We're all invited back for Christmas breakfast at ten in the morning," he finished. "You, me, and Vessel."

Teddy wrapped the remaining food into its paper container and pushed it toward Justin. "When's this meeting again?"

"The day after tomorrow. We'll spend tomorrow with the Joshua family, and then the next day I've got to get through that meeting." He rubbed the stubbly hair on the back of his head and tried to smooth it down. "Penny's going to be there watching my every move. And boy is she tough to please."

Teddy yawned again.

Justin picked up the small bundle of food. "We've got to get to bed, or we'll meet ourselves getting up. It's close to two a.m."

"Tomorrow I may prop myself in a corner somewhere and sleep," Teddy said. "I'm bone weary."

"You could come later," Justin told him, relieved at the thought. "If you want to sleep in, I'll leave directions on the table here so you can find your way when you're ready." The less time Teddy spent with Penny the better.

"We'll see how I feel in the morning," he said, shuffling toward the hall. "Merry Christmas," he mumbled and gave a little salute as he disappeared into his room and closed the door.

Justin took his time putting away the food and turning out the lights. Tonight in Penny's parlor he'd had a feeling of living in a world that wasn't real. The Joshua family lived a quiet, simple life. Their lot was hard in some ways, sure. But so was his. So was everyone's, when it came down to it. The problems were different, but they were still problems.

He changed his clothes and slid into bed. Did he dare to dream that Penny would someday live in his world? Would she want to?

He turned over and closed his eyes. *You can stop dreaming, you big dolt*, he thought. *Once she finds out that you've been holding back on her, she'll be so disgusted with you that she'll probably refuse to see you again.*

An ache swelled in his chest, and he shoved the thought aside. It was too painful to dwell on, even for a minute.

No one in the Joshua house stirred until nearly nine o'clock. Christmas was the one day of the year when they had nothing to do. The restaurant was closed every Sunday, but there were church services to prepare for, so a day of complete rest was extremely rare.

Farley was combed and dressed when Penny first ventured from her room. She wore a robe and her hair hung about her shoulders.

Farley kissed her cheek. "Merry Christmas, sis," he said.

She gave him a soft smile. "Merry Christmas." She looked at his starched shirt. "Are you going so soon?"

"If I'm going to stop in on Margaret and Catherine, I'll have to leave in a few minutes."

"Wait! I've got presents." She hesitated. "I hate to wake up Daddy."

"Don't. The presents will keep until I get back. I should be here around noon. After breakfast, Diane's folks are going to visit her grandmother. It's a family time, and I'm going to bow out."

"That will be fine," she said, relieved. "Justin will be here in an hour, and I still need to dress."

"He's a nice fellow," Farley said, giving her a wry smile.

She beamed. "I noticed."

He kissed her cheek again. "I hope it works out for you. He's a nice guy."

Her cheeks felt warm.

Farley glanced at the mantel clock and hurried away, leaving Penny to her primping.

Justin started the day by washing up to clear the fuzz from his brain. He shouldn't have stayed up so late talking to Teddy. Now he was paying for it.

Half an hour later, he and Vessel left the penthouse as quietly as they could so Teddy could catch up on his sleep. Justin pulled the door closed behind him with a feeling of intense relief. He'd left directions and a hand-drawn map on the table. With any luck, Teddy would sleep until two p.m. It wasn't unheard of.

Justin carried a small bundle under his arm. As was the family custom, he'd given Vessel a generous cash gift that morning. Arrangements had been made last fall for every servant in every one of Justin's homes to receive something as well, from parlor maid to stable boy. The Van der Meers were frugal but definitely not cheap.

The snow had stopped during the night, leaving the town with a clean-washed feeling. Mercifully, the wind had died down. The air was crisp, and the snowy sidewalks crunched beneath their shoes.

Justin drew in a cleansing breath and energy flowed through him. In five more minutes he'd be with Penny.

When they reached the stairs, they were already swept clean. Penny opened the door before they had a chance to knock.

"Merry Christmas!" she cried, stepping back to let them in. "You must be frozen. Come in where it's warm." She wore a dress of soft brown fabric with a hint of red in the color.

Justin laid his bundle on the bench beneath the coat hooks and took off his coat.

"Farley has already gone to Diane's house," she said. "He'll be back in a couple of hours." She beamed at Vessel. "Daddy's in the kitchen downstairs. He'll be up soon with our breakfast tray."

"It must be strange having a father who cooks," Justin said, following her into the dining room. The table was set for six.

"Not to me." She let out a small, enchanting laugh. "He's been cooking all my life."

Mildly embarrassed, Justin showed her the bundle. "I brought a gift—a thank-you for having us over."

"Justin, you shouldn't have gone to any trouble," she said,

eyeing the rolled-up cloth. "Why don't you leave it by the Christmas tree? Farley went out before Daddy was up, so we haven't exchanged our gifts yet. We can do it all at once." She smiled. "Thank you for being so thoughtful."

He swallowed and tried to fight back the heat crawling up his neck and into his cheeks—a lost cause.

A booming voice brought Vessel to the door of the inside stairs, and Michael Joshua stepped in carrying a tray wider than his girth. It was loaded with scrambled eggs, sausage, bacon, golden biscuits, and a stack of pancakes eight inches high. "Coffee's still in the kitchen," he said. "And there's another tray with the butter and syrup for these hotcakes." He set the entire tray in the middle of the table.

Penny headed for the stairs with Justin at her heels. Oh, the glory of a chance to speak to her alone.

"Does he always go all out for Christmas breakfast?" he asked her when they reached the bottom.

"This year is special," she said, gazing up at him. "He feels it, too." A hint of sadness touched her smile. "You've been good for us," she said. "Even for Daddy. You've made us look ahead instead of behind."

He thought about that for a moment. "So have you," he said. "I'm afraid I was caught in the same trap." She reached for the tray, and he had to fight back the urge to stop her and take her in his arms.

Lifting the coffeepot with a potholder lying beside the stove, he caught up to her on the fourth step. "Be careful you don't trip," he said.

She sounded a little breathy when she said, "I'm used to these stairs, Justin." She laughed then said, "Don't worry. I won't fall on you."

"It's that open pitcher of syrup I'm worried about," he retorted.

She was still laughing when she stepped into the dining room.

They took their places at the table, and Mr. Joshua offered thanks.

Reaching for the nearest dish, piled high with bacon and sausage, Vessel said, "When I was a boy in England, we'd always look forward to having Crackers beside our plates at Christmas breakfast."

"Crackers?" Penny asked, wrinkling her dainty nose. "For breakfast?"

He chuckled. "They were party favors, my dear," he said, "a fascinating invention." He forked meat onto his plate and passed the platter to Justin beside him. "They were about this long." He held his hands about eight inches apart. "A tube shape decorated with brightly colored paper. Each end held a string or a loop, so two people could pull each end, like a wishbone. When the middle gave way, it made a great cracking sound and some kind of treat would fall out. Whoever got the biggest half kept the treat."

"Candy?" Mr. Joshua asked.

"Sometimes. But it could be a small toy or a gaudy hat made of tissue paper." Vessel smiled at the memory. "We used to wear those hats and run about like little hooligans until Mother would have enough of it and set us down with a picture book or some such." He sighed. "Wonderful days."

Penny said, "Mother always gave us something she'd made with her own hands—a scarf, some gloves, a sweater. . .sometimes a dress or a coat."

A warm silence gave them a moment to enjoy the food.

When they finished, Penny said, "Daddy, would you mind if we read the Christmas story from the Bible before we leave the table?"

"Not at all," he said. "I'd enjoy that. I haven't heard it for years."

She hurried to her room and brought back a thick book with a worn black cover. "This was Mother's," she said. She handed it to Justin. "Would you mind reading for us?"

He opened the yellowed pages and began to read, " 'And it came to pass in those days, that there went out a decree from Caesar Augustus that all the world should be taxed. . .' " He read slowly and with feeling for the next five minutes. Then he gently closed the book.

"That was beautiful," Penny breathed. "I can never listen to that story without being touched."

Mr. Joshua cleared his throat. "Would you like to move into the parlor?" he asked. "We can take our coffee in there." He glanced at Penny. "We'll clear this up later. There's plenty of time today."

They had scarcely sat down when Farley burst in, stamping snow from his boots and grinning widely. "It's a gorgeous day," he said. His cheeks were red and his nose, too.

Penny laughed at him. "You look half frozen. What are you talking about?"

Leaving his boots in the hall, he dropped his coat over its peg and padded into the parlor in his stocking feet. "It's sunny, very little breeze. The snow is sparkling."

She slanted a look at him and gave him a sly grin. "Sounds romantic."

He let out a loud laugh but didn't comment on that. Instead he said, "For your information, both Margaret and Catherine are coming over this afternoon. And. . ." He hesitated to give his announcement a build up, "Catherine's father is going to hitch their sleigh for us after dark. The streets are covered with snow, perfect for a ride."

Penny let out a delighted gasp. "That's wonderful!" She looked at Justin. "Can you stay for that? You won't have to work early in the morning, will you?"

He grinned. "I can stay. I wouldn't miss it for anything."

Farley pulled a chair from the dining table, placed it next to the Christmas tree, and sat down.

"Now that you're here," his father told him, "we can exchange our gifts." He spoke to Vessel. "I hope you don't mind. We didn't have time to do this earlier today."

"By all means," Vessel said.

Wrapped in brown paper and tied with string, or bundled in brightly colored cloth, the gifts were distributed and quickly opened.

When the Joshua family had finished their exchange, Justin reached for his own bundle. He felt awkward. "I brought this as a thank-you for your hospitality," he said, handing it to Penny.

With a wondering glance at him, she unwrapped it and gasped with pleasure. Inside lay a small wooden box, carved roses covering the sides and lid.

"How lovely!" she exclaimed.

"It's something that's been in our family for a while," he told her. "I thought you might like it."

"I love it!" She turned it one way and then the other, admiring the workmanship. "Thank you, Justin!" Her sparkling eyes made him want to shout or dance or sing. Or all three.

He had to limit himself to a softly spoken, "You're quite welcome, Penny."

"And now, let's set up a game of Parchessi," Mr. Joshua said.

"How many can play?" Penny asked. She carefully set the box on a small table near her chair and stood up.

"Only four," her father said. "One at each corner of the board."

"In that case, Justin and I will clear the food away, Daddy," she said, looking at Justin for confirmation. "Would you mind sitting out this time?" she asked him.

"Not at all," Justin said, eager to help. He'd wash dishes for six hours straight if it meant five minutes alone in the kitchen with Penny.

Chapter 9

Farley picked up the wide tray and loaded it with dishes. "I'll carry this one. You get the plates," he said. "Go ahead and start without me," he told his father. "I'll get in on the second round."

To Justin's chagrin, Farley seemed to be planning to stick with them until the job was finished.

Scraping food into small dishes to put into the icebox, Farley said, "Don't you think Justin has vastly improved, Penny? I don't think he needs any more practice at all."

Wiping a cup, Justin waited for her reply.

"You're right. No more practice." She flicked a small bit of suds at Farley. "Who wants to practice on Christmas Day anyway?"

Farley dodged the suds. "You don't want to open that can of worms, sis," he warned.

She laughed. "Who said I don't?"

He pointed to the clock. "Diane will be here in half an hour."

"Spoilsport." She dug into the dishpan for another plate and the dishes began to fly as they finished cleaning up. Ten minutes later, Penny set the cider on the back of the stove to simmer.

Mr. Joshua and Vessel had the Parchessi game set up when the young people returned. Farley joined the men while Justin and Penny sat in the parlor. Minutes flew by, and Justin wished that for the second time in history the sun would stand still.

In the middle of the second game, a light tapping at the door brought Farley to his feet. "That's Diane!" he said, moving to the hall. "She's got the girls with her," he called back to the dining room two seconds later, then swung open the door.

Giggles and gasps filled the hallway. Penny left the parlor to join her friends and soon returned with them. "This is Catherine Bagley," she said with a small wave at the dark-haired girl. Three inches taller than Penny, Catherine had a regal bearing, yet a sincere and friendly smile as she said hello.

"Margaret Meadows," Penny said, beaming at the second girl. Smaller and slighter, she had a boyish smile and hair the color of honey. She wore a yellow dress with a large orange scarf tied about her shoulders.

Farley appeared behind them with his arm around a third girl, an olive-skinned beauty. "And Diane Wallace." He winked at her. "Soon to be Joshua."

Her blush gave her a radiant glow.

Farley looked at the Parchessi board. "Sorry to bow out, but I'm part of the entertainment committee." He stretched to remove his pieces from play.

"Well, Entertainment Committee," Catherine said, "what are we going to do?"

At that moment, another tap sounded on the door. Farley looked at Penny. "Who else is coming?" he asked.

"Teddy!" Justin exclaimed, remembering him for the first time that morning. "A friend of mine. I'd forgotten all about him."

Penny let the young man in, and he joined the group. Justin made the introductions, then he and Farley moved still more chairs into the parlor so that the seven of them sat in a circle along the walls of the tiny room.

"Charades!" Penny announced, clapping her hands. She grinned at Justin. "We've quite a few people here who are strangers. This way we'll get to know each other."

Justin stiffened. He had never been comfortable playacting. Teddy sent him a wide grin and hooked one arm over the back of his chair. He'd been a thespian at Berkeley and thoroughly enjoyed Justin's discomfort.

"Do you have a list of items?" Farley asked.

Penny drew a folded page from her dress pocket and waved it in the air. "I'll have to be the moderator because I already know what they are." She surveyed the group. Catherine wore an amused half-smile, and Diane chewed her bottom lip.

Penny stood. "Would you mind trading chairs with me, Margaret? That way I'll be in the center. Each side of the room is a team."

"Of course," Margaret said and quickly moved into Penny's chair, which put Margaret between Teddy and Justin. Teddy straightened in his chair and pulled his arms in a little. Margaret licked her lips.

"Farley's team starts," Penny announced. "Who's going to be first?"

Catherine stepped forward. Penny folded the paper back so only the top line was visible, then showed it to her.

Catherine shrugged and quirked in one side of her mouth. She faced Farley and Diane, pointed from one of them to the other, and then touched the fourth finger of her left hand.

"Married!" Farley burst out.

Catherine shook her head and tugged at her finger again.

"Engaged!" Diane cried.

"Point," Penny said. She turned to the other team.

"You go," Justin told Teddy. "You're a lot better at this than I am."

Teddy rubbed his palms on his pants legs as he stood. When he got the word, he grinned. Whirling, he pointed directly at Justin's midsection.

"Chest!" Justin said.

Teddy shook his head and pointed again, this time at Justin's head.

Margaret guessed "hair," "face," and "eyes," but got nowhere.

Justin tried "man," "boy," "American," "friend," and finally "handsome" as a parting joke, then gave up. "What was it?" he demanded.

Teddy shook his head, disgusted. "Wealthy. What else?"

Penny looked worried and sent a suspicious glance toward Justin, then asked Teddy, "Why would you point to Justin for that word?"

Justin glared at Teddy, and his friend's freckled face quickly turned the color of a ripe tomato. He covered his mouth with his palm and pulled his jaw downward. "I'm sorry," he said, letting his hand drop. "I did a bad job on that one." He turned to Penny. "Am I disqualified?"

She glanced at Farley. "Can we give them another try?" she asked. "I think that was a mix up."

Farley nodded. "Beginner's grace," he said.

Relief in the slope of his shoulders and angle of his chin, Teddy came to Penny for another word. "I apologize," he said. "I'll get the right of it this time."

They played for the next hour with Teddy on his best

behavior. Farley's team won the final point by guessing "signature" when Diane pretended to hand herself a bill and then she scribbled on the bottom of it with her finger.

"Anyone for spiced cider?" Penny asked as they broke up. "I have some in the kitchen downstairs."

Justin lingered toward the back of the group when the others filed out, expecting Teddy to naturally join him. When the young men had a brief moment on the stairs out of earshot of the others, Justin whispered. "You just cost me a year of my life, pal."

"I'm so sorry," Teddy said, shaking his head at his own stupidity. "I lost my mind for a few seconds. That's all I can say."

Justin clapped him on the back. "No harm done, but let that be a lesson for you. Watch it!"

Teddy nodded then grinned. "She's special," he whispered. "I can see why you're worried." He picked up speed and joined Catherine at the bottom of the stairs.

Continuing at a slower pace to give himself time to settle his mind, Justin arrived at the kitchen door as steaming mugs were passed around. They moved into the dining room and pushed two tables together so everyone could sit together.

While the rest were occupied, Penny drew near to Justin and whispered, irritated, "Did you tell Teddy about our arrangement?"

He felt a shock go through him.

Her eyes were wide and probing. "Why did he point at you for the word 'wealthy' if you hadn't?" Her lips tightened. "You shouldn't have done it, Justin. It could ruin everything."

Unable to defend himself, Justin didn't reply. She turned her back to him and joined the others, sitting near the opposite end of the table, far away from him.

Farley said, "This is great cider, sis."

Murmurs of approval went through the group.

Still looking disgruntled, she sipped from her mug and didn't reply.

"How about playing Twirling the Trencher?" Catherine asked. "That would be fun."

"Oh, no," Farley said. "Remember what happened last time we played that."

The girls giggled and looked at each other.

"Who wants to play?" Catherine asked. She raised her hand, and the rest of the girls followed her lead. None of the men moved.

"It's four to three," she announced.

"We can stand in front of the kitchen doors," Penny said. She dashed into the kitchen and soon returned with a brown wooden tray they used for carrying clean dishes to the drying racks.

The young people arranged themselves in a circle.

"I'll start." Catherine said, moving to the center of the ring. As Penny handed the tray to her, Catherine told her, "You can't have all the fun," and gave her a queenly smile.

Leaning over, she balanced the tray on one rounded corner and gave it a quick spin. It wobbled around. Catherine called out, "Teddy!" and stepped back.

Teddy lunged for it but the tray fell flat before he touched it.

"Forfeit!" the gang called. Every eye sought Catherine to see what punishment she'd mete out.

Teddy stood with his chin tucked in, a doubtful expression on his face, watching his tormenter.

Catherine said, "What was the name of your worst girl-friend and why?"

He shoved his hands into his pockets and grinned. "I don't mind telling that one," he said. "It was Alice. She dumped me on Christmas Eve—with no warning."

Diane and Margaret looked sympathetic.

Catherine lowered her dark lashes and smiled at him. "Now it's your turn," she said.

Teddy gave the tray a spin. It stood upright, a brown, fat blur. "Farley!" he cried.

Farley dove into the center and caught the tray before it toppled over. Holding it in one hand, he looked triumphant and grinned at Diane. He gave it a spin and called, "Justin!"

Caught off guard, Justin dashed into the center, overshot, and collided with Farley. The tray landed at his feet.

Farley took his time, savoring the moment, then he asked Justin, "What was the name of your last girlfriend?"

Teddy gasped and started to laugh. His face turned the color of an old brick.

Sending a warning look toward his erstwhile friend, Justin was actually glad for Teddy's distraction. His last girlfriend was Louisa Morgan, eldest daughter of J. P. himself, the famous tycoon. There was no way he could utter her name. Every girl in the room would immediately know who she was.

He lifted his chin and sent a last sharp glance at Teddy, who was still chuckling and coughing by spells, and said, "Double-forfeit."

Farley looked surprised. "Double-forfeit?"

Justin nodded and braced himself. A double forfeit meant drastic measures. He only hoped this penalty had nothing to do with his true identity. If he refused again, he could end up washing dishes for Farley for the next week.

Farley looked around as though finding inspiration for an extreme sentence. Focusing on Justin again he said, "Pick someone in this room to slap you in the face." He glanced at

Penny. "And if they don't do a proper job of it, I'll pick someone else myself."

Justin took his time looking at each one. He felt like a kid sent out to cut his own switch. Grandma had pulled that one on him too many times. Bring back one that was too small, and she'd go out and find a tree limb to work him over, at least that's the way it seemed to him at the ripe old age of eight.

He looked at Teddy—all too eager. The twist of Catherine's shapely lips showed she would love to show off her audacity. Diane and Margaret would probably give him a little tap and have Farley bellowing, "Foul!"

He gazed at Penny and didn't like the intent expression on her face. But. . .all in all, she was his best bet. "Penny," he said.

Without giving him a chance to set himself, she marched up to him, swung, and connected with his cheek. He felt the reverberation to his toes. His head snapped sideways. An inferno blossomed in his cheek.

"Oh!" she cried, her lips forming an oval. "I'm so sorry! I didn't mean to hit you that hard." She reached out as though to touch his cheek. Instinctively, he drew back. "It's all red. . .my fingerprints. . . . You need a cold cloth." She turned as though to head toward the kitchen.

He lunged forward to catch her arm. "It's all right," he said. "Don't bother with that. It's all right."

She looked at him and winced. "It hurts me just to look at it." Turning, she glared at Farley. "That was mean, Farley Joshua. No more forfeits like that."

Farley laughed at her. "You're the one who hit him," he said.

Justin's head was reeling a little. Blinking once, he tried to shake it off.

Blushing to her roots, she returned to her place and stared at the floor. Teddy looked like he was about to pass out from a laugh attack.

"Your turn, old man," Farley told him.

To show he was a good sport, Justin quickly spun the tray and shouted, "Teddy!"

Still laughing, Teddy had hardly moved before the tray hit the floor. Justin's eyes narrowed. "Teddy, tell us the exact circumstances of how we first met," he said.

92

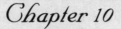

Chapter 10

Teddy's jaw dropped.

Locking eyes with him, Justin repeated the question, already sure what Teddy's answer would be. "Double-forfeit!"

Grinning, Justin tilted his head back and said, "For your double-forfeit you must wear Margaret's scarf on your head and sing the Yum-Yum song, the finale from *The Mikado*, like the girls actually did it." Teddy had performed a major part in that play just a month before graduation. He had a terrific memory, and Justin was certain Teddy could remember the first few lines anyway.

"Aw, c'mon, Justin," Teddy complained. "You know I can't sing."

Catherine spoke up. "No whining, Teddy." She smiled provocatively. "We'd love to hear you. Wouldn't we, gang?"

Farley and Catherine clapped, and Diane joined them. Farley put two fingers in his mouth and whistled.

Penny pointed toward the swinging doors. "You can stand over there so we can all see you."

With a grimace and the loud sigh of a martyr, Teddy took

the orange scarf from Margaret's outstretched hand. He flipped it over the top of his head and held the ends beneath his chin. He swayed side to side with the singsong of the rhyme and raced through the words in a shrill falsetto, "For he's gone and married Yum-Yum (Yum-Yum), Your anger pray bury, For all will be merry, I think you had better succumb (succumb) and join our expressions of glee!"

Catherine covered her face with her hands, fingers spread so she could still see him. Margaret turned red. She shook with laughter, tears streaming down her cheeks. Farley and Justin guffawed. The commotion was so loud they almost drowned out his last few words.

Whipping the scarf off, Teddy smoothed his hair with his free hand. As Teddy passed him, Justin clapped him on the back and said, "Good show!"

Handing the scarf back to Margaret, Teddy surveyed the group with a calculating eye, picking out the next victim before he spun the tray.

The game went on until the room grew dim and they had to stop to light some lamps. Justin got up to help Penny with them.

"Are Daddy and Vessel still playing that board game?" Penny asked Justin when the last lamp was glowing. After the slap, she'd seemed to forget her annoyance with him.

He shrugged. "More than likely. Vessel can play that game from dawn till midnight without any breaks. I've never seen anything like it. If he can't find an opponent, he'll play against himself."

"You're joshing," she said, chuckling. "They're two of a kind then. Daddy's always been that way about chess. At least he used to be before Mama died." She turned to the rest of the group and raised her voice. "Anybody hungry? I can bring out some leftovers."

"Sounds great," Farley said. "I'll help you." He put his arm around her shoulders and walked with her to the kitchen. Justin glanced at the table and noticed Teddy sitting next to Margaret. They seemed to be deep in conversation. So were Catherine and Diane.

Shoving his hands into his pockets, Justin strode to the kitchen doors and pushed inside. "Need some help?" he asked.

Penny looked up from a tray she was filling. "You can get the cheese. It's wrapped in cheesecloth in there." She nodded toward the pantry door.

He found the cheese and brought it back. As he returned, he caught sight of Farley's back disappearing through the doors.

"Still mad?" he asked Penny, sidling up to her at the table.

Her lips came out to form a thin ribbon. "Maybe." Taking the cheese bundle from him, she glanced at him. "Are you?"

He touched his cheek. It still burned a little. "I guess not. You were just playing the game."

"Something you need to learn to do," she replied archly. She cut ten slices of cheese in as many seconds, deftly arranged them, and handed him the tray. "You can carry that out. I'll bring a pitcher of water."

Wishing he could say more, Justin did as he was told. He figured it was better to run away and fight another day instead of trying to hash it out with her now. Tomorrow she'd understand everything. . .unfortunately.

The gang dug into the food like they hadn't eaten in two days. They were scarcely finished when a knock sounded at the dining room door.

"It's Daddy!" Catherine said.

Farley hurried to the door, and Mr. Bagley stepped inside. A small, thin man, he was completely covered except for a small slit for his eyes between his wool hat and his scarf.

"Have some hot coffee," Penny said when he approached the table. She looked at Farley. "I'm wondering if it's too cold for a sleigh ride," she said.

Farley replied, "We'll bundle up with blankets." He picked up a slice of cold ham and took a bite.

Pulling his scarf down, Mr. Bagley accepted the hot cup of steaming brew. "I'm much obliged, Penny," he said. He glanced at his daughter, Catherine, who stood two inches taller than he did. "We'll have to keep it short. That wind cuts like a knife. I'll run around the park and then head back." He looked at the plates in the young people's hands. "The horses are standing in the cold. We need to get moving."

Teddy gulped down the last of his dried apple pie, and Margaret set her plate on the table.

Penny turned to Justin. "Will you help me fetch everyone's wraps? They're in the upstairs hall."

Teddy said, "I'll go, Penny. You don't need to worry with that."

When they reached the stairwell, Teddy said, "Thanks for asking me over, man. That Margaret is a peach. A real honey."

Justin's brow lowered as he sent Teddy an unbelieving look. "I'm beginning to think that Alice wasn't so far off. If you could get interested in another girl that fast. . ." They reached the upstairs door, so he never finished the sentence.

Gathering two full armloads of coats, they headed back without any further conversation, and the group headed outside.

A large vehicle with double benches behind the driver, the

sleigh was painted a glossy black with gold trim. Farley and Diane took the front seat. Then Margaret climbed in beside them, and Teddy leaped up after her. Catherine was already in the back, so Penny and Justin joined her.

Four thick rugs lay on each seat and four heated bricks wrapped in burlap were on the floor. It took a few minutes to get everyone wrapped and bundled, but they were finally ready to set off.

Mr. Bagley gave a shout and flapped the reins. The horses leaned into the weight and set the sleigh in motion. One black and one gray, their combined breath formed a wide steam cloud that trailed behind them, almost like a miniature locomotive. Frigid air blasted the faces of the young people. Penny wrapped her green-plaid scarf around her face. In a few moments, everyone else followed suit.

"Let's sing," Catherine said, her voice muffled.

Farley shook his head. "Let's not." He settled a little closer to Diane. "I don't feel like it right now. Can't we just have some peace for a few minutes?"

Justin was glad Farley had spoken up. With the brim of Penny's green felt hat brushing his cheek from time to time, the dark night, and a pale moon, singing was the last thing on Justin's mind.

If only this Christmas Day could last forever. He had the girl of his dreams close beside him with a soft smile on her lovely face and a gentle spark in her eyes whenever she looked at him. Even when she was irritated she was the sweetest, most attractive woman he'd ever met. Who needed a sloe-eyed debutante when an angel miraculously crossed one's path?

Tomorrow everything would change. She'd no longer need him to meet Mr. Gold Britches. At some point he would have to tell her the truth as well. From what he knew of Penny, when she found out who he really was, she would be furious and humiliated. Would she ever forgive him?

"Isn't the night beautiful?" she murmured.

He shifted so he could watch her from the corner of his eye. "Gorgeous."

"Are you ready for tomorrow, Justin?" she asked, her voice still soft and warm.

He stifled the urge to put his arm around her. "I'll never be ready," he said.

She sent him a questioning glance, and he went on, "After tomorrow I won't have any more excuses to see you. Do you think I could ever be ready for that?"

She beamed. "Must you have an excuse?"

His answering grin started at his heart and worked its way out. "I guess not," he said.

She moved a fraction of an inch closer.

He let out a silent groan. What was he going to do?

All too soon, they rounded the last curve in the park and crossed the exit. The sleigh jostled into the street and settled down with a soft hiss as it slid across the smooth pavement.

Ten minutes later, they reached the restaurant. The sleigh slowed, then stopped.

Mr. Bagley turned to look down at them. "I can take Catherine, Margaret, and Diane home now. It's too cold to walk."

From the slant of their shoulders and their sober expressions, none of them wanted to go. But practicality won out. Farley, Justin, and Penny stepped down. Teddy took a moment to say something to Margaret. She blushed and nodded. The next moment Teddy was on the ground, grinning. The four of them stood on the sidewalk and waved as the sleigh took off. The moment it turned the corner, they headed for the door.

"My feet are numb," Penny said. "Let's go into the kitchen. The stove probably still has some coals in it. We can make hot chocolate and sit close to the stove to drink it."

"Close enough to put our feet under it?" Teddy asked. He nudged Justin with his elbow. "A profitable evening," he said. "Thanks for the invitation." He turned to Penny with a deep nod. "And thanks to you, too."

She gazed at him, obviously trying to figure out what he was talking about. "You added a lot to the party, Teddy," she said with a teasing smile. "I've never seen *The Mikado*, but if that song is any indication of how funny it is, I'll save up for two years just to buy a ticket."

Teddy smirked. "Thanks...I think."

The warmth inside felt so good, but they still had a chill in their bones. Penny hurried to the kitchen to start the hot chocolate while the men cleared up the mess in the dining room. They stacked the few dishes beside the sink.

"I'll take care of the food while I'm waiting for this to get hot," Penny said, stirring a pan of milk on the stove.

Farley spoke to Teddy. "Let's see how the game's going upstairs."

"Great idea!" Teddy said. "Call us when the chocolate's ready."

They headed out the door and soon their heavy shoes thumped on the stairs.

Justin looked at the trays on the table. "What can I do to help?" he asked.

"How are you in the dishpan?" she asked.

"I've done my share," he replied, for the first time infinitely grateful that his dear grandmother had decreed he do kitchen chores. He rolled up his sleeves and turned on the hot water. "Do you have a boiler here?" he asked, watching the steam spiraling from the sink.

"The boiler heats the building and supplies the kitchen and bath with hot water. Daddy had it put in last year. Now I wonder how we ever lived without it."

He nodded. "I'm thinking of having one installed myself."

She looked surprised. "You are?"

"One of these days," he said, making a show of placing silverware and mugs into the dishpan. He paused to ask, "What time should I arrive at the restaurant tomorrow?" He looked at her. "We are meeting there, aren't we?"

She nodded. "At fifteen past three at the Regal Astoria. Did I tell you that before?"

"I'll be there with bells on."

She loaded the tray with four white mugs and picked it up. "Don't get too far ahead of me with those dishes. I'll be right back."

The clock on the wall said nine o'clock. He was tired, and he knew Penny was. Maybe he should say good night when they finished clearing things up.

Penny came in laughing. "Daddy and Vessel have gotten those guys tied up in a game. Somehow they've figured out how to play teams—the old men against the youngsters. They're really going at it." She picked up a dishtowel. "I hung that suit in the hall, so you can pick it up on your way out. You'll need it tomorrow, you know."

"I was just thinking that we'd best head home."

"Already? It's only"—she glanced at the wall—"9:05."

"I don't want to wear out our welcome," he said.

She smiled at him. "You're not."

"Penny. . ." He tried to think of how to go on.

"Yes?"

"I just want to say that. . .no matter what happens tomorrow. . . the past two days have meant a lot to me."

"They've meant a lot to me, too, Justin." She set down the dish she was drying. "But you don't have to become a stranger when it's over. How would you like to come for dinner here tomorrow night at seven? We could talk about what happened with Mr. Matthews, whether our plan worked or not."

"Penny. . ."

"Are you trying to tell me something?" she asked. Her brow was crinkled, and she looked directly at him. "If you are, just tell me."

"There are things you don't know about me," he said. "My background and my past, things like that. When you find out, please don't make any hasty judgments. Can you promise me that?"

"Are you worried I'll think less of you because your family is poor?" she asked. "You don't have to worry about that, Justin. I don't care about those kinds of things."

Drying his hands he moved closer and smiled. "Try to hold on to that thought. I may ask you for it later."

"I'm glad you were the one in the dining room that day," she said. Her eyes were the color of forget-me-knots in May. Her face, so sweet and earnest.

He lowered his head and kissed her. She was precious, uncomplicated—everything he'd ever wanted in a woman.

"I have to tell you—" he said in a moment.

"Don't talk," she said, resting her cheek in the curve of his shoulder. "Everything's going be all right. You'll see."

Chapter 11

When Justin first awoke the next morning, the one thing he knew for certain was that everything was *not* going to be all right.

He was in love with Penny Joshua, hopelessly and helplessly in love with her. And he was a fraud, a big fat phony. At dinner tonight, he had to tell her everything. If she turned away, then he'd have to live with that. He couldn't sleep again before she knew.

Easing out of bed, he went into the bathroom to wash up.

He should have never agreed to the subterfuge. He could almost hear his grandmother's voice with her Dutch accent, "Vhat goes around, comes around." Well, things were surely going to come around like a bullwhip before nightfall.

He took his time dressing, then found Vessel in the dining room. For once the valet wasn't playing a game.

"Would you like me to call for breakfast, sir?" he asked.

"I'll have some cheese and bread with coffee," Justin told him. He noticed Teddy's open bedroom door. "Where's Teddy?"

Pouring them both a cup of coffee, Vessel said, "He went out at eight o'clock."

"In the morning? Where did he go?"

"I believe he had a date, sir. With Miss Margaret."

Justin laughed. "You're kidding me. Wow, that is rich." He sat at the table and sipped his coffee. Picking up a piece of bread, he carefully covered it with a slab of cheese and took a bite. "Things are getting out of hand," he said, swallowing. "What's going to happen when Margaret finds out who he is?"

Not a muscle of Vessel's face moved. "She'll be delighted, if I may say so. Her mother, too."

Justin moved his lips to one side. "You are so dry, Vessel. A real sober-sides."

Vessel's thin brows raised just a fraction. "Would you rather I tell you an untruth? I'm being perfectly frank."

Grinning in spite of himself, Justin said, "I only hope Penny will be delighted when she learns the truth about me. Somehow, I seriously doubt it."

"One never can tell, I'm sure."

Justin finished the last bite and stood. "You're a good friend, Vessel," he said. "Thank you for going with me yesterday. It was a great time."

He nodded. "A marvelous time, Master Justin. I won best out of five."

"Did you now? You and Teddy were going on so much about the game on the way home, I never got the final tallies."

"I'm to go over each Saturday afternoon while we're in town. The restaurant closes at three, you know. No dinner served on Saturday evening."

"Congratulations," he said. "I'd say you've finally met someone almost as intent as you are."

"Michael Joshua has a head on his shoulders, he has."

Justin took two steps toward his bedroom door. "I'm going

to read awhile. The meeting is at three-thirty, too late for my liking. I want to get it over with."

"I've brushed that suit and hung it on the rack," Vessel said, clearing away the remains of breakfast. "I'm glad this is the last time you'll have to wear borrowed clothes. It's humiliating."

"I'm glad it's my last time, too, but for very different reasons," Justin retorted. He picked up his copy of *Ivanhoe* and found a soft chair. Whatever happened, at least everything would be over by tonight. At least he'd know one way or the other if he had a future with Penny Joshua.

When Penny had retired the night before, she'd expected to lie awake all night. Her mind was so full, her heart so overrun by wonder and excitement and pure joy. She had found *him*. And he was wonderful.

Father, she prayed, *thank You for being so good to me. . . .*

The next thing she knew, Daddy was pounding on her door. "It's six o'clock!" he bellowed then trudged away, his heavy footsteps shaking the planks on the floor.

She had to be in the dining room by seven. She rolled over and snuggled into her pillow for just one more moment, remembering Justin's smile, the look in his eyes when they were close together in the sleigh. . .that glorious kiss. How could she live for six whole hours until she saw him again?

Moaning, she threw back the covers and grabbed her thick robe. Shoving her feet into icy slippers, she shuffled into the single bathroom. When Daddy knocked at her door, it was his signal that he was finished and she could go in.

Half an hour later, she lingered in front of her bedroom mirror and smiled at her reflection. *Is this what love's like? I don't know what else it could be. It must be love.* Sighing, she tied on her apron and headed for the stairs.

Farley was finishing a plate of eggs and bacon when she arrived. "Nervous?" he asked.

"About what?"

"Our date with Montgomery!" he exclaimed. "Did you forget already?" He looked at her with narrowed eyes. "You look like the cat that swallowed the canary. What are you up to?"

"Up to?" She tried to look innocent. "Why, nothing. That is, the same thing you are. What do you think?"

"You look different." He peered at her. "It's Justin, isn't it?"

She felt her face grow warm.

He stood up and picked up his empty plate. "Be careful, Penny," he warned. "He's nice enough, but he has no family and no prospects. When you marry, you should move up. I'd hate to see you waiting tables for the rest of your life."

She reached up to kiss his cheek. "With you watching out for me, how can I go wrong?"

Justin arrived at the Astoria at precisely three fifteen. He felt tingly in his stomach, a feeling that had nothing to do with hunger. Ducking into the men's room to check his hair and straighten his tie, he drew in a calming breath and lifted his chin. Penny would be watching his every move. This must be his *magnum opus* when it came to etiquette.

The room had only three patrons when he arrived. He stood a moment in the doorway. Before him lay forty round tables covered in white with ten chandeliers hanging above them, glittering even at midday. Every empty table held four crystal goblets, an intricately folded lavender napkin inside each one.

As Justin scanned the room, Farley stood to show him where they were seated. His hair glossy with tonic, Farley was decked out in a gray suit and blue tie. He remained standing until Justin reached him.

"Have a seat," Farley said. "Mr. Montgomery hasn't arrived yet. He'll be here shortly."

Justin sat in the chair next to Penny. She wore a blue dress that made her eyes glow. "Hello," he said. "How are you today? I'm afraid we kept you too late last night."

"Not at all." Her cheeks turned a delicate shade of pink. "Anyway, the restaurant closes at three on Saturdays, so I won't have to work tonight."

"But you're having a guest for supper," he said, smiling.

She slowly blinked her eyes. "That's not work," she said.

"Here he comes," Farley whispered. "That's Mr. Montgomery in the black suit."

Justin drew up when he caught sight of the hotel owner. He was short and stocky with broad shoulders and meaty hands. He had a dark fringe of hair around a shiny dome top. The closer he came toward them, the more familiar he looked.

Trying unsuccessfully to keep from staring, Justin stood along with Farley as the newcomer arrived. Farley stuck out his hand. "Thank you for coming, Mr. Montgomery." He turned toward Justin. "May I introduce Justin—"

The older man boomed, "Van der Meer! Good to see you, son. My sympathies on the passing of your grandfather. Gustaf was a good man, the best."

Farley looked from Montgomery to Justin. "You know each other?"

Montgomery's fleshy cheeks curved in a wide smile. "Why certainly. Justin Van der Meer, the new owner of the Nevada

Salt Company. I've known his family for years."

Penny let out a small gasp. She covered her mouth with her hand. How could that be? He was a waiter. . . . She turned to look at his face, and his guilty eyes told her all she needed to know.

She fumbled for her purse. She'd never been so humiliated, so mortified in all her life.

Justin reached out to stop her, but she brushed his hand away. What kind of a game had he been playing with her? Whatever it was, it was cruel.

Without a word to anyone, she grabbed her coat and set off in a half-run toward the hotel lobby. She wanted to hide behind a closed door where no one could see her cry.

What a fool she'd been. Telling him about her writing, mooning over him like an idiot, letting him kiss her. He must have had a good hearty laugh when he got back to his hotel.

Tears blurred her vision, and she almost tripped on the hotel steps.

Justin stood paralyzed for ten seconds, then charged after her. He didn't catch her until they were on the hotel steps. She was sobbing and gasping for air, slapping at her face to brush the tears out of her eyes.

"Penny, stop! Please let me explain." His fingers found her forearm.

She pulled away from him. "Explain? That you've been making a fool of me the whole time? Laughing at me? Telling me lies and charming me into believing them?"

"I never told you a lie," he said, his voice quiet and serious. "Never once."

"But, you. . ." She found her handkerchief and pressed it to her nose.

"I didn't tell you the whole truth, Penny," he said. "That was wrong. I regretted it within twenty-four hours of meeting you. But by then it was too late to confess."

"Too late? Why too late?"

A small crowd had gathered on the steps to watch the drama. If Justin hated anything, he hated a scene. He put his arm about her shoulder. "Let's talk over here out of the way."

She followed him around the corner into an alley. They stopped behind a carriage, out of sight of the street.

"I'll tell you why it was too late," he said. "Because I was falling in love with you. I was afraid that if I told you who I really was, you'd run away from me." His lips twisted. "It seems I was right."

She didn't seem to hear him. "Why did you agree to help us in that ridiculous charade? Why would you want to?"

"I thought it was a lark," he said with an attempt at a smile. "Something fun. It is ironic, you know. And I've always loved a prank." He grew sober. "I never intended to hurt you or anyone else." He paused then went on. "There's more to the story than this. Can you hear me out?"

Sniffing and wiping her damp cheeks, she nodded.

"I came to Colorado Springs because I was sick of the holiday debauchery of the so-called upper class—the drinking, the immorality, the fake fun that really isn't fun at all. Besides that, half the mothers in the country have their scouts watching for me every time I come into a town so they can hound my every step to draw my attention to their daughters." He grimaced. "The *Times* calls me the most eligible bachelor of the decade."

He leaned down until they were almost nose-to-nose. "Do you know how that makes me feel? How could I ever trust a girl? How could I ever know that she wants me and not my money?"

He rubbed the back of his head and smoothed it down. "I came here because I just had to get away from people and have quiet for a change. When I met you, I'd been here several days without a single thing to do besides read or play that game with Vessel. I was desperate for something to pass the time." His expression softened. "Then you came along."

"You deceived me. How can I forget that?"

"Penny, stop and think about what you just said. What were you planning to do to Mr. Montgomery? How is that different from what I did to you?"

She bent her head down and rubbed her forehead.

He pressed on. "You made an assumption, and I let it stand. That's exactly what you had planned for this meeting. Except for one difference. You *created* the situation for that purpose. I happened into it."

He clasped her by the shoulders. "I'm not condemning you, dear. I'm only asking you to forgive me. No, I'm begging you to forgive me. I love you, Penny. With all my heart I love you. Please don't send me away."

She looked up with deep questioning in her eyes. "You weren't laughing at me?" she asked.

"At the situation, not at you. Never at you."

"I suppose I have been rather foolish," she said. "I thought I was helping Farley, but all I did was make a big muddle of everything."

He drew her into his arms. "One thing you did not make a

muddle of. . ." He lightly kissed her.

She leaned closer to him and put her arms around him. "What's that?"

"Us. If you hadn't gone off the deep end, we never would have met."

She smiled for the first time. "That's true, isn't it?"

"Sometimes God does let some good come out of our foolishness," he said. "Every once in a while, that is. And that leads me to my next point." He kissed her nose. "No more scheming after we're married. Promise?"

"Anything you say, dear Mr. Van der Meer," she replied with an arch look on her face.

He kissed her, and she clung to him. After all the hours of dreading his confession, Justin could hardly believe it was true. He closed his eyes and lost himself in the warmth of her embrace.

Penny's head was spinning. She melted in Justin's arms. If only this moment could last forever.

Farley's voice brought her back to reality. Pulling away, she looked up to see Farley hurrying toward them. The carriage had moved away, and she hadn't even noticed.

"I've been searching all over for you," he said, a crestfallen look on his face. "Mr. Montgomery just left. He won't help me."

"Won't he?" Justin asked. His grin could have lit up a city block. "I guess that makes him the loser." He winked at Penny, and she leaned her cheek against his coat sleeve.

Putting his arm about her and holding her close to his side, Justin said to Farley, "Don't worry about that, old man. I'll wire my accountant right away. Will ten thousand be enough to get you started?"

Epilogue

267 Atlanta Blvd.
New York, New York
January 11, 1892

Dear Priscilla,

  I hope this letter doesn't upset you too much, dear, but I just had to write to let you know the recent developments with Gustaf Van der Meer's grandson, Justin. He always seemed like such a nice boy, but he's shown a horrible lack of judgment once he inherited his grandfather's millions. Since you left for your tour of Europe, he has been a very busy man.

  First (and worst of all) he married a poor girl with no family ties whatsoever, a nobody from start to finish. She's never come out into society, and from the looks of things, she never will.

  Can you believe that? I know you had such hopes for your daughter, Veronica, when Justin visited New York again.

  The newlyweds were married last month in the local

church on the edge of town with only a few family members and close friends present. The wedding didn't even make the social column of the Post. The only reason I heard about it was that Madge Jefferson was in Colorado Springs at the time, and she told me while she was here for a Christmas party.

It seems Justin has built a house in Colorado Springs, a very tiny place with only ten rooms. Not only that, but the bride and groom intend to make it their principal residence. They've only three servants: a cook, a housekeeper, and a valet.

I don't know how in the world they will manage. I think the boy has lost his mind. You know his mansions in Nevada and Wisconsin are so elegant. Much more fitting for a man of his means.

Well, I must get this in the mail, Priscilla. The postman is due within the half hour. I hope you are having a grand time in France. Please send me a letter soon with all the details about what they are wearing this year. And tell Veronica she'll have to look elsewhere for an eligible bachelor. (Think of all those millions gone to waste!)

With all my love,
I remain your sister,
Gladys Rothschild

Center Point Large Print

Also available in Center Point Large Print by Sarah Strohmeyer:

Love by
Accident

Dedication

To my son, Jonathan Dow, my in-house idea man.

Chapter 1

Colorado, December 23, 1882

Liza Wainright was covering a large pan of bread dough so it could rise when she heard the first rumble. It sounded like an odd groan, followed by a muffled sound almost like a man's shout. Ten seconds later the floorboards shook beneath her feet.

Her seventeen-year-old brother, Caleb, burst into the cabin, his boyish eyes wild, "Liza, it's the Hogback! Avalanche!"

With a small cry, she dashed onto the front porch of the cabin in time to see the side of Hogback Mountain disintegrate and slide into the valley below. Though almost a mile away, the rumble was deafening, the power horrifying. Ten feet of snow since the first of December, then a warm spell yesterday and today had made conditions ripe for a catastrophe.

Liza stared, unable to move a single muscle. That morning her other two brothers, Bryant and Harvey, had gone to the canyon to check on their cattle wintering there. Every other day the boys had to pull out bales of hay and break the ice on the stream so their longhorns could survive the harsh winter.

So weak she could hardly stand, she whispered, "Did it get into the canyon?"

Caleb's muscular arm circled her shoulder in an awkward hug. His chin touched her right cheekbone though he was only five feet six. "I'll saddle Midnight and ride out there," he said. "If Bryant and Harvey are in trouble, they'll need me." He stepped off the porch and trudged across the ranch yard.

The front doors of the barn and the cabin faced each other, separated by a stretch of earth now covered with eighteen inches of partially frozen snow. As Caleb disappeared into the dim interior across the way, Liza noticed a trickle of black smoke rising from the avalanche area. It grew until it was a wide, dark column.

Heading back inside for her coat, she returned to the porch. She couldn't take her eyes off the sooty plume in the distance. She stood and watched, absently pushing her brown hair behind her left ear where it had sprung loose from her bun.

When Caleb reappeared, he was in the saddle. Liza pointed to the smoke. "Is that a train?"

"Looks like coal smoke," he said. He squinted as though he could peer through a mile of misty morning. "It's got to be a train. I wonder if it got caught in the downfall."

"Check on the boys, then go and see if anyone's hurt," Liza said. "If people are stranded out there, they'll be desperate for help. You'll have to bring them back here." A feeling of deep dread filled her midsection. This was the third bad year for the Running W Ranch, and the larder had barely enough food to last the four surviving Wainrights through the winter. How could they feed a large group of hungry people for even one day?

She hurried inside and took a dozen long steps through the kitchen and dining room, then onto the back porch. In a closet-like room to the left—known to the family as cold storage—a frozen side of beef hung from the rafters. Although useless in summer, this place was mighty handy in winter. Hacking off a ten-pound chunk, she heaved it into the kitchen to chop it up for stew. Despite her five-feet-two stature, she could work alongside women twice her size. She had been hauling and carrying since she could remember.

She partially filled two large pots with water from the pitcher pump by the kitchen counter and dropped the meat inside them. She added more wood to the cook stove to get the oven hot enough for the bread. Narrow and squatty, it was a cast-iron relic her great-grandfather, Matthew Wainright, had hauled into the Colorado foothills more than sixty years before.

Matthew and his partner, Harold Anderson, had framed this cabin with their bare hands and lived in it while they tried to build a herd of longhorns. Even after Matthew married Priscilla Connolly, Harold had stayed on. Later, Harold had also married. He and his bride had lived in a cabin where the bunkhouse stood now.

Coaxing the cranky stove to full heat, Liza wished for the thousandth time that Great-Grandpa Matthew had picked out a nickel-plated Empire stove with a hot-water reservoir instead of this wheezing, gasping iron crate.

Holding her skirts high and to the left, she climbed the loft stairs to search for quilts and woolen blankets. The loft encompassed the entire second story with a small hole cut into the floor for the ladder to come through. It was one large room with a partition at one end for storage.

She found the blankets in an old trunk and threw them down the ladder, carefully climbing down after them.

As soon as the bread was fully risen, she put it in the oven then pulled on boots and her coat. The bunkhouse had been empty for more than a year. She must light the stove and sweep it out in case the worst happened. At least there were eight beds out there that could be used for stranded passengers.

Liza was back in the cabin and eight loaves of bread sat on the table, hot out of the oven, when a rider finally came into the yard. She caught a glimpse of him through the front window over the kitchen counter and hurried out to hear the news.

The rider was nineteen-year-old Harvey, her middle brother who was one year younger than she. He had a smooth, wide face and piercing dark eyes.

A small boy huddled against him in the saddle. All that could be seen of the child was a brown coat and matching hat. He had his face buried in Harvey's chest.

"Train wreck!" Harvey called. "We're having to bring the passengers out on horseback. There's no way to get a buckboard or even a sleigh in there. The trails are too muddy, and the tracks are buckled on the mountainside."

He rode up next to the porch steps. Holding onto the boy by his upper arm, Harvey eased him to the porch floor. "This is Mikey O'Bannon," he said. "His grandmother will be one of the first to come. We promised him that."

"That's my sister," Harvey told the child. "Go into the house, and she'll give you something warm. Your grandma will be coming soon." He straightened and said to Liza, "I'm changing to a fresh horse then I'm off to the neighbors. We've got to have food and blankets for about two dozen passengers. There's no way we can take care of that many ourselves."

Relief flooded Liza. "Good thinking, Harvey," she said. She reached out to the boy. "Hello, Mikey. My name is Elizabeth, but most folks call me Liza. You can, too." She took his hand and led him inside. His freckled face was smudged with tears and grime. She found a clean cloth and wiped his face. He avoided looking directly at her but didn't cry anymore.

Sitting Mikey at the table, she cut him a piece of warm bread and poured milk from a covered pitcher that she brought from cold storage. The child ate like he was starved. The rest of the passengers probably were, too.

"Would you like to take off your coat?" she asked him a few minutes later.

Tucking his chin down, he shook his head. Figuring he was still cold, she didn't press him further.

Liza opened the doors of her meager pantry and took a sack of cornmeal from a shelf. Mush was quick to cook and filling to an empty stomach. The stew would never be ready in time.

The porridge was just thickening when boots thudded on the porch and the door flew open. With a blast of cold air, Caleb came in supporting a small woman who was bent over and trembling. She wore a black bonnet and black cape. Liza rushed to help her into a chair at the dining room table, then found a quilt to wrap around her.

Caleb paused just inside the door, his boyish face looking more man-grown every day. "I'm going to saddle four horses so we can bring back more folks next time. Most of them are still inside the cars, but there's no heat and they're freezing."

"I've got the stove going in the bunkhouse," Liza said. "Harvey went to round up more help."

Nodding, Caleb pulled the door open and disappeared.

Liza turned to the shivering woman and poured her some hot coffee. She told her, "Put your hands around the cup to warm them and breathe in the steam." The woman pulled off her bonnet and laid it on the table nearby. Her white woolly hair was combed back into a tight bun. Coming behind the old lady, Liza hugged her close to lend her own body warmth to the poor trembling creature.

"Thank you, my dear," the woman gasped. "I'm ashamed to be such a baby."

"You're not a baby, Grandma," Mikey said, in clear, round tones. He'd straightened in his seat and was wisely watching his grandmother.

"You're right, Mikey," she said. "I need to stop acting like one, don't I?"

She drew in a full breath of the warm cabin air and lifted the cup with both shaking hands to take a sip. Setting the cup down, she said, "My name is Olivia O'Bannon. Mikey is my son's boy. His mother has been ill, so he came to stay with me for a while. Now we're on our way to take him home for Christmas."

Moving to the chair across the table, Liza introduced herself. "My brothers and I live here alone," she added. "Our parents died of cholera two years ago."

Olivia's seamed brow puckered with concern. "You poor dear. Where were they when it happened? Surely not in this valley. I would have heard of it even as far away as Canton's Corner where I live. I've been there since I married. I plan to die there, too." She took another sip. "Although, today I had my doubts about the dying part. When we heard that mountain shaking loose, I thought it was all over."

Mikey said, "It was all over in a minute, Grandma. Soon as the snow fell down." He raised his pudgy hand and made a diving motion toward the oak tabletop.

Olivia smiled and reached out to squeeze the boy's hand. "How right you are, young man. It was all over in a minute." She looked at Liza, waiting for her answer.

"My parents were on their way to Cheyenne when the cholera took them," she said. "It was an anniversary trip my mother had planned for three years." She bit back the sweeping grief that still choked her whenever she spoke of them.

The concern in Olivia's watery blue eyes held a spark of faith. "God had a reason, Liza," she said. "I know your heart is sore, but God has His own plans about our lives. Are you a Christian?"

Running her index finger under her lower eyelid, Liza blinked and nodded. "Yes, ma'am. I received Christ when I was about eleven years old. Mama and I joined the Congregational Church in Wiley's Corner. Pa and the boys. . ." She shook her head and didn't finish the sentence.

"We'll pray for them." Olivia finished her coffee and pushed the cup slightly back. Shrugging out of her cape, she said, "Now, tell me what I can do to help you." At Liza's protesting frown, she said, "I'm just fine, my dear. I was cold to the bone, that's all."

"Would you like something to eat first?" Liza asked. "I've made some cornmeal mush. I thought that would be warm and filling."

"That sounds wonderful," Olivia said, smiling at Mikey. "Doesn't it, son?"

His chin touched his chest, then swung high and back down again. "With milk!" he said.

"Of course, with milk," Liza said. She hurried to fill their bowls and joined them in the small meal. Who knew when she'd have time to sit down and eat again.

In a few minutes, Liza stood to fetch a basin and sack of potatoes. "I've got meat stewing. We'll need potatoes peeled. Would you like to do that while you sit here?"

"Of course, child. Anything you need."

Liza found her favorite paring knife and handed it to the older woman. "I need to check the stove in the bunkhouse. I lit a fire out there awhile ago, but it probably needs stoking about now."

Olivia smiled and her face took on a wholesome, sweet glow. "We'll be fine right here, Liza," she said, winking at Mikey, who was leaning onto the table with his knees in the chair, choosing a potato from the sack. Flicking the tip of the knife through a partially sprouted potato eye, Olivia had half the potato peeled before Liza had her coat on.

In the bunkhouse, the fire had almost gone out. Liza lingered a few minutes to blow the coals and coax tiny blue flames from the kindling, then she added larger pieces. Several minutes later, the wood crackled and the first rays of heat came through the sides of the potbelly stove.

Satisfied, Liza bent over to pull the back hem of her flowing skirt between her ankles and up to the front of her waistband. She pinned it there. Buttoning her coat, she headed back to the house. The yard had become a churning mass of mud and slushy snow. It sucked at her shoes and slowed her progress.

She had slogged partway across the yard when Bryant and Caleb rode in, each double-mounted followed by three more horses double-mounted as well. Ten people. Liza hurried as quickly as she could to meet them.

Again, the horses sidled up to the porch. Without stopping for a word with her, the boys headed for the barn to switch out horses. A horse carrying two adults tires after just a mile, and their own mounts had been working in mud since early morning.

Slipping out of her damp, slimy shoes, she left them on the

porch. When she reached the inside of the cabin, Olivia was already pouring steaming cups of coffee and shepherding the folks into chairs—eight girls and ladies at the dining room table and two men, a distinguished gentleman with a gray beard and spectacles and a young red-haired drummer, in the sitting room in front of the roaring fireplace.

Mikey had found a box of wooden blocks hidden under the sofa, relics of the Wainrights' childhood. He sat on the braided rug and practiced making towers, clapping when they fell down.

"I'll take care of serving everyone," Olivia told Liza. "You've done the hard part by cooking all this in the first place. You'll need all your energy getting everyone settled. Who knows how long it will be before we can get folks on their way."

"Does anyone know how many more are coming?" Liza asked.

An older man in a broadcloth suit spoke up. "Ten or twelve men," he said. "Cowpokes mostly."

Liza nodded. They'd have to set up bedrolls in the barn. The tack room had a stove in it. That was the logical place to begin. Of course, some of them would be able to leave before nightfall.

She moved to Olivia, who was ladling mush into bowls. "When Mikey gets tired, you can put him on my bed," Liza murmured to her, nodding to the door off the dining room.

The single bedroom made the remaining open area an L-shape, with the kitchen at the front corner and the dining room table inside the back door. The sitting room was on the front wall, joining the kitchen on the other side. From the kitchen sink or the stove, one could see both ways through the entire cabin, east to west and north to south.

"We're much obliged to you, Liza," Olivia replied. The

warmth of her words somehow soothed Liza's sore heart. She suddenly wished that Olivia could stay with her for a while.

When Olivia began serving, a young woman with rouged cheeks and an intricate blond hairstyle threw off her cape and stood to help carry bowls to the table. She had dancehall written all over her, from her kohled eyelids to her dangling earrings. The other woman avoided looking directly at her.

"My name's Charlene," she said, to no one in particular.

"Thank you for the help, my dear," Olivia said with a gentle smile.

Over the next three hours, the remaining passengers arrived to make twenty-three in all. When the first group had finished their coffee and mush, Bryant and Caleb took the doctor and the drummer to the barn to set up sleeping quarters, while Liza led seven women and girls to the bunkhouse.

Heavenly warm air met them when Liza opened the bunkhouse door. She handed a blanket to each of the ladies and let them choose their bunks. "My brother, Harvey, has gone for more supplies," she said. "Is there anyone here who lives close enough to return home?"

Four women raised their hands. Liza nodded. "When the neighbors come, I'll ask about getting you rides out of here." She opened the stove door to shove in another log.

A middle-aged matron stepped forward. She had steel gray hair and wore heavy black boots. "I'll take care of that, missy," she offered. "You've got enough on your hands." She glanced toward her teenage daughter, standing uncertainly among the women. "Sharon will help me."

"So will I," an olive-skinned young woman spoke out. "Don't worry about us, Miss Wainright. You've got enough on your mind."

"Why, thank you," Liza said. "There's a lean-to out the back door. That's where the woodpile is for this building."

She looked around at their weary, anxious faces. "A pitcher pump and some tin mugs are just outside the back door, too. Try to rest. Hopefully this will all be over soon."

A murmur of thank yous swelled toward her.

Embarrassed, she hurried outside. She wasn't used to gratitude and didn't know how to respond to it.

She had just reached the porch steps when a wagon pulled by four straining horses zigged and zagged into the yard. The ruts left behind it bore no trace of wagon tracks. It was sliding all the way. Who would be so foolhardy as to bring a wagon out in these conditions? Every fifty yards would be a monumental task.

Peering closely at the tall, muscular form holding the reins, she suddenly stiffened. He pulled the wagon close to the steps and took off his hat.

"Good afternoon, Liza," he said. His words sounded relaxed and casual, but his eyes were anxious. "One of Brown's boys came running over to tell us about the accident. Ma thought you could use a few things. With the road so bad, we figured that no one else would be able to get to you with very much."

Liza opened her mouth but no sound came out. The wild driver was young Garrett Anderson, whose ranch bordered theirs. She knew him from school, but the Andersons and the Wainrights hadn't spoken for more than fifty years.

Chapter 2

Liza had never understood why such animosity had existed between the two families for so many years, but her brothers—the oldest one, Bryant, especially—had been in several fistfights on the school playground with Garrett Anderson. They never talked about the bad blood, but everyone for miles around was all too aware of it.

Instinctively, Liza scanned the ranch yard looking for her brothers. What would they do if they came out of the barn and found Garrett here?

While she hesitated, the young man stepped down from the wagon. His black boots sank three inches deep into the mud. He turned toward the buckboard, filled with lumpy objects and covered with a canvas. "I brought some rice, canned goods, flour, and coffee. Blankets, too. Ma sent extra dishes." He looked apologetic. "She asked if you could send those things back when you're through with them."

He glanced toward the house. "Do you want to unload this now?"

Liza finally came out of her shocked trance. "Thank you, Garrett. I'm so glad you came. The boys are setting up sleeping quarters in the barn for the folks who can't leave by nightfall. We have twenty-three people, but some of them will be leaving." She held up her hand, motioning for him to wait as she headed inside the cabin door.

Opening it and leaning in so her head cleared the threshold, she said, "Has anyone here finished eating? We could use some help unloading a wagon."

Four cowboys stood up. One was tall and lean, the other three were shorter and of stocky build. They all wore the stoic expressions of Western outdoorsmen. Without a word, they marched outside and within seconds had formed a lineup to get the goods onto the porch.

Soon, two more men came out to help. Liza marshaled them to carrying boxes and crates to the kitchen, where Olivia and Charlene began unpacking them. The blankets, they piled onto the sofa.

Joining the women in the kitchen, Liza fought back a growing lump in her throat. Here was abundantly more than she could have ever asked or imagined.

She was setting canned peaches on the pantry shelf when she heard loud voices outside and rushed out to see what was happening.

Garrett had backed the wagon to the edge of the grass and unhitched his two horses. He was standing between them, holding their bridles. Bryant stood in mud ankle deep not far from the barn door with his shoulders back, chest out, and his face like stone. "I thought you knew better than to come on my land," he ground out.

Liza flew to the porch steps. "Bryant, he came here to help us," she called. "He brought a wagonload of food and blankets. He could have stayed home, Bryant, but he didn't! He fought that wagon through the mud all the way here. How can you be so unreasonable as to send him away? The least we can do is let his horses rest and give him a cup of coffee." She got into a stare-down with her brother and didn't flinch.

The horses sensed the tension and bobbed their heads. Garrett had a job of holding them down.

Finally, Bryant turned and headed back into the barn. Caleb appeared at the barn door for just an instant, then disappeared again.

Liza turned to the group of cowhands hovering on the side of the porch. "Would one of you mind taking his horses to the barn?" she asked. "We should have some neighbors coming in sometime later this afternoon. They may be able to give some of you rides out, if you want. Meanwhile, the men are setting up a bunk room in the barn if you'd like to lend a hand."

To Garrett she said, "You can leave your boots here and come inside."

Despite what she said to Bryant, she had never cared for Garrett Anderson herself. He had teased her unmercifully from the time she was six years old and he was seven in Wiley's Crossing Grammar School. Dipping her pigtails in the inkwell was the least of her problems when it came to Garrett Anderson. But right was right, and the man had done them a great service.

When they stepped inside the cabin, Garrett was the only man present. Liza introduced Olivia and her grandson, but before she could address the young woman, Charlene stepped forward with a wide smile.

"I'm Charlene," she said, offering him her hand. "*Enchanté.*"

He awkwardly shook her hand and immediately dropped it. "Ma'am," he said, removing his Stetson.

The resemblance between Bryant and Garrett was immediately obvious. Both men stood just over six feet tall with a full head of hair that was curly and dark; although Bryant's hair was dark brown while Garrett's was a glossy black.

Taking his coat, Liza said, "We just finished feeding everyone cornmeal mush and coffee. I've got a few slices of fresh-made bread, also. Would you like some?" She hung his coat on a peg and took off her own to hang next to it.

"Coffee and bread sound great to me," he said, scraping back a chair at the table. Watching her pour the black brew, he added, "I came to help, Liza. I can chop wood for you or peel potatoes. It doesn't matter much to me."

As Liza set the cup before him, Olivia brought the plate of bread and put it on the table. "You'd be smart to take him up on that," the older woman said. "Even if it's just to help carry things for the kitchen. Those cowpokes are willing enough, but they're pretty nigh useless when it comes to kitchen work." She eyed Garrett. "Of course, you may not be much better."

He grinned at her. "You may be surprised, Miss Olivia."

Mikey ran up to the table with three blocks balanced between his hands against his chubby chest. He set them down and ran back to the living room for more. While Garrett drank coffee and munched down three slices of bread, the little boy stacked blocks.

"Do you know how to make a wall?" Garrett asked.

Mikey shook his head.

"Let me show you." Garrett placed five blocks in a row with wide spaces between them. Mikey watched intently. Garrett made a second row of four blocks by stacking them over the gaps, then a row of three, two, and one.

Mikey clapped his hands. "Look, Grandma! A wall!"

Garrett laughed. "Now you make one."

Immediately, Mikey's hand shot out and knocked it all down. With intense concentration he rebuilt it.

"That's great, Mikey. Maybe one day you'll be a carpenter." Garrett picked up his plate and cup and carried them to the dishpan where Charlene was washing bowls.

She gave him a sidewise look. "Thank you kindly," she said.

Garrett did not return her smile. "You're welcome, ma'am," he said. He turned to Liza. "Where would you like me to start?" he asked.

"We need firewood split," Liza replied, a bit shy at giving him chores. "I've been emptying the kitchen wood box with all this cooking." She pointed toward the back door, just three feet from his chair. "The wood pile is out there."

He stood. "I'll fetch my boots and carry them out back to put them on," he said. Pulling on his coat, he opened the door to lean out and snag his boots. Liza held her breath, watching those muddy soles hovering over her floor. So far, the mud had been kept at bay with everyone removing footwear at the door.

When he closed the back door after himself, one of the matronly ladies asked Liza, "How can we help you?"

"We're chopping vegetables to put into the stew for supper," she said. "But the bread is all gone. We'll have to make some more."

"And biscuits," Olivia added. "Biscuits for supper and bread for breakfast. How's that sound?"

"Biscuits would be better for tonight," Liza agreed.

Charlene spoke out. "I make some mean biscuits," she said. "If someone will carry that burlap sack of flour to the table and find me some lard, I'll take care of that deal."

Olivia said, "You know, there will be people trailing in and out of here all day long with folks coming in to help. It wouldn't hurt to go ahead and make a pan or two of biscuits now to feed those hungry souls who ride in." She glanced at Liza. "Don't you think so?"

Liza nodded. "Olivia, God put you on that train to help me get through this. I'm so befuddled at the moment that I can't put two thoughts together in a straight line."

The older woman smiled. "You're doing fine, my dear. Just fine."

At that moment, a man's voice hurrahed the house. Liza grabbed her coat and hurried outside.

It was Miles Henshaw, one of their closer neighbors who lived only two miles away. He had two packhorses with him.

"We heard you have some trouble here," he said, staying in the saddle. "The missus sent some things to help out."

Liza said, "We've got twenty-three people here. Thank you so much for coming. If you can bring your pack horses close to the porch, we'll unload them."

Garrett stepped forward. "Howdy, Henshaw," he said.

The rancher looked at him in surprise. "Garrett. Good to see you."

Reaching for the first box, Garrett said, "I just got here with a wagonload of goods. I wish I could carry some of these folks out of here, but the road is too muddy. I slid most of the way here. If it hadn't been that I hitched my two strongest plow horses to the buckboard, I never would have made it."

Henshaw dismounted and untied the parcels. "There was another avalanche northeast of here, so this section of the tracks is cut off. No trains running for weeks, maybe months. Anyone leaving the area will have to go by horseback. With the snow melting so fast, we're looking at flood conditions in the next day or so."

Liza lifted a canvas sack of coffee. "If you can take a few out on these pack horses, that would be wonderful," she said. "Several people here are from Wiley's Corner or they have family nearby where they could stay." She lifted a tin. "It's a shame this had to happen so close to Christmas."

"Of course," Henshaw said. "I'll be able to mount two of them. If you don't mind, I'll take back a couple of those blankets to pad the horses' backs. I wish I had thought to bring a couple of saddles."

Before they had finished unloading Henshaw's goods, two more ranchers arrived and Harvey with them. Several cowhands trudged from the barn to help with the unloading. The passengers were sorted and labeled according to who could leave and who had no place to go. More coffee was served. Dozens of biscuits were devoured and dishes washed.

When suppertime came, they were left with fifteen passengers at the ranch, including seven cowhands, Dr. Samuel Grotz, and young Joshua Minnick, who sold brushes along the railroad towns. Among the women left were the matronly woman and her daughter, the olive-skinned young woman, Olivia, and Charlene. Mikey, of course, remained with his grandmother.

Garrett stayed busy. He chopped wood for the kitchen stove and carried hot water to the bunkhouse so the ladies could wash up. He found some straw to put on the porch to keep some of the mud out of the house and kept all the fires alive—even at forty degrees outside, the cabin stayed cold. It seemed like Garrett Anderson was everywhere Liza looked.

The group gathered in the cabin for the evening meal, nineteen people to eat with only thirteen seats in the entire house.

Bryant and Harvey found some boards in the barn and nailed together two rough benches to put along the walls of their sitting room. Everyone was elbow-to-elbow and knee-to-knee, but no one seemed to mind.

No one, that is, except Bryant. He was fine with the railroad refugees, but he avoided Garrett with obvious disdain. Liza ignored her oldest brother. As long as there weren't any words, she would wait out Bryant's bad mood until Garrett went home and things got back to normal.

Seated at the dining room table, Joshua Minnick said, "This is great stew, Liza. You're a good cook."

Liza shook her head. "Not me. That's what is known as gang stew. A whole gang of people helped to make it." She held up a large cloth-lined basket piled with golden biscuits. "Anyone want more biscuits? These are gonna get cold and stale before morning."

A grizzled-faced cowboy named Cody drawled, "I'll take that basket, Miss Liza, and thanks to you."

She passed the basket to Garrett next to her at the table and it made a trip around the entire room. When it returned, two lonely biscuits lay on the bottom. Garrett palmed them. He smiled at Charlene. "Looks like you've got yourself the job for the duration," he said, biting into one of them.

She beamed at him. It was the first natural look she'd shown since she arrived.

Liza said, "Where are you from, Charlene? I mean originally." The girl couldn't be much more than Liza's age.

"My folks have a ranch near Austin, Texas," she said. Looking uncomfortable, she lifted her fork to her mouth.

"I went to Austin once to a big horse auction," Garrett said. "My dad took a string down there to sell. He wanted some fresh stud stock, so he traveled all the way to Texas looking for new blood. That's when he got the contract with the army." His voice trailed off as though he was unsure whether he should give out personal information in hostile territory.

Charlene brightened. "You raise horses?"

Garrett nodded. "Morgans."

"We raised a few ourselves," Charlene said. "But the ranch was mostly beef cattle. My daddy said it doesn't hurt to diversify in case the market drops."

One of the cowboys spoke up. "He was right about that. Last summer the bottom dropped out of the beef market, and we've all been hurting ever since." Several men nodded.

Bryant spoke for the first time. "This is the third year we've had rotten luck."

Joshua said, "You aren't the only one. My business has dropped because the cattle business is bad. Who wants to buy brushes when they need food?"

The conversation continued along those lines for several minutes. Finally, Cody mentioned a game of checkers.

Caleb said, "There's a board and some checkers in the tack room. Harvey and I made them when we were kids." He rose from his seat on a bench and set his plate and cup on the table. "I'm sure I can find them without any problem."

With that, most of the men, including Bryant, headed toward the barn. The ladies stayed to wash up and then drifted out, also. Olivia lingered in the kitchen to fill a pot with beans for soaking overnight.

When Charlene said good night, Olivia hugged the girl. "Thank you for your help today, dearie," she said.

Charlene received the hug but acted self-conscious afterwards. Wrapping her cape about her, she carefully lifted her silk skirts before she even opened the door. How she could reach the bunkhouse without ruining that dress was anyone's guess.

The doctor excused himself and headed for the barn, but Harvey lingered. He sat at the end of the table for a few minutes without saying anything.

When Garrett returned to his seat there, Harvey said, "There's a place for you in the loft, if you want it, Garrett. You can't go home with your wagon this late. It's full dark out there."

Something around Garrett's eyes tightened. "Thank you, Harvey. I'm obliged." His words were softly spoken, but somehow they had a hardness to them.

Without another word, Harvey headed for the loft stairs and climbed out of their sight.

Olivia and Mikey were in Liza's room settling in for the night. Liza now occupied her parents' room with their over-sized iron bedstead. There was plenty of space on the massive feather tick for two small women and the boy.

"Would you like some more coffee?" she asked Garrett.

With a slight shake of his head, he said, "No, thanks." He rubbed his lower lip with his little finger. "Would you mind sitting here with me for just a few minutes?" he asked. "There's something I need to say."

Fighting back a rising tide of suspicion, Liza found a chair some distance away and sat down.

Garrett hesitated, then said, "My mother sent me over today. Since Pa had that heart attack last year, she's been wanting to speak to you, but she hasn't known how."

"To me?"

He nodded but didn't meet her eyes. "She feels bad about the. . .discord. . .between our families. She says that nobody knows why the feud ever started, so we should settle our differences and make peace."

Liza said, "I'm not sure if that's possible. You saw how Bryant feels about...anyone from your family. I don't know what it would take to overcome that."

"Ma says that Christians shouldn't have such bad feelings between them." He looked at her for the first time. "Your brothers aren't believers, Liza. I know you can't answer for them, but what about you? Can you forgive us? Can you let us forgive you?"

Chapter 3

Liza had always considered Garrett Anderson a boor of the first level. Now that she'd actually talked to him, she wasn't so sure.

They did belong to the same little church. She saw Garrett Anderson every week unless sickness or rough weather kept one of them away. He was the guy who set up the benches, passed out the hymn books, and stood up to take the offering—a fixture that everyone took for granted, at least Liza did.

"God commands us to forgive, Garrett," she said, swallowing and pulling at her skirt seam beneath the table. "I know it's my Christian duty." She finally found the courage to look at him.

"But?" he probed, watching her closely. His brown eyes were deep enough to drown in.

She didn't want to say it, but she had to. "You made my life pure misery when we were in school, teasing me all the time. I used to dread going because of you. I have a hard time forgetting that."

His expression grew pained. "I was too high spirited in those days. I should have had more sense." He leaned closer. "Can you please forgive me?"

He waited for her answer, a softly pleading look in his eyes.

Something inside her melted. She cleared her throat. "I do. . .forgive you. It was wrong of me to hold a grudge."

"Friends?" he asked, smiling kindly.

She nodded and smiled back, willing but still troubled. "I wish I could speak for the boys," she said. "I agree with your mother that there's been too much bad blood between the Wainrights and the Andersons. I wish we could call a truce and forget the whole thing. . .whatever it was."

He grinned at her. "At least we've made a start," he said.

The next morning Garrett came down from the loft within five minutes after Liza reached the kitchen. His curly hair was a mop on top of his head and made him look fifteen years old.

"Would you like me to fetch you some wood?" he asked her. "I can take care of building the fire, too, if you'd like."

"Thank you, Garrett," she said. She pulled on her coat to go outside to cold storage. When the last of their helpful neighbors had left yesterday, the back-porch pantry was crowded, the kitchen shelves overflowing. She had to leave one burlap sack of flour and another of cornmeal propped in one corner of the kitchen for lack of any other place to put them.

Shivering, she brought back a long slab of bacon and set about slicing it. Olivia appeared soon afterwards, every hair in place though it was only four thirty a.m. Next to her, Liza felt scruffy, but she had too much to do to spend more than five minutes dressing. There would be fifteen hungry people at her door before much longer.

"I'll take care of the coffee," Olivia said, reaching for a large cooking pot. The family coffeepot was far too small for this size crowd.

"I wonder if Charlene will come to make some more biscuits," Liza said. "The Craddocks sent a big basketful of eggs. We can have those this morning."

"I'll take care of the beans," Olivia asked. "They can simmer all day. We'll make lots of cornbread, and that'll make a good supper tonight. Cheap and filling is our motto around here."

Liza chuckled and gave the older woman a hug. "What would I have done without you?" she asked.

Olivia cleared her throat. "One of the other women would have stepped up," she replied, smiling. "You would have been fine."

When Garrett had the cook stove roaring, he moved into the living room to add logs to the fireplace.

Liza was frying bacon when she first heard Bryant's voice, loud and strident, coming from the bottom of the loft steps. "I'm not sure what you're up to, Anderson," he ground out. "But I want you off my place by nightfall, you understand?"

"If that's what you want, Wainright," Garrett replied, tightly.

Liza marched to the living room to see Garrett squatting in front of the fireplace with Bryant standing over him. "Bryant!" she said. "How ungrateful can you be? Garrett brought us a wagonload of food and supplies through an awful muddy mess. He could have stayed at home instead, you know. And he's been working without a break ever since he got here." Her lips formed a determined line as she bore in on her older brother. "How dare you speak to him that way!"

"Liza, I'm still the man of the house, and don't you forget it!" He grabbed his sheepskin coat from its peg and slammed out of the house.

Immediately, a shrill cry came from the bedroom.

"I can't believe him," Liza fumed. "He woke up Mikey."

Olivia hurried into the bedroom to soothe the frightened little boy.

"I apologize for him, Garrett," Liza said, her face flaming.

"It's not your fault," he said, dusting his hands off and standing. "I'm afraid I'm as much to blame as Bryant is. I did my share of picking fights when we were in school."

A boyish voice came from the top of the loft ladder. "I'll say you did," Caleb said, climbing down into view. "I remember that, even if I was only seven years old back then."

He stepped off the ladder and gave his sister a hard look. He jerked his head toward Garrett. "Liza, you'd best be careful how you talk to him. Bryant's already sore." He reached for his coat. "I'm going to help with the chores." He yanked the door open and strode out.

Liza stepped over to close the door properly, then let out a discouraged sigh. Suddenly, the smell of burning bacon made her fly back to the stove.

The door opened again, and Charlene stepped in. Her face was free of all traces of powder or rouge. She wore a denim dress and carried a pair of black shoes in her hand. "Good morning, all," she said, a shy cheerfulness in her voice. "I wore my boots over and carried my shoes. It's still a pond of mud outside."

"Maybe it'll freeze over," Garrett said wryly. "Then we can skate to the barn and back instead of swim."

She gave him a wide-eyed smile. "And that would be better?" she demanded, a lilt in her voice. She sat in a wooden chair to slip her stockinged feet into her shoes. "I came to see if you needed help," she told Liza.

"I was hoping you would," Liza said. "Would you mind

making more biscuits? They were a big favorite last night."

"My specialty," she said, standing. "If you'll move that sack of flour to the table, Garrett, I'll get started."

Olivia came out of the bedroom. "He went back to sleep," she said. "Poor thing, he's really exhausted. Too much excitement by far."

"I'm sorry, Olivia," Liza said. "Bryant didn't think about a child sleeping in the house."

"It's not your fault, honey. No harm done," Olivia said, lifting the lid on the pot of coffee. "Does anyone want an early cup of coffee? It's ready."

A chorus of *me*'s rose up. She chuckled. "That's what I figured." She found four cups, and they sipped while they worked.

"Today's Christmas Eve," Olivia said as they dished up eggs and set platters on the table.

Liza let out a gasp. "Christmas is tomorrow! I forgot all about it! Do you think some people may have to stay over that long?"

"If the weather stays like this, Mikey and I will," Olivia said. "I haven't ridden a horse for thirty years. I don't think I can start now."

Charlene spoke up. "I was going to spend the holiday with a girlfriend in 'Frisco. There's no point in going out there now. Traveling by stage to the next train station, I'd get there after everything was over. My next gig doesn't start until next week."

At the word "gig" everyone in the room focused on Charlene. Noticing the attention, she said, half apologetic, "I'm a dancer," then blushed at her admission.

Liza set the bacon on the table and said, "The boys and I

hardly do anything for Christmas. No tree or presents, usually. But we ought to do something special for those who have to stay over. It's awful being stranded when you could have been with your family for Christmas."

Olivia said, "We have plenty of food and plenty of hands to cook it. Why don't we make a big Christmas dinner?"

Liza warmed to the idea. "The Henshaws brought a couple of wild turkeys. We could thaw those out."

Garrett added, "I love cornbread dressing. Does anyone know how to make that?"

Olivia gave an unladylike grunt. "Since I was ten years old," she told him. She turned to Liza. "After breakfast we'll look over the pantry and plan a menu. How about that?"

Liza smiled. "I was dreading another dreary Christmas. Now I can't wait. It's going to be fun."

By six o'clock the entire group had gathered in the cabin for breakfast. When they had all been served, Bryant stood. "We're going to make two runs into Wiley's Corner today," he said. "We can saddle as many as five horses at a time. Those who have no place to go besides a hotel room are welcome to stay. We have plenty of food and the quarters aren't too uncomfortable, are they?"

"They're warm and dry," Joshua Minnick said. "What more could we ask?"

Words of approval came from every side of the room.

"How many can leave today?" Bryant asked.

Ten hands went up.

"We'll set out after breakfast. You'll have to decide among yourselves who will be in the first group." He sat down and picked up his coffee cup.

A buzz rose among the passengers.

"You can go ahead," the olive-skinned lady told the matron and her daughter. "The only place I have to go is back to the boardinghouse. It won't matter if I get there in the morning or evening. You have a family to think of."

Dr. Grotz said, "I don't mean to put myself forward, but I've got patients to attend to. I was only going to a day-long conference, and I should have been back last night."

"You're going, Doc," Bryant said. "No question about that."

Finally, they divided themselves into two groups. The first group—two women and their daughters, plus the doctor—left the cabin to get their things together. The remaining ladies—the olive-skinned beauty, whose name was Rosita, plus a red-haired woman named Ginger and her teenage daughter Betsy—stayed in the cabin to help clear away the remains of breakfast.

Before the first plate was washed, Mikey came stumbling from the bedroom. His straw-colored hair stood up on one side.

Olivia hurried to pick him up. "Well, you finally decided it was tomorrow, did you?" She hugged him, and he rested his face against her shoulder, surveying the world from his privileged perch.

Charlene scraped and stacked plates at the table. Speaking to no one in particular, she said, "We should have a Christmas Eve party tonight. Play some games, have some fun. Don't you think?"

Rosita said, "That sounds like a good idea. Of course, I'll be gone by then, but for those who must stay."

Liza finished pouring bacon grease from the cast iron skillet into a tin can on the back of the stove. She looked up and said, "That sounds nice. I'll ask Bryant if we can use the barn, though I don't see why not." She scanned the faces of the women, looking for volunteers. "We ought to set up an entertainment committee to think of activities and organize everything."

Charlene said, "I'll do that." She looked at young Betsy. "Would you like to help?"

Before her daughter could reply, Ginger shook her head in a commanding gesture.

Charlene flushed but didn't give any other sign that she'd noticed. She turned to Rosita. "Would you help me before you leave this afternoon?"

"Of course." Rosita turned her back on Ginger and scrubbed the plate in her hands with a vengeance.

As soon as the dishes were dried and put away, Charlene and Rosita moved into the living room to discuss the party while Ginger and Betsy worked over a large basin filled with bread dough. Mikey had his blocks out on the rug, but he soon tired of them and began distributing them to every adult in the room calling out, "Special delivery," for each one.

"They're leaving," Rosita called out, bending to peer out the window.

Everyone headed to the porch to say good-bye. With Bryant in the lead and Caleb bringing up the rear, they rode toward the road in a single file. The horses' hooves disappeared into the mud, then reappeared with a squishy sucking sound. The doctor tipped his hat as he passed the porch. "Thank you, Miss Liza," he said. "You've been wonderfully kind to all of us."

"My pleasure," she said, smiling and waving.

When they disappeared around the bend, the others went back inside, and Garrett came to stand next to Liza on the porch. "Do you want me to go home?" he asked. "If you do, I'll ride one of my horses bareback and lead the other. I can fetch the buckboard later."

"Do I *want* you to go?" She had to strain her head back to look him full in the face when he stood this close. "I can't say that I do, Garrett. Honestly, I don't know what I would have done without you yesterday or today. My brothers are never so quick on the draw when it comes to helping in the house. I'll need a man's strong back to help now and then as long as these people are here."

She sent an anxious glance toward the barn. "I don't want you to go. . .but. . ."

"But your brothers," he finished. "If I told you that they don't bother me, what then?"

"Won't your mother miss you?" she asked. "It's Christmas."

"She sent me over here. She gave me orders to stay as long as I'm needed." He looked serious. "That's why I'm asking you."

"Do you want to stay?" she asked.

"If you want me to, then I want to." He chuckled. "Your turn. Try to break the stalemate, will you?"

A smile forced itself out, and she gave up. "Could you at least stay for the Christmas Eve party tonight?" she asked. "After all this work, you deserve to be in on the fun."

He grinned and his face lit up. "I was hoping you'd see it that way," he said.

She turned to go into the house, and he fell in step with her. "Liza. . ."

She paused beside the door and looked up, waiting for him to go on.

"You know why I used to tease you so much in school?"

He had her full attention as she waited for the answer.

"You're the prettiest girl in these parts, and I wanted you to notice me."

Chapter 4

Garrett's lips pursed out in a rueful grimace. "I guess I got what I wanted, but not exactly as I'd planned."

Liza's cheeks were on fire. Moving away from the door, she walked to the side of the porch that faced away from the yard. If anyone saw her blush, she'd be mortified.

"Did I upset you?" he asked anxiously, coming behind her.

She shook her head. "Surprised, not upset," she said. She drew in a long breath and swallowed. Finally, she turned to him. "Thank you, Garrett. That's the nicest thing anyone has ever said to me."

His brown eyes held a soft light. "I meant it."

Suddenly, Liza forgot she was tired. Suddenly, her feet felt light, and her heart hummed a tune.

Harvey appeared in the barn doorway, and Liza said, "We'd best go inside."

The cabin was bustling with bread-makers, bean-stirrers, and party-planners. Liza set out the turkeys to thaw and discussed lunch options with Olivia. Garrett split wood out back and kept the fires burning. Liza didn't talk to him again for several hours, but she was constantly aware of his presence as he moved from the fireplace to the cook stove, supplying the fires' insatiable appetites with fuel. His warm looks told Liza that he was aware of her, too.

How could this be happening? She'd always dreamed of catching a young man's eye, but Garrett Anderson's? That she'd *never* dreamed of.

Despite Bryant's disapproving presence, they managed to accidentally sit together at lunch, and they lingered over their coffee cups when everyone else was through.

The second group to leave would be Rosita and four of the cowhands, Bryant and Harvey acting as escorts and bringing the Running W horses back.

"I'm sorry to leave you all with the dishes," Rosita said, swinging her long wool cape around her shoulders.

"You go ahead, dearie," Olivia told her, propping the stirring spoon on a plate beside the stove. "Once those men are ready to leave, they won't want to wait. You'd best put your things together in a hurry." She came over to hug the young woman. "God bless you, my dear."

"Thank you," she said. Turning to Liza, she added, "I almost hate to miss the party." She included Charlene, at the dishpan, in her smile.

Charlene gave her a sudsy wave.

Liza stood to see Rosita to the door. "I hope you reach your family soon," she said, glancing into the yard. "Be careful out there. It's looking wetter and more dangerous all the time." She watched Rosita gingerly step into the muddy swill, then closed the door against the breeze. It must be more than forty degrees out there. Maybe the sun and the constant wind would dry out the yard a little.

When she returned to her seat next to Garrett at the table,

she said, "I feel like a slacker, sitting here and watching all of you so busy."

"You deserve a rest," Ginger said. "Betsy and I are going to the bunkhouse for an hour or two when we finish here. We'll have some time to rest then."

"I'm going to take a nap with Mikey," Olivia added.

Crumbling the last of a biscuit onto his plate, the boy let out a howl.

"Hush," his grandmother told him, "or you'll go right now instead of waiting for me."

That quieted his protests. He rubbed the biscuit bits into a tiny pool of sorghum and stuffed the gooey mass into this mouth.

"What needs to be done this afternoon?" Garrett murmured to Liza.

"Olivia has supper mostly taken care of," she said. "There's precious little to do for that. But we should make some goodies for the party tonight and maybe bake some dried-apple pies for tomorrow."

"How about some Poor Man Cookies?" Charlene suggested. "Flour, brown sugar, oatmeal, and a few other things. No eggs. They're simple to make."

"I'll help," Betsy said, glancing hopefully at her mother.

Ginger held her daughter's gaze for a short moment, and Betsy shrank. "We'll do the pies," she told her daughter.

"I'll help you later when I get up from our nap," Olivia told Charlene. Now very familiar with the kitchen, the grandmother found a clean washcloth. Dampening it in a bowl of warm water, she came toward her grandson.

"Show me those patties," she said.

He held up his crumbly, sticky hands for her to wipe.

"What would we ever do without little boys?" she asked, taking the last bit of biscuit from his cheeks. She bent over and kissed his forehead. "Come to Grandma, honey." She picked him up and carried him to the bedroom, his feet dangling around her knees.

"He's big enough to walk," Garrett said, when the bedroom door closed.

"But there's something special about being carried," Charlene told him. "For the boy and for the grandma."

Ten minutes later, the women finished the dishes and set out for the bunkhouse. Charlene hesitated after Ginger and Betsy left. "I'm tired, and I need to rest," she confided, "but I hate going out there with that old biddy. She cuts me every chance she gets." Pulling the door open, she went out.

"Would you like me to fill your coffee cup again?" Liza asked Garrett.

He nodded. "That would be fine."

Glad he said yes, she took her own cup to the stove as well and ladled them full.

When she returned, he said, "Tell me about your folks, Liza."

She tried to think of where to begin. "They were wonderful parents. The best. They loved each other, and they loved us. I guess that's what really counts."

She absently rubbed the wood grain on the table next to her cup. "We've never been well off, but we've never lacked either. Pa believed in hard work and honest dealings with his neighbors. Ma was up before everyone else and went to bed after we did. She worked her hands raw sometimes."

"Did your father ever think about running anything besides longhorns?" he asked.

She shook her head. "He knew cattle. That's what he always said when anyone mentioned trying farming or logging or breeding horses, or whatever. I don't think he could have done anything else. Bryant's the same way. He's stuck in one groove. I don't think he'll ever do anything else."

"Harvey seems different."

She nodded. "Bryant calls him 'Professor' sometimes. Harvey loves books and learning. He'd like to go to college, but there's not enough money to pay his tuition. So, he saves up and buys books. The loft has a shelf full of them."

Garrett nodded. "I saw them up there. *The Age of Reason* by Thomas Paine, *Principles of Nature* by Elihu Palmer, *Walden* by Thoreau—pretty impressive."

"Expensive, you mean. The philosophies in those books scare me. They don't agree with the Bible at all."

He nodded. "I'm not much of a reader," he said, "but I remember those titles from school."

"I'm afraid that Harvey believes that everything written down in a book must be so. Bryant, on the other hand, thinks the exact opposite. He doesn't trust book learning." She shook her head. "He's too much like Pa, set in his ways and his opinions." She turned to him. "What about your folks? Your mother sounds like a fine person."

He nodded. "She is. She's seen a lot of trouble in her life, though. Since Pa passed away last year, she's had a tough time of it."

"At least she had you," Liza said.

"I don't know why God let me be the one to grow up," he said. "She had three other children, you know. They all died before they reached a year old. Except for me. Sometimes I wonder what the good Lord was thinking when He let that happen."

"I'm glad it was you," she blurted out, then blushed and wished the words back.

He grinned at her. "You know, at this moment, so am I."

Liza's cheeks grew warmer still.

At that instant, the door burst open and Bryant stepped in. When he saw Liza and Garrett so close together at the table, he drew up. His chin lifted.

Not looking at Garrett, he spoke to Liza. "We're heading out for the second run. Last time it took four hours to make the round. I'm expecting to be back around nightfall. If we're not back, wait until morning and send some men after us. The ground's getting slicker by the hour. I'm afraid we may have a horse fall and break a leg."

She stood. "Are you sure you should go?" she asked. "Maybe you should wait a few days, so the ground can dry out."

"We'll try it. If it gets too bad, we'll turn back." Without a good-bye, he ducked out the door.

Liza moved to the door to check that the latch caught. From the look on her older brother's face, she was surely in hot water now. With a small sigh and a little shrug, she returned to the table.

The silence between her and Garrett was taut.

"Garrett," she said, "if the road is as bad as Bryant says, you may not be able to get out if you wait much longer. Are you sure you want to stay?"

"As long as you don't chase me away with a stick," he said.

Chapter 5

They talked until Charlene returned to start the cookies and Olivia came out of the bedroom. Excusing himself, Garrett went out to split some more wood.

Liza moved to the pantry to pull out baking ingredients when Caleb came inside. He looked all in.

"It's a muddy mess out there," he said, sinking into a chair at the table. "The horses have been milling around in the corral churning it up and wearing themselves out. I finally had to put them all in the barn. I wonder how the cows are doing in that canyon, but I'm going to have to wait until tomorrow to find out."

Liza poured him a hot cup of coffee. When any of her brothers came in and sat down, that was a given. "On Christmas Day?" Liza asked. "You've got a few cowboys out there in the barn. Why don't you get a couple of them to go with you this afternoon? Then you can have tomorrow clear."

"What are we doing tomorrow?" he asked.

"A big Christmas dinner," she said. "A holiday celebration, like most folks have. We're planning to eat turkey, dressing, and fill more serving dishes than this table can hold."

"And then some," Olivia agreed. She found a large mixing bowl and brought it to the table. "All right, Charlene," she said, "come and pour out the ingredients for those cookies. I'm going to watch you, so I can make these later."

Caleb finished his coffee about the time that Ginger and Betsy arrived. Tipping his hat to the ladies as they came in, he set off for the barn. A short time later, he rode out with two other men, heading northwest toward the canyon.

Charlene was sliding her first pan of cookies into the oven when a commotion in the yard brought the ladies to the porch. Seven horses were heading through the yard, their steps lagging.

Bryant stopped near the porch. "The creek's flooding the road," he said. "We can't get through. It's too dangerous."

"Caleb and a couple of the men went to check on the canyon," Liza told him. "Could you and Harvey ask the men to set hay bales around and get the barn ready for the party?"

Bryant surveyed the yard. "We've got to do something about this mud," he said. "I think we have some old boards around somewhere. Maybe we can make a boardwalk from the barn to the house, but it's at least a hundred feet. I'm not sure if we can round up that much wood." He shook his head. "All we can do is try."

Rosita brought her mount to the porch stairs and swung down. She handed her reins to Bryant. "Thank you," she said, when he reached for them. "I'll stay here and help the ladies."

"Welcome back!" Charlene said. "We missed you." She turned to Liza. "The party will be more fun with everyone here, at least."

Liza smiled. "You're right, Charlene. It's best to look on the bright side."

Strangely, the party spirit seemed to flow through the cabin as soon as Rosita stepped inside. The younger women told stories and laughed as they baked cookies. Mikey woke up, and Betsy played with him on the carpet while her mother rolled out pie crusts.

Liza tried to blend in with the rest, though her eyes often trailed to the window where Garrett's tall form bent over the chopping block. How long did it take to split a few logs, anyway?

Finally, Garrett came inside for a break and a drink of cool water. He was sitting at the table when Bryant came in. In his stocking feet, he stood by the door to ask Liza, "Are you sure you want to have this party in the barn? The boardwalk sank into the mud. You can't even see it, especially not in the dark."

Liza turned to Charlene. "What do you think?"

"We're going to play Blind Man's Bluff and Musical Chairs," she replied. "There's not enough room in here for them."

Liza nodded then said, "Maybe we should put sawdust on the porch to absorb the mud. At least that'll help keep some of it out of the house." She looked at the splotchy floorboards in the dining room. "I've given up on trying to keep it clean in here, but we can at least try to put a limit on what tracks in."

Garrett stood up. "If you'll show me where the sawdust is, I'll take care of that for you."

Bryant gave him a grudging look. "It's in sacks in the barn. We use it to keep the barn floor dry."

Garrett picked up his hat from a nearby chair and put it on. He sent Liza a wink an instant before he walked out after her brother.

That evening at supper, Garrett sat across from Liza. In some ways, that was worse than sitting beside him because she couldn't stop looking at him. She tried to pretend that nothing had changed, but her heart was singing too loudly to hide it.

Once she caught Bryant frowning at her, and she lost her breath. He was seriously vexed with her. So seriously that it frightened her.

She found an excuse to get up from the table. Her bowl of beans sat untouched, her cornbread growing dry and hard, but she poured coffee and offered the basket of bread to everyone in the room twice over, ignoring the meal. There would be time for it later. She didn't return to her seat until Bryant had gone out.

When she did, Garrett gave her a sardonic smile. None of the by-play was lost on him. The glint in his eyes told her he knew exactly what had happened.

As usual, Charlene was the first one to set up the dishpan for washing, and Rosita soon joined her. Ginger and Betsy piled cookies into a wide, cloth-lined basket while Olivia took care of a fresh pot of coffee.

As soon as the last dish lay in the cabinet, the group set off in a troop toward the barn. With the cookie basket on Ginger's arm and the cooking pot of hot coffee in Garrett's padded hands, they set off single file. Charlene carried Mikey, so Olivia could hold Rosita's arm with one hand and her black skirts with the other. Liza was last across with a double stack of tin coffee mugs in her hands.

They reached the barn with laughter of relief, congratulating each other on a safe trip. Harvey had found an old dusty table and set it along the wall for the refreshments.

The barn was square-shaped with horse stalls running down two sides, leaving a wide rectangular area open in the center. A dozen hay bales formed a circle along the edges, and the floor held a layer of fresh straw. The area glowed from lanterns hanging on posts all around. Nearby, horses muttered and stamped, mildly irritated at the commotion.

When they'd set out the food and found places to sit, Liza said, "Charlene, you do the honors. You know what's planned."

Charlene turned to Harvey and handed him a scrap of paper. "You call them out," she told him. "I can't stand up in front of all these people."

Liza looked at her, surprised. If Charlene was a dancer, she certainly couldn't be shy.

Harvey headed to the front of the area and called out, "First off, we're going to divide into two teams and play Twenty Questions." He eyed the group and held up his hand with the palm vertical. "We'll divide the room here. Pick your captains and let me know when you're ready." He scanned down the list and glanced at Charlene. "Say, these are pretty good."

Charlene beamed.

Rosita giggled.

They played for an hour, then broke up for cookies and coffee. Garrett picked up several cookies and moved to a seat on the hay bale next to Liza. He offered her one and grinned when she took it. "You're welcome," he said, though she hadn't said thanks.

"You're going to get me into trouble," she said with mock rebuke. "Bryant is watching you. I hope you know it."

"Absolutely," he replied, taking a big bite.

When everyone was seated with food in hand, Olivia said, "How about some testimonies? Has the Lord done anything for you this week? Or maybe this year?"

The cowhands looked uncomfortable.

Harvey, usually the moderator, stayed silent.

Olivia waited a few seconds then went on, "I'm thankful that we're all safe. If the train had been moving just a little faster, we wouldn't be sitting here enjoying this good food and fellowship."

Amens and nods from all directions brought warmth to the room that hadn't been there before.

She continued, "I know that God has His hand in those things. The way I see it, those of us who were on board the train have a special responsibility. God spared our lives. That couldn't have been an accident."

Rosita looked sober.

Charlene looked like she was about to cry.

Garrett cleared his throat. "I wasn't on the train," he said, "but the Lord did bless me last year, and I'd like to tell about it." His voice was mellow, but it carried throughout the room.

"My father had a heart attack last March at the age of forty-three. It was a big shock to Ma and me. He lived for almost a whole day after it happened. The doctor said there was nothing that could be done for him. We knew he wasn't long for this world, and he knew it, too."

He swallowed and rubbed the bridge of his nose. "I'd just like to say that I'm grateful that God let us have that time with him. We got to sit with him and tell him how much he meant to us. He and Ma had a chance to say their good-byes and promise to meet again on the other side." He paused a moment then went on. "When I miss him, I think about that time, and it helps me feel better."

Glancing around, as though unsure how to end, he said, "That's all."

Liza felt a lump coming into her throat. Her parents had

died far away. She and the boys hadn't even seen their bodies. Folks with cholera had to be buried right away and their possessions burned.

In the darkness, she felt Garrett's fingers close around hers, so warm and comforting as though he knew what she was feeling at that moment. She swallowed back her tears and hung on to him.

Finally, Olivia said, "I'd best get to the house. I'm too tired to go on. Mikey's getting cranky, too."

Harvey looked at Liza. "I guess we'd best call it a night," he said. "Thanks, everyone! It was a great time."

Next to Liza, Garrett said, "A wonderful time!"

Liza beamed.

Taking two lanterns, the bunkhouse ladies left first. Those from the cabin tried to pick out the boardwalk under the mud as they made their way across the yard.

Carrying the empty basket, Liza was almost to the porch when her shoes slipped on the slimy board. With a cry, her arms flew up and the basket hit the sludge. Behind her, Garrett's hand shot out to grab her arm. They did a little two-step but managed to keep their balance. Laughing, they made it to the step and climbed to the porch floor.

Liza was about to go inside, when Bryant's arm came across her waist to stop her. Ahead of her, Garrett disappeared through the door, not realizing she wasn't with him.

"I want to talk to you, missy," Bryant said, his eyes hard in the darkness.

Liza gulped and waited, trying to brace herself for what was coming.

"You're making a fool of yourself over that lying Anderson whelp," he said. "I'm warning you, Liza. I'm not taking this."

"Lying?" she demanded. "What makes you say lying? He's never lied to you."

"All Andersons are liars," he retorted. "They have been for generations. You know that as well as I do."

She drew herself up to her full five feet, two inches. "I do not!"

He bent over with his face close to hers. "I'm not going to argue with you, Liza. I'm *telling* you. You'd better mind what I say."

With that, he took two quick steps and disappeared through the cabin door.

Liza remained on the porch for a few minutes, trying to compose herself before she went inside. She wanted to cry, but she was also furious at Bryant for being so uncaring. She was only a year younger than he was. Why couldn't he trust her judgment enough to give her a chance to tell him what she'd learned about Garrett? It wasn't fair.

On the other hand, her brothers were all she had in the world. Bryant was hotheaded enough to make things really tough on her if she didn't give in to his demands. Were her feelings for Garrett strong enough to warrant such a struggle?

She wasn't sure. She'd never felt for a man like she felt for Garrett. But it could be only a passing thing, the product of unusual circumstances or maybe the phase of the moon. She'd heard that a full moon fostered romance. Or was it the new moon?

She peered out from under the eaves to see what the moon looked like. It was quarter-sized crescent, smiling down at her foolishness.

Shaking her head at her own idiocy, she went inside. The kitchen counters were loaded with a dozen loaves of bread, six pies, crumbled cornbread in a large bowl, and a platter of left-over cookies from that evening's festivities—all covered with dishcloths.

She went to her room, undressed in the darkness, found her way to her edge of the bed, and crept under the heavy eiderdown quilts.

Mikey sighed, a sweet, soft sound.

Although she had to be up at four to make the dressing and put those turkeys in the oven before breakfast, she lay awake long into the night. How could she talk some sense into Bryant? How could she give up Garrett?

Chapter 6

C hristmas morning dawned with an icy wind coming from the mountain. It crept in around the windows and under the doors. Garrett was up early, stoking the fires to try to chase away the bone-aching cold. Still, Liza's feet felt like half-frozen stumps as she stuffed both turkeys with cornbread dressing in the pre-dawn. She'd been forced to lay aside her wool shawl for fear of dipping it into the food.

Finally, the birds were in the oven. She was washing her hands when Olivia came out of the bedroom.

"Good morning, Liza," she said. "You know, despite the interruption of our holiday plans, it has been good to see the Wainright cabin again."

"You know this place?" Liza asked, reaching for a hand towel.

"I believe my mother may have worked here when I was a girl," she said, setting the coffeepot under the pitcher pump's spout. "That was more years ago than I care to count." She gave the pump handle four hard, quick pushes. Water gushed out and hit the bottom of the pot with a metallic sound.

Charlene arrived as Olivia was setting the pot on the stove.

The younger woman's face was swollen around the eyes, her nose and cheeks red.

"Charlene," Olivia said, concerned. "Are you ill?"

Sniffing, she said, "Only inside, Miss Olivia. I didn't sleep hardly at all last night." She dabbed at her nose and her eyes filled with tears.

Immediately, Olivia went to her. "Honey, what is it?" She drew her to the sofa and sat beside her.

With her ear tuned to their conversation, Liza pulled out the half-empty basket of eggs and started slicing bacon. Garrett moved away from the living room fireplace to join her. They shared a glance but didn't speak.

Charlene's tears grew into soft sobs.

Olivia held her and patted her back. "What is it, child? Did someone say something hurtful to you?"

Charlene shook her head. "It was your test. . .testimony last night," she quavered. "About God sparing us for a reason." Her breath came in gasps. "I'm so ashamed."

Olivia let her cry for a few moments until she'd settled down a little.

"Charlene, God loves you. He loved you so much that He sent His Son to die for your sins. . .in your place."

Charlene nodded.

She lifted Charlene's chin so she could look into her watery eyes. "Honey, if you had been the only person in the entire world, He would have still died for you."

Tears overflowed onto Charlene's ruddy cheeks. She nodded.

"Tell Him about it," Olivia urged, her voice gentle. "Tell Him how ashamed you are and that you want Him to take away your sin. Let's do it right now."

Again Charlene nodded.

Olivia bowed and Charlene bowed with her so their heads were touching, temple to temple. "Father," Olivia prayed, "your child, Charlene, has come to understand that she needs Your forgiveness. Lord, please hear her and grant her a new life."

When she finished, Charlene said simply, "Lord. . .be merciful to me. I'm a sinner." Her voice broke. "Please take my life and make it new."

They hugged each other with more tears.

Liza had tears on her cheeks as well.

With a smile that was just for her, Garrett squeezed her arm then made himself scarce at the woodpile. Liza had seen the same reaction in her brothers. Whenever they saw tears, they wanted to be far away.

Finally, Charlene came to the kitchen.

Liza hugged her hard. "I'm so happy for you," she said. "I wish you were going to stay around here. We've got a good little church in Wiley's Corner. Our pastor is a wonderful man of God. You'd learn a lot from him."

Charlene dipped her hands in the washing-up basin beside the back door and patted her cheeks. "I'm tempted to do that," she said. "I just wish folks hereabout didn't know where I came from."

Olivia said, "It's best to be out front with that instead of trying to hide it away. God's grace is for everyone. If there're people who don't see it that way, then you've lost nothing by not associating with them."

Liza said, "Think of it, Charlene. You received Christ on Christmas morning. What better gift could you ever have?"

"That's right," she said, beaming. "That's right!"

A noise at the door brought them around to see Rosita step inside. "What's right?" she asked, taking off her wool scarf and smoothing her black hair.

Charlene said, "I received Christ on Christmas morning."

Rosita looked puzzled.

"I'll tell you about it after breakfast," Charlene promised. She washed her hands and dried them. "What's next?" she asked. "Do you want me to make more biscuits?"

"We're eating bread this morning," Liza told her with a grin. "The oven is full of turkey."

The news of Charlene's conversion met with mixed reactions. Liza expected Ginger to be happy for the girl, but she gave no reaction at all. Harvey, surprisingly, seemed enormously pleased.

There were fifteen people at breakfast that Christmas morning: ten passengers, the four Wainrights, and Garrett. After the meal, the men brought the checkerboard to the house, saying that the barn was too cold. A couple of them had found scraps of wood to whittle, and Harvey kept everyone entertained by retelling stories he'd read in Plutarch's *Lives*.

Near noon, Mikey sat at the table with a frown on his dimpled face. "I want my mama," he said, a chant he'd picked up at breakfast and had continued for hours.

Garrett found a seat across from him. Without speaking to the child, he placed his hands together in a prayerful pose then twisted them so that his hands faced each other with a finger wiggling out each side. He held his hands up and examined each wiggling finger as though fascinated.

Mikey stopped whining. He stared at Garrett's hands.

Garrett held them out for Mikey to take a better look, and the boy smacked at them. Tucking his chin down, Mikey grinned.

"Do you want to see how I do it?" Garrett asked, pulling his hands apart.

"I do!" Caleb said, coming away from his position as spectator of the checkers match.

Garrett waited for Caleb to join him at the table. Placing his hands together again, he twisted them.

"Wait!" Caleb said. "I didn't get it."

Garrett spoke to Mikey. "Want me to show him on your hands?" he asked.

Mikey nodded and held out his chubby fingers.

Garrett placed the boy's palms together, pushed down one finger from each hand and twisted the palms.

Mikey let out a delighted squeal as he wiggled his displaced fingers. "Look, Grandma!" he cried.

Olivia laughed. "My brothers used to do that one," she said. "I haven't seen it for years."

Caleb tried to imitate Garrett's moves but failed. Finally, Garrett pressed the boy's hands into the right position.

"I got it!" he said, separating them and fitting them together again.

Setting a pot of potatoes on to boil, Liza chuckled. "Where did you get that from?" she asked.

"Our old foreman," Garrett told her. "He knew all kinds of tricks, and he kept me entertained when I was this age." He ruffled Mikey's straw-colored hair.

Careful to keep his hands together, Mikey eased out of his chair and made the circuit around the room to show his fingers to each adult in turn. Halfway around, he tripped and his hands came apart. Running to Garrett, he said, "Do them again!"

"Please," Olivia told him.

"Please," he said, his former pout totally forgotten. When Garrett had him set, he ran back to the last cowboy, then moved into the kitchen to show the ladies.

"That was good of you," Olivia told Garrett.

He stood and reached for a stick of wood in the box beside the stove. "I'm glad it worked," he said, grinning at the happy child.

That Christmas dinner was the biggest meal Liza had ever overseen. There were so many serving dishes that they had to set up a side table just for the food. Turkey and dressing, mashed potatoes, sweet potatoes, pickles in several forms, corn, cabbage salad, boiled greens, fresh rolls, and plenty of pies. By one o'clock, everyone had eaten his or her fill, and there was still food to spare.

Clearing away the leftovers, Liza remarked to Olivia, "Before the avalanche, we had barely enough food to last the winter. Now look at all this food just a couple of days later. I feel like the four starving lepers while Samaria was under siege. The prophet promised that by tomorrow this time there would be more food than they all could eat."

Olivia said, "I know that story. One of the king's men said, 'If God opened the windows of heaven, could this be?'"

Liza nodded. "Then the lepers went out to the enemy camp and found more to eat than they could carry away."

Olivia smiled. "In your case, the food came in on horseback."

"And wagonload," Garrett added.

Carrying plates to the dishpan, Charlene was listening intently. "Where is that story in the Bible?" she asked. "I'd like to read it sometime."

"I think it's in the Kings," Olivia told her. "We'll look it up later. I have a Bible in my case."

Rosita carried the old dishwater out the back door to pitch it onto the ground. When she returned, she said, "What are we going to do with the rest of the day?"

Ginger stretched her back. "I'm going to take a rest. We'll likely be heading home tomorrow, and the washing pile that will be waiting for me will be a sight to behold. I guarantee it."

"Do you think we'll be able to leave tomorrow?" Rosita asked.

Bryant answered from across the room. "I rode out to check the stream after breakfast. It's going down. As long as we don't get any more rain, we may be able to cross it in the morning. No promises, though." He again focused on the checkerboard.

Charlene looked troubled, but she stayed busy with drying the dishes and didn't say anything.

Olivia said, "I've got to have a couple of days at home. Then we'll take a stage to the next open rail station so Mikey can get home to his mother. She's frantic to see him, I know."

"I'll hate to see you go," Liza said. She turned to include those in the kitchen. "All of you. I know that this has been a problem for you all, but you've been a blessing to me."

"You're sweet to say that," Olivia said. "I hope this won't be good-bye forever. Canton's Corner isn't so far away. Please come and see me sometime."

One by one, folks wandered off to their own places, leaving Bryant and Joshua intent on a checkers game and a couple of cowboys dozing in chairs beside the fire. Olivia took Mikey for a nap, and the house grew quiet.

"How about a walk?" Garrett asked Liza, speaking softly so no one else could hear.

"In this cold?" she whispered back.

"We could find someplace out of the wind, I reckon."

"I'll get an extra sweater," she said and tiptoed into the bedroom to find one. In a moment, she returned.

Bundling into coats, scarves, and hats, they left the house

by the back way and eased the door closed behind them.

"Where to?" he asked, when they were in the yard.

"Let's go around the mud in the yard and get behind the barn. There's a high fence on that side of the corral that would give some shelter."

The wind snatched the breath from their lungs. It crept down their collars and up their coat sleeves. By the time they reached the corral, Liza was shivering.

"We won't be able to stay long," she said. "We shouldn't anyway. Bryant will be missing me before long."

Shoving his hands deep into his coat pockets, Garrett said, "Is tomorrow going to be good-bye for us, too?"

She hesitated. With all her heart she wanted to say no, but she wasn't sure. "What should I do? Bryant won't listen to me. He's got his mind made up, and nothing will change it. I know that just as sure as I know I'm standing here."

"Why does that have to affect us?" he asked. "Aren't you an adult now? Can't you make up your own mind?"

"My brothers are all I have," she said. "They're Wainrights, all three of them. I can't forget that I'm one, too."

He leaned back and looked straight up at the blue sky. "Why did our grandfathers do this to us?" he asked. He looked at her once more. "No one knows how the bad feelings started, so how can we make an end of it?" He peered at her. "What do you know about the feud, Liza? What was the story that came down through your family?"

"That the Andersons are liars and cheats," she said.

He bristled.

She tugged at the middle button on his coat. "You asked me. That's what I heard. That's what the boys have heard. That's all I know."

"Nothing else?" he asked. "Surely there must have been something more, some reason for such a reputation."

She shook her head. "My father only spoke of it once or twice that I remember. And that's all he said."

Turning sideways to her, he leaned against the fence. "I hope you'll believe me when I say that my father was an honest, God-fearing man. So was his father before him. They were men of faith who prayed and read the Bible to their families every morning of their lives."

Liza stared at him. She could hardly believe what she was hearing. Why had her grandfather been so adamant that the Andersons were wicked? She said, "What did you hear about us?"

He drew in a breath before answering. "I hope you're ready to hear this," he said. "Remember, it's what I was told, not what I personally think about you." He caught her hand and held it. "I was told that the Wainrights are malicious liars, that they set out to destroy people for no reason."

Liza said, "My father scorned religion of any kind and so did my grandfather. But I've never known either one of them to tell a lie, Garrett. A man's word is his bond. You know that. That's what they lived by." Her eyes narrowed. "If either of our grandfathers had been dishonest, they would have never been able to do business with anyone in these parts."

"But both of them were respected in their own right," he said.

"The only people who had misgivings about them were each other." She looked at him. "Does your mother know anything?" she asked. "Maybe you should ask her for more information."

"As soon as I get home, that's exactly what I'll do," he said. "I've got good reason to find where this all started." He hesitated, watching her closely. "At least I hope I do."

"Garrett. . ."

"I know I may be rushing things," he said, interrupting her. "But the fact is, I don't know when I'll have another chance to talk to you. Your brothers may run me off with a shotgun if I come back later."

She wanted to deny it, but she knew what he said was true.

Standing, he looked into her eyes and went on. "You've been special to me since we were kids in Miss Casey's school. When Ma suggested that I bring over food and supplies, I agreed to it because I'd have a chance to see you again." He searched her face. "I love you, Liza. Is there any hope for me?"

"Garrett. . ."

He put his gloved hand over her mouth. "Don't tell me what Bryant wants you to say. Speak what's in your own heart. Please." He removed his hand to let her speak.

The anguish on his face tore at her heart. "I love you, too," she said simply. "But I. . ."

She didn't get any further. Drawing her close, he leaned down and kissed her until her head was spinning.

She'd never felt so sheltered as she did at that moment.

"We've got to fight," he said, whispering into her hair. "We can't let a fifty-year-old argument keep us apart."

She nodded, her rounded cheek brushing the front of his black coat. "I want to," she said, "but how?"

He drew back enough to look into her face. "I'll talk to my mother. Maybe she can remember something that will give us a place to start."

"But what if finding the reason doesn't make any difference? What if Bryant won't listen?"

"If Grandfather Anderson was wrong, I'll make restitution if it takes giving up my entire ranch," he said. "No one could argue with that. If Grandfather Wainright was wrong, then at least the Andersons can have a chance to forgive him." Garrett's voice had new steel in it. His arms tightened. "I'm not going to lose you now that we've found each other."

He kissed her again.

Breathless, Liza pulled away. "We've got to go back inside. Bryant will come looking for us, and then I'll really be in trouble."

"You're right," he said, kissing her cheek. "If I go home tomorrow, I'll meet you right here at dusk two days from now."

She nodded. "I'll be waiting for you."

Chapter 7

Peering around the corner to be sure the way was clear, hand in hand they hustled around the yard. Releasing her, Garrett headed for the woodpile to gather wood.

Liza paused outside the back door to calm her breathing and then returned to the warmth of the house. She quickly shrugged out of her coat and eased open the bedroom door to lay her wraps inside. Olivia and Mikey lay sleeping quietly under the nine-square quilt.

To stay out of Bryant's range of sight, Liza busied herself with sweeping the dining room floor near the back door.

Garrett came in and dropped a dozen split logs into the wood box next to the kitchen stove. "It's bitter out there," he remarked, his tone casual.

"Would you like some coffee?" Liza asked. "There's still a little left."

"Bring us some, too," Bryant called from the living room.

When Liza brought her brother his coffee, he muttered, "Where have you been?"

She felt her face flush. "Out for some air," she said, avoiding his eyes.

Bryant didn't speak again. His harsh stare told her all she needed to know.

A few minutes later, she joined Garrett at the table. "He's on to us," she whispered.

Under the table, he squeezed her hand. "It's going to be all right," he murmured. "I promise you that."

Her chin lifted. "I'm tired of being Bryant's bondslave," she retorted, still whispering.

The door opened and Charlene stepped inside, her blond hair blowing across her face. She pushed the door shut and tried to smooth it back, but several wisps hung about her face, giving her an ethereal look.

Shrugging out of her cape, she came to join Garrett and Liza. Harvey came in behind her and moved to the living room without saying anything to those in the kitchen.

Watching the other girl's downcast face, Liza asked, "What's the problem?"

Charlene shrugged. "I don't know where to go," she replied. "I can't go back to my old job. My parents have. . . That is, they don't want me to come home." She looked down at her hands. "When we leave tomorrow, what should I do?"

The bedroom door clicked shut. "Come home with me," Olivia said, stepping to the table. "I've got a spare room, and my house will be mighty quiet once Mikey goes home." She placed her hand on Charlene's shoulder. "God will make a way for you, my dear. He's already begun."

Charlene nodded, fighting tears. "You're a saint, Miss Olivia," she whispered.

The older woman shook her head. "No, Charlene. I'm a sinner. . . reborn by the grace of God. The same as you."

Leaving Charlene, Olivia turned toward the kitchen. "What

shall we do to feed those hungry mouths this evening?" she asked. "It's almost five o'clock. We're going to start hearing from the crowd pretty soon."

"Let's just set out leftovers," Liza said, getting up from her seat. "I set some bowls out into cold storage. I'll get them." She rushed outside without stopping for her coat, Charlene right behind her.

Returning in less than a minute, both girls gasped as they shut the door behind them, their hands full of dishes.

Garrett was piling still more wood into the kitchen stove.

Olivia came to relieve them of their burdens. "What were you thinking?" she gasped, shivering. "You should have taken your wraps out there. I'm getting a chill from standing next to you."

She poured food into pans and set them to warm while Liza made more coffee. Charlene began setting up the dishpan for the after-dinner cleanup.

Harvey moved to the kitchen table. Leaning back, he stretched his legs straight out. "Say, Charlene," he said. "How about another game of Twenty Questions this evening? Do you think you can come up with some more good ideas?"

She turned, surprised. "I suppose I could," she said hesitantly.

He turned to Liza. "Sis, find us a piece of paper. We can plan it out now." He looked at Charlene. "Ten things would be enough, don't you think?"

"That should be plenty," she said, moving to sit across from him. "But we can't stay up late tonight again."

He nodded. "We'll be leaving before daybreak, if I know Bryant."

A *harrumph* sounded from the living room. "Six o'clock," his older brother called.

Harvey went on. "You'll have to sit here, Charlene." He

pulled out the chair next to him. "Otherwise, everyone will hear what we're saying."

Liza looked up and caught Garrett watching her, an amused expression on his face. When he sent a pointed glance toward the couple at the table, Liza's eyes widened. She looked at Garrett and he winked, then leaned down to check the fire in the cook stove.

When the passengers had gone to their quarters, Harvey lingered in the living room watching Bryant put away the checker pieces. Harvey glanced at his sister in the kitchen and directed his question to her. "You could use some help around here, right?"

She nodded. "Who couldn't," she asked, wiping the counter and wondering where he was going with this.

He looked at Bryant. "How would you feel about Charlene staying on and helping Liza around here?" he asked. "She has no place to go."

Bryant considered. "Olivia offered her a place, Harvey. Why do you want her to stay on here?"

Harvey's sensitive mouth tightened. "I'd like her to stay, that's all."

"Are you sure that's wise?" Liza asked. "You've only just met. Why don't you ride to Canton's Corner every couple of weeks to see her instead?" She glanced at Bryant. "I think she'd benefit from being with Olivia for a while. They are good friends, and Olivia would be a good influence on her. Charlene needs that now."

Bryant nodded. "There is some sense to what Liza says, Harv."

"But Canton's Corner is half a day's ride," Harvey protested. "How about if we give Charlene the option and let her make up her own mind?"

Liza had a sinking feeling. Harvey wasn't a Christian. With all that twisted philosophy he read, he wouldn't be a good influence on Charlene.

Listening from the dining room where the brothers couldn't see him, Garrett gave Liza a nod. She went on. "Let's sleep on it," she told the boys. "We'll talk to Charlene before breakfast. She always comes early to help with the cooking."

With no more work to do, Liza had no excuse to stay up later. Bryant seemed determined to wait up until Garrett also retired, so she said good night and went to bed. Garrett had wanted to say something to her, but she hadn't had a chance to find out what it was.

Sometime during the night, a tapping on her window brought her awake. Frightened at first, she finally woke up enough to realize that it might be Garrett. She slipped into the hard leather of her frigid shoes and found her coat in the dark, still lying where she'd thrown it yesterday afternoon.

She crept out to the back porch, and Garrett's lanky form appeared from the shadow of the cold storage wall.

"What is it?" she asked, shivering.

He drew Liza into his arms and quickly whispered, "Talk to Charlene and tell her that my mother would pay her forty dollars a month to help with the cooking and cleaning."

"But what about Harvey? He's got his eye on that girl, Garrett, and he's not a good influence on her."

He let out a mirthless chuckle. "Do you think Harvey would come to the Anderson ranch for any reason? Do you really?"

She sighed. "I see your point. Okay. I'll speak to her in the morning." She pulled away. "My feet are numb. I've got to get back inside."

He let her go. "I've got to figure out how to get back up that ladder without waking the crew."

She reached up to kiss his cheek. "Thanks for caring about Charlene," she said. "Just be careful you don't start caring too much!"

He grabbed her back to him and kissed her. "No danger of that." He kissed her again.

Giggling, she freed herself and hurried back inside.

Despite her soft bed and warm blankets, she didn't sleep much for the rest of the night. Tomorrow everything would change. She dreaded seeing how much.

Out of bed and dressed long before the others awoke, Liza stoked the fires and put on the pot for coffee. She prayed that Charlene would wake up early enough to give them a chance to speak privately.

A few minutes later, the young woman arrived. "I couldn't sleep," she said, "and I figured I may as well come over and start breakfast."

Liza hugged her and urged her toward a chair at the dining room table. "I've been up praying that you'd come," she said. "I've got to talk to you."

Keeping her voice very low, she outlined the three choices that lay before Charlene without mentioning Harvey. "I'd love to have you here," she said, "but I'm not sure how wise that is at this point."

"What do you think I should do?" Charlene asked.

"As much as I love Olivia," Liza replied, "I think the Anderson ranch is your best bet. What if you can't find work in Canton's Corner? Olivia can't afford to keep you for long herself. From what Garrett says, his mother needs help."

Charlene nodded. "I'll do that, then."

"She's a Christian woman," Liza said. "They go to our church, so I'll see you there every week."

Charlene brightened. "Say, that's all right."

"You can go with Garrett this morning. I think he's leaving before breakfast."

"Before? I've got to get ready."

Liza smiled. "Go ahead. I'll make the biscuits this morning."

The breakfast crowd seemed small with Garrett and Charlene already gone.

"Where's Charlene?" Harvey asked Liza, coming close beside her at the stove to speak privately.

"She had a job offer. She left an hour ago," Liza replied. "She's going to be a housemaid and cook at the Anderson ranch. Mrs. Anderson needs help, from what I understand."

"You're kidding! Why that. . ."

Liza's chin lifted. "That what?"

Clamping his mouth tight, Harvey picked up his hat and headed outside. A few minutes later, he came out of the barn on horseback and trotted toward the canyon.

Before the sun peeked over the mountaintop, the remaining women were exchanging hugs and saying good-byes. With promises of letters, they boarded the wagon and tied their bonnets more tightly against the fitful wind. Mikey laid his head on his grandmother's lap, and she covered him with a rug.

When the wagon lurched forward, Olivia waved at Liza. "Good bless you, my dear," she called.

Liza remained on the porch until the last cowboy disappeared from sight. Caleb had gone with Bryant, as usual, so she was the only one left on the place. It seemed like a graveyard after all the excitement of the past three days.

She stepped inside and closed the door. Leaning against it, she looked over the cabin. It seemed different to her.

Pulling off her coat, she rolled up her sleeves and set about clearing away the breakfast dishes. The boys would be starving when they returned. She had to get bread started and decide what to make for dinner. In spite of the massive meals they'd prepared for the stranded passengers, the pantry still seemed overloaded.

"Though I open the windows of heaven. . ."

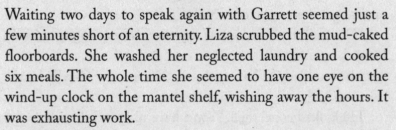

Waiting two days to speak again with Garrett seemed just a few minutes short of an eternity. Liza scrubbed the mud-caked floorboards. She washed her neglected laundry and cooked six meals. The whole time she seemed to have one eye on the wind-up clock on the mantel shelf, wishing away the hours. It was exhausting work.

Finally, the sun sank below the horizon on the evening of the second day. She bundled into her coat and two scarves and hurried toward the corral.

When she arrived, Garrett was waiting.

She fell into his arms.

"I've missed you something fierce," he murmured into her hair.

"Not as much as I've missed you," she declared.

"I've got so much to tell you," he said, keeping her close. "Charlene sends her love, by the way, and her thanks. She and Mother are getting along famously."

"I'm so glad." She drew away from him. "What did you find out?"

"Mother doesn't know many details about the original argument, but she said that I should pay a visit to my father's maiden sister, Johanna, who lives in Canton's Corner."

"I want to come," she said.

His brow creased as though he were wondering if she'd lost her mind. "Is that possible? How could you get away?"

"I'll tell Bryant I'm going to visit Olivia," she said. "And I will."

"Are you sure? Who would cook for the boys while you're away?"

"Harvey is a pretty good hand in the kitchen. I'll make some extra things and leave them in cold storage. How long would it take to get there and come back?"

"One full day, I reckon. If we leave early enough, we could be back by nightfall."

She nodded. "That settles it. I'm going. They'll hardly miss me."

He looked concerned. "You'd have to spend the whole day in the saddle. Are you up to that?"

"You haven't had a chance to know that about me yet, Garrett," she said with a daring look in her eye. "Horses are my passion. I can ride most men out of the saddle."

He suddenly grinned. "You don't say!" He leaned down to kiss her. "You're getting better and better all the time." He moved to kiss her again.

She pulled back. "We've got to make plans. When are you planning to leave?"

"Before daybreak in the morning."

She nodded. "I'll meet you by the lightning-struck oak tree." Stepping away from him, she peeked around the corner. "The boys are still in the canyon, but I'm expecting them back any moment. You'd better ride while you have a chance."

He grabbed her hand and pulled her back into his arms. "Not without a proper good-bye."

Chapter 8

The next morning, the rising sun found Garrett and Liza more than halfway to Canton's Corner. North and east of their ranches, the small town lay on the Colorado plain. Once the riders came out of the foothills, they made good progress.

Liza rode Sassy, her favorite bay mare, named for her spirit and staying power. Wearing jeans with a full skirt over them, she had an easy posture in the saddle and a gentle hand on the reins.

On a feisty black, Garrett sat a full two hands higher than Liza. With his added height, he made her feel like a child riding next to him.

When they stopped to let the horses rest and drink from a small spring, they sat next to each other on a flat rock. Liza pulled out a packet of biscuits and fried ham.

"Do you think your aunt will know anything about the argument between Jacob and Ryan?" she asked.

He munched and swallowed. "It's hard to tell. I'm amazed at how little the older generation talked about their family's history."

"Maybe it was too painful," Liza said, lifting her canteen for a long drink. She screwed on the metal cap. "If we get there early enough, we can spend an hour or so with Olivia. I'd like that."

"Let's go," he said. Standing, he gave her his hand and pulled her to her feet.

They arrived in Canton's Corner just after ten o'clock and found Johanna Anderson's cottage a few minutes later. She lived in a tiny cabin near the church's graveyard. It had a small yard with window boxes at both front windows.

"Why, Garrett!" she exclaimed, opening the front door to his knock. A tall, husky woman, Johanna Anderson was almost the same size as her nephew. The family resemblance was striking, from the dark curly hair to the strong jaw.

"Come in!" She stepped back to let them enter.

"This is Liza Wainright," Garrett said, his arm about Liza's shoulders.

"Nice to meet you, Miss Anderson," Liza said, suddenly nervous under the older woman's scrutiny.

"Nice to meet you, too," she replied, a touch of irony in her voice. "Won't you come in? Would you like some tea?"

When they said they would, she left them in the sitting room to put on the teakettle. Garrett found a spot on the sofa. An ornately carved piece, it must have come from New York or Paris.

Liza hesitated until he patted the place beside him. "Don't go weak-kneed on me now," he teased her. When she sat down, he went on, more seriously, "Aunt Johanna is a straight shooter. She'll help us if she can."

The lady in question appeared at that moment and took a seat in the matching chair nearby. "What can I do for you,

Garrett?" she asked. "I have a feeling you had a definite purpose in coming here."

Garrett relaxed on the sofa and said, "Aunt Johanna, what can you tell us about the disagreement between your father and the Wainrights? Do you know what caused the bad blood between our families?"

She glanced from Liza to him. "Papa was very bitter about it, and he wouldn't speak of it. He wouldn't let your father or me mention the name Wainright in passing when we were talking of schoolmates or anything else."

The teakettle whistled, and she hurried to make their tea. In a few minutes, she returned with a small porcelain pot and three china cups on matching saucers.

"However, my mother told me the story. . .as much as she knew of it," she went on as though uninterrupted. Serving the tea, she said, "My father, Ryan Anderson, was the foster son of Matthew Wainright. Ryan was the son of Wainright's partner and good friend. When his parents both died of cholera, Matthew took Ryan in at the age of twelve and treated him as his own son."

She paused to sip. "Matthew had a son of his own who was a year older than Ryan. That was Liza's grandfather, Jacob Wainright. The boys didn't get along. That was the root cause of all this evil. Jacob resented Ryan's coming into the family. Ryan was jealous of Jacob's standing as the natural-born son of Matthew."

"This is getting a little confusing," Garrett said. "Would you mind if I write some of it down so I can keep it straight in my mind?"

She set down her cup. "Of course. I have some writing paper in the secretary." She moved to a small desk with an inlaid design in the fold-up cover and found a single page. Picking up a pencil, she brought them to him with a book to rest them on.

Garrett wrote quickly. "So the two boys, Ryan and Jacob, didn't like each other." He glanced at Liza. "They were our grandfathers."

Johanna nodded. "They each had one son. Jacob's son was. . ."

"Luke Wainright," Liza said when Johanna hesitated. "My father."

The older woman nodded.

Still writing, Garrett said, "Ryan's son was Robert, who was my father."

"Back to the story," Johanna went on. "When Ryan was eighteen, the trouble started. One of the only things that Ryan had left from his parents was a small locket that had belonged to his mother. He treasured the locket and kept it close to his bedside in a drawer. One day it came up missing. He accused Jacob of stealing it, just to spite him. Jacob denied it, but the locket was never found. From the way the story goes, they never spoke to each other again."

She shrugged. "That's not much to go on, I know. But that's what my mother told me. Two years later, Matthew was killed by a bull. The boys split up the ranch with a long stretch of wire, and you know the rest."

Liza was disappointed. She wasn't sure what she'd hoped to hear, but it wasn't something this intangible. Had Jacob stolen the locket for pure meanness? She thought of Bryant and his sometimes-spiteful ways. Was Jacob like that?

Johanna finished her tea. "Would you like some more?" she asked. When they refused, she set her cup on the tray. "I never could figure out why my father didn't sell his half of the ranch and go somewhere else. Why did he stay right there, neighbors with the Wainrights for the rest of his life? If it had been me, I'd have moved to Texas. What's worse, my father didn't like cattle. He didn't love horses either."

She looked at Garrett. "How is your mother?" she asked. "I haven't had a letter from her in more than a month."

They chatted of family news then Garrett told her of the avalanche and his stay at the Running W. Finally, they stood to go.

"We've got another visit to make before we move on," he said. "We need to be back tonight."

Johanna saw them to the door and kissed her nephew's cheek. "You are so like your father," she said. "I still miss him terribly."

He hugged her. "So do we." When he let her go, he said, "Liza lost both her parents a few years ago. Cholera."

"My dear," Johanna said, "I'm so sorry!"

They talked a few more minutes, then said their final good-byes. As Garrett and Liza returned to their horses, Liza said, "She's a fine person."

Garrett smiled sadly. "Mother asked her to come and stay with us, but she loves her little house and doesn't want to leave it. I only wished she lived closer."

Back in the saddle, they wound their way through Canton's Corner and finally stopped in front of a clapboard structure on the main street near the local school.

"I hope this is the right place," Liza said, swinging down.

"If it's not, we can ask here. Surely most folks around would know Olivia."

But the lady herself answered the door. She gasped and then laughed. "Well, you took me at my word, I see," she said, reaching for Liza's arm. "Come in out of the cold, child. I'm so glad you've come."

"Mr. Garrett!" Mikey's shrill voice came from inside. He

ran to Garrett and clasped him about the knees.

Laughing, Garrett lifted the boy and gave him a hug. "Hello, old man. I bet you didn't expect to see us so soon."

"Let's go in here," Olivia said, fitting a key into the first door to the right. "I keep it locked when my company is less than ten years old."

The cold inside hit them with a force when they entered. "Garrett," Olivia said, "would you light the fire? There's kindling already laid in the firebox and some matches in a tin on the shelf."

He found the matches and knelt to light the wood.

It was a room the size of Liza's sitting room and furnished with two padded rockers, a short, plush-covered sofa with dark wood trim, and several small tables. Liza chose one rocking chair, Olivia the other to catch the first warm rays from the fire. When the blaze rose higher, Garrett sat on the sofa with Mikey on his lap.

Liza said, "We came to Canton's Corner to visit Garrett's aunt. We couldn't be so close to you and leave town without stopping to see you."

Olivia looked puzzled. "I barely got home before you arrived. You must have come here for a special reason."

Watching Mikey play the finger game, Garrett replied, "We came to ask Aunt Johanna what she knows about the feud between our families."

Liza added, "We're on a quest to find out why our grand-fathers hated each other. They were foster brothers, you know."

Olivia nodded. "I know. The missing locket."

Sitting bolt upright, Liza gasped. "You know about it? Why didn't you tell me?"

She looked slightly offended. "It wasn't my place, child. I didn't want to put my nose where it didn't belong." She glanced at Garrett. "Besides, I wasn't fully sure how matters stood between the two of you until now."

"Bryant has forbidden me to see Garrett," Liza said. "If only we could put this feud to rest." She leaned forward, urgency in her voice. "Can you tell us what you know about the locket?"

Olivia watched her intent expression. "Why is it so important? What can be changed after so many years?"

Garrett replied, "I'm determined to do what I can to make amends. If Jacob was falsely accused, I want to make that public. If he was guilty, I want to forgive him posthumously. Whatever it takes to put this animosity to rest."

"If that's possible," Liza added ruefully. "Bryant is very bitter about an argument he knows little about. But that doesn't mean he'll be quick to change his mind. He never is."

The older woman nodded and pursed her lips. "Fifty years ago my mother was hired help to Priscilla Wainright, Matthew's poor wife. When the incident with the locket happened, my mother was at their home to help with holiday cooking because Priscilla had been ill." She thought back for a moment. "It was a few months before I turned sixteen. That would make it Christmas of 1833."

She absently rocked for a few seconds. "My mother came home very upset that day. She liked Priscilla, felt sorry for her in a way, I guess."

"Why was that?" Liza asked.

"Matthew could be difficult. He had a way of making up his mind in a snap judgment, and nothing could dissuade him, least of all his wife."

Liza nodded.

"Well, the boys, Ryan and Jacob, ended up enemies from that horrible day onward. Priscilla was heartbroken to have such a rift within their family. She and Matthew loved Ryan as much as if he'd been their own son."

Suddenly, Mikey struggled to get down from the sofa. "I'll get my soldier!" he cried and ran from the room. His shoes thumped loudly on the hallway floor.

Garrett asked Olivia, "Is there any way that we could find out whether Jacob really took the locket? Did it ever come to light again? If he had taken it, what did he do with it?"

"He could have thrown it into the creek," Liza said, "but what good would that have done him? I think it would have been better for him to drop it somewhere where it could be found and clear his name. Then the unpleasantness would have disappeared. I just can't believe that he would have been so callous toward his mother, if she was that upset about it."

"I can't either," Olivia agreed. "When he saw what a stir followed, he would have given it back somehow. From what I knew of those boys, neither of them was that mean spirited."

"You knew them?" Lisa gasped.

"Of course I did, child. Ryan came to call on me a few times." She smiled at Garrett. "I thought of him when I first saw you. You are very like him. He was a kind man, a devoted Christian."

"As my father was," Garrett said, leaning forward to prop his elbows on his knees and clasp his hands. He looked at Liza as though to confirm what he'd already told her about his family.

"Did he sell it and regret it later?" Liza asked.

Olivia said, "That time of year folks stayed at home. Anyone leaving the ranch in winter weather would have been examined for insanity. I doubt that Jacob left the area."

"What else could have happened to the locket?" Liza asked.

Olivia sighed. "That's the big question. But how to answer it after all these years?" Her expression suddenly changed. "Wait a minute." She closed her hazel eyes in an expression that told she was thinking hard. "Mother told me that Priscilla was quite a writer. She spent hours writing letters and recording things that happened with Matthew's business. She must have had a special friend or a relative that she wrote to. Those letters could shed some light on what happened that day."

Liza clapped her hands. "What a brilliant idea! If she wrote to someone, that person would have written back to her. If we find out who wrote to Priscilla regularly, we may be able to track him or her down and find Priscilla's old letters. They're probably in a box in some dusty attic." She turned to Garrett. "We've got a storage room at one end of the loft. There's where we'll find them, if they're still around."

He said, "That's right. Ryan and Jacob slept in the same loft where your brothers sleep now, didn't they?"

Olivia nodded. "It's the same cabin where my mother worked. I lived in Wiley's Crossing until I married Mr. O'Bannon the following year."

They talked a few minutes more then the young people rose to leave. "We have to be back home by nightfall," Liza said. "It isn't fitting for us to be out alone after dark."

Olivia hugged her. "I'm so glad you came to me. Please come again before too long." She saw them to the door. "My prayers go with you," she said before she closed it after them.

They got back in the saddle. Before they set off, Liza said, "I hate to mention this, but I'm starving."

Garrett laughed. "So am I. Let's see what we can find to eat while we ride. That sun is moving way too fast for my liking."

Half an hour later, they each carried a fat sandwich wrapped in paper. They cantered until the town had disappeared behind them, then slowed to eat the food and talk.

"What did Bryant say when you told him you were coming with me?" Garrett asked, reaching for his canteen.

"I didn't tell him," Liza replied, keeping her face turned downward. "I left a note on the table with breakfast. There was a pot of beans on the back of the stove for their lunch and supper meals."

Garrett gulped a mouthful of water. "You didn't tell him?"

"He wouldn't have let me go. I know he wouldn't."

"Right. But what's he going to do when you get back?"

She shrugged. "I guess I'll find out when I get there, won't I?"

"Liza, I hate to see you in trouble because of me."

She sent him a wry look. "It's a little late to think of that, isn't it?"

He grew quiet, and they finished their lunch. Stuffing the empty paper into his saddlebag, Garrett urged his horse close to her so that their legs brushed.

"I'm going back with you to face him," he said, his jaw set.

"What? Do you want to get shot?" she asked, horrified.

"I'm not going to hide around corners anymore. Bryant is the one who's wrong. Why should we be acting guilty?"

"I have to live with him, though," she said, weakly.

"Maybe not. We'll see about that." He leaned over to kiss her on the cheek. "Bryant's not the only one who can make up his mind, my love. I'm not going to have you taking the pounding for both of us."

She looked into his deep brown eyes. "One part of me wishes you could just take me away from there."

He reached for her hand and kissed it. "One of these days, I will do just that."

But I love my brothers, too, Liza thought as they picked up the pace again. What was she going to do?

Chapter 9

They reached the Running W on the edge of dark. Leaving Garrett's black horse tied on the edge of the property, they led Sassy into the barn. The yard was still spongy, but not soupy as it had been before.

When they walked into the barn, Caleb was inside tending the stock.

He strode to Liza, his face an angry mask. "You've bought yourself a peck of trouble, Liza," he ground out. "Going off with that no-account..."

Her chin came up. "His name is Garrett, and you will call him that."

Her little brother backed down a fraction. "Bryant is furious. He's in the cabin waiting for you." He grabbed the horse's reins. "I'll take care of Sassy. You'd best get to the house." He turned his back on her and led the horse further inside.

Liza's stomach churned. For a second she thought she might be sick. The last thing on earth she wanted to do was face Bryant with him in a temper.

Garrett slipped his arm about her waist. "I'm here, Liza. If it gets too bad, I'll take you home. One way or the other, meet me at that same tree in two days at sundown. Can you do that?"

She nodded, then turned to face him. "At first I didn't want you to come here tonight, but now I'm so glad you did."

He touched her chin. "Can you trust me to take care of this?"

She nodded.

"Let's go fight a lion," he said, winking.

They strode to the cabin, up the porch steps, and through the front door.

Bryant had a single lamp lit. It was in the center of the dining room table. He rose from his chair when they came in, his face eerie from the lamp's yellow glow beneath him. He didn't speak, just stood and stared at them.

Leaving Liza at the door, Garrett strode to him. "Bryant, I want to make peace between us," he said. "You have my apologies for all the childish fighting in the school yard. I shouldn't have taken on my father's grudges. It was wrong."

Bryant still didn't speak. The corner of his mouth twitched.

Garrett went on. "I'm in love with your sister. I want to court her, Bryant. I'm asking you all right and proper for your blessing."

"That's something you'll never get," Bryant snarled. "I ought to get my Sharps .56 and run you outta here."

Liza came to stand beside Garrett. "That wouldn't do any good. Asking your blessing is a sop, Bryant. I'm going to see Garrett one way or the other. I'm a grown woman, and I can make my own choices."

"Not and live in this house, you can't," he said, focusing his blistering stare at her.

At that point, Harvey came down the loft stairs. He stood near Liza, his eyes on his older brother. "That's not the way

I see it," Harvey said, his voice calm. "Liza has every right to choose her own man. Just like you and I have a right to choose our own wives."

Bryant's expression turned to disbelief. "You and I will hash this out later," he threatened.

Harvey straightened to his full height. "I'm not afraid of you, Bryant. You can whip me, sure, but you can't change my mind. I'm not ten years old anymore."

Bryant turned his attention back to Garrett. "If Liza's fool enough to want you, she can have you, but only off this property. If you come back on my land again, I'll shoot you. Brother-in-law or not."

Garrett reached for Liza's hand. "As you wish," he said. He glanced at Harvey, a flicker of thanks in his eyes, but didn't speak. Giving Liza's hand a quick squeeze, he headed for the door and walked out.

Liza stood stock still beside her bedroom door. One part of her was afraid of Bryant's anger, but another part was furious. Who did he think he was, ordering her around like a child?

The tension in the room was taut as a banjo string. Glaring at each other, Bryant and Harvey seemed to have forgotten her.

"So, you're taking the bit in your teeth?" Bryant ground out. "I may just kick you out, too."

"Oh yeah," Harvey threw back. "Do you think you and Caleb can run this place alone? Just the two of you without Liza or me?" His dark brow came down. "You need us, Bryant. It's about time you admitted it."

Another stare down and Bryant strode out of the cabin, the door flying back to thud against the doorframe.

Liza let out a trembling breath. She found a chair and sank into it. Her knees were shaking, her insides quivering. "Thank you,

Harvey," she stammered. "I never expected you to side with me."

He came to the table and sat. "I didn't either. I never figured it would come to that."

"Garrett is a good man," Liza said, strength returning to her. "He's an honorable Christian man. Not just a churchgoer, but a believer. I love him, Harvey."

"Yeah, it's a joke, isn't it? A weird, ironic joke."

Pulling at the buttons on her coat, she stopped and looked at him. "Are you talking about me and Garrett? Because if you are. . ."

He shook his head. "Not you. Me." He slicked down his black hair where it curled up in the back. "I may as well confess. It's going to come out anyway." He met her eyes. "It's Charlene. I'm crazy about her."

"I knew it," she said.

He scoffed. "Was it that obvious?"

She chuckled. "Only as obvious as a red shirt in a hospital ward."

He leaned back in his chair and stared at the ceiling.

"Don't worry," she told him. "I don't think she noticed it. I didn't see any signs from her, anyway." She reached out to clasp his arm to get his full attention. "She's a Christian now, Harvey. That means she's a changed person. It also means she shouldn't be in company with an unbeliever."

He met her eyes, unblinking.

"I've never asked you before," she went on, "but how do you stand with the Lord? Have you ever admitted you are a sinner and received Christ?"

He swallowed. "I've never told anyone about it, sis, but we went to a brush arbor with Mama when I was twelve and I asked Christ to save me just sitting there on the bench." He looked regretful. "I was afraid that Pa and the boys would laugh at me if I let on that I was a Christian."

"But those philosophy books," she said. "Why do you read them and not the Bible?"

"Who said I don't read the Bible?" he asked. "I've been reading the Bible and comparing it to what those men teach. They are way off the beam, I tell you. Paine worst of all." He leaned toward her. "I want to go to a good, strong Christian university where I can learn to speak out against all that hooey those 'learned men' are spouting."

"Harvey! I never dreamed. . ."

He cut her off. "Do you suppose Garrett would let me call on Charlene sometime?"

"I don't see why not. She's only working there. She can see whomever she pleases."

"She's the sweetest gal I've ever met, Liza—hardworking, kind, and sensitive. She's got a humility about her none of the church girls around here have."

"More power to you, Harv," she said. "We may both end up over there. From what Garrett tells me, it wouldn't be such a bad thing either." She got up to hang up her coat and clear away the remains of dinner, still spread out on the table.

Harvey returned to the loft. She was left alone until Bryant and Caleb came in half an hour later. By that time it was full dark. Caleb sent her several dark looks, but Bryant didn't glance her way once. They sat in the sitting room before the fireplace for a few minutes, then climbed to their beds.

A few minutes later, Liza gratefully closed her bedroom door behind her, relieved to be alone within her own sanctuary. What a day it had been: so many conversations to remember, so much new information to process.

Pulling on her warmest gown and nightcap, she slipped into a double layer of wool socks and pulled the quilt around her ears. She was looking forward to meeting Garrett's people. From what she had seen so far, they were a wholesome group, one she could be proud to be a part of.

Excitement and exhaustion finally won out, and she fell into a deep sleep.

Liza awakened to find a dim stream of light pouring through her window. Blinking, she tried to make her mind focus. Suddenly, it hit her. Breakfast was late.

She flung back the covers and dashed into the kitchen. Crumbs of bread crust on the table and the remains of coffee told the story. The men had eaten a cold breakfast and started their day without waking her.

Her heart sank. It was a sign of Bryant's disapproval. Normally, he would have called her if she wasn't in the kitchen when he came down.

She cleared away the few dishes and set a pot of stew on the stove. As soon as she finished, she headed for the loft ladder. Her biggest fear about Bryant's disfavor was that he would ask her to leave before she had a chance to look for a box of letters.

The loft was a second floor that covered the entire span of the house with a three-foot square opening for the ladder. With only four windows, it was always a little dark unless the summer sun streamed through it—a rare happening.

The small door to the storage room had cracked leather hinges that were so dry the door was difficult to move. Inside, the windowless area was too dark to see much. She had to find a lantern in the boys' quarters and return with it to begin a search.

Old trunks, forgotten pieces of broken furniture, wooden crates—all covered with thick dust and cobwebs. Liza shrank away as her face brushed a spider web.

Leaving for a second time, she found a kerchief to completely cover her head. Bringing a broom this time, she knocked down every cobweb she could see and looked more closely.

She searched for almost an hour and found nothing. In the far back corner of the room, deep in the shadows, a wooden crate held a box made of thick paper and tied with twine. Liza pounced on it.

Moving to a three-legged table propped on two crates, she pulled off the twine and peered inside. It was full of letters in chunky handwriting, the ink thick and dark. The envelopes were all addressed to Priscilla Wainright.

Quickly, Liza replaced the lid on the box and hurried out, returning the lantern and closing the groaning door behind her.

She checked the stew pot as she passed through the kitchen, then hurried to her room to spread the letters on her quilt. Getting comfortable on the bed, she sorted the envelopes according to the writer. There were five in all, but most of the letters by far had come from someone who signed her name Suzanna, Priscilla's sister. Organizing the letters by date, she read each one.

The writer was Suzanna Mayfield. She lived in Granite City, Oklahoma, where her husband, Alexander, owned the *Bugle,* a local newspaper. She had five children. One of them was a late-comer, a little girl named Magdalene who was born when the oldest was seventeen.

When Liza reached a letter dated December 30, 1833, her hands began to tremble as she read:

Dear Priscilla,

> *I'm so sorry about the trouble with your boys. They can be difficult when they reach a certain age. I can tell you from experience now that my David has reached twenty. He's a sweet boy, no doubt, but so determined. I guess it is part of coming of age, not that we mothers like to see it happen.*

> *I wish there were some way that I could relieve your mind. All I can say is that time heals wounds. I hope that is true in your case.*

After that she moved on to her own news.

Holding the letter, Liza considered. If Suzanna's husband had owned a newspaper, maybe his sons took it over after he died. It was a place to begin anyway. She scanned the rest of the mail but found nothing of interest. Keeping out that one letter, she packed everything neatly into the box once more and took it back to the storage room.

Intent on returning the box to its original place, she held the lantern high in one hand and had the box under her arm. She was about to replace it when she realized that there was a second box under the first. This one was dark and crumpled with no lid. Inside lay a dozen or more small books with their crumbling bindings upward.

Intrigued, Liza set down both lantern and letter box. She lifted one of the books and opened it. The leather crackled under her hands. The pages were yellowed and crumbled along the edges wherever she touched.

The first one had the following inscription on the first page: Private Journal of Priscilla Cartwell Wainright, 1855–1857.

Liza gasped. This was more than she'd ever hoped. Had

Priscilla kept a diary in 1833? She dug through the diaries, checking the dates, and finally found the one she was looking for. She quickly turned to the ending pages of the book and read the entry for Christmas Day. It said basically the same thing as the story Johanna told, about the missing locket and Ryan's accusation of Jacob.

Disappointed, she turned back a few pages and read about Christmas preparations. Then on November 23, she found something interesting:

> *My sister, Suzanne, two of her sons, and her daughter came to visit today from Granite City. I was scared to death to have them traveling this time of year, but Suzanne insisted. Her husband had to travel to Europe on business, and she couldn't stand to be at home alone over the holiday.*
>
> *Their little daughter, Magdalene, is so sweet. She's a handful at times, full of questions and so curious about her surroundings. They're planning to stay right through Christmas. I'm so glad to have Suzanne with me, especially since I've been feeling poorly for the past few weeks.*

Liza read through to Christmas and then read that entry again. One phrase caught her eye. It had been meaningless before: "We caught Magdalene up in the loft this morning. How she managed to climb the ladder without falling, I'll never know."

So, there had been someone else in the loft that day. Changing her mind about returning the box of letters, she picked up both boxes this time and carefully climbed down to the first floor. She hid them under her bed, pushed far up against the wall.

Suddenly, she realized that she was starving. It was near noon and she hadn't eaten a single bite today.

Tomorrow at dusk, she was to meet Garrett. If only she could get word to him to meet her today instead. How could she live another whole day before she could tell him what she had found?

She was finishing the last bite of a cold bacon-and-biscuit sandwich when Harvey came in. He paused inside the door and then slowly closed it after himself. "Bryant's in a cold fury, Liza," he said. "I'm not sure how long either of us can stay here with him like that. He's nigh impossible to work with."

"Where is he now?" she asked, getting up to pour him some coffee.

"In the canyon. He had Caleb pack them some lunch, so they probably won't be back until later this afternoon."

She set the coffee before him. "Harvey, how would you like to ride over to the Anderson ranch?" she asked, making him two bacon-and-biscuit sandwiches. "I just found out something about the feud, and I need to speak to Garrett."

"The feud?" he asked. "What are you up to now?"

Without answering, she swallowed the last drop of her coffee, then headed for her bedroom to change into riding clothes. "I'll tell you on the way," she said. "Eat your lunch so we can leave. We must be back before Bryant and Caleb come home."

Chapter 10

The Anderson ranch was surrounded by a whitewashed board fence that glowed brilliantly under the winter sun. As Harvey and Liza drew near the house, horse stables came into view, also whitewashed and clean. Paddocks and riding paths crisscrossed the wet fields like a maze. Everything was tight and strong, well-formed and well-maintained.

The riders drew up a moment to survey the place before they rode in. "I never dreamed it would look like this," Liza breathed.

He grunted. "Me neither. I've always considered the Andersons beneath us. Now I'm wondering which of us is the poor cousin." He urged his sorrel mare forward.

The ranch house was a two-story structure with a wide verandah on each level. It was as wide as it was deep, forming a cube shape with two chimneys on the east side and two more on the west. It was the biggest house Liza had ever seen.

Suddenly, she wondered if she should have come.

Before she could voice her fears to Harvey, Garrett came bounding from the house to meet them. He raised his arms to Liza to help her down, laughing in delight. "So, you couldn't stay away from me!" he said, his face glowing. He glanced at Harvey, still in the saddle. "Come on in, Harvey. Mother wants to meet the both of you."

Putting his arm about Liza's shoulders, he started toward the house with her.

She glanced back to be sure that Harvey was behind them.

That he was, peering toward the house as though searching for something.

Before they reached the front steps, Sarah Anderson came out to the verandah. She was a small woman with dark glossy hair pulled back into a bun low on her neck. She wore a full-skirted gown with a small white shawl pinned about her shoulders.

"Mother, this is Liza," Garrett called when they reached the steps.

Liza waited to speak until they reached the porch floor. "Good afternoon, Mrs. Anderson," she said.

"How good of you to come," Sarah said warmly, reaching for Liza's hand. "I'm so glad to meet you." She turned to Harvey. "And this is. . ."

"Harvey Wainright," Garrett said. "The second brother."

"How do you do, ma'am," he said, his Adam's apple bobbing.

"Please come inside where it's warm." Sarah opened the door and led the way inside. "Charlene," she called when she stepped through the door, "please bring us some coffee." She turned to Liza. "Or would you prefer tea, my dear?"

"Coffee is fine," Liza said.

Inside the front double doors, they entered a wide hallway that ran the entire length of the house. To the left was a formal dining room and to the right a parlor complete with Belcher furniture and a massive gilt-framed mirror over the fireplace.

Sarah Anderson moved into the parlor and sat in a chair beside the hearth.

Overcome by the size of the room and the richness of the furnishings, Liza stopped on the threshold until Garrett's arm about her urged her inside. He led her to the red-velvet sofa and sat down. She sat, too, and rubbed her right hand over the soft fabric beside her.

Harvey found a chair and sank into it, his head turned to watch the doorway.

Sarah made polite inquiries about Liza's health and the welfare of her family while they waited for the coffee to arrive.

When Charlene appeared, Harvey's face lit up.

The china cups on the silver tray rattled when she caught sight of him. Seconds later, she recovered herself and served the drinks.

"So, what brings you here?" Garrett asked when Charlene had returned to her duties elsewhere. "I know this isn't a social call."

Liza blurted out, "I found Priscilla's diary in the loft. I couldn't wait to tell you."

"How wonderful!" Sarah said. She was genuinely pleased, and that surprised Liza a little.

"I brought it with me," Liza said. "It's in the saddlebag. I forgot to bring it in."

"I'll fetch it," Harvey said, getting to his feet. He strode out and closed the door behind him.

"There were visitors in the house when the locket disappeared," Liza went on. "Pricilla's sister, Suzanne, and some of her family came for Christmas that year. Two sons and a little girl about three years old named Magdalene came with her. The little girl managed to climb the loft steps and scared them all because she could have fallen and hurt herself."

She turned to Garrett. "Suzanne's husband, Alexander Mayfield, owned the *Bugle* in Granite City, Oklahoma. We could trace the family from that, couldn't we?"

"We could, but I think we'd have to travel to the town."

Sarah said, "Why not send a telegram to the courthouse there asking for information about Magdalene Mayfield and her brothers? That would save you a possibly useless trip."

"That's a good idea, Mother," he said.

He turned to Liza. "Wouldn't Suzanne's sons have slept in the loft?"

Liza said, "More than likely, they did."

"One way or the other," he replied, "we need to find any of those children and learn if they know anything more."

"I wonder where Harvey is," Liza said, looking toward the door.

Garrett quirked in one side of his expressive mouth. "He'll turn up when he's ready to, I reckon."

Holding her cup near her lips, Sarah looked thoughtful. "I wonder why no one ever considered that someone else in the house could have taken the locket instead of Jacob. Why did Ryan accuse him exclusively?" She sipped her drink.

Garrett set his cup down and replied, "Probably the jealousy between them."

Liza added, "He would also hesitate to accuse one of his cousins, I imagine."

Sarah shook her dainty head. "As godly as Ryan was in his later years, he had that one Achilles heel. He could never forgive Jacob. So much turmoil has come into the lives of so many because of that one fault."

"Lest any root of bitterness. . ." Garrett said.

Liza added, "Unfortunately, the people in our generation are the many who are defiled." She gazed into Garrett's face. "I hope we can break the cycle of hurt. It seems to grow with each new branch on the family tree."

"That's our prayer, too," Sarah agreed. "I hope you young people can put an end to it all."

Finally, Harvey reappeared carrying the decaying journal. They spent the next thirty minutes reading the entries aloud and discussing them.

Finally, reluctantly, Liza said, "We've got to be heading home. If we don't leave right away, Bryant and Caleb will get back to the house, and we won't be there."

"How is that situation going?" Garrett asked.

Harvey scoffed. "About as bad as it can get. I don't know how much longer I'm going to be able to work with Bryant. He's as prickly as an old cactus. And Caleb takes Bryant's side in everything. He always has."

Sarah stood, and they all followed her lead toward the door. "If things get too difficult for you," she said, "you are both welcome here."

Garrett grinned at Liza. "More than welcome."

Harvey stepped forward to shake Sarah's outstretched hand. "Thank you, Mrs. Anderson," he said, a hearty note in his voice.

"Yes, thank you," Liza said. She came closer to take Sarah's hand, but the older woman drew her into a hug. "You're as sweet as Garrett described you," she said. "I'm awfully glad to know you. Please come back any time you are able."

The warmth of Sarah Anderson's acceptance and approval spread through Liza and brought a glow to her face. "Thank you, ma'am. I'm so glad I came."

Without time for long good-byes, they were quickly back in the saddle and trotting down the trail.

On the ride home, Harvey remarked, "That was quite a different picture than we've been painted, isn't it, Liza?"

"Totally different," she agreed. "I'm only sorry that we didn't venture over there sooner."

"I'm sure Garrett is, too," he said wryly.

"Say, what about you and Charlene?" she demanded. "You were gone an awfully long time getting that book."

His lips came out as he tried to stifle a smile. "We're going to sit together in church next Sunday," he said smugly.

"Harvey!" she gasped. "Garrett and I are just now getting to that point. Are you sure you're ready for that?"

He kept his gaze straight ahead. His voice was dry. "I've never been so sure of anything in my whole life."

The ranch yard was empty when they arrived home. Liza helped Harvey tend to the horses so they could be turned into the corral as soon as possible, and then she hurried to the house to get supper finished. Whipping up a small pan of biscuits, she stirred the stew and added a hint of salt. She brought a leftover dried-apple pie from cold storage and set it on the back of the stove to warm it.

She had arranged to meet Garrett the following evening to plan their next move. If they had to travel to Oklahoma, they shouldn't travel alone. It was too far to venture without a chaperone. Who could they get to go along? Harvey was needed at home.

At the edge of dark, Bryant and Caleb rode into the yard. They took their time coming to the house, and when they entered, their faces were rigid. They ate their food in disapproving silence, then retired to the loft.

Liza was relieved to hear their boots on the floorboards overhead.

Harvey found a book in the sitting room and sat near the hearth to read by lamplight.

Liza finished washing up the dishes and closed herself in her room. She slowly changed for bed and brushed out her waist-length hair. Mrs. Anderson might have to make good on her promise to take them in. Liza wasn't sure how much more of the ice treatment she could take from those boys. She certainly wasn't going to tolerate being made to feel unwelcome in her own home.

The next day, Liza set to cleaning the cabin like a winged fury. Scrubbing the last speck of mud from the floors, including both porches, she cleaned the hearth and polished every surface in the kitchen. Reorganizing the pantry after lunch, she kept one eye on the clock. She had to meet Garrett at the big tree this afternoon.

Finally, it was time to go.

As before, he was already waiting for her there. Pulling her behind the tree, he kissed her soundly and held her close. "It seems like forever since I saw you last," he said. "We've got to put an end to this distance between us."

She giggled, breathless. "It's not more than a mile," she said.

"Ten feet is too much for me." He kissed her again.

"Garrett, what did you decide?" she asked when she could speak again. She couldn't linger here too long.

"I sent a telegram to Granite City asking for information about Magdalene or her brothers. So, now we'll play a waiting game until they answer."

"How long?"

"It could be one day. . .or a week. There's no way of knowing," he replied. "I'm going to ride to town every morning to see if an answer has come."

He kissed her nose. "I guess we'll have to meet here every afternoon until then."

She shook her head, regretfully. "I'm afraid I can't do that. If Bryant and Caleb come in early, I won't be able to get away. That's bound to happen soon."

"If you don't come, I'll sneak around behind the cabin and tap on the window at the back porch."

"Garrett, I'm afraid. Bryant could start shooting and claim he thought you were a prowler or a thief."

"That's not likely. I doubt he'd take a chance on hanging for it."

She sighed. "Last night, neither Bryant nor Caleb spoke a word to Harvey and me when they came in. They gulped down their suppers while they glowered at us and then went straight up to bed."

He squeezed her to him. "I can't stand to think of you having to put up with that."

"At least he isn't threatening me," she replied. "Not yet, anyway. I'm afraid one of these days he's going to come home and order Harvey and me to pack our things."

"That wouldn't be such a disaster, would it?" he asked, smiling down at her. Looking deeply into her hazel eyes, he grew sober. "Just as soon as we can try to set things straight with your brothers, I want you to marry me."

"What if Bryant won't listen?" she asked.

"Honey, I said *try* to make amends. Whether he accepts what we say or not, I still want you to marry me." He searched her face. "Will you do it, Liza? Do you love me at all?"

"I do love you," she whispered, a cold knot of dread in her throat. "But I love them, too." She leaned her forehead against his chest. "What am I going to do?"

Chapter 11

Two days later, Garrett was waiting for her, a yellow page in his hands. When she reined in Sassy, he waved it at her.

"It came yesterday," he said. "I picked it up this morning."

Swinging down, she said, "What does it say?"

Grinning, he shoved it at her. "Here. Read it."

She scanned the page then went back to read it more closely.

Garrett hovered over her, watching her face.

Scott Mayfield current owner of *Bugle*, grandson of
Alex M. STOP Family still in Granite City STOP Invite
you to come for a visit STOP Telegram your arrival date
to SM before coming STOP

"When can we go?" she asked.

He took her hand and leaned against the tree's massive trunk. "We can't go alone," he said, "and Bryant would have to know you'd be away for two or three days."

She nodded. "I can take care of the second part, but what

about the first? Harvey can't come. He's got to help at the ranch."

"Mother says she can spare Charlene for a couple of days. What would you say to Charlene coming?"

"I'd be delighted," she said. "I'd like to get to know her better."

"It's settled." He lifted her hand to his lips. "I've got to run, my love. So many things to do before we go."

"But when?" she said with a laugh. "When do we leave?"

He chuckled. "Didn't I tell you? At daybreak tomorrow. The train leaves Wiley's Corner at seven o'clock."

After a quick and excited good-bye, Liza returned to the cabin. When she stepped inside, Bryant was at the kitchen table, a coffee cup in front of him. He stood when he saw her.

"Where have you been?" he demanded harshly.

"Down the road a mite," she said, closing the door firmly behind her. She took off her coat and hat. "I've been to see Garrett," she added when she was ready.

His scowl deepened. "You insist on defying me. What do you hope to gain by it?"

With calmness she didn't know she had, she met his stormy gaze. "I'm going to uncover the truth about what caused this bad blood between us and the Andersons," she told him. "I'm going to find out, and I'm going to put it to rest. For fifty years we've hated each other, but no one even knows why. There's something very wrong about that, Bryant."

"There's something very wrong about ignoring your elders," he retorted.

"My elders?" she demanded, heat rising in her. "You're fifteen months older than I am, in case you've forgotten." Shoulders squared, chin high, she took two steps toward him. "You're not the old man of the family! We're a team. We all have a say, and we all work equally hard. That's what we agreed to when Pa and Ma died."

His expression remained like flint.

She went on. "I'm going on a train trip with Charlene and Garrett. We're leaving in the morning, and we may be gone for three days."

"If you go, Liza, don't bother to come back. I'm warning you."

She felt that old fear rising, but she pushed it back. "There was a family visiting here the day the locket disappeared," she said.

"What locket?"

Caleb came in and closed the door. He stood just inside without moving to even remove his coat.

"This entire fight was caused because Ryan Anderson lost his mother's locket. It was all he had left of her. After both his had parents died, he was the foster son of the Wainrights. He and our grandfather, Jacob Wainright, were about the same age. There was jealousy between them. When the locket came up missing, Ryan accused Jacob of taking it for spite. Jacob hotly denied it, but the mystery was never solved. No one found the locket."

Caleb's chest swelled. "My grandfather was no common thief!"

She turned to him for a second. "That's what I'm trying to prove! Don't you see? If I can prove that Jacob was innocent, then we can forget the whole thing. Garrett and his mother are willing to forgive and forget."

Harvey came in at that point. He sized up the situation and moved three steps into the kitchen where he could see everyone at once.

"Where are you going?" Bryant asked.

"Granite City, Oklahoma. It's just across the border from Colorado, not far from Boise City. I'll be gone for two days, possibly three if we can't find the right person. There must be someone in the Mayfield family who's old enough to remember that day. It was exactly forty-nine years ago, Bryant. They'd be grandparents or great-grandparents by now. There's not a day to lose."

"You're grabbing at straws," Bryant scoffed.

"What will it hurt to try to find the truth? We may just clear our family name." She flung both hands out to him. "We've been living under the shadow of that accusation long enough. Don't you think it's time to give our family a clean slate?"

"She's right," Caleb said, his chin lifting a little. "I want to know what happened."

"So do I," Harvey added.

Hearing Harvey's voice, Bryant's gaze fastened on him. "And you! You're in on this, too. I can smell it." His mouth formed a grim line. "That's what too much book learning does to a man. Makes him *weak*." His face twisted as though he had tasted something disgusting.

Harvey swelled up. "Oh, so hating someone without knowing why is a sign of strength, is it? Turning on your own blood kin because of something that happened half a century ago is strong, too, I suppose." His chin tightened. "I'm sorry, Bryant. You've got it wrong. It takes guts to step out of the mold and stop the course of things. Letting things run their course is *easy*."

For a moment, Liza feared they'd come to blows, but then Bryant backed off. He pinned Liza with his dark gaze. "Go," he said, "but take Harvey with you. I'll not have my sister going off with a man for days at a time without a brother with her."

Liza said, "But the stock. . ."

"We'll take care of it," Caleb put in. "Go ahead, Liza. Maybe you can get this whole ugly mess settled. I'm tired of it. It's time things got back to normal around here."

She glanced at Harvey. "We leave at daybreak. The train leaves Wiley's Corner at seven."

He nodded, then hustled toward the door. "In that case, I've got some stuff to take care of before nightfall." He grasped the latch and went out.

Liza took off her coat and hung it up, ignoring the still forms of her brothers. Were they frozen like that? Why couldn't they go outside or sit by the fire?

Finally, Bryant moved into the sitting room. "How about some checkers, Caleb?" he asked, his voice surprisingly mild. "I brought the game back to the house last night."

"Sure." The youngest brother hurried out of his coat and sat across from Bryant near the fireplace.

Heartsick at the growing void between herself and her boys, Liza checked the roast in the oven and stirred the pot of beans on the back of the stove. Despite the pain they caused her, those boys were everything to her. Was there any way to keep the family together?

That evening, she knelt beside her bed, her knees on the icy floor. "Oh, Lord," she prayed aloud, "I believe You brought Garrett into our lives to settle this awful feud. Please make a way of peace between our houses and between my brothers and me." She got up and crawled between the frigid sheets, shivering and waiting for the bed to grow warm. How would she ever be able to sleep?

The next thing she knew, Harvey's call came through her door. "Liza!" he called, his voice husky. "We've got to be leaving. Are you up?"

Instantly awake, she threw back the covers and bolted upright. "I'll be there in a few minutes," she called. "Make some coffee, will you?"

Twenty minutes later, they were in the saddle. Their breath came out in steamy billows as they talked.

"What about our horses?" Harvey asked. "We can't leave them tied to a tree for three days."

"Garrett will have thought of that," she said. She told him of the telegram and of their hopes for this trip. They talked of it for the entire ride.

When they reached the big oak, a buckboard and three people waited for them—Garrett, Charlene, and a young Hispanic boy about Caleb's age.

"Well, what do you know?" Harvey breathed when he saw Charlene.

"Sorry. I forgot to mention that she was coming," Liza said.

He didn't seem to mind at all.

Garrett came near. "Jorge will bring the buckboard back from town and take all the horses to our stables," he said, reaching for Liza to help her down. "We've got to hurry."

The men moved the cases into the waiting buckboard. Sitting on the bench seat with the ladies, Garrett held the reins while Jorge and Harvey climbed in back, then shook the leather straps and called to the twin blacks. They set off at a rumbling, lurching pace.

An hour later, the four young people were settled into facing plush seats, their faces gleaming with excitement.

Harvey laughed aloud. "Who would have ever imagined that we'd be traveling together today?" He grinned at Charlene beside him. "I'm not complaining."

Dressed in a dove-gray gown with a white crocheted collar,

Charlene looked calm and at peace. Her bold stares and flashing glances had totally evaporated. With her clean-washed face and her hair drawn back into a bun, she could hardly be recognized as the same girl who had arrived at the Running W just days before.

As the car rattled down the rails, the day passed in quiet camaraderie. They reached the station at Granite City a little past four in the afternoon, then waited fifteen minutes in line before they could disembark from the train.

"Where to now?" Liza asked when they reached the platform. She wished for her woolen shawl that hung in her room. The icy wind cut like a knife.

"To the newspaper office," Garrett said. "I'll check at the station to see if we can hire a cab or rent a wagon." He set off and returned a few minutes later. "I found a cab driver. He'll take us to the *Bugle*."

At least it was a closed carriage. Her feet were still throbbing from cold, but getting out of the wind was a mercy. The four of them sat in nervous silence. Whatever they learned here would set in motion a course of action that would affect all of their lives.

A young, pock-faced clerk was about to lock the office door when they reached it. He opened the door a crack, waiting to hear their story.

"We've just arrived from Colorado to see Mr. Mayfield," Garrett said. "He's expecting us."

The young man pulled the door open and let them pass. His first words to them were, "Second door on the left down that hall." He pointed in the general direction with his sharp chin.

Walking single file through a warren of oak desks piled high with papers, the four young people found the office. Garrett knocked on the door.

A woman's voice called, "Come in, please," and they entered a waiting room with six wooden chairs in formation along the west wall. The secretary was a matronly woman with a blond-gray pompadour hairdo. "Yes? May I help you?" she asked in cultured tones.

Garrett replied, "We're here to see Mr. Scott Mayfield. We're relatives of his just come from Colorado." He introduced each one in the party.

After a few minutes of fuss and bother, she returned to say, "He will see you now."

Mayfield's office was tastefully done in dark wood and darker leather, the furniture well turned out, the artwork refined. However, every level surface was covered with papers, most of them newsprint in some form of production. One wall held a bulletin board with paste-up squares covering it.

Mayfield himself was a short, round man with a bald head the shape of a mosque dome. He seemed worried. When he came to greet them, he offered an apologetic smile. "I'm glad to meet you," he said and carefully got each of their names. "You're like a vision from the past."

"We're here on a mission," Garrett told him. "We were wondering if you could answer some questions."

"Here, sit down." He moved some piles to form an awkward stack on the floor in front of his desk.

When they found seats, he returned to his own desk chair and Garrett continued. "The event we're here about happened on Christmas Day of 1833 at the Wainright cabin. From what we can gather, some members of your family were there for the holiday."

He frowned and his bald head creased high above his eyes.

"In '33 I would have been... twelve years old. Let me see..." He stroked his thick neck and squinted at the pressed tin ceiling.

Liza gave him a few minutes then said, "Your little sister, Magdalene, climbed the loft stairs and gave everyone a fright. She was three years old."

His mouth fell open. "Right! We spent most of the visit riding in the corral with Jacob and Ryan. It was bitter cold, but you know how boys are. They don't have sense enough to come in when they should."

"Mr. Mayfield," Garrett said, "this is very important. Do you remember anything about a lost locket that day?"

Still frowning, he slowly nodded. "As I recall, Ryan was in a temper over it. It spoiled the end of our holiday. No more riding, no more checker games. Neither of the boys would pay my brother Fred or me the slightest mind after that. It ruined everything."

"Did you see the locket?" Harvey asked.

Mayfield shook his head. "Not once."

"Who slept in the loft?" Liza asked.

"Fred and me...and the other two boys, of course."

Garrett leaned forward, his face intent. "What about Fred?" he asked. "Would he know anything?"

Scott Mayfield shook his head. "Freddy was killed at Gettysburg," he said.

After a moment of awkward silence, Garrett said, "I'm sorry to hear that. We had no idea." He went on. "Does Magdalene live nearby? Would she mind seeing us, do you think?"

Mayfield's face cleared. "She'd be delighted. Family, no matter how distant, is a thrill to her. She lives on Haygood Avenue, six blocks from here. Her name is Dixon now. She's been a widow for fifteen years."

He wrote on a scrap of paper and handed it to Garrett. "Here is her address. Head east on this street for two blocks, then turn left on Haygood and go down four more blocks. Her house is on the left, white with a huge porch."

Garrett shook the little man's hand. "It's good to know you," he said. "Thank you for your help."

"I'm afraid I didn't help at all," he said, shaking hands all around. "Please do me a favor and tell Magdalene that I'll stop in on her later this evening."

They promised to do so and left. The same clerk let them out and quickly locked the door after them.

Holding her hat down to keep it from flying away, Liza clutched her overnight case in the other hand and hustled down the street after Garrett, whose long legs ate up the distance. She could hardly keep up.

Around the corner, they found Magdalene's house without a hitch, and Harvey knocked.

"I hope she's close by," Charlene groaned when a strong gust hit them.

The next moment, the door swung inward and a small woman appeared. She had brown hair with gold highlights in a high chignon, with no hint of gray despite her fifty-two years. Round cheeks and hazel eyes, she looked exactly like Liza with thirty-plus years added on.

The two women stared at each other for a short moment then Magdalene laughed. "I'm not exactly sure who you are, but we've got to be related," she said, moving back to let them in.

"I'm Liza Wainright," Liza said. "This is my brother, Harvey, and some friends, Garrett Anderson and Charlene Thomas."

"Anderson?" Magdalene asked. "Kin to Ryan Anderson?"

"He was my grandfather," Garrett said.

"I should have guessed it." She looked at each one. "The apple doesn't fall far from the tree, and that's a fact." She ushered them into her tiny parlor. "It's bitter out there. Would you like something hot to warm you up?"

When they gratefully accepted, she hurried out.

"Wow, that's Magdalene," Liza murmured. "Pinch me to make sure this is real. I *must* be dreaming."

Garrett pulled out his pocket watch. "At this rate, we may be able to head back home early in the morning."

Harvey grinned at Charlene but spoke to Garrett. "Don't hurry back on my account, old man," he said.

The older woman arrived with a tray and china cups. She handed everything around and set a plate of teacakes and sandwiches on the table.

The men and Charlene helped themselves.

Liza's stomach reminded her that she hadn't eaten since before dawn. She picked up half a sandwich and nibbled.

"So," their hostess said, sitting and spreading her full dark skirts about her, "what brings you to Granite City?"

Garrett repeated his story, ending with, "We came to ask if you might remember that day. I know you were very small. Honestly, we aren't holding out much hope that you can help us."

She nodded and the wisps of hair about her face swayed. "Of course I remember," she said. "How could I forget?"

"Did you see the lost locket?" Liza asked.

Tears filled the woman's eyes. For a moment, she didn't speak. Then she nodded. "I took it," she said.

Chapter 12

Sniffing, Magdalene pulled a handkerchief from her pocket and loudly blew her nose. "I found the locket in a small drawer, under some other things. My mama would have been furious if she caught me snooping like that. I would have gotten the spanking of my life. Even now, at fifty-two, I'm sure of it."

She paused to sip from her cup. "The locket was tiny and made of gold. It had a rose carved in the front of it. I'd never seen anything so lovely. I was mesmerized, and I hid under the bed to look at it where no one would see me." She paused, remembering.

"Mama started calling, 'Magdalene Esther Mayfield,' and I knew I had to go right away. I just dropped the locket under the bed and ran to the ladder." Her lips formed a wry smile. "I almost got spanked anyway, for climbing to the loft."

"Did you hear the boys arguing about the locket?" Garrett asked.

She nodded. "I watched the whole ugly scene, but I couldn't say anything. At three years old, the danger of a spanking outweighed every other thought in my childish head. We left the next day, and I've never mentioned that incident to a living soul since."

A tear spilled over. "I'm so sorry. How could you ever forgive me for the damage I've caused? Once I got older, I was too ashamed to admit that I'd covered up my part in that tragedy. It was so much easier to ignore what I had done."

Liza got up to hug her. "We didn't come to condemn you," she said, kneeling in front of the older woman's chair. "We came to set things right. Of course we forgive you." She glanced at Harvey.

He cleared his throat. "Yes, ma'am. We sure do."

Garrett added, "It was a child's folly. Please don't blame yourself anymore, Miss Mayfield."

"Maggie," she said, wiping her eyes. "Please call me Maggie."

She got up to hug each one in turn and say, "I'm sorry," another dozen times. Finally, she sat down again, exhausted.

"Maggie," Liza said, "which bed did you hide under? Do you remember?"

She blinked, thinking back. Her pixie nose was red, her eyes swollen. "There was a woodpile out the window beside the bed," she said. "Not that it's still there."

"But it is!" Harvey declared. "That's my bed now."

She focused on him. "You don't say! You still live in that cabin?"

They talked another hour, telling her of their families and their dreams until shadows filled the room.

"We must be going," Garrett said. "We've got to find a hotel for the night."

"A hotel?" Maggie demanded. "You're staying over with me. I won't have it any other way." She looked at the girls. "Would you mind helping me throw together some supper?"

"Oh," Liza said, "I just remembered. Mr. Mayfield at the *Bugle* said to tell you he'd be over later."

"Did he now?" she asked, beaming. "Scotti is my favorite brother. He spoils me terribly."

The rest of their visit was like a homecoming. Scotti Mayfield joined them for supper then left to bring his brother, Michael, and Maggie's two daughters to see their long-lost relatives. That evening the house was filled with people who were strangers but somehow very familiar—their looks, their mannerisms, even their opinions on certain matters.

The next morning, Maggie hugged each one of her guests. "God bless you, dear," she repeated four times in succession. She stood back so she could see them all. "You don't know what you've done for me," she said. "I feel like a thousand pounds just lifted off my back."

Liza smiled. "You've done a very brave thing, Maggie. You were honest. You could have sent us away, but you didn't."

The older woman's eyes filled with tears. "God bless you all!"

The young people filed out of the house and headed down the street. Garrett flagged down a cab, and they climbed aboard. The breeze was chilly but not as cold as it had been before.

The train ride home passed all too quickly. As the engine pulled into the Wiley's Corner station, Garrett whispered to Liza, close beside him, "I hate to send you back to that house, Liza."

She nodded. "I hate to go back," she admitted, "but it has to be." She squeezed his arm. "I just hope that Bryant will stop being angry long enough for Harvey and me to talk to him."

Garrett looked over at Harvey and Charlene, who were deep in their own private conversation. "How about if we pray before we get off the train?" he suggested, breaking into their tête-à-tête.

"We need the Lord's help to get everything straightened out for the four of us."

Nodding, Harvey sat up a little straighter. "Good idea." He glanced at Liza. "I hate to think what Bryant's attitude will be when we get back."

Bowing, Garrett said, "Dear Lord, overshadow us all this day. Grant Your grace to face what is ahead and please have mercy to help us settle the angry spirit that moves among us. Bring glory to Your name, I pray. Amen."

Clasping Garrett's arm, Liza felt a lump forming in her throat. She was so blessed to have someone like Garrett watching over her. She was afraid to be so happy, lest something snatch it away and break her heart.

In a buckboard rented from the livery stable, they traveled to the Anderson ranch. Sarah and Charlene put together a quick supper for them, then Liza and Harvey set out for home.

At the end of their own long lane, Harvey remarked, "It's a shame we don't live further away. We're getting home way too soon for my taste."

Liza smiled at his foolishness. "I know what you mean, Harv, but we may as well get the showdown over with."

But when they reached the cabin, it was empty. There was no note and no signs of life. The kitchen was fairly clean, supper sitting cold in a pot on the lifeless stove.

Immediately they both set about building fires in the cook stove and fireplace. A few minutes later, the cabin felt the first hint of warmth.

"Do you think they decided to camp on the range?" Liza asked, worried. "It's bitter cold out there. What is Bryant thinking?"

Harvey scoffed. "I hope he gets cold enough to cool off his hot head." He added a fat log to the fireplace. "That should carry us through the night." Dusting off his hands, he moved to the foot of the ladder. "I'm tired. Unless you need something from me, I'll turn in now."

"Good night, Harvey," she said. "I'm going to do the same."

She went into her room, intending to retire, but once she got changed she was suddenly wide awake. Turning up the lamp beside her bed, she got down on her knees and pulled out the boxes hidden underneath. She had a detailed family history in those journals. Suddenly, it was imperative that she read them.

She pulled the quilts high around her and dumped the journals into her lap. There were more than a dozen of them. As she turned the box upright, she spotted a yellowed paper wedged into the bottom of it.

Carefully, she dislodged the document and held it up to the lamplight. At the top in curly script was: The Last Will and Testament of Matthew Zachary Wainright.

Liza's hands were trembling, and not only from the cold. She peered at the words of the will, reading them slowly, trying to decipher the legal jargon. Then one paragraph jumped out at her:

The land holdings of the Running W, I leave to my sons, Jacob Wainright and Ryan Anderson, to be held in joint ownership by them and their heirs, providing that my wife, Priscilla Wainright, may choose to live in the cabin as long as she lives. The joint ownership will continue forever until both brothers or their heirs do willfully and voluntarily sign a bill of sale.

Liza read that section again and then a third time, forgetting the cold that was numbing her nose and the growing stiffness in her fingers. The Running W and the Anderson ranches were actually one large section. The fence was purely arbitrary. It meant nothing as far as ownership went.

She remembered Sarah Anderson's words: "I never could figure out why my father didn't sell his half of the ranch and go somewhere else. Why did he stay right here, neighbors with the Wainrights for the rest of his life?"

Ryan didn't sell because he couldn't sell. No wonder he was bitter against Jacob.

She refolded the will and sorted through the journals to begin reading at 1834. Scooting deeper into the covers, she held up the journals to catch the light until her arms grew weary and her eyes drifted closed.

The next thing she knew, it was morning. One of the books lay on the quilt near her head. The rest of them were in a heap to the side.

Blinking, she pushed her hair from her eyes. What a lazy dolt she'd become. She couldn't remember the last time she'd been in bed when the sun rose, and now she'd done it twice in just a few days.

She pulled on her robe and went to find Harvey. He was in the living room, sitting before the fire, gazing dreamily into it.

"What about the chores?" she asked.

"Done," he said, looking at her with a dull expression in his eyes.

"I'm sorry I slept so late. I was up reading. . ." She held up one finger. "Just a minute." Dashing into the cold bedroom, she found the will and brought it to Harvey. Pointing at the essential paragraph, she said, "Read here," and sat in the rocking chair while she waited.

He bent his head over the paper, progressing slowly through

the flowery writing and dense jargon. Glancing up with a puzzled expression, he read it again. Finally, he laid the paper on his lap and focused on Liza. "We don't own the ranch free and clear," he announced. "The Andersons have joint ownership." He cocked his head. "Just wait until Bryant hears this. He'll turn to charcoal from the inside out."

"This is getting worse and worse," she said. "Would you mind eating cold biscuits this morning? There are a few in the tin on the counter. I want to look through the rest of those diaries to see what happened between Jacob and Ryan after Matthew died."

He folded the will and handed it back to her. "Make some coffee and I'll help you look through them," he said. "I'm not hungry anyway."

She suddenly smiled. "Lovesick, huh? Can't eat, can't sleep?"

He grimaced. "You should be talking, sis. I watched you and Garrett all the way to Granite City and back again."

She felt her cheeks growing warm. Turning toward the bedroom, she said, "I'll fetch those journals so you can start looking at them while coffee's brewing."

They pored over the journals dating from 1836 to 1845. They abruptly ended with an entry dated July 19.

Liza closed the last book. "Priscilla must have passed away sometime around then," she said. "She wrote all of this in the quiet of her own home, but what a treasure she left for us."

"She was a great lady," Harvey agreed. "I feel like I know her."

"Sarah had it right. Ryan did want to sell his half of the land and move away."

"But Jacob refused to sign."

"We still hold joint ownership, you know," Liza said. "The four of us and Garrett."

"I wish Grandpa Wainright had said a majority instead of a unanimous agreement."

She stood to gather the books. "I've got to get busy. It's near noon. The house needs cleaning, and I haven't set anything on for supper yet."

"I'll help you until I have to go to the barn for the evening chores." Pulling on his coat, he filled both wood boxes and stoked both fires.

Liza put a roast in the oven, then stirred together bread dough. While it was rising, she peeled potatoes.

Harvey swept the cabin beginning at the fireplace hearth and ending at the back door.

Her paring knife whipping through a potato skin, Liza said, "Jacob was so offended at being falsely accused that he wouldn't speak to or even look at Ryan from then on."

"Can't you see Bryant doing that now?" he asked.

She grimaced. "I'm afraid I can. All too well."

Flipping the last of the dust onto a sheet of stiff paper, he tipped the paper over a metal trash can. "I wonder what happened to that locket," he said. "It was never found."

"Maggie said she dropped it under the bed and ran to the ladder. No one saw it after that."

"I'm going up there to look for it," he said, carrying the broom with him.

"It's not there," Liza called after him. "It couldn't be there after almost fifty years. Think of all the times the loft has been spring cleaned. I bet it got swept out years ago."

His voice sounded muffled when he called down. "There's no hurt in trying to find it. No one else has until now."

Fifteen minutes passed. Liza heard him shuffling around, the scraping of wood on wood a couple of times, then nothing.

"Liza," he called, "bring me a blunt knife, like you'd use to spread butter."

She dropped the last potato into the pot. "Give me a minute. I'll be right there." She set the pot on the stove and put on the lid. Picking up a table knife, she climbed the stairs.

Harvey was on his stomach with his face inches above the floorboards where his bed used to be.

"Wasn't the bedstead nailed in?" she asked.

"Yep. Old rusty nails. They didn't give me much trouble," he said, turning. "Did you bring that knife?"

She handed it to him.

Carefully, slowly, he slid the knife blade through the wide cracks in the floor, beginning at the wall and coming out four feet, then going back to the next crack.

Liza sat on the displaced bed, then soon lay down on it, her arm under her head, watching Harvey's slow progress. Her eyes drifted closed.

"Whoa!"

His shout brought her fully awake. She sat up. "What is it?"

Hunching over, he worked the knife back and forth a few times. "There's something wedged in a crack of the floorboards." He picked it up. "Look at this," he said. He handed her a black lump.

She rubbed it on her skirt and held it up to the window to catch the light. It was a heart shaped object no more than half an inch long with a string dangling from it. She looked closer. It wasn't a string, but a fine chain clogged with dirt. "Harvey!" she cried. She scrubbed the piece against her sleeve, turning it from one side to the other. A rose-shaped indentation appeared against a tarnished background.

Harvey knelt beside her to look at it.

"This is it! Look!" Holding it up for him to see, she placed it in his outstretched hand, then flung her arms around him. "You found it! I can't believe it!"

Chapter 13

Harvey held her for a moment then spoke, his voice dry. "Not that it will do us any good."

Liza pulled back, her smile dimming. "You think Bryant won't care about this?"

"Bryant makes up his own mind, regardless of the facts," he declared. He moved to sit beside her on the bedstead. "But does that matter to us?" he asked. "We can make decisions just the same as he can, Liza. Why should his stubborn prejudice change our thinking or our plans?"

She nodded, her mouth sad. "I wish Caleb weren't so tied to him, though. I'm afraid we're going to lose Caleb, too."

He hugged her again. "Let's let the Lord take care of it for us," he told her. "If they don't come around now, then maybe they will sometime in the future." He gave her back the locket.

She shrugged and looked down at the locket in her hands. "That's what Priscilla hoped, too. She died hoping that."

"Hey." He shook her gently. "This isn't a funeral. We just made a miraculous discovery. Wait until the boys hear about it. Maybe they won't be as negative as you're thinking." He stood. "Meanwhile, I've got to get this bedstead back in place." He grinned down at her. "I may be strong, but I can't move it with you sitting on it."

She shot him a disbelieving look and swatted at him. He dodged, laughing. Smiling in spite of herself, she left him and headed for the ladder, the locket safely in her skirt pocket.

She returned to the kitchen to check on supper. A few moments later, a loud rapping sounded at the door. She jumped at the sound, then went to see who it was. Harvey shinnied down the ladder as she crossed the room.

She pulled the door open and her heart jumped when Garrett strode inside.

"What's wrong?" she asked, sure there must have been a catastrophe to bring him to her front door.

"I had to come and see if you're all right," he said. "Liza, I've got to get you away from here. I can't stand it. I'm worrying about you from dawn till midnight and losing sleep worrying about you after that." He clasped her hands. "Please come back with me."

"I can't come now," she said, "but that may change this afternoon. I've so much to tell you. Let's sit down."

They moved to the sofa before the fireplace, and Harvey sat in the chair nearby.

Liza glanced at Harvey as she reached into her pocket. "Look what Harvey found this afternoon," she said, pulling out the locket. She held it toward Garrett.

He peered at the blackened object and slowly reached for it. The chain slithered through his fingers and hung in two crooked, filthy lines below his hand. He turned the locket over several times. "Where was it?" he asked finally.

Harvey answered. "Under my bed where Maggie said she dropped it. It had fallen into a big crack between the floorboards and gotten covered with dirt."

Liza added, "It probably got swept into the crack by someone bending over to push a broom under there. The bedstead was nailed to the wall, so it was almost impossible to see what you're sweeping. And the loft is always a little dark."

He gathered the chain into his palm and hefted the tiny object. "It's so light. I can hardly feel it in my hand," he said. "To think this little thing caused so much grief."

"We have to show it to Bryant and Caleb," Liza said. "Depending on their reaction, Harvey and I may be going back with you this afternoon."

"That's not all we found," Harvey said.

Liza paused to look at him, a question on her face.

"The will," he said.

"Oh, I forgot about it! I was so excited about the locket." She ran to the bedroom and brought the yellow page out to Garrett. Pointing, she said, "Read this paragraph."

With his brow furrowed, Garrett bent over the paper. "Well, if that don't beat all," he said in a moment. "I had no idea our properties were tied together."

Harvey said, "That was Matthew Wainright's idea of forcing peace between the two boys, I guess." He shrugged. "Whatever it was, it didn't work."

"We need to get this legally undone," Garrett said. "If we all agree to divide the property between us, then we won't have to wait for everyone to sign again."

"What do you mean?" Harvey asked.

"There are five of us," Garrett said. "We can split the land up five ways. I suppose that will mean I'll have to give up some acreage in order to make it come out right, but I'm agreeable to that."

"What about your mother?" Liza asked.

"Pa left his claim to the property to me."

"Why didn't anyone explain all this to us?" Harvey exclaimed.

Garrett said, "Both of us lost our fathers in a sudden tragedy. They probably figured they had plenty of time to tell us how things stood." He looked from Harvey to Liza. "The Anderson-Wainright situation wasn't a topic for the dinner table, was it?"

Both of them shook their heads. "We never talked about it."

"Neither did we," Garrett said. "But now that we know, it's our responsibility to take care of it while we can."

"Now's the time to do it," Liza agreed. "If we don't deal with it now, the next generation will have many more people who have to sign off. It'll end up a hopeless tangle."

Garrett handed the will to Liza. "Put that back in a safe place. We have to take it to a lawyer as soon as possible."

She took the thick pages. "Would you like some coffee?" she asked.

"A glass of water," he said. "I'll come to the dining room, so I can talk to you while you're in the kitchen." He stood and handed her the locket, then paused by Harvey's chair. "How are you doing?" he asked.

Harvey stood. "Not too good, I'm afraid. Bryant is unbearable. I don't know what makes him so difficult."

"He's angry," Liza said, pumping water into a pitcher. "He always gets angry when he doesn't get his way."

Harvey looked out the window. "They're back early," he said. "Bryant's coming to the house, and Caleb is right behind him."

"I tied my horse in front of the house," Garrett said. "I'm tired of hiding around corners."

Harvey hitched his belt a little higher. "Let them come. It's time we had it out."

Liza's heart was thumping so hard she couldn't pour Garrett's water into a glass. She set down the pitcher and turned toward the door, leaning against the edge of the table.

Bryant shoved the door open and it hit the end of the kitchen counter with a bang. He stepped inside with his chest swelled, his hands curled at his sides.

Caleb came after him and closed the door.

For a moment no one spoke, then Liza said, "We found the locket, boys. It was in the loft where Maggie said it would be. She was right, Bryant. Jacob didn't take the locket. It was all a mistake."

Her brother's upper lip drew up. "What do you want me to do, Liza?" he fumed. "Shake hands and be best buddies? Well, it's not happening."

"There's more to it than that," Harvey added. "We found Matthew Wainright's will. You've got to look at it. It still affects all of us—all five of us in this room."

For the first time Bryant looked uncertain. "What does it say? Tell me."

Liza said, "Matthew Wainright tied the land up with a restriction that it can't be sold unless both Ryan Anderson and Jacob Wainright *or their heirs* all sign off on the bill of sale."

Harvey added, "We don't have two ranches. The Running W includes the Andersons' place. That fence is just smoke and mirrors, Bryant. They put it up the same way people hang a blanket down the center of a room. It keeps other folks out, but they're all still inside the same four walls."

Caleb moved to a chair. "Well, if that don't beat all," he drawled.

Bryant scowled at Harvey. "Well, it happens that I don't want to sell," he said.

Garrett spoke for the first time. "Neither do we. We only want to divide up the property, so each person can make a decision about what to do without having to wait for anyone else to agree." His voice softened. "In order to divide the entire section into five parts, I'm going to have to give up claim to some of my acreage. But I'm willing to do that, if it'll make peace between us."

Bryant scoffed. "You'll grow old holding out for that to happen, Anderson. Locket or not, you're still a. . ."

"Bryant!" Liza cried. "Stop it! I'll not have you talking to him that way." She stepped closer, her voice shrill. "I'm going to marry him, do you hear me? You can be miserable all you want, but that's not going to stop me from being happy." Tears ran down her face. "I don't know what I'll do without my boys," she sniffed, "but I've got to make my own choice about this."

Caleb stood and came to her. He looked back at Bryant. "I respect you as my oldest brother," he said, "but it's not right to make Liza's life a misery. Who else is she going to marry if she turns him down?"

Dashing the tears from her eyes, she tried to smile at Caleb. "I'm not marrying him because he's my last chance," she said. "I love him, Caleb." She started crying again. "But I love you, too!"

Caleb leaned over to hug her.

Bryant watched them. His expression remained the same, but something in his stance softened. "You can visit us, Liza," he said, "as long as you come alone." With a hostile look directed at Garrett, he stalked out of the house.

The tension in the room immediately relaxed.

"I don't want you to go," Caleb said. "Things have been pretty awful around here since you've been leaving us to go everywhere."

Liza hugged him again. "I'm not going anywhere right away,"

she said. "We'll work all of that out before the time comes." She blinked away the last traces of tears. "Anyone hungry?" she asked. "We missed lunch."

Garrett stayed around until Liza's three brothers left the cabin to do their chores. She was busy at the kitchen counter, washing up the last of the lunch dishes when they went out.

Without saying anything to her, Garrett came behind her and turned her around.

"I've got soapy hands," she said, laughing at him.

"We've got to talk," he said. The intense look in his eyes told her that he wasn't going to be put off.

She turned and quickly dipped her hands in the rinse water. Grabbing a towel, she said, "What do we need to talk about?"

He pulled her into his arms. "It's about what you said to Bryant. I'm here to tell you that I'm holding you to it."

She looked doubtful. "What did I say?"

"That you were going to marry me." He kissed her. "I have to admit, I would rather you said that to me first, but I'm not that choosy. Just hearing you say it at all is good enough for me."

She melted into his arms for a long, sweet moment. "Garrett, is it ever going to be over?" she murmured.

Holding her close to his heart, he said, "Things will settle down after awhile, darling. Harvey and Caleb love you dearly. They're not going to count you as an enemy, not by a long shot. Even Bryant may come around eventually."

"I don't deserve you," she murmured. "You came up here with that loaded wagon like a gallant knight straight out of Harvey's Sir Walter Scott novels. I couldn't believe my eyes."

He took his time scanning her face. "I couldn't believe mine either. I thought an angel had come down to light on your front porch."

"An angel?" she retorted.

"Don't be so skeptical," he replied with a little laugh. "I *still* think so." He grew serious. "God brought us together, darling. I'm sure of it." He drew her closer for another kiss. His voice was husky when he said, near her ear, "Our romance may have begun with a train wreck, but believe me, it was no accident!"

Epilogue

The Rocking A Ranch
Wiley's Corner, Colorado
September 17, 1883

Dear Cousin Maggie,

It seems like so long since we've seen one another. I wanted to come to Granite City to give you this news in person, but I can't get away right now. There's so much to do. Garrett and I have set our wedding date for November 1. We do hope you and your family will be able to come.

Garrett wanted to get married last spring, but we were still in the middle of that legal muddle, and I wanted to wait until it was all settled. It's all over now, a mostly happy ending but a little sad.

The sad part is that Bryant has left us. After we discovered the locket, he moved his things into the bunk-house and lived there for more than nine months. He still took his meals in the cabin, but he never talked to anyone besides Caleb. For a while, I was scared that Caleb would go out there with him, but he stayed in the house with us and slowly got to know Garrett. They're friends now.

It took us until spring to reach an agreement on dividing the land. Garrett's and my sections will be one ranch. Harvey's and Caleb's sections will be one ranch. Bryant got it into his head to leave, so he sold his rights to the rest of us for $1,000 each. He said he wants to go to Nebraska or Montana and build his own ranch. With $4,000, he'll have plenty to do that.

Now, for the good news. Harvey and Charlene are going to join us for a double wedding! Everything has worked out perfectly. I'm moving to Garrett's house and relieve his mother of overseeing the housekeeping staff. Charlene is moving into our cabin to take care of the boys. Harvey and Charlene have joined our little church, and they are so happy. Even Caleb is whistling these days.

We hope you can join us for the wedding. It would be wonderful to see you and your brothers and all their families there.

I remain your faithful cousin,
Liza Wainright

P.S. Please remember to pray for Bryant.

CHARLENE'S POOR MAN COOKIES

2 cups oatmeal
1 cup brown sugar
½ cup white sugar
1 cup flour
¼ teaspoon salt
1 teaspoon baking soda
¼ cup hot water
½ cup shortening, melted and cooled

Mix dry ingredients. Add wet ingredients. Mix well. Roll into 1-inch balls. Bake at 350° for 8–10 minutes. Makes about 3 dozen cookies.

A Wife in
Name Only

Dedication

To my dear friends at the
Calvary Baptist Church ladies Bible study.
You enrich my life.

Chapter 1

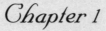

Colorado, October 1884

The sky over the mountains was dark and lowering when Katherine Priestly and her brother, Johnny, left their ranch to head south. Traveling on horseback in late October was always risky business in Colorado, and the sky wasn't making any promises. Huddling deep into the shawl wrapped around her head and shoulders, Katie squeezed her eyes shut. The last thing she needed was to add frozen tears to her misery.

The night before, she and Johnny had made their decision to leave home. It had been so hard leaving Ma and the four younger kids behind with just a little cornmeal and some flour in the larder and a small deer hanging in the smokehouse. It had been hard hugging them all good-bye and hearing their sniffles, especially Ma's. But facing the bitter wind and the steely sky were hardest of all.

They had to make it to Musgrove, the mining camp twenty miles southeast of their ranch. It was the only place they could think of to find work, a tiny spark of hope because this time of year the camps were almost shut down. Everyone with any sense headed home for the winter—except those desperate enough to stay there. . .or desperate enough to go there.

Doggedly heading into the wind, the Priestly siblings qualified in that respect. They were desperate enough to do anything that would feed their family through the frigid months ahead.

Their ranch had never been prosperous, but Pa had eked out enough to feed his six children and keep them in shoes. Until last August when anthrax had wiped out their herd. Within days, they were penniless and living on what Pa could shoot and Ma could scratch out of the ground in her kitchen garden.

When fall days shortened and the icy wind swept through, Pa gathered the children around. With Ma close to his side, he said, "I'm leaving in the morning to take a job with the railroad. It only pays twenty-five dollars a month, but with God's help it will feed us through the winter." He looked at Johnny. "You'll have to take care of them for me, son."

He squeezed his wife's hand. "I'll be back come spring."

That was six weeks ago, and they hadn't heard from him since. Had he met with an accident? Had the railroad refused him work?

These questions gnawed at Katie's mind as the terrain grew rugged and the road all but disappeared. "How much further?" she called to Johnny ahead of her.

He pulled his horse up and waited for her to come up to him. "What was that, sis?" he asked. His sandy brown hair blew across his eyes. The top of his nose was red above the scarf covering the lower part of his face.

"How much longer?" she asked. "My feet are numb."

"We'd best find some shelter and build a fire," he said, scanning the area for a hollow or an offset in the rocky terrain.

"There's a place." He urged his horse forward.

Half an hour later, they sipped weak coffee and held their feet toward the flickering fire.

"They hurt," Katie whispered, gazing at her boots.

"Don't take them off, sis," Johnny said. "You'll never get them back on." He glanced at the sky. "We can't stay here too much longer. What if it starts to snow?" He took a closer look at his sister's pinched face and drew her into his arms. "Here. Let's try to keep each other warm. That's what Pa and I did when we were out in that blizzard that time. We huddled up and waited it out."

Katie pulled her shawl higher until it completely covered her face. She pressed her cheek into Johnny's coat and tried to stop shivering. Johnny was a good brother. A year older than she, he'd always looked out for her.

All too soon, they were back in the saddle. The wind had died down a little. Now and then the sun tried a peek at the landscape.

When they rode into Musgrove, it was suppertime. The streets were clear. Not a person, a horse, or a wagon in sight. Katie was so cold and so exhausted, she could hardly stay in the saddle.

Johnny led the way to the hitching rail at the general store, a shanty with board walls and tent canvas for the roof. He helped Katie down, kept his arm around her, and supported her inside.

The warmth of the store almost felt painful to Katie's frozen cheeks. A potbelly stove glowed in the center of the room, and a slim, white-haired woman sat close by it in a rocking chair. When she saw them, she stood.

"Bring her here by the fire," she said, reaching for Katie's arm. "Where did you kids come from? You can't be from around here, and it's much too cold to be traveling."

Katie sank into the chair. It felt like a tiny spot of heaven. Her eyes drifted closed.

She heard Johnny say, "We rode down from our ranch, about twenty miles from here. We had to stop twice to thaw out. . ."

The rocking chair was soft with padding on the back and the seat. It wrapped around Katie's cold form while the heat from the fire seeped into her weary, aching muscles. Her head relaxed on the back of the chair, and she soon fell asleep.

"Katie!" Johnny's voice brought her out of the delicious warm stupor. She blinked and pushed away his hand.

"Here's some hot tea for you," he said, his voice insistent. "Drink it, sis. You need it."

She tried to focus on his face. The smell of the sweet tea caught her attention. "Thank you," she said, sitting up straighter and reaching for the blue enamel mug. She hadn't eaten anything since cornmeal gruel for breakfast.

"You'll stay for supper, of course," the storeowner said. "It's not much, but it's hot."

"We're obliged," Johnny said. He had his hat and coat off and was standing near Katie with his hands out to the stove. "My sister was all tuckered out."

Katie sipped the tea and savored the warmth traveling through her. "Did you ask about work?" she asked Johnny.

"Mrs. Sanford is going to hire me for the winter," he said. "Room, board, and five dollars a month."

"There aren't many customers this time of year," the store-keeper said. Her face was drawn and she had a hollow-eyed look. "But I can use someone to keep the snow shoveled away from the door and carry wood for me. Come spring, I want to start building a real store with a tin roof and windows in it. He can help with that, too, if he's a mind." She nodded, pleased.

"Five dollars?" Katie murmured. Even in these hard times, it was a meager amount.

Johnny knelt by her and whispered, "It's the best we can do, sis. No one else is hiring here. At least Ma won't have to feed me along with the others. I'll send the five dollars to her like clockwork."

She touched his chin, still soft as a child's though he was nearly twenty. "What about me?" she asked, speaking louder and looking at Mrs. Sanford. "I need work, too."

Setting three bowls on a rough-hewn table nearby, the older woman looked up and shook her head. "There's nary a place hiring this time of year, girlie," she said. "I wish there was." Suddenly her gray eyebrows drew together. "Wait a minute. Wait a minute. There was someone in here..." She bent her head low, drumming her fingertips on the tabletop. Suddenly, she straightened, her finger pointed toward the canvas ceiling. "Masten! Brett Masten needs a cook at his ranch. He stopped in last month to see if anyone was pulling out of Musgrove and needing work."

"How far is that from here?" Johnny asked.

"Ten miles west," she replied. She looked at Katie. "You're not going anywhere tonight," she announced. "It don't cost nothing to loan a body a cot and a blanket now and then. You'll sleep here and head over there in the morning."

Katie nodded. "Thank you, Mrs. Sanford," she said, and she meant it.

Johnny got up to help Mrs. Sanford, and Katie finished her

tea while she waited. What if the rancher had already found someone? What then?

Near noon the next day, Katie rode into the Masten ranch alone. It had been a nerve-wracking two hours, alone in the saddle, cold and scared, watching the landmarks and praying that Mrs. Sanford had been accurate in her directions. Katie wanted nothing more than to find a place, any place to roll up her sleeves and work. Preferably some place with a roaring fire, but any place would do.

The entrance to the ranch was marked by two tall posts with an arched piece of iron over the lane. It had the word "Masten" welded into it and a six-pointed star on each side.

The ranch yard was bare, free of trash but also free of any decoration. The bare wood of the buildings was gray and weathered, strong and sensible, with a long rambling cabin to the left of the lane and the barn door facing her straight ahead as she rode in.

She scanned the area, looking for someone to talk to. The cabin had two front doors, one at the closer end and one in the center. She had no idea which place to knock or where to put her horse. She also feared she'd fall if she tried to dismount alone. She'd stopped feeling her feet half an hour ago.

She brought her horse to a halt in front of the ranch house when a tall man stepped out of the barn. He paused in the doorway, his bushy white eyebrows raised in surprise. Rubbing his nose, he came toward her in a kind of sideways gait unique to old cowboys. He wore a stained Montana Stetson that had long ago lost its shape and was now only a rounded dome with a floppy brim.

"Help you, ma'am?" he asked. His voice was creaky and higher toned than Katie had expected. He had a round face and blue-gray eyes.

"I've c-come to see about a j-job," she stammered, partly from cold and partly from stark terror. What if Masten turned her down?

The cowboy turned toward the house. "The boss is inside, rustling up something for dinner, I reckon. He'll be mighty glad to see you." He pointed to the door in the center of the long building. "That's the kitchen door. Go on in."

She tried to kick her boot free of the stirrup, but it wouldn't come loose.

Without any fuss, he pushed the toe of her boot through the metal arch and offered her his hands.

She gladly leaned on his strength and eased to the ground. Schooling herself to walk a straight line with those two frozen stumps she called feet, she headed toward the second set of steps and made it to the door. Knocking, she waited, willing her breathing to stay silent and slow.

"It's open!" a man's voice called.

She pushed and the wooden door moved inward. Feeling the warmth meeting her, she quickly entered and shut out the cold behind her.

After the wonderful heated air, the first thing she noticed was the smell. It was a mixture of charcoaled bacon and stale beans with a background aroma of fresh coffee. A lanky man bent over the stove, his left side facing her. He wore a blackened apron over jeans and a red-and-white checked shirt, his sleeves rolled to the elbows.

Behind him, a small square worktable was piled high with vegetable peels and dirty cooking pots. The table had soiled dishes stacked in the center where someone had simply moved the dirty dishes inward and set the table with clean ones—which were now dirty, too.

For a full minute Katie stood without moving, trying to decide whether to be pleased or disgusted. If this was the boss, he hadn't found a cook yet. On the other hand, what she was looking at would take two days of hard work to set to rights, besides the cooking she'd have to do as well.

"I'm here about a job," she faltered at last. "Mrs. Sanford at the general store in Musgrove. . ."

"Can you cook?" he demanded, looking at her for the first time. His voice was strident with an edge of desperation.

"Yes, sir."

"How old are you?" he asked, a little softer.

"Eighteen," she said, lifting her chin.

He pushed the smoking skillet away from the hot spot on the Franklin cook stove and picked up a grimy towel. "What brings you here, if I may ask?" he cocked his head a little, squinting one eye as he sized her up.

She licked her lips. Her feet were beginning to ache as they warmed up. "We lost our cattle to anthrax. I'm trying to find work to get through the winter."

He nodded. "That anthrax outbreak scared me spitless. We were spared, thank the Good Lord."

He pulled a chair away from the worktable. "Here. Sit down. We need to talk." When they were seated, he went on. "I'll pay you thirty dollars a month. You can sleep in the room off the kitchen. It's back there." He nodded toward the hall that went off from the back of the room beyond the stove. "And you'll get your meals, of course."

She swallowed. "I'd like forty dollars," she said. "I have to send money home to Ma."

His eyes narrowed. He studied her, working his mouth outward. "There's one more thing we have to get settled. I have a rule here at the Masten Ranch. Once burnt, twice shy, as they say. I only hire married women. A single woman on a ranch full of single cowhands is a recipe for big trouble. As much as I need kitchen help, you'd end up being more of a problem than I can even describe if I don't enforce that rule."

Katie gulped. She felt the safe, comfortable warmth of that filthy kitchen slipping from her frantic grasp.

"That's all right then," she said, her voice tight. "I'm married."

Chapter 2

She cleared her throat and plunged ahead. "My husband just got a job with Mrs. Sanford at the general store in Musgrove. He sent me here since there was no work for me there. The town is all but closed down."

Still watching her closely, Masten slowly nodded. "I reckon we have a deal then," he drawled. "I'll have Duffy bring in your things."

"There's just a saddlebag," she said.

He pointed toward the stove. "Throw out that mess in the skillet," he said. "It's not fit to eat. We'll skip dinner today and wait for supper. The men won't mind one bit, believe me. I've been fighting a mutiny around here for six weeks. Not one of them will lift a finger to do 'women's work,' and I'm no account in the kitchen. Never was and never claimed to be."

"What happened to your cook?" she asked, untying her wool bonnet. Strands of her dark wavy hair fell around her face. She smoothed them back.

"He caught pneumonia. We did everything we could for him, poor hombre, but with no doctor and no medicine..." He sighed. "I'm mighty glad to see you, Mrs..."

"Priestly," she said. "Please call me Katie."

"I'm Brett," he said, smiling a little. He stood and found his ten-gallon hat. "I'll go out and spread the good news." Lifting a long buffalo coat from a peg, he whipped it on and stepped outside.

Pulling at the buttons on her black coat, Katie slowly made her way toward her room. Past the stove, a door opened off the tiny back hallway. She turned the knob and went inside. The room was medium sized with a narrow bedstead, a nightstand, and a small chest of drawers under the only window. At least the bed had a warm quilt on it. She laid her coat across the end of the bed and placed her bonnet on top of it.

She moved closer to look out the bare window into the back yard. How could she dress in here with a grand view of her entire room readily available to anyone who had a hankering to use the outhouse?

The same old cowhand appeared in her doorway. He was holding her saddlebags. "Here you are, ma'am," he said, bobbing his head.

"Thank you. . .Duffy, is it?" she asked, taking them from him.

"That's me all right."

"I'm Katie," she said. "Duffy, I'll need a bucket, a broom, and a mop. Can you find those for me?"

"Gladly," he said with a loose grin. "The hands are powerful glad to see you, Miss Katie. I guarantee they are."

"Just Katie," she said, trying out a timid smile. "No Miss."

His head bobbed again. "Suit yourself," he said. He turned away. "I'll rustle up a bucket and them other things for you." He disappeared toward the back door, and she heard him go outside.

Rolling up her sleeves, Katie set to work. Adding wood to

the cook stove, she set on a pot of water to heat and started scraping plates. She'd never have the kitchen cleaned before suppertime, but she had to clean enough to begin to cook a meal. What had those males been doing? Re-using dirty pots? It was disgusting to even think about it.

Piling the first dishpan full of cups coated with dried coffee, she left them to soak while she put on a second pot of hot water. At this rate she'd have to take a break from cleaning to split some wood.

The kitchen was a wide room spanning about thirty feet. At Katie's right, a long work counter had a pitcher pump at the end nearest the door and cabinets beneath it. A window over the counter gave a broad view of the front yard. At the far end of the counter was a door on the south wall. She opened it and found that it led to a sitting room with a stone fireplace. After a quick peek, she closed the door.

The cook stove sat a few feet from the sitting-room door with a wood box nearby. The back hall opened up beyond the stove.

To Katie's left, a second window faced the front yard. She opened the side door on the north wall to see a row of six cots along the wall in front of her. On the other side of the room stood a potbelly stove and a small table with four chairs around it. Feeling like an intruder, Katie quickly closed that door, too.

A dining table and ten chairs filled the north end of the kitchen, and the back wall held a long bank of built-in cabinets. Every level surface was covered with dirty pans and dishes, many of them moldy. She found an apron and tied it on, ignoring the dark stains on it. She had to start somewhere.

Three hours later, Katie stepped out to the stoop to jangle the triangle. It was just past four o'clock, early for supper but mighty late for dinner.

Within seconds, five men appeared in the barn door and aimed for the house like they had a purpose. Katie stayed on the stoop just long enough to get a look at them.

Besides Duffy and Brett Masten came a big bruiser of a man with wiry blond hair and a big, bulbous nose. He had a slow walk and an easy way of moving his shoulders, like a sleepy bear.

After them marched two younger men, one of them no more than five feet three inches tall, the other about five eight. The short man had wavy red hair and moved like he had springs in his shoes. The other one might have been Hispanic. He was about the same age as her brother Johnny. He was as dark as Johnny was fair and by far the handsomest of the cowhands.

Katie moved inside to set the food on the table while the men milled around the pump and basin, washing up.

"Boy, don't that smell good!" the bruiser said.

Red made a moaning noise. "My stomach thinks my mouth's sewed shut!"

Katie smiled at their enthusiasm. Biscuits and chipped-beef gravy wasn't exactly fancy cooking, but there was plenty of it. And it was good. She'd fixed herself a plate earlier. If there were leftovers, she was going to have a second helping and not feel guilty.

The men gathered around the table and waited while Brett bowed and thanked the Lord for the food. Then they dug in.

Ten minutes later, Katie refilled the serving dishes and wondered if there would be leftovers.

When the men were about finished with the meal, Brett held up his hand to silence their chatter. "Men, I'd like to introduce the lady who rode in today and saved our lives." He held his hand toward Katie.

Standing beside the kitchen's pump, she felt her face glowing.

Red gave a hoot and said, "Welcome home, ma'am!"

Brett said, "That's Rollie Barker."

The bruiser called out, "Yeah, his bark is worse than his bite."

Someone shoved the man's shoulder, and the rest laughed.

Brett laughed, too. "The one with the smart mouth down there is Lew Mullholland and beside him is Duffy Reed, our local weather man. And this," he clapped the Hispanic-looking guy on the back, "is Henry Hadley."

"Enrique!" Red called out, clapping.

The man in question endured the attention with a look of long-suffering. "Call me Hank," he said, speaking to Katie directly.

Red went on. "You'll have to forgive him. He's from Texas." He laughed at his own joke.

Brett said, "Everybody, this is Mrs. Katie Priestly, sent by the Good Lord to save us from starving."

From poisoning, more like it, Katie thought. She smiled. "Please call me Katie. Not Miss Katie, just Katie."

She got some salutes and a couple of nods.

"Great cooking!" Duffy said, reaching for yet another biscuit.

"The best!" Lew agreed, sopping up the gravy on his plate with a scrap of biscuit.

"I'll try to do better tomorrow," Katie said, apologetic. "There wasn't much time today."

Duffy chortled. "If it gets much better than this, my tongue'll beat my brains out."

The talk moved to ranching matters, and Katie turned her attention to cleaning up the pans from that meal and then moved to working on the dirty piles stacked on the counter.

She was drying a thick meat platter when the last of the hands drifted out. Brett Masten was still at the table. When the door banged closed, he stood. "Katie, you're welcome to sit at the table with us," he said, pulling his coat from its peg. "I didn't say anything just now because I didn't want to embarrass you if you'd rather not. The men are kind of rough. . ."

Her hand stopped wiping the platter. "That's kind of you, Mr. Masten." She hadn't expected this.

"Brett," he said with that small smile. He put on his ten-gallon hat. "You don't have to give me an answer or anything. If you want to, you can set yourself a place next time, that's all." He tipped his hat to her and headed out.

Katie set the platter on the far end of the counter where the clean dishes were stacked. She let out a small sigh of relief. This wasn't going to be so bad after all.

With a lighter heart and renewed energy, she cleared the table and quickly washed up the dishes from that meal. Washing up right away was so much easier than waiting until the food had turned to stone.

She opened every cabinet door along the back wall—five above the thick oak counter and five below it. Her mother had never enjoyed this much storage space. It was pure luxury. But the contents were a total shambles—food containers beside pottery dishes, pots piled with silverware.

Darkness fell, and Katie lit a lamp. Although she couldn't wash dishes by lamplight, she could surely empty those cabinets and start organizing.

Sometime later, the door on the south side of the kitchen opened and Brett stepped in, concern on his face. "Are you still at it?" he asked. "It's nigh on eight o'clock."

She set down the sack of rice she was holding. "I was hoping to set this to rights before I retire," she said. "It's so much easier to cook when things are in order."

His keen eyes seemed to look right through her. "All that stuff will still be there tomorrow. You rode in from Musgrove this morning, remember?" He made a shooing motion with both hands. "Please, go and rest. I didn't hire you to do everything in the first twelve hours."

She wiped her hands on her apron. "I suppose I should," she said. Her shoulders were aching. She felt them now. "But there is one thing." She hesitated, feeling a flush climbing her neck.

He waited for her to go on.

"I need a curtain for the window in my room," she said.

"A curtain?" He pulled in his chin as though uncertain of her meaning.

"To cover the window. . .for privacy." Her face was flaming. Did she have to spell everything out to him?

His mouth opened a little as he slowly nodded. "Oh, yes. That." He seemed puzzled. "I'm afraid curtains are something I've never worried about up to now." His gaze wandered over the kitchen. "I wonder what we could use. . ."

"A sheet? A tablecloth?" she asked, hopefully.

He shook his head.

"A quilt," she went on, a little frantic now.

"A quilt! Yes, I have an extra one of those." His hand went to the doorknob behind him. "Let me see. . ." He disappeared into the shadows beyond the door.

Katie followed him, hesitant to enter his domain. Standing in the doorway, she took in a massive room, at least thirty feet long and fifteen feet wide. To the left was a stone fireplace that covered almost half of that tremendous length.

The room was practically bare. Four wooden chairs sat in a

half-circle around the firebox that glowed orange from a large bank of embers. The floors had no rugs. The three mullioned windows gave her a cold, black stare.

Brett lit a lamp and moved through one of the two doors on that long back wall. He returned in a moment with a tattered blanket over his arm and held it out to her. "This is the best I can do, I'm afraid," he said. He looked sheepish. "Since that bad experience with that *single* female cook ten years ago, I haven't had a woman on the place. No womenfolk at all. I'm afraid things are a little rough."

"Thank you," she said, taking the blanket. She turned back to the kitchen. "Good night." She softly closed the door after herself. A little rough indeed.

She found a couple of tacks in a tin can that had been shoved back into a cabinet. Using the heel of her shoe, she held the center of the quilt's edge in her teeth and pounded in three tacks. Miracle of miracles, it held.

The room felt like an icehouse. She made a mental note to leave her door open in the evenings from now on to warm it up before she went to bed. She didn't feel secure leaving the door open while she was sleeping, so she laid her coat over the quilt and tried to ignore her cold toes. Spring seemed a hundred years away.

When Katie woke up, her knees were touching her chin, and the quilt was over her head. What was it? Some kind of a noise that woke her? She peeked out of the covers. The room was dark. Another noise. Someone at the woodpile outside the back door was stacking logs.

It must be morning. Scratching around in the darkness, she

found a match and scraped it against the bedpost. Shivering, she lit the lamp and hurried into her clothes. She was fastening the buttons on her shoes when heavy boots passed her door. The wood box rumbled with the sound of dropping sticks.

She combed her dark hair and pulled it back into its usual high ponytail. She'd been blessed with natural waves, but that made it hard to catch all the strands at one swipe.

Finally, she was ready. She picked up the lantern.

When she stepped into the kitchen, Brett was squatting before the cook stove, holding a match inside its front door. "Morning," he said, barely glancing at her. "Fire went out. I forgot to stoke it last night." He peered inside the stove and carefully added a sliver of kindling.

"You mean I forgot," she said. "I'm sorry. It won't happen again."

He kept his gaze on the tiny flames. "Don't worry about it. I should have mentioned it. It was completely my fault."

She went to the pitcher pump and filled the washbasin. Patting ice-cold water onto her face, she reached for the hand towel hanging beside the pump. "How about eggs?" she asked, turning to face him. "Do you have chickens?"

He nodded. "We keep the eggs in a box in the henhouse this time of year to keep them cold. Whenever you need any, ask one of the boys and he'll fetch them for you. I'll have Rollie bring some in now."

"That won't be necessary," she retorted. "I can fetch them just fine."

His eyebrows raised a fraction of an inch. He added a small log to the fire. "The chicken house is out the back door and to the right about a hundred feet. It's up against the corral fence. You can't miss it. Just follow your nose."

She looked at him to see if he'd meant that as a joke, but his face was as calm and serene as ever. "What time do you usually have breakfast?" she asked him.

"Six o'clock or thereabouts," he said, clanging the door closed. Dusting his hands, he unfolded his legs like a lady opening a fan and stood up.

Watching his face, Katie's head bent back further and further. He was at least a full foot taller than she. Why hadn't she noticed it until now? She stepped away to ease her embarrassment. "We'll have hotcakes and sorghum for breakfast, if that's all right," she said.

"Katie, if you fixed scrambled wagon tracks and fried cow chips, the boys would think it's just fine," he told her with a small smile. He looked around. "Is there anything else you need before I see to the chores?"

"I'm perfectly fine," she said. "We may be a few minutes late this morning, but I'll call when I'm ready."

"Jangle the triangle on the stoop, and they'll come a-running." He lifted his buffalo coat from the wall and gave her a nod. Then he went out.

Setting the coffeepot on to brew, she got busy. At fifteen past six, she called the hands in. This time she sat with them, at a corner far from Brett at the head of the table and with one empty chair between herself and Rollie.

"Hot cakes!" Duffy exclaimed, eyeing the tall stack of golden discs. "I haven't eaten hotcakes in nigh on five years."

Rollie turned to Katie. "Old Cappy didn't cook anything but bacon and biscuits for breakfast."

Lew added, "Once in a blue moon he'd work himself up to a pan of sweet rolls."

"Every other Christmas or so," Duffy added.

"Let's pray," Brett said, and all bowed their heads.

A few minutes later, Rollie leaned a little toward Katie. "So, where are you from?" he asked.

"We have a ranch a little west of Muddy Creek," she said, reluctantly.

"You still have it?" Lew asked.

She nodded, her eyes on her fork as it cut a piece of bacon. "We got hit with anthrax last summer."

A heavy silence settled around them. "Too bad," Duffy said. He glanced at Brett. "But for the Good Lord. . ."

"There goes us," Brett finished. "At least a dozen ranchers were wiped out. Others lost everything, but they're too stubborn to call it quits."

"I guess we fall into the second category," Katie said, trying to smile. She had a sudden image of her five-year-old sister, Arlene, hugging her arms tight across her hungry stomach and crying. Suddenly, Katie's breakfast tasted dry.

"Anyone want more coffee?" she asked, getting up to fetch the pot.

Brett began to discuss the business of the day, and the mood was broken. For the men, at least.

After they left the kitchen, Katie's tears dripped onto her shirtwaist. If only she had money to send her family now.

That evening after supper, the hands headed through that door on the north wall.

A few minutes later, Brett came into the kitchen and sat at the table with his account books. Katie was rinsing pinto beans. She planned to start them soaking before she retired.

"Tomorrow I'll make a passel of bread," she said. "I finished cleaning out the cabinets this afternoon."

He gazed around the room. "It looks like a new place," he

said warmly. "You've done better than I ever imagined. The boys like you, too." He smiled at her, then wrote something in his ledger.

"Mr. Masten," she said, closing her mouth before she could go on.

"Brett," he replied, looking over at her. "What's troubling you?"

"I need to send some money to Ma," she said. "Could you advance me twenty dollars on my pay so I can get it to her right away?"

His brow creased as he looked at her anxious face. "They're in dire need, aren't they." It was more of a statement than a question.

She nodded, her lips pressed together.

He pulled his tally book from his shirt pocket. "I'm going into Rosita tomorrow," he said, slipping off the rubber band. "There's a Western Union there. Give me her name, and I'll wire the money to her. She'll have it within a few hours."

Katie blinked. She'd dreaded asking, but now she wondered why she had. "Her name is Betsy Priestly," she said. Immediately, her breath stopped. Gasping, she rushed on. "She's actually my husband's mother. She's at the Tumbling P Ranch west of Muddy Creek."

"What's your husband's name?" Brett asked, sliding the tally book back into his pocket. "I may know him."

Chapter 3

J ohnny," Katie replied. How could the lies fall off her tongue so easily? She hated herself for it, but she was on a dangerous sled ride and couldn't get off.

Brett continued his bookwork and didn't say anything more. Finishing her duties, Katie stoked the fire in the stove and went to her room. She was too ashamed to talk to Brett anymore tonight. He was a good man, and she had never felt so lowdown in her entire life.

A woman of strong faith, Betsy Priestly had tried to instill that trust into her children. When Katie was nine years old, she had accepted Christ at her mother's knee. For the next eight years, her mother's prayers had been something she took for granted, like the sunrise or the cold spring behind their house.

That was before their lives had changed in a few short days last summer. When their cows began dropping in the fields by the dozens, Ma had prayed. Pa and the children prayed, too. They'd prayed and prayed while they watched their livelihood disintegrate in the cleansing fires that burned the swollen carcasses and their barn and everything else the cows had come near.

They'd prayed, and the garden had produced twice as much this year as any year before. Pa and Johnny had shot meat, and they'd had plenty.

But then harvest time was over. Wild game moved into winter hiding. Again, they'd prayed, but this time the heavens were silent.

"Don't lose hope," Ma had said twenty times a day. "God will see us through."

Katie had tried to hold onto her faith. Truly she had. Then Pa went away, but no money came. For weeks and weeks they'd prayed, but it never did come. *Where was God then?* she wondered in the most secret place in her heart. *Where is He now?*

Closing her bedroom door, she quickly changed into her flannel gown and lay down on her bed. The room was warmer tonight, the quilt soft and the pillow welcoming. She closed her eyes. *I'm going to sleep*, she told herself. She almost believed it until the wetness of her pillow made it cling to her cheek. *Oh, Lord*, she cried in her spirit, *where are You now?*

Katie was up early the next morning and had the fire going before Brett appeared through the sitting-room door. "Morning," he said. "Duffy and I will be leaving before the men come for breakfast. Could you feed us something that's quick to make and pack a couple of sandwiches to take along?"

"Of course," she said.

He reached for his buffalo coat. "I'll saddle my horse while you're doing that." He opened the door and strode out, still settling his hat onto his head.

Duffy appeared shortly afterwards. "It's going to turn cold tonight," he predicted. "I can feel it in my bones." Without another word, he followed Brett.

Katie involuntarily shivered as the second cold blast hit her through that open door. Hurrying to her bedroom, she found her coat and ran out to the henhouse.

When Brett and Duffy arrived, she had six eggs scrambled and waiting for them with two day-old biscuits and some fresh, crisp bacon. She set their plates before them and poured steaming coffee into their mugs.

Duffy set his round hat on the table beside his plate. "Say, I could get used to this," he said. He paused while Brett said the blessing then sipped coffee. "That goes down just right, don't it?"

Brett methodically emptied his plate and his cup without talking, but that didn't stop Duffy's chatter. "There's snow in the air," he said. "Mark my words. I kin smell it."

The men finished about the same time and stood to leave. Katie handed Brett a tin of biscuit-and-bacon sandwiches. He thanked her and said, "We'll be back before suppertime, Lord willing."

"Thank you kindly for that breakfast, Katie," Duffy said with a loose-lipped smile. "If you wasn't already married, I'd have my proposal all writ out and memorized." He chuckled at his own joke and followed Brett out the door.

Katie stood beside the kitchen counter a moment to watch them go. Ma should have her money by tomorrow. With her first paycheck, she'd buy some writing paper and write Ma and the kids a letter.

Before she knew it, Katie had been there two full weeks. Now that the kitchen was clean and in good order, she enjoyed her work. The hours were long, but the company was good. She looked forward to meal times for the fun of listening to the hands' teasing and bantering with each other. She also looked forward to Brett's evening visits to the kitchen. Some days he worked over his account books and others he simply read his Bible.

One evening near the middle of November, she was giving the stove a final wipe-down for the night when she worked up the nerve to ask him to read aloud.

"What would you like me to read?" he asked. "Do you have a favorite passage?"

She paused with her cloth in mid-swipe. "Oh, I have lots of favorites. Psalm 23, Psalm 51, Psalm 127, lots of them."

"Are you a Christian?" he asked, watching her keenly.

Suddenly shy, she nodded. "I received Christ when I was nine years old. But there's no church near our place, so we never could go to church much."

He thumbed through the worn pages. "We don't have one near here either, unfortunately. A circuit rider comes through once a year or so." He stopped at a page. "Here's one. 'I will lift up mine eyes unto the hills, from whence cometh my help. My help cometh from the LORD, which made heaven and earth. He will not suffer thy foot to be moved: he that keepeth thee will not slumber.'" He read on to the end of Psalm 121.

She listened to his smooth voice and those words sank into her soul.

When he finished, he said, "Katie, I've been thinking of something." He pulled his lips inward then dragged his lower lip out from between his teeth. "If you'd rather not, just say so. You don't have to do it."

"What is it?" she asked.

"Would you mind adding to your duties for an extra ten dollars a month? I'd be obliged if you'd clean my quarters once a week. That is, if you don't mind."

An extra ten dollars when she'd already bargained him up to forty? Fifty dollars a month seemed like a king's ransom. "I'd be glad to," she said. "I'll do it on Saturday mornings."

"Good," he replied, that small smile on his face. He nodded. "Good. Thank you." He turned a page in the Bible and began to read again.

At noon the following day, Katie was on the stoop ready to signal for dinner when Duffy rode into the yard on his blue roan mare. Katie waved at him, then stared. As he drew near, the tinkling of a tiny bell reached her. It grew louder until she realized the sound was coming from Duffy's saddle. He had a small bell tied under the pommel. As long as she'd been around cowboys, she'd never known anyone to put a bell on his saddle before.

Remembering her manners, she stopped staring and jangled the triangle. As always, her five boys came on the double. Grinning at their hurry, she stepped inside to get out of their way while they washed up at the pump.

When they were all seated and Brett had offered thanks, Katie handed a bowl of fried potatoes to Lew and looked at Duffy. "Duffy, why do you have a bell on your saddle? I've never seen that before."

Rollie gave a loud hoot. "I can answer that one," he said, handing her the platter of fried chicken. "We put a bell on him because one of these days he's going to forget how to come home and we'll need to be able to go out and find him."

That brought up a general howl. Duffy laughed with the rest. When the commotion died down, the old-timer said, "He's teasing you, Katie. Don't pay him no mind."

She glanced at Rollie's freckled face and said, "I stopped doing that the first day I came."

That brought another uproar.

Rollie grinned at her. "Nice shot, Katie, my gal. I didn't know you had it in you."

She smiled and picked up her fork. "Save some room, boys," she said. "I baked bread pudding. It's still warm, and there's cream to put over it."

Lew said, "You're spoiling us."

"Don't talk her out of it," Rollie told him. "She's doing just fine."

Katie glanced down the table and found Brett smiling at her. Not one of his usual small smiles, but a wide, big, natural smile. He met her gaze, and her heart stepped up its pace. That smile reached his eyes, too.

Suddenly, she realized what she was doing. A married woman shouldn't be so pleased at the way a man looked at her. It wasn't fitting.

She got up to serve dessert, a wonderful excuse to leave the table for a few minutes and calm her treacherous heart. She didn't look at him again, not once until the men all went outside.

That's the end of that, she told herself as she washed up after the meal. No more smiling and definitely no more looking.

That evening Brett came to the kitchen with his Bible in hand. He sat down and read for a few minutes, then said, "I'm going into Rosita tomorrow with Rollie and Hank, so I'm going to pay your first month's wages tonight." He pulled some coins from his shirt pocket. "Here's the thirty I still owe you. Is there anything you need from town?"

"You can send another twenty to Ma," she said. "There are a few things I need. Can I make a little list?" She opened a cabinet door. "There are a few things we need for the kitchen, too."

"Whatever you say," he replied absently, turning pages. "Put whatever you need on a list, and I'll bring it home." He stopped and ran his finger down a column. "How about Isaiah 40 for tonight?"

Her work was finished, so she sat at the table a few chairs away from him while he read. He spoke the words like he meant them: " 'Even the youths shall faint and be weary, and the young men shall utterly fall: But they that wait upon the LORD. . .'"

When he finished, he quietly said, "How about if we pray?"

She nodded, and he said, "Lord, You know how weak and needy we are. We're working hard and doing our best to scratch out a living out here in the wilderness. Please look down on us and bless us. Help us to stay close to You. Help us to speak a word for You when You give us a chance. Please help the Priestly family. They've had a bad time, Lord. Meet their needs, I pray. In the name of Jesus, amen."

Katie kept her head bowed after he said, "Amen." She felt tears building behind her eyelids, and she didn't want him to see. Finally, she pulled her handkerchief from her pocket and pressed it against her eyes.

When she looked up, the Bible was closed, and Brett sat quietly with his hands in his lap. His eyes were open, but his head was bowed.

She sniffed and scraped her chair back. "Thank you, Brett," she faltered. "Good night." She turned and escaped to her room. Lying on top of the quilt fully dressed, she curled into a tight ball and sobbed. She could see them so plainly—Bonnie and Mark, almost teenagers with their dark wounded eyes and a set to their young jaws that told of their determination to survive,

Georgina, with her crooked braids and boundless energy, and Arlene, so gentle and sweet. She missed them all so.

Rubbing the heels of her hands into her burning eyelids, she reached down to pull her coat over her, snuggled into her pillow, and fell into a deep and troubled sleep. She dreamt of wild animals chasing Georgina, of Arlene lost in the dark, of Ma crying at night. When she awoke she felt like she'd hardly closed her eyes.

The men were riding out early that morning, so she had to get moving. Her bones ached, and so did her feet. She'd worn her shoes all night.

What can I give the men to take along for a nooning on the trail? she wondered as she quickly combed her hair. There was a large piece of bread pudding left. That would do for starters.

Moving automatically, she went out to add small sticks to the orange coals in the cook stove. While she waited, she found the tin for packing food and went to the counter to put the bread pudding inside it.

Suddenly, she blinked and wondered if she were still dreaming. The pan of bread pudding was completely empty, like someone had licked it clean. Had one of the men come in for a midnight snack? Maybe.

She stopped to add bigger wood to the fire and put on the coffeepot. Beef sandwiches would have to do for them today. Not that they minded much. She went to the box on the back porch where they set food to keep it cold and lifted the lid. It was empty. Even the plate was gone.

A knot formed inside her chest. Something was very wrong.

Katie headed for the sitting-room door and knocked. Brett

appeared thirty seconds later, his face half covered with white lather, his straight razor in his hand.

"Someone took food from the back porch," she said. "I had a big piece of roast beef out there. I was going to make you beef sandwiches for the trail. When I went out, the box was empty."

"It could have been a raccoon," he said. "This time of year, they turn into real scoundrels."

"Would a raccoon take the plate, too?" she asked.

"Now, you've got a point there," he said. He waved the straight razor in the air near his right ear. "Would you mind if I finish shaving? I'll come back as soon as I'm through."

A giggle burst out. "I'm sorry. I guess I got pretty spooked."

He grinned. "Who wouldn't?"

Half an hour later, the three men bound for Rosita had gathered in the kitchen. They were drinking coffee and eating cornmeal mush.

Katie picked up the bread-pudding pan. "Did anyone finish this off?" she asked. "A large piece was in this corner last night, and now it's clean."

Rollie and Hank shook their heads.

Brett looked thoughtful. "Check with Duffy and Lew," he said. "If neither one of them took it, have Duffy put a couple of hooks on the kitchen doors. I don't like the idea of someone coming inside."

"It could be an Indian," Hank said, spreading butter on a slab of bread.

"Or a drifter," Rollie added.

Letting out a harsh sigh, Brett looked disgusted. "What's the world coming to? Worried about strangers coming in at night. A body should be safe inside his own four walls."

Katie's eyes widened. "How about my door?" she asked Brett. "Could I have a lock on my door, too?"

He looked at her surprised. "Of course you can. Just mention it to Duffy. He'd crawl through an ice floe without his shirt on if you asked him to."

Sniggers went up from the younger men.

Brett ignored them. "When Lew and Duffy come to breakfast, ask them about the bread pudding. It's possible one of them raided the kitchen in the middle of the night."

But when she asked them an hour later, both men shook their heads.

"It must have been a drifter," Duffy said, rubbing the fuzz on the top of his head.

"But this area is so sparsely populated," Lew objected. "They usually like to stay closer to towns." He pulled out a chair and sat at the table.

Duffy's white eyebrows came low over his frosty blue eyes. "Whoever it was, he's had his last night of fun on us," he declared. "I'll get those hooks attached right after breakfast."

Chapter 4

Katie was on edge for the rest of the day. Walking to the henhouse, she had the skin-crawling sensation that someone was watching her. An hour later, she dropped a cupful of milk on the floor while she was making cornbread.

At noon, Duffy dipped a wedge of cornbread into his stew and said, "I scouted around the yard and found nary a sign of footprints. The ground is froze hard, but there should still be some sign." He shook his head. "Nothing."

Lew hooked his long arm around the back of his chair. "It was probably someone passing through and needing grub for his journey. Most likely, he won't be back."

Duffy nodded. "Those hooks should take the wind outta his sails, anyway."

Brett and his men returned shortly before supper. Rollie had a young buck thrown over the front of his saddle. He veered off from the rest of the men and circled the house to carry the meat to the smokehouse in back.

Venison would be a nice change from beef. Katie knew a recipe for barbeque using molasses and vinegar. It was Johnny's favorite, her pa's, too.

Brett came directly to the house and ground-hitched his horse near the kitchen steps. Katie saw him dismount. She hurried to turn her potatoes sizzling in a skillet before he walked in.

He carried a canvas sack and a package wrapped in brown paper and tied with twine. He set the goods on the table. "Here's your receipt for the money transfer," he said, digging into his shirt pocket for the paper. He handed it to her. "How have things been around here?"

Thanking him, she took the page and glanced at it. "Duffy put on the hooks. He said there are no tracks around the house at all. He can't understand how someone could have been prowling around without leaving any sign."

Brett's tired features creased with concern. "I'll have a talk with him." He hesitated. "I'm sorry about this. If you're feeling nervous, don't be afraid to ask for help, even if it's just going to get the eggs."

"I'm all right," she said. "Lew thinks it was a traveler, passing through and needing food for the trail."

"He's probably right." He backed away. "I'd best tend to my horse." He turned and headed outside, his boots loud on the plank floor.

Katie pushed the receipt into her skirt pocket and picked up the metal spatula. Maybe she was making too much of nothing.

Rollie was the first one in for supper. He turned a chair backwards, straddled it, and sat down. "What's the news on our food thief?" he asked.

Lifting a cloth-lined bowl full of hot biscuits to set them on the table, Katie said, "No news at all, I'm afraid." She told him of Duffy's unsuccessful search.

Rollie reached into the pocket of his blue flannel shirt. "I brought you something from town," he said. He handed two small paper envelopes toward her.

She hesitated then took them. "What are they?" she asked. If these were something personal, she'd have to refuse.

"Cinnamon and nutmeg," he said. "They'd just got some in, and I've got a powerful hankering for sweet rolls or maybe some pumpkin pies."

She sniffed the bits of brown paper. The aroma brought up several delightful images. "That's thoughtful of you, Rollie," she said. Carrying them to a cabinet, she opened a tin and carefully set the papers inside. "I'll see what I can do with those."

When Duffy came in, Rollie stood to turn his chair around and set it back to the table. "Say, Katie," he said, grinning. "I know why Duffy has a bell on his saddle."

The old-timer took off his hat. "I can't wait to hear this one," he said as Lew and Hank stepped through the door.

Rollie went on. "Hank put the bell on there so's old Duffy can't sneak up on us. We can say anything we want about him and be sure he's too far away to hear."

Lew chuckled. Hank tapped the back of Rollie's head with his palm, and Rollie grabbed Hank's wrist.

Duffy shook his head. "That was good, Rollie," he said. "Go to the head of the class."

Hank chuckled. "Yeah, that's where the dunce sits on a stool."

Brett arrived, and Katie took her place at a far corner of the table. The banter died down while Brett prayed, then began again soon after his amen.

"How about a game of checkers after supper?" Duffy asked Lew.

The big man shook his head. "I'm turning in early."

The old-timer scanned the table for another likely opponent.

"I'll play," Brett told him, "after I finish my accounts."

While the men played their game, Hank entertained them all with his fiddle. He didn't play that well, but any music was a welcome diversion. Watching the checker game, Rollie sang a few bars now and then.

Katie took her time finishing the dishes. She wiped every surface and fed her sourdough starter. Setting out a large pan of apple-pandoughty for the men to snack on, she said good night and went to her room. The excitement of that day had worn her out. She wanted some time alone before she retired.

In her packages, she'd found a writing tablet and two sharpened pencils along with her change. She wanted to start a letter home tonight. She'd write a little every day until one of the men want back to town to mail it for her.

She left the door open, so the warmth of the kitchen stove could come in. Lighting the lamp, she folded back the cardboard cover on the tablet and wrote the date in careful script: November 18, 1884. She began by telling all about the ranch and the hands. She told how much she liked working there and about Johnny's job in Musgrove.

Her eyes were drooping by the time she finished the back of the second page. She closed the tablet, slid it under her thin mattress, and shut her door. Thank the Lord for Duffy and this new hook. She'd sleep better with it there. A few minutes later, she snuggled in her warm flannel gown under the quilt and closed her eyes. Sleep covered her like a goose-down comforter.

Suddenly, she came full awake. The room was black as ink.

The house was silent except for the normal creaks.

Katie lay motionless, her eyes wide, her ears tuned for the slightest sound. All she heard was the rattling of the wind against her windowpane.

Turning over, she pulled the quilt closer around her neck. If someone was out there, she was the last person to check. Let the men see to it.

After a few minutes, she dozed and didn't wake up until morning.

She was dressed and in the kitchen a few minutes past five, moving mechanically to build up the fire and put on coffee. Crossing to the table to gather the mugs and plates left from the men's late snack, she suddenly stiffened. The apple-pandoughty was completely gone, the dish licked clean.

She let the pan stay where it was.

When Brett came in a few minutes later, she pointed at the table. "Did the men finish that whole pan last night?" she asked, a hint of accusation in her voice.

Brett looked from the object in question to her pointing finger. "Well, yes. I believe they did." He looked a little sheepish. "I'm afraid I ate four pieces myself."

Blinking, she let out a great sigh of relief. "I was afraid someone had been in here last night."

He went on. "I made a fresh pot of coffee after you turned in. Me and the boys had a time eating pandoughty and swapping stories until late. It must have been nine o'clock when we called it a day."

She held up her hand with the palm toward him. "That's all right. I don't mind if you ate it. That's not it at all."

He grinned. "Maybe I should leave a note from now on: Here lies an empty pan left by five hungry cowpokes."

She chuckled at his foolishness. "I've got to get busy or breakfast will be late." She picked up the lard can. "Would you mind bringing in that last haunch of beef from the smokehouse? It'll have to thaw awhile before I can cut it up."

"Sure thing," he said, picking up his coat.

She handed him a basin, then opened the cupboard door to find the flour bin.

Brett had his hand on the door latch when she said, "Brett, didn't you buy a fresh sack of cornmeal yesterday?"

"That's right."

"I'm sure I put it right here," she said, her hand on the empty shelf. She turned to look at him. "It's gone."

"What?" he demanded. In two strides, he was next to her, peering into the cabinet.

She opened all the doors. No cornmeal anywhere.

He said, "You'd best check through all the cabinets and see if anything else is missing. I'm getting mighty tired of this, and that's a fact."

Picking up the basin, he headed outside. He was back in five minutes, the enamel basin hanging from his hand. "The beef's gone," he said. He set the bowl on the table.

Still stirring biscuit dough, Katie felt her throat tighten. There *had* been someone inside last night, latched doors or no.

The breakfast mood was somber that morning. The men poured sausage gravy over their biscuits and forked them down while Brett talked. "The doors were still locked when I came in the kitchen this morning," he said. "I can't figure it out, but we've got to put a stop to it."

Duffy said, "Should we set up a guard?"

Brett replied, "I hate to think of watching through the night. That would be hard on all of us."

"Maybe it's a ghost," Hank said, only half joking. "How could a person come through a latched door?"

Brett's lips twisted. "Does a ghost need to eat?" he asked. "Could a ghost take food through the door with him?" He turned to Katie. "Just exactly what was taken last night? Did you figure that out?"

She nodded and listed off, "Five pounds of cornmeal, a small jug of sour milk, and a cooking pot."

Rollie said, "Someone's hiding out. They're getting hungry, and we're the grocery store."

Katie swallowed. "An escaped prisoner, do you think?"

Brett said, "It's not likely, but it is possible. The closest jail is in Pueblo. A man on foot could cover the distance in a couple of weeks, I reckon."

"This time of year?" Duffy asked. "I'd think a man in that shape would head south and get out of the state the quickest way he could. He'd hop a train, most likely."

Duffy shook his head. "It's going to turn bitter cold. Whoever it is out there can't make it much longer."

Rollie said, "If you can spare me, I'll scout around on horse-back today, looking for tracks."

"Take the whole morning, if you need it," Brett said. "We're going to be working the fence line south by the spring. You can ride out to meet us when you're finished." He scraped back his chair. Before he stood, he said, "On second thought, Rollie, just come back to the house when you're through, in case Katie needs something. I don't like to have her here alone with all this going on."

Rollie nodded, and Katie breathed for the first time that morning.

She tried to go about her usual chores as though nothing

had happened, but her attention was elsewhere. She burned the first batch of sourdough bread, not badly, but enough to make her irritated at herself.

When Rollie came in, she was scrubbing the kitchen floor. At least that was something that couldn't be botched.

"Mind your feet," she said as he stepped inside. "Take big steps and sit down at the table. I'll bring you a hot cup of coffee in a few minutes."

He took off his coat and hat then did as she said. Sitting down, he propped his boots on the chair across from him and said, "My mama would chase us out of the house with the mop handle if we stepped on her wet floor. She's a terror, my mother is." He grinned. "She raised six of us boys and not a scoundrel among us."

Katie sat back on her heels and smiled at him. "She sounds like my kind of woman. I have been known to chase the young'uns outside from time to time."

He said, "Do you have children?"

"My brothers and sisters," she said, leaning down to wipe the cloth over the floorboards. "There are six of us, four girls and two boys. I have an older brother and the rest are younger."

"You married young," he said. "You can't be more than sixteen yourself."

"Eighteen," she corrected. She clamped her mouth shut. She was talking way too much.

Finishing the mopping, she carried the bucket to the back step and flung the dirty water to the ground. She set the bucket on the porch beside the door and returned to Rollie in the kitchen.

"Did you find anything?" she asked as she poured his coffee.

He shook his head. "Duffy was right. Whoever it is, he knows enough to cover his tracks." She set the mug in front of him, and he picked it up. "That could be Indians."

She gulped. "You think so?"

Glancing at her face, he said, "I'm guessing. I don't know anything for sure." He took his time looking around the kitchen. "Is there any place else that a man could come through?"

"I've been thinking about that myself," she said, her arms crossed tightly about her waist. "This room is tight. I checked it out myself."

He drained his cup and set it down. "I'm going to look around the smokehouse. Maybe the fellow made a mistake out there and left a shoeprint or a hoofprint." He paused beside the door. "Don't worry, Katie. We're going to watch out for you. Believe me, not a man here wants anything to happen to you. You saved our lives, you know that? You surely did. If you weren't already married, I'd lay odds that you'd have three or four proposals by now." With that he went out and closed the door firmly behind him.

Katie rubbed her forehead. Well, that proved Brett had known what he was doing when he made that rule about no single women. Not that she wasn't flattered, but on this side of things she was very glad she didn't have to fend anyone off. She could be just friends with all of them.

That evening at supper, Brett announced that there would be no guard unless it was absolutely necessary. "Keep in mind that you may have to miss some sleep before this is all over," he told them. "I'd suggest you all turn in early."

However, the night was calm. Nothing awakened Katie. She felt rested and refreshed when she arrived in the kitchen the next morning. The weather had suddenly grown a little milder, so her feet weren't quite as cold. Maybe she'd stir up some hotcakes this morning. The boys would like that.

Stoking the fire, she put out her hand to pick up the coffee-pot and fill it. A cold wave traveled down her back, sucking her breath from her. The blue enamel coffeepot was gone.

Chapter 5

B rett came immediately in response to her banging on the sitting-room door. He had a towel draped around his neck. One look at her and he said, "What is it? Are you all right?"

When she didn't answer right away, he covered her hands with his. His fingers were warm.

"The coffeepot!" she croaked. Her throat was too tight to say more.

He rushed past her to the cook stove and looked at its bare top. Suddenly, he snapped the towel from around his neck and flung it to the floor. "Duffy!" he bellowed.

He strode to the bunkhouse door and tore it open. "Duffy!" He charged inside, leaving the door ajar behind him.

Katie moved aside to be out of the line of sight. The last thing she wanted was for one of the hands to see her peering into their quarters as they rolled out of bed.

She stood near the stove, her hands twisted inside her apron. What was she going to do now? A missing cooking pan and now the coffeepot—at this rate, she was going to have to get creative or stop cooking altogether. If she had any food left to cook, that is.

Men's sleepy voices drifted out of their quarters until some-one had the sense to close the door to the bunkhouse.

Katie found a saucepan. She poured coffee grounds into it, then filled it with water and added a few eggshells. It would probably taste like mud, but at least they'd have coffee for breakfast.

The men drifted into the kitchen long before she was ready to signal that the meal was ready. Lew carried a dented tin coffee-pot. He handed it to her. "This is from our trail pack," he said. "It's not very big, but you can use it until we can get to town and buy another one."

She took the scuffed and stained pot. "Thank you," she said and set it on the washing-up counter. It looked as though it had been rubbed with sand the last time it had been used.

Despite the impropriety, Katie considered asking Brett if she could sleep in one of his rooms until all this was over. She felt so alone and out of reach in her own place. If someone tried to storm her door down, would anyone hear her call for help?

Brett came in and told her, "This morning we'll do the chores *after* we eat. First, the men and I have to powwow."

When everyone was at the table, Brett poured coffee from the saucepan into five mugs. "Let it set awhile to settle the grounds," he told the men as he handed the cups around, then he joined them at the table.

Still frying bacon, Katie listened to their talk.

Duffy said, "I believe we can rule out a few things, boss. Indians don't give two wooden nickels about coffee nor coffeepots."

Lew added, "Drifters almost always carry a camp coffeepot.

They wouldn't have no use for a big kitchen pot like ours. Besides, they don't stay in one place too long. It's nigh onto zero degrees out there. They wouldn't be camping out around here. They'd want to find a place closer to civilization where there are other men to share a fire with and more places to scrounge for food."

Brett nodded. "So, no Indians and no drifters. What does that leave us?"

"Someone on the run," Hank said. "An outlaw or a convict."

Duffy shook his head. "Someone on the run would keep on running. This has been going on for more than a week."

An idea suddenly came to Katie. She turned from the stove to speak. "Someone in trouble," she said, feeling her stomach contract in sympathetic hunger pains. "Someone destitute."

The men sat in silence for a few minutes.

Brett lifted his coffee cup and tried out a sip. He grimaced and set it down. "If there's someone in genuine trouble, we have to find out who it is, so we can give some proper help. He'll freeze to death out there if we get a blizzard or a real bad cold spell. Last winter it got down to thirty below."

He turned to Lew. "You and Duffy take off for town after the meal," he told him. Turning toward Katie, he went on, "Make them a list of supplies to buy for the kitchen and give it to them. Get plenty."

Back to the men, he said, "Rollie, scout around the outside of the ranch grounds. Look for hiding places where there's shelter from the cold. He'd need a fire, and he'd need water nearby. Think it through from that angle and see what you can come up with."

Katie set bacon and eggs on the table along with a plate of sliced bread. Brett bowed and prayed, "Lord, if there is someone hungry hiding outside in the cold, please help us to find him. We've got room in the bunkhouse, and we've got plenty to eat. But for Your protecting hand, we'd have lost our cattle and everything here. Thank You for Your care. Amen."

Katie picked up her fork and tasted the eggs. They were cooked to perfection, but she couldn't force herself to swallow more than one bite. Mercifully, the meal was over soon and the hands dispersed to begin their day.

Katie got out of her seat to clear the table. Still in his chair, Brett slowly sipped his coffee. When she came near him to pick up Hank's dishes, he said, "Sit down for a minute, will you? Please?"

She glanced at him, surprised, and sank into Hank's chair at the corner beside him.

"I'm getting a little worried about you," he said gently. "Are you afraid of staying in here alone?"

Avoiding his gaze, she nodded. "A couple of times I woke up thinking I heard someone come in, but I've been too scared to cry out. He could come and get me next."

He nodded. "I know. I thought about that myself." His mouth worked outward as he considered that. "We'll have to come up with some kind of signal so you can alert me without giving yourself away at the same time. I'll talk it over with Duffy when he comes back from town."

Watching her hands knotted together in her lap, she nodded. "Thank you."

He made a move to push his chair back.

She looked up. "Brett. . ."

He stopped, waiting for her to go on.

"Would you mind if I. . ." she paused, nervous about asking him.

"Probably not," he murmured with that small smile. "Go on."

"Could I start setting some stuff out for him? Cooked leftovers and things like that?" She met his gaze for the first time. "It makes me feel sick inside, thinking about someone starving out in the cold."

He cocked his head so one eye focused on her and the other eye squinted. "You know what they say about feeding strays," he drawled.

"This is a human being, not a dog," she retorted. She clamped her lips shut. That statement was far too forceful.

He smiled, his blue-green eyes scanning her face for a long moment. "You're thinking about your own family, aren't you?"

She nodded.

He placed both his hands flat on the table. "Go ahead. Between all of us, we should be able to smoke him out, so we can bring him in out of the cold altogether." He stood and picked up his coat. "Hank and I are going to ride the fence line today to check for breaks. We may not be back in time for dinner."

Standing, too, she nodded. "I'll save the main meal until this evening."

He put on his coat and hat then stood near the door, unmoving, watching her.

Wondering why he'd hesitated, she looked up at him. Those blue-green eyes held hers for an endless moment, so full of concern, so warm and. . .

Suddenly, she gasped. "I have a letter! I almost forgot it. Tell Duffy to come and pick it up before he goes." She scurried toward her room, then remembered her manners and called back, "Please!"

He chuckled. The door banged as he went out.

Her hands were shaking as she pulled out the paper tablet.

Her knees were weak as she tore out the pages with writing on them. What was wrong with her? She'd told herself, no more looking, and what had she done? Gone right ahead and looked anyway. She let her head fall back until her chin pointed at the ceiling. Closing her eyes, she drew in a deep breath. *He thinks you are a married woman! Start acting like it!*

Folding the five pages together, she realized she didn't have an envelope. She dug in her coat pocket for the coins Brett had given her weeks ago.

She sat on the edge of her bed for a few more minutes, forcing calmness through her clenched hands and tense mouth. Nothing had happened between her and the boss. It was all in her foolish, stupid mind.

When Duffy arrived fifteen minutes later, she had everything neatly on the counter waiting for him. She handed him the pages and pointed to the top sheet. "I've written everything here," she told him. "If you would buy two envelopes, you can address one to my mother and bring the other one back to me for next time." She gave him a coin. "Here's five dollars. It's the smallest amount I've got."

He slid the letter into his inside coat pocket. "Is there anything else you need from town?" he asked. "Besides a coffeepot, that is?"

She nodded. "Cornmeal, lard, and pinto beans." She paused then went on. "Use some of my money to buy a wool army blanket."

"I kin remember that," he said, nodding. "We'd best get there and back in a hurry. We're in for some snow any time now. I don't hanker on getting caught in a blizzard."

She handed him a cloth bundle. "Here's something to eat while you're on the trail. It's not much, but I wasn't expecting you to be riding out again so soon."

He took it from her. "I'm obliged, Katie," he said. "You're number one in my book."

She smiled. If he had been her natural-born uncle, she would have hugged him. "You're very welcome, Duffy," she said.

Grinning, he repositioned his floppy hat and shuffled out.

Deep in thought, Katie cleared away the remains of breakfast. Brett was so patient even through all this trouble. What lay under that silent, gentle exterior? Suddenly, she had an overwhelming urge to find out.

The day passed in peace and silence. Katie stayed busy baking bread and cleaning Brett's part of the house. She liked to clean when he was away. Handling his things with him looking on was too embarrassing. When she finished, the floors glowed with a fresh coating of linseed oil and the fireplace stones had a brilliant sheen.

She saw Rollie ride in shortly after three o'clock that afternoon. Ten gleaming golden loaves made a double line down the back counter, filling the house with a rich aroma.

He went into the barn for a few minutes, then sauntered to the house. Despite his short stature, he walked like a big man with his chest out and his head high. He came inside and unbuttoned his denim coat. "Boy, if that don't smell good!" he said, eyeing the loaves set out to cool.

Katie asked, "Did you find anything?"

"Nothing I could say for sure," he said, taking off his black flat-crowned hat. "Whoever it is, he knows something about tracking. Otherwise, he'd leave more traces of his coming and going. The average person would." He looked at the stove. "Have you got any coffee?"

"I've got better than that," she replied. She pulled a dish towel off a large pan of warm sweet rolls and set the pan on the table.

With a gasp of anticipation, he pulled out the head chair and sat down. Katie brought him a plate and a steaming mug of coffee. She left him alone for a full ten minutes while she finished peeling potatoes for supper.

Finally, she joined him and helped herself to a sweet roll. It was buttery and warm. "This is some of that cinnamon you brought me," she said. Reaching for a second one, she giggled. "We're spoiling our supper."

He laughed. "I won't tell if you won't." He drained his coffee cup and stood to refill it from the camp pot on the stove.

"Rollie," Katie began when he sat down, "where is Brett from? Originally, I mean. Is he from Colorado?"

"Wyoming," he said, draining the second cup of coffee. "Far as I know, his parents still live there."

"I wonder what brought him down here."

"Why don't you ask him?" he said, standing. "It's late. I'd best see to the stock. Thanks for the rolls!" With that he lifted his hat and coat and strode out.

An hour later, Duffy and Lew rode in. Duffy came directly to the kitchen without even taking his horse to the barn. He set a burlap sack on the table. "Here's the goods you needed," he said. Reaching into his inner pocket, he pulled out two envelopes. "These are for you."

Katie took them. The first was the new envelope she'd asked for. The second was thick with her name scrawled on the outside of it—a letter from home.

Hurrying to her room, she tore it open and sat on her bed to read it. It was in her mother's handwriting.

Dear Katie,

I'm so glad to have good news for you. I received a letter from your father last week along with forty dollars. He's been riding the rails in the caboose. His pay was delayed because of some kind of mix up, but he's all right. I got your twenty dollars as well, so the children and I are living like kings. We've plenty of food, and I bought some coal to keep us warmer. I hope you are well, my dear. Thank you so much for what you are doing for us. I haven't heard from Johnny yet. I hope he's doing all right. Please write me when you can.

All my love,
Ma

Katie held the page to her heart and breathed a heartfelt prayer of thanksgiving. The family would be fine. Next spring, they'd all come home and everything would get back to normal. Her shoes had wings when she returned to the kitchen. God really had heard their prayers. He really was there.

That night after supper, she waited for Brett to come into the kitchen, the same as she waited for him every night. That evening he brought in his account books to record the expenses from that day's trip to town.

Katie was used to his routine now. Those quiet moments after the supper dishes were finished had become her most cherished part of the day.

When he finished with his records, she joined him at the table. "Duffy brought me a letter," she said. "It was good news."

He leaned back in his chair and grinned. "You don't say. I'm glad to hear that."

"I just wanted to say thank you for giving me that advance. It made all the difference for Ma and the kids. She said they've got plenty to eat and she bought some coal, too."

"Well, I want to say thank you to you, too," he said. "You've turned this cold cow camp into a home, Katie. The food's good and the place is spotless. I couldn't ask for any better."

She beamed under his praise. "I like it here," she said. "The men are fun to be around."

"As you can probably tell, they like you, too."

"What made you choose Colorado?" she asked him. "Why did you buy land here?"

He tilted his head in that familiar way and said, "I met a man in Cheyenne who wanted to sell. The price was right, and the land was good. So I bought it."

"Didn't you want to stay near your folks?"

He leaned back in his chair, his legs stretching straight out. "I'm the youngest of four boys. My three brothers are all married and have big families. I guess I figured they were enough family to take care of the folks." He quirked in the side of his mouth in a vaguely cynical smile. "Besides, every single girl in the territory had me on her list of possibles. I got tired of trying to outrun them."

She laughed at that.

He chuckled, too.

She said, "I would think you'd be flattered. Most young men would be thrilled."

He rubbed his five o'clock shadow. "I guess I'm too independent. I always figured I'd pick my own gal, not *get* picked." He shifted in his chair. "Say, I've been thinking that maybe we could set a little trap and catch our prowler."

She waited, listening.

"How about if you set a nice meal in that box on the back porch. The boys and I will take turns watching. When he comes, we'll grab him. It's that simple."

She looked sheepish. "I'm afraid I'm ahead of you. After supper I put a new blanket on top of the box and a pan of sweet rolls inside it."

"You don't say!" He got to his feet. "Let's see if they're still there." He headed toward the back door with Katie behind him. He paused to lift the lantern from the center of the table as he passed it.

When he reached the porch, he stopped in the doorway and cried out. "I'll be a jackrabbit's hind leg!"

"What?" She edged past him.

The blanket was gone.

"If I was a betting man, I'd lay odds that the rolls are gone, too!"

Katie lifted the lid and gazed forlornly into the empty box. Disgusted, she dropped the lid. "I'm sorry. I should have told you what I was doing. We could have caught him and no one would have lost a wink of sleep."

Holding the lantern up so he could see her face, he said, "You're too quick to blame yourself. We'll try again tomorrow."

Standing so close to her that she could see the gold flecks in his eyes, he gave her that slow smile, and Katie forgot to breathe. For a moment she feared. . .no, hoped. . .he was going to kiss her.

Then he moved back, and the moment was gone.

Katie lifted her skirt to clear the doorsill and headed back inside.

Brett paused beside her bedroom door. "I hope Duffy's contraption works," he said, looking overhead at the string crossing the ceiling. It began next to Katie's bedstead and ended tied to a bell in Brett's bedroom. If she got scared, she could pull the string and, hopefully, it would ring and wake Brett up.

She stopped beside him to look at the string, too. She looked doubtful. "If I hear a noise, you'll find out if it works, all right. Unless you sleep right through it."

He grinned down at her. "I won't sleep through that. I promise you."

She suddenly became conscious of the man-smell from his blue flannel shirt, his collar open just below his Adam's apple, the warm look in his eyes.

Forcing herself to look away, she said, "Good night," and stepped into her room. She firmly closed the door and hooked the latch.

Leaning against the oak door, she rubbed her face with both hands. She could hear her mother's voice so clearly echoing in her head, "Oh, what a tangled web we weave. . ."

How was she going to get out of this? Brett was the dearest, most desirable man she'd ever known. He was tall and strong and handsome. He was a Christian, true and honorable.

She closed her eyes and let out an anguished sigh. She was fighting a losing battle, and she'd better admit it now. She'd condemned herself by her own impulsive words. Brett thought she was married, and she was hopelessly in love with him.

Chapter 6

S he dressed for bed and turned out the light. Under her thick covers, she closed her eyes. The best thing for her to do was to confess her lie to him before breakfast. That was the right thing to do. But did she have the courage to do it?

She knew she didn't. She was a hopeless coward without a speck of principle. When Brett found out the truth, he would probably turn her out. She deserved it, too.

Despite her agitation, she slept well and woke up early. She took her time dressing, thankful for a few extra minutes of quiet before the morning flurry of activity began.

Brett was already in the kitchen when she came in. The stove was glowing and the new coffeepot giving off steam.

"Good morning," she said, pausing at the end of the hallway. Just seeing him made her heart beat a little faster.

He looked up from reading his Bible. "Good morning. Did you hear anything last night?"

She shook her head. "With those easy pickings he got last night, I'm not surprised. Why come back when you've already had a windfall?"

He nodded. "You're right about that."

She pulled out the flour sack and the tin of lard. "How about pancakes this morning?" she asked him.

"Duffy will be delighted," he said.

She looked at him and he smiled, a soft, gentle smile that was somehow different. Or maybe it was the tenderness in his eyes that was different.

Turning her back toward him, she used a metal cup to scoop flour from the bag.

"Maybe we'll get another deer today," he said. "Sometimes when we first go out, we'll spot one or two. Rollie can usually bring one down if he has a mind to."

"That would be good," she said. "The smokehouse is almost empty."

They chatted about the insignificant details that people usually talked about before breakfast, but Katie's mind was definitely not on their words. She couldn't wait for breakfast to be over so he'd ride out and she wouldn't have to watch her every syllable, fearing that she'd give herself away. Yet, at the same time, she wanted to throw her arms around him and beg him to stay with her forever.

She had serious fears that she was losing her mind.

Finally, the hands trooped in from the barn, chores finished and all of them famished. The usual *oohs* and *aahs* went up over the pancakes.

After the prayer, Rollie forked three tender, golden circles onto his plate. "Hey, I've got an announcement," he called out to no one in particular.

"Sandra Matins finally said yes," Hank called back.

Rollie smirked. "You think that's possible?" he demanded, a bit too hotly. He turned to Katie and said, "Sandra Matins is the daughter of Rosita's mayor. She doesn't condescend to notice a mere cowhand."

Hank called out, "He sure is sweet on her, though."

Rollie stuffed a triple-thick piece of sorghum-coated pancake into his mouth and chewed. Swallowing, he said, "What I meant to say was"—he gave a mock bow to Hank—"I know why Duffy has a bell on his saddle."

A chorus of groans went up.

Brett shook his head. "Hurry up and tell us. You're killing us with suspense." He shifted in his chair and picked up his coffee cup.

Rollie laughed. "He uses it to turn his horse. When he taps it on the right side, the horse turns right, and when he taps it on the left side, the horse turns left." He waited, eyebrows raised.

The room was silent for several seconds. Finally Lew said, "Save your energy for the fence line, Barker. You'll do all of us more good."

Several chuckles followed.

Unruffled, Rollie reached for a second helping. "These are great, Katie," he said. "It's a shame you're married, 'cause—"

Brett interrupted him. "We know. We know," he called out, "but we're tired of hearing that one, too."

Rebuffed, Rollie clamped his mouth shut and poured sorghum.

Surprised at Brett's abrupt words, Katie stole a glance at him over the rim of her coffee cup. He had his face turned down, his attention fully on his food, so she couldn't get a good look at his expression.

She caught the cowhands exchanging looks over Brett's bowed head. Whatever that was about, they were as clueless as she was.

Half an hour later, the men rode out. Relieved, Katie

watched them from the window. She had the whole day to herself. She needed some quiet to sort out her thoughts and calm down her treacherous emotions.

She picked up the broom to sweep through the entire kitchen and moved into Brett's quarters to sweep there, too. His bedroom was the back room closest to the kitchen, a room that was also large but spare. A wide bedstead took up the center of the space. Half of one wall held a row of pegs for hanging clothes and other items. The other side had a narrow dresser, and that was all. No rugs or curtains in this room either.

Using a dust rag to touch here and there as she made her way through, she finished his room and closed the door. Moving further, she opened the door that led to his office, not that he used it much. He almost always came to the kitchen with his books, saying that it was warmer in there.

Pushing inside, her eyes on the floorboards as the broom swished across them, she glanced up and froze. A scream formed at the back of her throat. She fought it down, her breath coming in small gasps at the effort.

The desk drawers had been pulled out to their maximum length, papers hanging out of them. The desktop had open books sprawled across it, some books pushed to the floor. Pens and pencils lay scattered across the floor as well.

Standing in the doorway for a long moment, Katie backed out and pulled the door closed behind her. She wouldn't touch anything until Brett had a chance to look at it. Besides, she wouldn't feel right touching his personal papers. How would she know where to put anything anyway?

Suddenly, she dropped the broom and dashed into the kitchen. Hooking the front and back doors, she made a circle around the room, testing every window and looking for weak spots where someone might be able to push in. She moved into Brett's quarters and did the same.

That's when she found it. The far window in his sitting room had a loose latch. It looked latched, but when she pulled on the lower sash, the latch slid away and the window moved up. That window faced the front porch, so it was easy enough to lift the window and step over the sill. The door to the kitchen had no latch. That single loose latch gave free access to the entire house.

Katie was as close to panic as she had ever been in her entire life. She picked up the broom and returned to the kitchen. If the door had swung into the kitchen, she could have braced it shut by shifting the wood box over to block it. Unfortunately, it swung into the sitting room, so she'd have to hold the door closed somehow.

But how? She had no tools, no boards, and no nails.

There was no bell attached to Brett's horse for her to ring him home. It was still mid-morning. How could she get through the day?

The only safe place she knew of was her bedroom. At least it had a latch on the door.

She picked up the bag of potatoes and carried it into her room. The stew was already simmering. She only had to peel the potatoes. That wouldn't be too bad. She could mix up biscuits after they rode in.

She had planned to make some more pandoughty and scour the counters as well, but those things would have to wait.

Working with nervous haste, she peeled the potatoes. Dashing around the kitchen, she set them to wait in a pan of water and hurried back into her room. What could she do with herself within these four walls for half the day?

She ran into the kitchen for the broom and other cleaning supplies and hurried back to latch herself in.

An hour later, the windows gleamed, the floors were clean enough for a baby to crawl on, and cobwebs had disappeared. *You're being an idiot*, she told herself as she stretched out on her bed. *No one has ever come into the house during the daytime.* Her eyes drifted closed. *What are you so worried about?*

The next thing she knew, the kitchen door banged, and Brett called out, "Katie?"

She flew off the bed, unlocked the door, and bolted into the kitchen. She met him in the center of the room and flung herself into his arms. Trembling, she clung to him.

"What on earth?" he said. "Did someone come in here while we were gone?"

She shook her head, her face buried in his buffalo coat.

Finally, she gasped. "I found out how he's getting in."

Gently loosening her grip on his waist, he said, "Show me. We'll take care of it right away." He kept his arm around her shoulders as she turned toward his quarters.

"I was sweeping up," she began, her voice faltering, "and I found your office. . ." She pointed toward the closed door.

He moved ahead of her to open it then drew up, his eyebrows pulled down. "What was he looking for?" he demanded, moving inside the room.

Katie stayed in the doorway, her arms wrapped about her waist. She wasn't cold, but she was surely shivering. "That's not where he's getting in," she said.

Brett looked up from his examination of his desktop. "Where is it?" He moved toward her.

She walked to the offending window, opened it, and then closed it again.

He looked at the latch and worked the sash to see how it had loosened. "I'll have Duffy take care of that right away," he said. Opening the window, he bellowed, "Duffy! Come to the house!" then closed it again.

"I was too scared to stay in the kitchen," she said. She wanted to act calm, but she couldn't catch her breath. "I stayed in my room with the door locked."

"All day?" he asked. He seemed as upset about that as he had about his office. He put his arm around her shoulders, and she leaned against him. "Let's get you something hot to drink. I believe I have a tin of tea in the cabinet."

She nodded. "It's in the second door from the left."

"Well, you're going to sit at the table and let me make you some," he said. "You're all in."

When they reached the kitchen door, Duffy burst in. "What's going on, boss?" he demanded, his eyes darting to Katie's face. "Did something happen?"

"No one was here," Brett told him, "but Katie's been scared half to death. She found a window with a loose latch. It's probably where the varmint has been getting inside. I want you to fix it right away." He jerked his head backward. "It's in there. The second window past the fireplace."

Duffy edged past them and disappeared through the door. Brett closed it after him, then stayed beside Katie until she sat at the table.

"I'm embarrassed," she managed to say. "I've heard stories of pioneer women fighting off bears or crawling through the brush for miles after they've been wounded. I feel like such a weakling."

He found the tin of tea and lifted it from the shelf. "Everyone's not cut from the same cloth," he said. He took off the lid and paused to smile at her. "There's no sense in blaming yourself because you're you, is there? God made you just the way He wanted you. I, for one, am glad He did."

He dipped up a cupful of hot water from the pot on the stove and added tea leaves. Stirring it, he added a little molasses and brought it to her. "Here. This should make you feel better."

"Thank you." She let the warm steam cover her face for a moment before she sipped.

He sat near her. "I feel rotten for leaving you here without one of the men nearby. With all that's been going on around here lately, that was pure foolishness. I'm so sorry, Katie. Can you forgive me?" He said it so sincerely and so caringly that she had a strong urge to cry.

She didn't know what to say, so she simply nodded. Cupping her hands around the mug, she bent closer to its calming warmth.

In a few minutes, her trembling had stopped and her breathing slowed to normal. To say that she'd overreacted would be the understatement of the century. How would she ever live it down—throwing herself at Brett like that and clinging to him like a drowning man overboard in a hurricane?

He didn't seem to notice her fiery cheeks because he said, "We need to bait that trap again tonight. Do you think you're up to it?"

Relieved to have something to talk about, she said, "Of course. I'll fix a plate with some of that stew and some biscuits. The smell alone should bring him down out of the hills."

Brett smiled. "Good." The front door to his quarters banged shut. "That's Duffy. I'll have him check all the other windows—in the bunkhouse and everywhere. I was so worried about the kitchen that I didn't check those other windows close enough. I just looked at them instead of trying every one." He shook his head. "I'm afraid I'm to blame for most of your distress, Katie. I can't tell you how sorry I am."

Uncomfortable, she got to her feet. "I'd best mix up those biscuits and get them into the oven," she said, turning away from him. She couldn't stop thinking about the feeling of his arms around her, the smell of his coat, the slow sound of his heartbeat against her ear. Yanking the mixing bowl from its shelf, she reached for the sack of flour. *You're pathetic*, she scolded herself. *Truly pathetic.*

An hour later, the men gathered for dinner. Katie set the pot of stew in the center of the table with a cloth-lined bowl of biscuits beside it, and they dug in.

Duffy started out the evening's conversation. "You don't have to worry about any more loose windows," he said, speaking to Katie. "I double-checked every one of them, even in the bunkhouse."

Rollie said, "Good. Let's keep him out of the bunkhouse. We don't want no prowler catching Hank with his hair messed up."

Lew drawled, "Catching lead is more like it."

"I'd like to ask for a couple of volunteers," Brett said, reaching for a third biscuit. "We're going to lay a trap tonight, and someone's got to watch it. We'll take hour-long shifts. It's too cold out there to stay longer than that."

Lew nodded. "I've got first watch."

"Second," Hank said.

"I guess that makes me third," Rollie said. "I'd best get to bed right after supper."

Brett said, "We may not have to call on you, Rollie. Last time he had the box emptied before we turned in. I hope he's hungry tonight."

When the boys were finished, Katie filled a bowl with stew and placed two biscuits on top of it. She covered the whole thing with a dishtowel and handed it to Brett.

"When Lew's in place, I'll set it out," he told her, putting the bowl on the freshly wiped table. "No sense letting that varmint get the drop on us a second time."

Ten minutes later, Lew went out. Brett followed a few minutes later.

Katie washed the dishes, alert for a shout or a scuffling noise from the back porch. She hung her towel to dry and pulled out the bag of beans.

Brett had just come to the kitchen with his Bible when a thud shook the house. Brett dashed for the back door.

Katie stayed in the kitchen. She had no desire to get in the middle of a fight.

Loud voices.

Duffy and Hank burst through the bunkhouse door. "What's happening?" Duffy asked. "Did they catch him?"

Katie shrugged. "I don't know."

The men headed for the back door. Before they could reach the hall, Lew and Brett came in holding a struggling kid. He had scraggly blond hair and a freckled face. He looked to be about twelve years old.

Chapter 7

L et me go!" he cried out, jerking his arms. "I've got to go."

Using the toe of his boot to pull a chair back, Brett said, "Sit down here, son. We've got to talk to you."

The boy's dirty face had a gaunt, haggard look. His green eyes had the roving look of a caged bobcat. "Please!" he burst out. "Please, let me go!"

"Sit!" Brett pushed him into the chair. Lew moved behind the boy to hold his shoulders down.

"We're not here to hurt you, son," Brett said, moving in front of the kid. He knelt down to be at eye level with him. "You're in some kind of trouble, and we want to help you."

"Then let me go," he ground out. "Let me go now!"

Brett stood his ground. "You're not going anywhere. It's near zero out there. You'll freeze to death if the temperature dips down much more." His voice softened. "Tell us why you're out in the cold. Please believe me. We're not your enemies."

The boy looked around the room, scanning the six faces watching him. His head twitched from side to side. His face screwed up.

"What's your name?" Brett asked.

"Albie Taggart," he said, tucking his chin toward his chest.

Brett reached out and pulled a chair over. He sat in it, facing Albie knee to knee. "What happened to you? Why are you out in the cold?"

His chin quivered but his words were strong. "Ma died two weeks ago. The Widow Hazelette said we'd have to go to an orphanage." He looked up to glare at Brett, his fists clenched. "But we ain't going! Do you hear? We ain't going!"

Brett leaned toward him. "That's not what we have in mind at all, Albie. We don't want to send you to an orphanage." He slipped the next question in without a pause. "How many children are in your family?"

"Me and Jane," he said.

"How old is Jane?"

"Ten."

Katie felt a physical pain go through her. She was just a little older than Georgina.

Albie went on without prompting, "She's sick. I tried to find some money to buy her some medicine, but I couldn't find any." Tears clouded his eyes. Angrily, he swiped at his face.

"Where is she?" Brett asked gently. "We'll bring her here where it's warm and take care of her."

Albie looked up, still afraid.

"She has to have help," Brett said. "You know she does."

Hanging his head, the boy nodded. "I'll show you where."

Brett turned to Hank. "Saddle four horses." To Duffy, "Bring me some rope," he said.

Katie gasped in alarm.

Looking at her, Brett said, "Don't worry. I'm not going to hogtie him, although I ought to." He turned to the boy. "Stand up, son. We're going to have to search you for weapons. You may just get it into your head to run off again. We can't take a chance on that."

Albie endured the humiliation with insolent patience.

Brett lifted a small knife from the boy's belt and a rope slingshot from his pocket.

"No gun?" Lew asked.

Albie looked behind him. "Pa took the Colt with him for the trail."

Brett drew up. "Where is your father then?"

"He went to find work on the railroad. Our cattle all died last summer, and Pa went out to find work. He sent us money a couple times, but then Ma got sick." His voice grew louder. "We couldn't find Pa. We didn't know where to look for him. He's going to come back to the ranch next spring, and he won't know where to find us neither!"

Brett put his hand on the boy's shoulder and stooped to look him in the eye. "We're going to help you, Albie. We'll help you find your father. Come spring you'll be able to go back home. Everything will be all right. I promise you."

Katie hoped he was right. A lot of things could happen to a man working for the railroad.

Brett glanced at his men. "Rollie and Lew, you'll come with us." He turned to Katie. "You'll have to get a bed ready for the sick child." He hesitated, thinking. "She ought to be in with you—ladies together and all that." He let out a breath as he made a decision. "We'll trade. You can take my room. It has a double bed, and you can look after the girl. I'll take your room."

Duffy returned with the rope and handed it to Brett.

Measuring off a loop, Brett went on to Katie, "It'll just be until we can make other sleeping arrangements."

He set a loop over Albie's head and worked it down to the boy's waist. "This is to keep you from running off in the dark. I'm sorry to have to do this, but I can't trust you just yet."

Sullen, the boy watched as Brett wrapped the loop around three times, tying each circlet with a separate knot. "That ought to hold you."

Katie grabbed two biscuits and handed them to the boy. His eyes lit up when he took them from her. He swallowed the first one in two gulps. The second one in three.

A few minutes later, they rode out. Duffy and Hank stayed in the kitchen to wait. Hank brought the checkerboard out, and they sat down for a game. Katie brought in the plate of stew from the box outside and returned the food to the pot. She set it on the stove to warm it up and hurried to Brett's room to get the bed ready.

Made of dark wood with four square posts and deep side rails, the bed was sturdy but not very attractive. Stripping back the covers, she wondered if Brett had made it or bought it somewhere. It had a rope-hung mattress that was stuffed with cotton, quite expensive for a frame as rough as this one was.

She stripped the bed and rolled the sheets into a bundle. Taking Brett at his word that there were no extra sheets in the house, she pulled up a quilt and smoothed it over the mattress. That would have to do until she could take care of some washing tomorrow.

Less than an hour later, Brett hello-ed the house. The men forgot their checkers game and dashed outside to help.

Katie went to the doorway and peered out. Lew had a child bundled in his arms, covered by the new army blanket Katie had set out. Lew handed the child to Duffy.

Katie stood aside so Duffy could pass her. She could see

nothing of the girl as he made his way inside.

"Take her to Brett's room," she told Duffy's back.

He didn't hesitate but marched right on through. He laid her down on the bed and pulled the wool blanket back from her face. "She's burning up," he said. He touched her flushed forehead and shook his head. "It hurts a body to see a little one so stove in."

Rollie came in holding a leather satchel. "Here are her things," he said.

Jane Taggart had thick black hair done up in two wide, frazzled braids. She had soft, curving cheeks with her dark lashes forming perfect half moons across them.

Her eyes stayed closed while Katie undressed her and slipped the nightgown on her that had been in her bag. The child was starved. Somehow, Katie had to figure out how to get some nourishment into her.

Pulling the quilts around the girl's chin, Katie hurried to the kitchen. Someone had dished up a bowl of stew for Albie. The boy was sitting at the table, shoveling food into his mouth. Poor kids. How had they survived at all?

Pulling a small pot from under the counter, Katie spooned some stew into it and added water. She poked and stirred the meat until it fell to bits and mashed the potatoes until she had a slightly lumpy broth. "I'm going to need some help," she said to no one in particular as she poured a glass of water.

Without a word, Brett stood up and followed her into the bedroom.

"We've got to wake her up enough to eat a little," Katie told him. "Can you help her sit up while I try to feed her some of this? The last thing we need is for her to choke."

"Poor tyke," he said. He sat on the edge of the bed and

slid his arm under the child's frail shoulders. "Come on, honey. Let's wake up." He gently shook her chin. "Wake up, Jane. Can you hear me?"

Jane's eyelid's fluttered. She let out a pouty moan.

Katie leaned in closer to speak directly into the girl's face. "Open your mouth, Jane. Eat." She held the bowl close to her face. "Smell that?"

The beefy aroma brought her around. She had large brown eyes, unfocused but obviously very aware of the stew. She opened her mouth, and Katie put a small spoonful on her tongue. She swallowed and opened for another until half the bowl had disappeared.

"Water," she said, her tongue thick.

Jane set down the bowl and held the glass to Jane's peeling lips. She swallowed three times, then relaxed.

"Let her rest now," Katie told Brett. She backed away to give him room to move off the bed and lay Jane back on the pillow. Carefully covering her, Brett stood watching Jane breathe for a few seconds.

Katie whispered, "Pray for her, will you, please?"

He glanced at Katie and for a moment she almost expected him to reach for her hand. But he didn't. He simply bowed and said, "Lord, we thank You for helping us find these poor children. We place them in Your care. Give Jane strength. Please help her to get well."

With that they tiptoed from the room.

Outside the bedroom door, Brett stopped to say, "We're putting Albie in the bunkhouse. He needs a bath in the worst way, but we'll take care of that later. I don't think the boy could stand anything more tonight. He's almost as done in as Jane."

Katie said, "I'll look after them in the morning."

He rubbed his jaw. "I guess they'll have to stay here until spring. I don't see any other way about it. We can't send them back to their ranch alone, and that widow woman isn't going to send them away, that's for sure."

Katie pressed her lips into a soft upside-down smile. "You're a good man, Brett," she murmured.

He grinned. "It's nice to hear you say so. I think you're fine yourself."

She stepped back to break the spell. "I'd best get some things from my room," she said.

Still watching her with that light in his eyes, he nodded. "You'd better do that."

She hurried away like a kid running from a brush fire when the wind had come up and blown sparks everywhere. If she wasn't careful, she'd get herself singed.

The next few days were a whirlwind of activity for Katie. She lost two nights of sleep tending to Jane. She washed sheets and scrubbed the children's filthy clothes. She cooked massive meals and watched Albie eat enough for two men.

Before dawn on the third morning, Katie woke up to find Jane lying in sheets soaked with sweat, her dark hair matted to her head. She was shivering.

Rushing for her own extra nightgown, Katie got the child changed and pulled off the sheets for washing yet again. When she had her comfortable, Katie brought her some soup and watched her feed herself.

"Your fever has broken. You're going to get better," she told the child. "Albie will be so happy when he wakes up this morning. I'll tell him he can come in and see you."

"Is Albie all right?" Jane murmured. "He's not sick, is he?" She had wide brown eyes that looked so helpless.

Katie took the empty bowl from her. "He's right as rain, Jane," she said in a singsong. "He'll come to see you in the morning without warning."

Jane smiled wearily, her eyes already drooping.

Katie set the bowl on the dresser and slid between the covers next to the child. She snuggled deeper into the pillow and fell asleep before she'd taken two breaths.

The next thing she knew, light was streaming through the window. She blinked and sat up. What on earth? She was so late for breakfast that the men had probably gone without eating. Why hadn't someone knocked on the door?

She flipped the covers back and pulled her brown skirt over her nightgown, topping it with a navy shirtwaist. Not waiting for her shoes, she scurried to the kitchen. It was empty. The biscuit tin was empty, too, and the coffeepot sat on the stove, about one-third full.

The bunkhouse door was open. Stepping over to close it, she caught sight of Albie sound asleep, his mouth open and one arm flung over his head. He was an attractive child when his defenses were down.

She gently closed the door and headed toward Brett's bedroom to dress properly. Before she reached the sitting-room door, he came in. She touched her hair. She'd totally forgotten to comb it.

He grinned when he saw her. "So there you are. I thought you might sleep till noon."

"What time is it?" she asked.

He pulled his pocket watch from his pants pocket and looked at it. "Seven-thirty."

She yawned and covered her mouth. "Jane's fever broke sometime before dawn. I had to change the bed and her, too. I warmed some soup for her and she ate all of it. She's sleeping now."

"Why don't you head back to bed, too?" he asked. "You're all in."

She frowned. "I've got to see to lunch."

"We'll eat biscuit-and-bacon sandwiches today. The men completely understand." His smile was soft and warm. "Go ahead. Sleep while those kids are snoozing. It'll do you good."

Her eyes did feel heavy. Maybe she could close them for just a few minutes. "All right," she said.

He patted his pockets. "Now why did I come in here? I was after something." Frowning, he stared at the plank floor. Finally, he shook his head. "Oh well, it'll come to me. I'll be back in a few minutes when it does." He grinned at her. "Katie, I'd be tempted to say you've driven every thought from my head." Chuckling at her shocked expression, he turned and went out.

Chapter 8

With the resilience of a child's constitution, within three days Jane and Albie had life in their eyes again. After three weeks no one would have known the ordeal they'd just come through, if it weren't for Jane's occasional nightmares.

Without being asked, Albie went to the barn with the men to help with the chores. He split wood for Katie and gathered the eggs. In the evenings, Lew and Duffy took turns playing checkers with Albie and teaching him their wily ways at the board. Jane loved to watch them and offer her brother her own brand of advice.

"How did you manage to come and go around here without leaving any tracks?" Lew asked Albie one evening over the checkerboard.

"My pa taught me to track," the boy said. He jumped two of Lew's men. "I wrapped my shoes in burlap whenever I left our camp, and I stayed out of the brush as much as I could so I wouldn't break no branches."

Lew made a move. "Sounds like you could teach me a thing or two," he said. "We'll go hunting later in the week.

How about that?"

The boy brightened. "Sure," he said. "Can I carry a Winchester?"

Lew chuckled at his sudden enthusiasm. "We'll see about that," he said.

The next morning, Jane watched Katie patting doughy globs into perfect circles at the worktable. "Can I help you make biscuits?" she asked. The top of the girl's head almost reached Katie's shoulder.

"I don't see why not," Katie replied, her hands still in motion. "Wash your hands, and I'll show you how."

Jane skipped to the pump and dipped her fingers in the washbasin. Drying her hands on the towel there, she came back.

Using her chin, Katie pointed toward the bank of cabinets. "There's an apron in the second door on the bottom."

Jane found the bleached bit of muslin and wrapped it around her waist. "Ma showed me how to do this," she said, a hint of pride in her voice. She wrapped the strings around her waist and wound them to the front where she tied a bow. "I used to help her with biscuits, too."

Katie moved the bowl of flour so it sat between them on the worktable. "This is the way I do it," she said. She dropped a spoonful of flour into her palm, scooped an egg-sized lump of dough on top of that with more flour on top, then she flipped the dough between both hands, shaping it into a smooth circle. She dropped it onto the half-filled pan and said, "Let's see you do it now, Jane."

With nimble fingers, Jane imitated Katie's actions perfectly. Her finished biscuit wasn't quite as smooth as Katie's, but it came close.

"That's excellent!" Katie exclaimed. "I can see you're going to be a big help around here."

Jane smiled with satisfaction. "Ma always let me help her." Suddenly, her smile faded. Her mouth tightened and she lowered her chin. She kept making biscuits, but she didn't talk anymore.

Katie wanted to pull the girl into her arms, but she didn't think Jane would respond to her in that way. Instead, she gave her some quiet and some space for her thoughts. If only they could help the children reunite with their father. There had to be a way to find him.

That evening at supper, Brett said, "We need to make a trip to town sometime in the next week. It'll be Christmas in a few days. I'd like to get some fixin's for a nice Christmas dinner." He glanced at Katie at the other end of the table. "That is, if you'd like to."

Katie smiled at Jane sitting in the once-empty seat between her and Rollie. "That would be fun, wouldn't it? We may be able to make some molasses cookies."

"Gingerbread men!" Jane said, her face shining. "We make those every year."

Katie raised her eyebrows and looked at Brett. "Gingerbread men," she said. Her eyes thanked him in a way that words could have never done.

He sent her that small smile and something inside her felt warm.

He looked at Duffy. "You're the one that's always looking at the sky. What's the weather sizing up to be?"

"Not a cloud in sight," the old-timer said. He dipped the edge of his biscuit in molasses. "Besides the burning cold, there's no bad weather heading our way that I can see. But that could change any minute. You know that."

Brett said, "Town's only a little over an hour's ride from here. Let's go tomorrow morning." He looked around the table. "It'll be a cold trip. Who wants to come along?"

After a long moment of silence, Katie said, "I would, if you don't mind."

"I'll go," Hank said.

Brett nodded. "That'll make three of us, then."

Katie added, "I'll set food on the back of the stove for those who stay."

"If we leave at daybreak, we should be back by noon," Brett said. He looked at Albie. "Take care of your sister while we're gone, son. And keep the fires stoked."

The boy nodded.

While Albie and Jane washed the supper dishes, Katie pulled out her stash of money, now hidden inside her pillowcase. She had twenty dollars saved from her cleaning money. She would buy some presents and send a package to Ma and the kids, something for Jane, too. Katie figured Albie was too man-grown even at twelve to appreciate a present from her when none of the hands were getting anything. She couldn't afford to buy a gift for everyone in the house. But something for Jane, definitely.

Tingling with excitement, she dropped the coins into her coat pocket and returned to the kitchen. She had to get beans ready for cooking. That was something even Duffy could heat up for lunch tomorrow in case they were delayed in getting back.

The morning was bitter cold, much colder than Katie's trip to the ranch almost three months before. She dressed in her warmest clothes, three layers deep with her coat over all.

When she reached the kitchen, Brett handed her a pair of cowboy boots and two pairs of wool socks. "Take off your shoes and put these on," he told her. "You can carry the shoes with you to wear while you're in town. Your feet will freeze otherwise."

"Thanks. I'll have to get my buttonhook." She set the boots near the table and quickly returned. When she finished unbuttoning her shoes, she slid the buttonhook into her coat pocket. The socks and heavy boots forced her to walk stiff-legged to keep from falling.

Brett held her arms to steady her on the kitchen stoop, then gave her a leg up into the saddle. When she was settled, he handed her a bear rug. "Wrap this around you to keep your face from freezing," he told her.

Huddled in the saddle, she felt like a furry package, but she was definitely warmer than she had been on her ride into the Masten Ranch last October.

They arrived in Rosita shortly after nine o'clock. A one-street town with a dirt thoroughfare, the main shopping center had two stores—an emporium and a milliner's shop. Brett helped Katie down and supported her into the emporium where a giant potbelly stove had four chairs pulled near it. She gratefully sank into a chair, closing her teary eyes and breathing in the warm air.

"Do you have some hot coffee?" Brett asked the storekeeper.

Within minutes a steaming cup nestled between Katie's hands. Every sip was heavenly. "I'm afraid we'll have to wait awhile before we can head back," she told Brett sitting across from her. Hank had taken the horses to the livery stable, then set out to find his own diversion.

"You've got all the time you need," he said gently. "The men lived without a cook for six weeks. They'll make it through the day without you."

She grinned, and her lips felt stiff. "They won't like it."

He smirked. "They'll survive."

When her hands thawed enough to manipulate the buttonhook, Brett helped her slide out of the boots, and she put on her shoes. "That's better," she said, standing and flexing her toes. "I almost feel human again."

Brett approached the counter where the shopkeeper waited. He was a tall balding man with bulging eyes. Permanently bent, his narrow back joined his long neck, forming a smooth arc that ended at the crown of his head. With his head permanently bent forward, he looked upward at Brett with those big eyes in an expression that seemed grotesque. "How can I help you, Mr. Masten?" he asked, his voice surprisingly smooth.

Brett said, "Mr. Sullivan, this is my new cook, Katie Priestly. She'll tell you what she needs for the ranch. Please, put everything on my bill. I'll be back with a pack horse in a few minutes."

Sullivan nodded and his whole upper body weaved. He hooked his thumbs beneath his black suspenders. "What can I get for you, little lady?"

Katie handed him the list she'd written the night before. "I've got some personal shopping to do as well," she said.

"I'll be back shortly," Brett said, heading for the door.

Katie took her time, letting her body soak in the warmth of the store while she browsed among the goods. Sullivan carried everything from canned goods to dried fruit, from bolts of fabric to kitchen wares. He sold lamps and carpets, seeds and garden tools.

She chose peppermint sticks for the children, six in all. She figured Albie wasn't so old that he'd be insulted by a piece of candy. She bought three books of paper dolls as well, figuring those would be easy to mail to her littler sisters, and Jane would like them, too. A pair of white gloves for Bonnie, a snap-brim hat for Mark, and four yards of fine calico fabric for Ma.

She was handing the fabric bolt to Mr. Sullivan for cutting when Brett strode in. He held an envelope in his hand.

"This came for you," he said.

He handed her a letter addressed in Bonnie's handwriting. Concern creased Katie's face. Ma was usually the one to write on the envelope.

Moving to a chair near the stove, she tore it open and scanned the message inside.

Dear Katie,

Ma is sick. She has a fever and hasn't eaten for two days. Georgina and Arlene are crying. I wish you were here.

Love,
Bonnie

She handed the letter to Brett.

He read it and handed it back. "How old is Bonnie?" he asked.

"Thirteen."

"Is she the oldest at home?"

Katie nodded.

"You'll have to go," he said with conviction. "I'll go with you."

"Just like that? What about the hands? What about Albie and Jane?"

"Let's take the children with us. The men can fend for themselves." He stepped up to the counter. "Mr. Sullivan, add two sides of bacon to that order, will you please? And we'll need those things wrapped up right away."

He moved to Katie's side and said, "Can you get those boots back on okay? I'm going to round up Hank and fetch the pack horse."

When she nodded, Brett headed out.

She unbuttoned her shoes with the methodical ease that comes with practice. She wouldn't have to mail those Christmas presents after all. But she hated the thought of leaving Rollie, Hank, Duffy, and Lew alone without a decent meal until she returned. There wasn't time for her to do much extra cooking for them either.

She pushed her padded feet into the boots. How in the world would they be able to get all the way home in this cold without freezing in the process?

As an afterthought, she picked up two pairs of leather gloves, one for Johnny and one for Pa. Neither of them would probably be there while she was at home, but she could save them for spring when she saw them again.

Twenty minutes later, Brett helped her mount up, and they headed home. Pushing the horses to their top speed for the distance, they reached the ranch yard in less than an hour. Brett led the horses to the porch stoop and swung down to help Katie. He handed the reins to Hank, who took the two saddled horses to the barn while Brett unloaded the pack horse.

As soon as Katie entered the house, Albie shoved his arms into his coat sleeves and strode out to help Brett carry in the goods. Jane was at the table, the checkerboard in front of her, when Katie came in.

"Jane," she said, "we came back early. I got some bad news from home."

Jane stood up. "What is it?"

"My mother is sick," Katie said. "She has a fever."

A look of horror crossed Jane's small face. She ran to Katie and threw her arms around her waist.

Katie leaned over to hug the child. "I'm going to her," she said into Jane's ear. "I want you and Albie to come with me. Do you want to?"

Jane nodded. She drew away and wiped her wet cheeks, sniffling. "When do we go?"

"First thing in the morning." Katie pulled off her coat and scarf. "We have so much to do. I'll need your help."

"We have to make biscuits," Jane said. "Lots of them."

Katie chuckled at the girl's unexpected insight.

"I can do it if you measure everything," Jane said.

Katie caressed the top of the child's dark hair. "You're a good girl, Jane. That would help me a lot."

She sat down to get out of those boots.

Brett and Albie came in with the goods from town, then left for the barn on some errand while Brett explained their plans to the boy.

Wearing her own shoes, Katie carried her things to Brett's bedroom. When she returned, Jane had everything on the worktable: flour, lard, salt, baking soda, and a large bowl.

Katie bent over to pull a wide, flat pan from the cabinet. "We'll need a lot of them, Janey, my girl—some for us to take on the trail and some to leave with the hands. If we set some biscuits outside in that box, they'll freeze for later. We can put a pot of beans out there, too. In that way, it's good to have it cold outside."

"We already have a pot of beans," Jane said, looking at their lunch that was still on the stove.

Katie reached for another bowl. "While you're doing that, I'll make cornbread, too.

When Albie came in, Katie had him bring in a haunch of beef for stewing and then she put him to slicing bacon with her sharpest knife.

She stayed so busy that she hardly had time to think of the trip. It was almost nine o'clock that evening when she finally packed her saddlebags. She had helped Jane pack her things after supper and then had sent the girl to bed, worried about her and the cold day to follow.

They ate a quick breakfast, preparing to leave shortly before dawn. Katie stepped outside and drew up, surprised.

Brett had the buckboard pulled near the steps, the back piled high with cowhide rugs and buffalo robes. "We put in three foot warmers with hot coals in them, two in the back and one in the front," he said. "That should keep us from freezing until we get to Musgrove. Mrs. Sanford at the general store will give us some fresh coals for the rest of the trip."

He helped her in. "We should be at the ranch by nightfall if all goes well."

Relieved beyond belief, Katie leaned on his arm and climbed aboard. Jane and Albie climbed in the back and immediately set about making a nest for themselves.

Jane looked up at Katie. "We can put the stew next to the foot warmer to keep it from freezing, can't we?"

Katie nodded, smiling. "That's a wonderful idea."

"Would you rather be in back with the children?" Brett asked when he climbed aboard. "You'd be warmer there."

She shook her head. "I'll ride with you for a while," she said. "If I get cold, I'll move back."

He grinned and shook the reins. With only one foot warmer

between them, they had to sit close together.

Katie looked back to see that Albie and Jane had completely buried themselves. Giggles and squirms lasted for a few minutes, then they were quiet. "They're asleep," Katie said.

"Oh, to be a child again," Brett said, glancing back.

"They've had their share of hardship," Katie reminded him.

"But they came through it like soldiers," he said. "They're good kids. I hope I have some like them one of these days."

Now that they were on their way, Katie's mind turned toward home. She missed Bonnie, Mark, Georgina, and Arlene something awful. Not to mention Johnny and Ma and Pa. She could hardly wait to hug them all.

Glancing at Brett, she felt a cold knot forming in her chest. The truth was sure to come out before this day was over. The best thing for her to do was tell him now.

Chapter 9

Unfortunately, making that decision was a thousand times easier than carrying it out. Musgrove appeared in the valley below them, and Katie hadn't said a single word about her falsehood. Several times she'd opened her mouth to speak, but the words wouldn't come. Brett was a good and honest man. He would surely scorn her when she told him.

But Johnny would give her away. He would run out to greet her and call her "sis" like he always did. She had to tell Brett herself before that happened.

"Brett. . ."

He leaned toward her, bending his head sideways. "Yes?"

"I have to tell you something." She shifted her feet trying to catch some last ray of warmth from the foot warmer.

"Did I ever tell you about the time my brother fell in the well?" he said. Without waiting for her to reply, he started into the story. Katie glanced back to see Albie and Jane with their noses uncovered, listening to Brett's tale. How could she stop him now?

With growing misery, she watched the shanty town of

Musgrove come closer and closer with the resigned dread of a convicted felon on his way to the gallows.

They reached the general store, and the children hopped down from the back of the wagon.

Katie eyed the door, sure that Johnny would appear at any moment. When he didn't she grew worried.

Brett didn't seem to notice her discomfort. He handed her down and led the horse to the watering trough, now topped by a layer of ice. He had to break through it for the horse to drink.

Katie hurried inside. "Hello, Mrs. Sanford," she said, anxiously. "Where's Johnny?"

The old woman shook her head. "He got word that his mother was sick, so he lit out day before yesterday." She peered at Katie. "Aren't you his sister?"

With a furtive glance at the children eyeing the candy jar, Katie quickly nodded. "I'm going home as well," she said, keeping her voice quiet. "We stopped to see if we can get something to drink and some hot coals for our foot warmers."

Mrs. Sullivan nodded. "I've got coffee on the stove," she said. "Coals are ten cents a shovelful."

Brett stepped inside at her last words. He carried the foot warmers in his hands with several small blankets over his arm. "We sure do appreciate the coffee," he said. "I hate to be a bother, but can you put about half milk in the children's cups?"

"It's no bother." Mrs. Sullivan bustled about filling the order while Brett and Katie sat near the fire.

"My face is cold," she told him, rubbing her mittens over her cheeks.

"How long did it take for you to get here from the ranch last October?" he asked her.

She held her hands toward the stove. "We left before noon and didn't get here until suppertime. But we had to stop every little while to warm up. My feet almost froze because I didn't have proper boots. That made the trip twice as long as it should have been."

He nodded. "I'm hoping we can make it there in a couple more hours. Even with the foot warmers, it's going to get cold before we reach the ranch. We may have to stop and build a fire."

They lingered at the general store for an hour to let their limbs warm up, then they set off again. Buried under their rugs, Albie and Jane's voices drifted upward, too muffled to understand their meaning. From time to time a single word like pa or ma would burst up like popcorn out of a roasting basket.

When Musgrove disappeared behind them, Katie said, "Brett, I must speak to you about something."

He pulled the buffalo robe further down over her face. "Lean on me," he said. "You'll stay warmer." He put his arm about her shoulders, and she naturally slid closer. The shoulder of his buffalo coat felt so warm under her cheek. "Don't worry yourself, Katie," he murmured. "Everything is going to be all right."

He went on, "Tell me, what do you think of my house? It's an odd setup having the bunkhouse attached, I know."

"It's a great setup," she said. "The hands don't have to go outside for their meals, but you still have the privacy of your own place. I think it's fine."

"It's rough," he said.

She chuckled. "You could use some curtains"—her eyes drifted closed—"and a rug or two, maybe some padded furniture. . ."

The next thing she knew, he was shaking her awake. "Wake

up, Katie. We've got to stop and build a fire. I was hoping we wouldn't have to, but my feet are like ice. I know the children must be cold, too."

Blinking, she pulled the buffalo robe off and shuddered at the cold blast that hit her cheeks. She looked around. "I know this place," she said. "It's about an hour from our house." She shivered. "Can we make it that far?"

Brett turned to call to the children. "Albie! Jane!"

Albie pulled the cowhide rug away from his face and looked at Brett.

"Are you freezing back there?" Brett asked him.

His chin quivered as he said, "Jane's really cold."

"We'll try to find some shelter and build a fire. If we can put some coals in these foot warmers, we can make it the rest of the way without any problem."

Katie squinted at the landscape. "There are two big rocks with a hollowed out place between them. They're somewhere near here." Suddenly, she pointed. "There! See them?" Orange-red and jutting up fifteen feet into the air, the boulders stood shoulder to shoulder a hundred yards ahead.

The wagon rumbled over the rough ground as Brett edged closer and closer to the crack between the rocks. "We need to get the horses as close in as we can to shelter them from the wind," he said.

"There's no water here," Katie told him when he set the brake.

"We'll manage," he replied, helping her down.

The children scrambled out of the wagon and began to search for wood. Katie went into the rocky shelter. Someone had been there recently. They'd kicked apart a half-burned fire. She knelt to rebuild it with the charred sticks. They would light much faster than fresh branches.

A few minutes later, Brett and the children came in with their arms loaded. Albie broke the smaller branches over his knee and made a small pile of them. Using his knife, Brett shaved a couple of dry sticks into tinder and pulled a small tin of matches from his pocket.

The fire caught on the first match and quickly grew.

"That was a blessing, having the wood already here," Brett said. "Let's gather around and pray for a safe journey the rest of the way, shall we?" The four of them circled the small fire and joined hands. Brett prayed a simple prayer, and peace settled over them. Albie lay on his side, propped up on one elbow. Jane sat with her boots near the fire, her knees bent with her chin resting on them.

Feeding the flames, Brett said, "Does anyone want to know why Duffy's horse has a bell?"

Katie smiled. "Is this another joke?"

He laughed. "No. Actually, it's the real reason. I figured now that we're away from the likes of Rollie and Hank, I could tell you the truth about that."

"What is it?" Katie asked.

He dropped a stick on the fire. "Have you ever heard of a bell mare?"

Albie said, "I have."

Brett grinned at him. "Go ahead, Albie. Tell her what it is."

The boy said, "It's a mare that keeps the horses in a remuda together. She has a bell on her and the horses stay near that sound. When the horse wrangler wants to find the remuda, he listens for the bell."

Brett grinned. "That's it. We run both longhorns and horses. Duffy uses the bell to keep our string of horses together on the range. It's amazing how they follow him around like little puppy dogs. He's a first-rate wrangler." He peered into the flames. "It looks like we've got some good coals brewing in there."

While they waited for the coals to multiply, Katie told the children, "I can't wait for you to meet the kids at the Priestly house. There are three girls and a boy your age, Albie. His name is Mark."

"How old are the girls?" Jane asked, tilting her head. Her top lip formed a perfect bow shape.

"Bonnie is the oldest. She's thirteen. Then there's Georgina. She's nine, and Arlene is five. Georgina has pigtails just like yours except they're a little lighter brown than yours. She's full of fun. I know you'll love to play with her."

Jane's face glowed with anticipation. "I always wanted a sister," she said, "but Ma said the Lord didn't will it."

Albie let out a grunt. "Me neither," he said, dropping a small stick on the fire.

Jane went on. "Ma was always sickly. She said she was glad she had the two of us. That was a miracle."

"You'll like Mark," Katie told Albie. "He loves horses and hunting."

Albie rested his chin on his hand and gazed into the fire. Jane chattered about Molly Chambers, her best friend at school.

Half an hour later, they were snug in the wagon and heading down the trail. They reached the ranch around noon.

The Tumbling P was a small affair, about half the size of the Masten Ranch. The house was a square cabin with three dormers coming out from the front of the roof. Those dormers shed light on the children's domain. As they entered the small yard, Katie looked up and saw a pixie face in the window of the center dormer. It immediately disappeared.

Beyond the house, the remains of the barn lay as charred and bleak as the Priestly family's current prospects. Katie's heart pounded in her ears. The family would begin pouring out to greet them. One of them would surely give her away. Why hadn't she told Brett the truth when she had the chance?

Still shrugging into his coat, Johnny was the first one to appear. He paused on the steps to gaze at the group, wondering who they were. Then he spotted Katie and ran toward her. She leaned over the side of the wagon for him to lift her down.

"Katie!" he cried, welcoming her into his arms. "It's so good to see you! We didn't think you'd be able to come."

She threw her arms tightly around his neck and hugged him hard. "Don't call me sis," she whispered into his ear. "Do you hear me?"

Puzzled, he tried to draw back and look into her eyes.

She hugged him all the harder. "Just don't call me sis, Johnny." With that she let him go and turned to hug Bonnie, who was at her elbow, and Georgina next to her.

Finally remembering her manners, Katie waved her hand toward the wagon seat and said, "Meet Brett Masten. He was kind enough to bring me here when he heard Ma was sick."

The Taggart children had already climbed down from the wagon and were standing shyly near Katie's back.

"Albie and Jane Taggart," Katie went on. She turned to Georgina. "Jane is about your age, Georgina. Why don't you take her inside and see if you can find something fun to do?" The girls looked into each others' eyes, giggled, and ran for the house. Two sets of pigtails bounced with each stride.

To Albie, Katie said, "Mark will show you where to put your things."

"Let's go inside," Bonnie said, shivering. She looked very like Katie except her features were smaller. They had the same brown eyes and fair skin, the same wavy dark hair.

Bonnie linked arms with Katie and rested her head on Katie's shoulder. "I'm so glad to see you I could just cry."

"How is Mother?" Katie asked, loosening her arm to slip it around her sister's waist.

"She's better, thank the Lord," Bonnie replied as they crossed the threshold into the kitchen. It had a warm smell from bubbling chicken soup.

Like the Masten place, the Priestlys' kitchen was in front and to the left of the door. The dining area was to the right. With a sofa pushed against the far wall, it doubled as a sitting room.

Bonnie went on. "Mrs. Andrews came and helped us. She stayed for two days. Ma started getting better right away. I don't know what we would have done without her, Katie." Strain still showed on the girl's face.

Katie hugged her. "It's over now." She rested her cheek against Bonnie's for a second. "We have *so much* to be thankful for. I'll tell you all about it later." She turned loose of her sister to unbutton her coat. Laughing, she said, "I've got to get out of these boots first thing or I'll fall over."

From behind her, Brett said, "I brought your shoes in."

Katie turned to beam at him. "Thank you. I forgot them. I guess I'm a little excited." She sat in a chair at the table to kick off the boots. "I want to go in and see Ma before I button those things on. They take too long."

At that moment, a short, thin man came from the back room. He had thinning gray hair and papery cheeks.

Katie gasped. "Pa!" She lunged up to run to him and almost fell. She still had one boot on.

Brett jumped forward to catch her.

With a little shriek she clung to him. "I'm all right," she said, laughing. "Help me off with this boot!"

He knelt to pull it off.

Once she was free, she skipped into her father's arms. His face was thin, but he had a smile in his hazel eyes. "Katie, girl!" He stroked her hair.

"When did you come home?" she asked. She couldn't stop smiling.

"Yesterday. I had the chance to take off a week for the Christmas holiday, so I took it. Bonnie had sent me word that Ma was sick. I had to come." He turned and put his arm about Katie's shoulders. "She wants to see you."

They entered her parents' room, and Johnny came in after them. On the bed, Ma looked so weak. Her dark hair was sprinkled with gray, and her skin looked pasty.

"Katie!" she breathed. "I'm so glad to see you." She raised her hand to touch her daughter's face.

Katie bent over to kiss her fragile cheek. Sitting on the edge of the bed, Katie said, "How are you feeling?"

The sick woman's voice was breathy. "I'm tired, but I'm going to be all right. I get stronger every day."

They talked for a few moments then Katie turned to her brother. "Johnny, would you please close the door. I have something to tell all of you."

Chapter 10

When she finished with her story, her father said, "Katie, I have to ask you something, and I want you to tell me the truth." He had a set look on his face that she recognized. There would be no weaseling out of anything.

"Of course."

"I saw you with him just now," he said, his hazel eyes keen as he looked at her. "What's between the two of you?"

Katie looked sheepish. "It's a big muddle, Pa," she said. "He's a fine Christian man, and I'd give anything to have him ask me to marry him."

"Do you love him, honey?" Ma asked.

Katie nodded. "But he thinks I'm married to Johnny. If I tell him I'm not, what does that make me?" She sighed.

Johnny scowled. "I can't believe you did that, sis! That puts me in a bad position, too."

Pa said, "Well, Katie's going to have to set him straight. It's not right to let the lie stand, child. You know that."

She nodded. "I'll tell him myself. Before we leave here, I'll tell him." She squeezed her mother's hand. "I may have to stay here with you after that."

"And welcome," Ma said, lifting Katie's hand to her lips. She let her hand fall back to the quilt. "I need to rest now."

The three of them left the room and softly closed the door.

In the dining room, Bonnie was skipping around setting bowls on the table.

Looking at all of them gathered there, Johnny said, "Tomorrow's Christmas Eve. Let's make this a special Christmas!"

He said to Brett, "Would you come with me to cut a tree? I know of one not far from here that would be perfect for that corner." He nodded toward an empty nook beside the sofa. "Mark and Albie, too."

Brett gave that small smile. "I'm game."

The boys looked interested.

Johnny picked up the coffeepot. "Who wants coffee?" he asked, lifting an enamel cup from the counter. He filled three mugs then lifted a jug of milk to fill several glasses.

"Let's make Christmas cookies," Georgina said, sharing a smile with Jane.

Katie sat at the table near the girls. "We've got one whole day to get ready," she said. "Let's make a battle plan."

Everyone gathered around the long table—the six Priestly children, Albie and Jane, Brett, and even Pa. He sat at the head of the table and watched them talking as though he couldn't get enough of looking at them all.

As they ate lunch and discussed Christmas fun, Katie had the strange feeling that she was watching herself from a corner of the room.

Eleven weeks ago she had left this house hungry and more discouraged than she could even describe. Today they were all together again, warm and fed, everyone talking at once about a happy holiday.

An hour later, they split up and set about their assigned tasks. Bonnie peeled sweet potatoes to make some pies. Katie supervised the cookie makers: Georgina, Jane, and Arlene. Mark and Albie headed outdoors with Johnny and Brett in search of a Christmas tree.

When Ma woke up from her rest, Katie took her a bowl of soup and told her of their progress. Pulling herself into a sitting position at the head of the bed, the older woman said, "Look in my sewing basket. I believe I have some white ribbon you could use to make bows for the tree."

She slowly ate the soup while Katie dug around to find the ribbon. "Here it is!" she cried, holding it up.

Ma handed Katie her bowl. "I'm so glad you're home, dear. All this excitement will do the kids so much good. This house has been too quiet for them."

Katie kissed her mother's forehead. "They've been awful worried about you, Ma. Sleep now. I'll try to keep the noise down."

Her mother smiled and reached out to catch Katie's hand. "Let them make all the noise they want," she said. "It does me good to hear them happy."

The rest of the day was a blur in Katie's mind. She laughed at Johnny's foolishness and giggled at Georgina's antics. It was so good to be home.

Always on the alert for a chance to speak to Brett alone, she hardly saw him. It seemed he was always with Johnny or else sitting with her father discussing ranching, the anthrax epidemic, or life in general.

That evening Ma was able to sit in a chair and eat her dinner. Katie sat with her and later helped her into bed. As Katie was fixing the quilt around her, Ma said, "He's a nice young man. I can see why you like him." She winked. "I'll tell you a secret. Your father likes him, too. I can tell by the way they talk to each other."

"Do you think so, Ma?" Katie said. "I haven't had a chance to tell Brett the truth yet. I've been watching for a chance, but he's always with someone." She picked up Ma's empty dishes and returned to the kitchen.

The Christmas tree stood in the designated corner, slightly bent at the top but otherwise beautiful with its popcorn garland and white bows.

All the children slept in the second-floor loft—one huge room with a blanket hung down the center of it. Boys on the right and girls on the left of that "Mason-Dixon Line." Two wide beds stood on each side, all piled high with quilts and comforters. Since Georgina and Jane wanted to be together, all three girls filled up one bed. Katie was alone in the other one.

She had a difficult time getting the three youngest girls to bed on Christmas Eve. They wanted to chase each other and giggle. Once she even caught them jumping on their bed.

"What are you doing?" she demanded in a hoarse whisper. "If Pa hears you jumping up here, he'll come up!"

The giggles stopped and finally they settled down. Kissing each of them, Katie found the package she'd hidden in her saddlebags and carried it downstairs. Without opening it, she laid the entire thing under the Christmas tree.

As usual, Brett was talking to Pa—Brett at the dining table and Pa sitting in a corner of the sofa. Albie and Mark were playing checkers at the other end of the table with Bonnie looking on. Johnny came down from the loft and sat beside Katie, who was at the table near her father.

"Since you work for the railroad," Brett was saying to Pa, "I was hoping you might know how to find their father. His name is Rudolph Taggart."

"I'll certainly do what I can," Pa said. "As soon as I get back, I'll ask at the office. They must have a way to track people down."

Mark spoke up for the first time. "Why can't they stay here until their pa comes back?" he said. "We have enough to eat now. Why can't they stay?"

Katie looked at Brett. From the expression on his face she knew he was waiting for her to speak.

"What do you think?" she asked Pa.

He nodded. "I don't see why not. Albie would give Mark some company. He has a lot on him keeping the wood box filled and the chores done."

"Jane's handy in the kitchen," Katie told Bonnie. "She's been a big help to me." She smiled at Brett. "I'd miss them."

His smile was slow and warm. "I'd miss them, too. On the other hand, they'd be happier here with the other children. Don't you think so?"

She nodded. "You're right. It's for the best. If Pa finds Mr. Taggart, he could bring him back here to fetch Albie and Jane home. It would be a lot easier that way." She looked at Albie. "What do you want to do? Would you mind staying?"

He shrugged. "I wouldn't mind staying," he said. He moved a checker piece. "Jane likes playing with the girls, too."

"It would only be about three months," Katie told him. "If you change your mind and you'd rather come back to stay with us, send a letter and we'll come and get you." She looked at Brett for confirmation and he nodded.

Johnny yawned. "It's been a long day. I'm going to turn in," he said. He patted Katie's shoulder. "Good night, everyone."

Pa stood up. "I'll stoke the fire."

Brett held up his hand. "I'll take care of that for you, Mr. Priestly," he said.

"Why, thank you, Brett. That's good of you." He touched Katie's hair. "Good night."

Brett left the room to pile wood into two stoves: the kitchen cook stove and the potbelly stove in the dead center of the room.

The boys finished their game, and the three older children went upstairs as well.

Brett clanked the last iron door closed and stood, dusting off his hands. He moved to the washbasin to rinse away traces of soot from his fingers.

"You have a nice family," he said, drying his hands. He looked directly at her, his eyes calm but also full of purpose.

Katie felt a lump forming in her throat.

He flipped the towel over its rack and sat next to her at the table.

"I've been trying to tell you something," she managed at last.

"But I wouldn't let you," he said.

She looked up at him, a frown between her eyes.

He leaned closer. "I wouldn't let you," he said more forcefully, "for a reason."

"Brett, I'm not married." The words burst out before she'd fully formed them in her mind. "I lied to you."

He clasped her hand and lifted it to his lips. She gazed into his eyes and couldn't look away.

"You may have lied to me," he said, his words soft and gentle, "but you didn't fool me. Not for a minute."

"You knew all along?" she gasped. "Why did you hire me then?"

He kissed her fingers. "Because you were desperate. I could see it all over you. I could also see that you weren't used to telling stories. It was eating you up. It still is." He grew serious. "I wanted to help you more than anything," he said, "but I was in a tough spot, too."

She nodded. "The more I got to know the men, the more I could see why you made that rule. The entire atmosphere of the ranch would have been different if any of the men were competing for my attention." She lowered her chin. "Not that they would have."

He lifted her chin so he could look into her eyes. "Don't kid yourself. Every one of the hands is half in love with you."

"They are?" She forgot to breathe.

He nodded. "All but me." He leaned even closer. "I'm not half in love with you, Katie. I'm deeply and passionately and irrevocably in love with you."

His lips suddenly twisted. She couldn't take her eyes off them.

"I was afraid I had a big red sign painted on my forehead for all to see, but I couldn't help it." He caressed her with his eyes. "I didn't want to help it."

He pulled her to him, and she lost herself in his arms.

When he turned her loose, she murmured, "But I lied to you, Brett. How can you love me when I did such a horrible thing?"

He chuckled, a soft, delightful sound. "You didn't have to *be* married in order to get the job," he said, a laugh in his voice. "You only had to *say* you were married. As long as the hands considered you off limits, then everything was under control."

He kissed her gently and said, "That makes me just as much a part of your deception as you were. I knew about the lie, but I let it stand."

She closed her eyes and let out a pain-filled sigh. "How can I go back? This is going to make so much trouble."

"Didn't you hear me?" he asked. "I love you, Katie. Will you marry me?"

She threw her arms around him. "Yes! I will!" Tears seeped out between her closed eyelids. "I've never wanted anything so much in my life."

They moved to the sofa to cuddle and whisper and ask the questions that all lovers ask: When did you know? What did you think of me when we first met? And a hundred more.

"When we lost our cattle, I started doubting God," Katie said. "I wondered where He was when the food ran low and we didn't hear from Pa. I couldn't understand why He'd allowed so much misery to come to us." She paused, gazing into the center of the room, forming her words. "I couldn't feel Him," she looked at Brett, "but He was always there."

"He led you to me," Brett told her. "There's no way I can properly thank Him for that."

Awhile later he got up to stoke the fires, then returned to her side. They talked of the future and marveled over the past.

When the thirty-day clock struck four times, Katie let out a sleepy giggle. "It's time to start breakfast. I'd best put on the coffeepot."

"This early on Christmas morning?" he asked.

"Especially on Christmas morning," she retorted. "Those kids will be down here in full force thirty minutes from now. After that no one will sleep, believe me."

He pulled her close for one last kiss. "Before you do that, there's something I have to ask you," he said.

"What?"

"I have this rule about no single women on my ranch," he drawled. "I can't change that now."

"Does that mean I'm out of a job?" she asked.

"Quite the contrary," he said with a grin. "It only means we'll have to travel to Pueblo when we leave here. Before we go back home, I've got to find a parson to make an honest woman of you!"

Epilogue

The Masten Ranch
May 24, 1885

Dear Pa and Ma,

Thanks so much for your last letter. I'm always thrilled to hear from you. I was glad to learn that Albie and Jane are safely at home with their father. Pa, please send directions to their ranch so Brett and I can visit them after the baby is born.

I've spent the last three days sewing curtains out of blue calico. Duffy has been hanging them up for me. Next project, we're going to move Brett's desk into a corner of the sitting room so we can make a nursery out of his office. He never uses that room anyway.

News flash. Rollie Barker is dating a girl from Rosita. She's the mayor's daughter, and he's got it bad. The hands are ribbing him from morning to night. He's the biggest tease around, so I have to laugh at him getting his payback.

I miss you all. I can't wait for you to come in the fall.

Love,
Katie

Dear Reader,

Although I was raised in an Amish/Mennonite family, my parents divorced when I was thirteen. Deeply wounded by an abusive stepfather, I was extremely shy. Through a series of very painful events, I was cut off from my parents for five years. As God healed my wounded heart, my true personality slowly unfolded. Now I love talking to people, making new friends, and sharing my faith.

I had been a writer for years, but had never sold a novel. During this healing time, my books began to be published. My first novel, *Megan's Choice,* was a reader's favorite, and I was a favorite new author with Heartsong Presents. *Fireside Christmas* received four stars from *Romantic Times* and appeared on the CBA best-seller list for three months. Then my historical mystery, *Reaping the Whirlwind,* won the coveted Christy Award in 2001. My last release, *Colorado,* has sold more than 167,000 copies to date. To God be the glory. Great things He hath done.

Because I spent so many years struggling as a beginning writer, I have a heart to help people who have plenty of talent but who need personal guidance to cross the hurdle into publishing. In 2006 I founded ChristianFictionMentors.com, a twelve-lesson interactive program that guides new writers through their first novel.

My husband, David, and I were missionaries on the tiny island of Grenada, West Indies, from 1987 to 2001 with our seven children. While there, I wrote *Survival Cookbook: For Americans Abroad,* 250 recipes for cooking-challenged

Americans who can no longer purchase convenience foods. The cookbook is now in its third printing.

I never dreamed that one day I'd love speaking and even appear on radio and television. God continues to broaden my horizons, and I can't thank Him enough.

Visit www.askroseydow.com to ask me any question you may have regarding the writing life, any future books on my horizon, from-scratch cooking questions, or anything at all. You'll see a date there for my next live interview by teleconference. Or visit my Web site at www.roseydow.com. See you there!

A Letter to Our Readers

Dear Readers:

In order that we might better contribute to your reading enjoyment, we would appreciate your taking a few minutes to respond to the following questions. When completed, please return to the following: Fiction Editor, Barbour Publishing, Inc., P.O. Box 719, Uhrichsville, OH 44683.

1. Did you enjoy reading *Colorado Christmas*?
   ❏ Very much—I would like to see more books like this.
   ❏ Moderately—I would have enjoyed it more if _____
   _____
   _____

2. What influenced your decision to purchase this book?
   (Check those that apply.)
   ❏ Cover   ❏ Back cover copy   ❏ Title   ❏ Price
   ❏ Friends   ❏ Publicity   ❏ Other

3. Which story was your favorite?
   ❏ *How to Be a Millionaire*   ❏ *A Wife in Name Only*
   ❏ *Love by Accident*

4. Please check your age range:
   ❏ Under 18   ❏ 18–24   ❏ 25–34
   ❏ 35–45   ❏ 46–55   ❏ Over 55

5. How many hours per week do you read? _____

Name _____

Occupation _____

Address _____

City_____ State_____ Zip_____

E-mail_____